DARK BIRTHRIGHT

A NOVEL

JEANNE TREAT

AHEAD
OF THE
HANGMAN
PRESS

AN
AHEAD OF THE HANGMAN PRESS
BOOK
PUBLISHED BY
BRUCE & BRUCE, INC.
Copyright © 2006 by Jeanne Treat

www.darkbirthright.com

Second Edition
CreateSpace

ISBN 978-1466469334

Manufactured in the United States of America

This work is fictional. Some characters' names and the events
depicted in this novel have been extracted from historical records,
however, neither these characters nor the descriptions of events
are held to accurately represent real people or their conduct. Every
effort has been made to present readers an exciting, interesting story
set in a reasonably authentic environment. No other purpose than
entertainment was intended or should be implied.

Cover design and illustrations by Charles Randolph Bruce- rebelking.com
Interior character drawings by Jane Starr Weils- www.janestarrweils.com

This book is dedicated to my husband, who helped me to realize a dream, to my mother, who told everyone I was an author before it was true, and to dozens of seventeenth century Scots who lived in my head, guiding my pen.

Book One
in the Dark Birthright Saga

It's 1619 in Scotland.
A child born of mysterious parentage is given to fisher folk to raise as their son. Dughall grows up in a family bound by honor, becomes a healer, and displays psychic abilities. His life is torn apart when he's claimed by his real father, a cruel and powerful lord who tries to mold him in his image. Dughall must define himself, in the midst of a struggle between a Duke, an Earl, and the family who wants him back. All the while, he's determined to marry the girl he left behind, a woodland lass with eyes as green as a peacock's feather.

Map of Scotland with insert of where the story takes place.

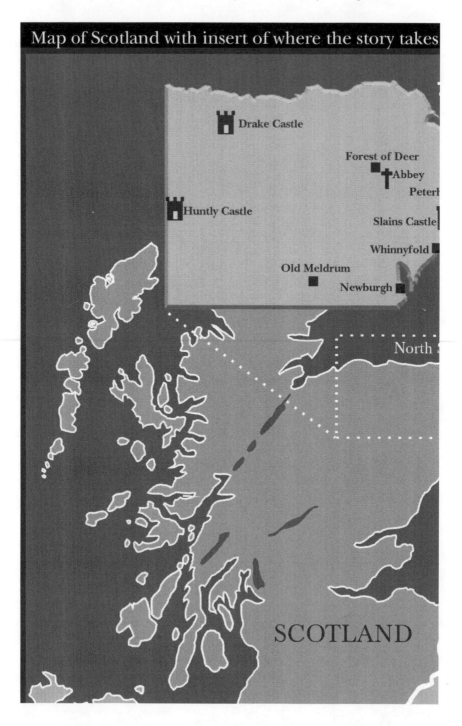

Map of Scotland with insert of where the story takes

"On the rocky coast of Scotland, an epic story unfolds. *Dark Birthright* delivers a heart-rending tale of love and survival amidst the greatest odds. Wonderful...Inspirational...Unforgettable."
- Linda A. Lavid, author of *Paloma, Rented Rooms,* and *Thirst*

"*Dark Birthright*, set in 17th century Scotland, will indulge fans of Diana Gabaldon's Outlander series and their interests in historical fiction. Jeanne Treat creates captivating illusions of benevolence, ruthlessness, and devotion, entwined within the hands of fate in this truly intriguing tale."
- Shannon Curtis, member of the Ladies of Lallybroch

"Bravo! *Dark Birthright* is an amazing read. Jeanne Treat deftly draws the reader into 17th century Scotland and the struggles of a goodhearted lad thrust into a world of cruelty and pain."
- G.L. Gumkowski, author of *A Glimpse of Heaven*

Reviewers say:

So complete and so intricate were the details of this novel, you would think that Jeanne Treat walked straight out of the seventeenth century to tell this story...
-Lighthouseliteraryreviews.com

Fantastic! Lucky me to be picked to review this book. In summation it's an adult equivalent of the Harry Potter series... Magnificent human creativity!
-Tregolwyn Book Reviews

Because of her strenuous research, this book has all the qualifications a historical novel requires to be truly head and shoulders above the rest of the genre, and you will simply love the fast paced action, the facts about the time period and the location, as well as the language that simply seems to flow from Mrs. Treat's pen. This book is highly recommended!
-Roundtablereviews.com

Jessie Hay

PROLOGUE

NORTHEAST SEA COAST
WHINNYFOLD SCOTLAND
OCTOBER 31 1619

The midwife wrapped the child tightly, opened the door, and walked a path to the stone cottage where Jessie Hay lived. It was the last day of October and the wind from the sea was bitter cold.

Maggie had been a midwife for forty years, and never witnessed such brutality. No one knew the young woman who came on horseback, showing signs of labor. Her body was dark with bruises and rope burns marred her wrists. She gave birth, held her son tenderly, and whispered something in his ear. Then she bled to death.

Maggie's heart ached as she walked the stony path. How could a man beat his pregnant wife? A fierce wind blew the skirt about her legs, chilling her to the marrow.

The small boy snuggled against her bosom, lifting her spirits. He was seeking a nipple, a good sign. "Poor laddie," she crooned. "What will I do with ye?"

Maggie's head throbbed as she considered the possibilities. The stranger never spoke her name, so it would be impossible to find her husband. Even if she could, would she want to? The man had beaten the lass nearly to death. He might blame her for the woman's demise or accuse her of sorcery. Her inner voice insisted that the child live.

She prayed for divine guidance. "Goddess, help me. Am I doing the right thing?"

The blanket was thick with the smells of birth, blood and mucous and the rose-like scent of newborn skin. It spoke of life.

Her first idea seemed right. Close by, a fishwife named Jessie Hay nursed a newborn son. Perhaps she would have enough milk for this wee orphan.

She arrived at the woman's door and hesitated. What would she say? Jessie was a good friend and fellow healer. For years she'd been childless, even called barren. It might please her to have two sons.

Maggie knocked.

Jessie opened the door and the midwife entered. The cottage was dark, but for the glow of the hearth and a single candle. Jessie held baby Ian in her arms, stroking his red hair. She laid him in the cradle. "What have ye got there, friend?"

Maggie shifted her bundle and uncovered the lad's face. "Poor child, he's shivering."

Jessie's eyes widened. "Let me feed the fire." She stoked the fire with a bundle of peat. "Whose child is this?"

Maggie took off her shawl and sat at the table, holding the precious bundle. She was weary to the bone. "Sit with me, lass."

Jessie left the hearth and joined her.

The midwife stroked the child's face. "His mother came on horseback, showing signs of labor. She was a lady."

Jessie's brow knotted. "How did ye know?"

"Her clothes and shoes were well made, of silks and fine leather."

"Who was she?"

"I asked her name, but got no answer. The lass removed her ring and pressed it into my hand. Payment, I suppose. I put her to bed and made ready for the birth."

Jessie leaned forward to get a glimpse of the baby. "The child looks good. What happened?"

Maggie's throat tightened. "Her arms were dark with bruises where a man's hands grabbed her. He'd taken a belt to her legs, leaving great welts. I wondered how she rode that horse."

Jessie's eyes widened. "What kind of devil would beat a woman with child?"

"That's not all! I saw rope burns on her wrists; she must have struggled."

"Poor lass. Did she say who did this?"

Maggie frowned. "Nay. She wouldn't tell and she didn't cry out, though the birth was hard. I would have thought her dumb if she hadn't spoken to the child."

"What did she say?"

"She held him so tenderly and whispered in his ear." Her voice cracked with emotion. "Oh dear."

"Please friend. What did she say?"

"Poor little one, yer father must never find ye."

Jessie shuddered. "Mercy! What happened to her?"

Maggie glanced at the blood under her fingernails. "She's dead. The afterbirth came and the bleedin' wouldn't stop. There was nothing I could do."

They were silent for a moment. Maggie searched her eyes. "Take this child. I'll swear he's yer own."

Jessie bit her lower lip gently. "Let me see him."

They placed the infant on the table and uncovered him. The wee lad shivered as they counted fingers and toes and admired his black curls. He was perfect but for a birthmark on his shoulder that looked like the head of a stag.

He fussed as they wrapped him, sucking his lower lip fiercely. Jessie picked him up and responded to his search for a nipple, nursing him until he fell asleep. When she put him in the cradle, the children stirred and touched each other.

Jessie smiled. "Two sons. My husband will be pleased." She touched the lad's cheek. "Wee stranger. We'll name ye Dughall, after my own dear father."

The midwife was relieved. "Bless ye, lass."

"Maggie, can ye tell the child's fortune?"

"Born on the day of the dead. This child will have the Sight."

"You said that about my son Ian."

"Aye."

Jessie frowned. "I must know the truth, and don't tell my husband. You know how he feels about the old religion."

The old midwife hesitated. Did she dare tell a fortune? Her body was weary, and her emotions were raw.

"Please, friend. I must know if we're to keep him."

Maggie took a breath. She touched the lad gently between the eyes, until her mind filled with a vision of another time. Two men rode horses along a dry riverbed. She reached out with her other hand and touched Ian between the eyes.

"This is not the first time these two souls have been together."

"Tell me, Maggie."

"Wait, lass." She closed her eyes. "They were brothers during a time of death and destruction. I feel love and admiration, and something else."

Maggie saw a vision of what had been, and touched Ian's crown. *Will ye stand by him this time, or let him die?* Pain and regret flooded her senses, and she pulled her hand back suddenly.

Jessie was startled. "What do ye see friend? What shall this child bring?"

The midwife hid her true feelings. "Sweet lass, he will bring ye luck."

Maggie pulled on her wrap and left the cottage, tears falling on her cheeks. She would tell no one. Her mother had been hanged a witch for less.

Alex   JANE☆

FISHERFOLK

NORTH SEA COAST
ABERDEENSHIRE SCOTLAND
NOVEMBER 1619

ONE WEEK LATER

For the second day, two fishermen paced the beach looking for a break in the weather. The sea was a mass of white-capped waves, breaking in foam against the shore.

Alex Hay shivered in the wind. He feared he would miss the birth of his child, and prayed that his wife would survive. "God help us! How long must we stay in Broadsea?"

Robert coughed into his mitten. "Watt says we can stay as long as we like."

"The child was due last week! I have to get back to my wife."

Robert frowned. "Hmmphh... It's your boat. We'll sail tomorrow and hug the coast."

Thunder rolled and rain fell in torrents. Alex grasped his shoulders. "Thank ye, friend. I won't forget this."

Icy rain dripped off their wool caps as they hurried back to old man Watt's.

***

They headed south at dawn, clinging to the shore. Black clouds tumbled like the sails of their boat and lightning streaked to the mountains at Braemar. The air was close, breathing an effort.

Alex was tempted to put ashore. The specter of death rose before him, as the men struggled with the sails. *Reckless,* he thought. *I condemn these men, as I risk all for her.*

The sea was fierce and the wind bitter. The scaffie struggled in six-foot waves, water spewing across her decks. William was pitched into the water, pulled under and tossed up aft, screaming as a wave pinned him to the hull. Alex held Robert's belt as he hauled the lad out, cold as ice, but alive. Frozen and weary, they sailed past Cruden to the Bay of Whinnyfold.

Alex felt his heart stop. The lone figure of Maggie waited on the beach, her shawl wrapped tightly about her. "Trim the mainsail!" he cried, struggling with the rudder.

The boat sailed on a starboard tack close to the wind, then into a port tack. Robert dropped the sail and they entered the narrow channel, hitting the beach.

"Thank God! Pull her higher and tie her off."

"We'll take care of the 'Bonnie Fay'," Robert said. "Go to her, man. Ask about your wife."

Alex climbed out of the scaffie and ran to Maggie, desperately trying to read her face. She shivered in the wind, her lips a shade of blue. He feared the worst. "My wife?"

Maggie smiled. "She's well. Ye have two fine sons."

"Two? Two sons! God answered our prayers." He hugged her. "You're like ice. Go home and get warm."

Maggie shivered. "I'll come back to gut the catch."

"Nay bother. There's not much. We were held up in Broadsea with bad weather."

"Go to yer wife, lad. She needs ye."

Alex helped his men secure the boat, telling them about his sons. Seagulls screamed above, threatening their meager catch. With frozen fingers, they loaded it into a creel.

Robert lifted the basket onto his back. "Storm's coming. Go to your lass, man."

"Thank ye, I will." Alex brought a burning finger to his mouth, sucking the spot where a hook pierced his skin. He walked the beach, thinking of his wife, a bonny lass with hair the color of burnished copper. "Ah, Jess." He sighed. "You're so fine to me."

Five years had passed since they wed, and they hadn't lost their need for each other. The only thing they lacked was a child. Now she'd given him two sons.

"They'll never call ye barren again."

Alex walked up the steep path and approached the four rows of cottages. With aching legs, he passed Maggie's house and looked to the right. Jessie stood outside their cottage, a plaid wrapped around her. She ran to him.

Alex pulled her close and kissed her forehead. "God in heaven."

"Husband, I have something I must tell ye."

His voice was husky. "I know lass; you've given me two sons."

The fog rolled in, rendering the air as damp as icy water. He could see their breath. He wrapped the plaid around them, holding her close until he felt her heartbeat. For a moment he was lost in her touch, body-to-body, and soul-to-soul. They separated and with heads bent against the rain, walked to the cottage.

***

Inside, Alex sat on a stool and took off his thigh boots, letting the water drip out. "I'm almost too tired to undress, lass." He stood and took off his coat, breeks, and flannel jersey, laying them over a chair. Water pooled under his feet.

She handed him a towel. "You're dripping."

He ran his fingers through his long brown hair, shaking off the water, and pulled on a dry pair of breeks.

"Did everything go all right, husband?"

"Nay. We almost lost William, but he's all right. We were up to our knees in icy water on the way home."

She held him close. "Oh, Alex."

"I'm alive and whole. I want to see the lads." He stood at the cradle and admired his sons. "Come to your father, wee ones."

Ian was awake, balling his fists and kicking the blanket.

Jessie smiled. "He won't break. Slip a hand under his neck and the other under his bottom."

Alex picked up Ian and cradled him in his lap. The child gripped his finger. "He's so like you lass, with fair skin and red curls. A sturdy boy, he'll make a fine fisherman." Ian frowned and sucked his lip. "You dinna like fish?"

"Give him to me. He needs to nurse."

Alex gave her the child and watched in awe as she lowered her shift and offered her breast. Ian calmed as the nipple was found. Alex's heart swelled. This was his wife, his son.

Jessie looked up. "I'll need Dughall soon. Wake him."

Alex went to the cradle and picked up the sleepy boy. Dughall stirred and opened his eyes. "A wee lad, but still a precious gift. His hair is dark like mine." His voice cracked with emotion. "Your father loves ye."

"What's wrong, husband?"

"Nothing, lass." He gave her a long look. "A man should be strong about these things."

Jessie smiled. "It's all right. When my brother was born, Father cried in front of us all. Sweet are the tears of a man who has held his newborn son."

✳✳✳

That night in bed, Alex held her tenderly. She nestled her face in his neck, rested her thigh on his and trembled. Alex placed a hand on her chest and felt her heart beating wildly. It was a silent signal between them. He slipped her shift over her head. "Lay back love."

Watching the candlelight in her eyes, he ran a finger across her cheek and pressed it to her lips. Jessie laid back, arms grasping the pillow. Alex kneeled above her, admiring the fullness of her body. She was his wife, the mother of his sons. Knowing that his pleasure was tied to hers, he stroked her body until her breath came in gasps. "Are you sure lass, it's not too soon?"

"I need ye, husband."

He was swept away in a sea of sensation, her scent, her spirit, the love in her eyes.

Alex pressed his body against hers and felt their hearts beat in unison. Struggling to control his passion, he made love gently. "God in heaven. I love ye lass. You've given me two sons."

"Husband, there's something I must tell ye."

He stroked her hair. "Two sons. They'll never call ye barren again."

"But Alex."

"Shhhh… My life is complete. Tell me tomorrow."

Earl of Huntly
"Blackheart"

OBSESSION

HUNTLY CASTLE
ABERDEENSHIRE
NOVEMBER 1619
ONE DAY LATER

Blackheart stood in his study, looking out the iron-grated window. The courtyard bustled with activity as inhabitants of the castle began their day. Two portly sisters opened the bakehouse and went inside to stoke the fire, and horses were led out of the stables to be groomed. The sounds of hammering could be heard against the rush of the River Deveron, its banks overflowing from a heavy rain.

Blackheart's expression was grim as he straightened his silk shirt and tossed his dark curls over the collar. He saw his manservant enter the courtyard on horseback and motioned to him. Perhaps there was news of his wife.

God damn her! I don't care whose daughter she is. She promised to obey me, not run from me. When I find ye lass, I'll make ye suffer.

He reached into his pocket, took out a riding crop, and fingered the three leather strands. "I've never used this on a woman." He raised the crop and brought it down on his hand, drawing blood. The pain cleared his head and intensified his anger. "Whore! No one takes my child from me."

There was a timid knock at the door. "Come!" Blackheart growled, as he placed the crop on the desk.

His manservant entered, still in riding clothes. He removed his hat and bowed respectfully. "My Lord, I have news." He stared at the whip and waited to be acknowledged.

Blackheart's impatience flared. "Speak up, Connor! Has my wife shown up at her father's house?"

Connor shifted nervously. "Nay, m'Lord. She's not there."

"Hmmphhhh... Then she's still on the run."

"My Lord. The Duke told me he plans to visit his daughter after the birth of his grandchild. He left this for you." He reached in his jacket, took out an embossed envelope, and handed it to his master.

Blackheart reddened. "That old bastard! We'll have to put him off. Have Hawthorne and Troup returned?"

"Aye, m'Lord. I was about to question them. They searched the eastern sector and found that a lady of her description stayed at an inn a week ago."

"Someone gave my wife safe harbor? Damn it! Why was I not told this?"

Connor hung his head. "Forgive me, my Lord. They returned this morning, with the innkeeper in tow."

"Excellent! Now we'll get some answers. Get Hawthorne and Troup in here immediately. Bring the innkeeper as well."

"Aye, my Lord." Connor backed out of the room slowly.

"Go!"

Blackheart fumed. "Christal can't survive on her own. She's heavy with child." He flexed his hand open and closed, and drove his fist into the desk. His voice was cold and deliberate. "I'll kill anyone who helps her."

He walked to the credenza and took the stopper out of an ornate crystal decanter. The twenty-year-old whisky was dark amber and smelled of peat. He poured a glass and belted it down, savoring the taste and the burning sensation. "There's no pleasure without pain."

Hawthorne and Troup entered the study, dragging an elderly man between them. His hands were tied and his face bore the marks of a beating.

Blackheart pointed to the floor in front of him. "On his knees, right there."

The white-haired man shook with fear as they forced him to his knees.

Blackheart picked up the riding crop. "Do ye know who I am?"

The man paled. "Aye, my Lord. The Earl of Huntly."

"That I am." He ran the strands of the whip along the man's arm and watched him flinch. "What's your name?"

"Milne. Donald Milne of Old Meldrum."

Blackheart's eyes flashed. "Old Meldrum! How in hell did she get that far?"

Milne tottered.

Blackheart snapped. "Straighten him up!"

Hawthorne and Troup sprang into action, supporting the old man until he kneeled on his own. Hawthorne growled a threat in his ear, "Pay attention to your master or you'll answer to me."

The old man nodded frantically.

Blackheart stared. "Let's get down to business. I'm told that my wife stayed at your inn a week ago."

Milne's voice was weak. "I don't know yer wife, m'Lord."

The Earl shook his head in disgust. "You disappoint me, old man. Let's see. Christal's a young woman with clouds of dark hair and startling blue eyes. She was riding a chestnut mare with a white streak on its forehead."

Milne took a ragged breath. "A pregnant lass?"

"Aye! She's carrying my child."

"Now I recall. She's a kind and gentle lady, m'Lord. I was pleased to make her acquaintance."

Blackheart reddened. "How dare ye! She's a witch. Save your skin and tell me where she is."

The innkeeper trembled. "Forgive me, m'Lord. She stayed the night and left the next day before anyone got up."

"Hmmphh... So you don't know where she went?"

"Nay."

"Not even the general direction?"

"Nay."

"Don't lie to me!" He raised the crop and struck the man across the chest.

Milne cried out.

"Stupid old man. We can do this the easy way or the hard way. Which will it be?"

Milne groaned. "My Lord. Have mercy! My mind is feeble."

Blackheart motioned to Hawthorne. "I grow tired of this game. Take him below and throw him in the hole. Let Fang have at him. Twenty strokes. Then we'll talk again."

The old man looked panic-stricken. "My Lord. Please. My heart is weak."

"Tell Fang to take care that he doesn't kill him."

Milne sobbed as they lifted him. "I don't remember."

Blackheart smiled. "A session with Fang will improve your memory. Take him below and send Connor to me."

"Aye, m'Lord."

***

Blackheart sat at the desk drumming his fingers, deep in thought. There was a knock at the door. "Come."

Connor entered and stood his distance. "How can I serve ye, my Lord?"

Blackheart frowned. "The innkeeper may not tell us where she is."

"Fang will persuade him."

"We shall see."

"My Lord. What do you wish me to do?"

"I must know what happened to my wife. If she's alive, I want her back to face punishment. If she's dead I want evidence of her death."

"What about the child?"

"The child is another matter. I can't have my seed scattered about the countryside. If it takes the rest of my days, I must know what happened."

"If she's dead, how will we know your child?"

"My son or daughter will bear the birthmark of the clan, somewhere on their body."

"The mark of the stag?"

"Aye."

Connor swallowed hard. "Do you want the child alive, m'Lord?"

"Only if it's a son."

Connor stood. "I'll take my leave and start the search."

"Spare no expense. Post a reward and establish informants in every town to the east."

"As you wish."

Blackheart took out a dirk and ran his thumb along the edge of the blade. "One more thing. When you find out who helped her, I want to be there to question them and take their lives."

Lord James Drake
The Duke

VISITATION

DRAKE CASTLE
ABERDEENSHIRE
DECEMBER 1620
ONE YEAR LATER

Lord James Drake, Duke of Seaford, sat in a brocade chair in his wife's bedroom. That morning the priest had performed last rites, crushing his hope for a recovery. His heart was heavy as he watched his son Andrew kneeling at his mother's bedside.

So this is how it ends, he thought. *God in heaven! How could ye take her before me?*

He fingered the ivory rosary beads, but words of comfort escaped him.

Andrew patted her limp hand and kissed her forehead. "Goodbye, Mother." He stood and faced the Duke, squeezing his shoulder. "Father. She's talking nonsense. She knows I'm here, but she sees Christal as well."

James' eyes filled with tears. "Christal! Oh God, my heart is an open wound. I can't bear to lose both of them."

"I loved my sister as well."

"She must be dead," he sobbed. "I offered a king's ransom for her return. No alliance is worth this agony! Why did I ask her to marry him?"

"Father. It's not your fault. The Earl is a despicable man." Andrew sniffled. "The end is near. I'll leave ye alone."

James trembled as his son hugged him. The young man sighed and left the room.

He moved his chair close to the bed and sat at her side, holding her hand. Jeanne's breathing was labored and body frail from the long struggle. Healers from as far away as Aberdeen had tried to save her, admitting defeat. She wanted to die.

Her sunken eyes focused on his face. "James..."

"Jeanne." A tear slid down his face. "Don't leave me, lass."

She smiled, reminding him why he stayed faithful all these years. His heart was breaking.

"James. Christal is here to help me to pass. Do ye not see her?"

He felt a chill, as though something passed through him. "Dear God." He gripped her hand. "That bastard killed her, didn't he?"

A shadow of pain passed over her face. Her body shuddered.

"Don't die."

"Shhhhh... I don't have much time. Christal asks that you find her son. He's in grave danger."

James felt a ghostly hand on his cheek and stiffened. His voice choked with emotion. "Christal's son? How will I know the child?"

Jeanne closed her eyes and nodded, as if to a presence in the room. "The lad bears the mark of the Gordon clan on his right shoulder."

James swallowed hard. "Where is he? Tell me."

Jeanne opened her eyes and tried to speak, but her voice was weak. "Look to the sea, husband."

"The sea? This is Scotland. It's all around us. Where does the lad live?"

Her lips moved, but no sound came out. He leaned forward as she whispered.

"Farewell, James. I love ye."

"Nay!" he cried, grasping her hand. "God help me. I can't live without ye, lass."

Jeanne closed her eyes, a smile fading on her lips, and released a last breath. She was gone.

James stood and held a hand on her chest, hoping to find a heartbeat. There was none. "Oh God! Let me die with her." He buried his face in his hands and cried, shaking in grief.

Andrew entered the room and made the sign of the cross. "Poor Mother. She never recovered from Christal's disappearance." He clutched his father's shoulders. "Her suffering is over. She didn't deserve it."

James sobbed openly. "She's dead. Oh God, why couldn't it be me? How can I go on?"

Andrew drew him close. "I need ye, Father. I'm not ready to be Duke."

The older man gulped air and steeled himself. "Of course. Duty calls. I love ye, Son." He stiffened as he remembered her last request. "I have to go on. There's a child I must find."

Andrew frowned. "What child?"

James' eyes were wild. "My grandson! Christal's son. She was in the room when your mother passed."

Andrew looked skeptical. "Father… You haven't slept in days."

"I tell ye she was!"

Andrew hugged him. "Come to the chapel with me. We'll pray for Mother's soul, and then you can tell me about it."

Maggie

CHILD'S PLAY

YTHAN SALT WATER ESTUARY
ABERDEENSHIRE
AUGUST 1627

SIX YEARS LATER

It was a hot summer day. Jessie, Maggie, and the boys walked eight miles to the Ythan Estuary to collect mussels for bait. Near the river, heather, crowberry, and weeping willow lived alongside marshland and water pools. Walking to the dunes, terns glided at their side, banking and diving for sand eels. Ian and Dughall ran ahead, spotting rabbits feeding on primroses.

Jessie tasted salt in the air. She knew the smell of low tide, of worms and snails and rockweed. As they approached the mussel flats, seagulls screamed and took to the sky.

"What's wrong, lass?" Maggie said. "I see dark circles under yer eyes."

Jessie nodded. "I had a bad day yesterday. The lads pulled everything out of the drying shed and left it to rot in the sun. I was so mad I could have spit."

Maggie raised her eyebrows. "Did the meat spoil?"

"Nay. I found it just in time."

"Thank goodness."

Dughall and Ian ran towards them. "Mother. Can we go to the pool?"

Jessie's head ached. "Aye. Take the basket and collect the things you love. Stay close to the small rock pool. Maggie and I will gather mussels and come back for ye."

Ian smiled as a copper butterfly landed on his hand. "Aye, Mother."

"We'll bring ye a giftie," Dughall said. "Violets or cowslips."

"Never mind that. Stay at the pool. Don't make me look for ye."

Dughall pouted. "This morning you said you wanted violets!"

Jessie rubbed her forehead. "Ach! I never said that. I was thinkin' it."

"Same thing!"

"Nay, it isn't."

Maggie frowned. "Lads! Give yer mother some peace. Go to the rock pool."

"Thanks, Auntie. Come on, Ian!" Dughall took the basket and ran towards the weed banks with Ian on his heels.

***

They took off their shoes and waded to the mussel flats, squeezing warm sand between their toes. The creel was placed between them.

Jessie twisted a mussel shell from a rock and tossed it into the basket. Her eyes teared. "Oh Maggie."

"What's the matter, lass?"

"The lads are driving me daft. I can't turn around without them getting into trouble. I worry that they're getting spoiled."

"They're high-spirited lads. What does Alex say?"

Jessie reddened. "I've asked him to discipline them, but he won't do it. He's their father! Yesterday, we had words about it." Tears rolled down her cheeks.

Maggie frowned. "Would ye like me to talk to him?"

"Nay. It would only cause trouble."

"Hmmphh…"

"I love Alex so much. I don't understand him."

Maggie straightened her back and sighed. "Did he not tell ye that his father beat him?"

Jessie's eyes widened. "Nay. I wondered about the marks on his backside. When did it happen?"

"About the time his mother died. He was nine."

"He never talks about his parents."

"Bonnie Hay was a friend of mine. On her deathbed, she asked me to look after Alex. I agreed, but his father had other ideas. Gavin

Hay wandered the beach cursing God, and took to the drink. Now some men are agreeable when drinking, laughing and sleeping it off. Gavin was plain mean, finding fault with everything Alex did. He beat that child with a leather strap, seemed like every day. One night, he wouldn't stop."

Jessie's heart ached. "Dear God."

Maggie frowned. "I stood outside that cottage, hearing the crack of the strap and Alex's cries, wondering what to do. A man has the right to discipline his son, but this was too much. I grabbed a broomstick and confronted him, knocking his whisky to the floor. He called me a meddling witch." She smiled bitterly. "That night, I took Alex home to treat his wounds. He didn't say a word. I feared for the wounds I couldn't see, the ones he carried in his heart. I hugged him and promised to make things right."

"No wonder he loves ye."

"It was a hard promise to keep. I fought with Gavin, and kept Alex when he got drunk. I couldn't stop the beatings every time. Ye asked why I never remarried. Gavin made sure I had a fearsome reputation. No man would have me as wife."

"Dear Maggie."

"When Gavin was drowned at sea, we buried him in the church yard and returned home. I saw Alex go into his cottage and get the strap. I followed him to the beach, where he ran his fingers through the leather strands, rolled it into a ball, and tossed it into the sea."

Jessie bit her lip gently. "Oh… He refused to name our son after his father. Now I know why."

"Enough said. Talk to yer husband, lass."

"Aye."

They worked for hours in the sun, twisting mussel shells from rocks. Eider ducks wailed overhead, eyeing the bait.

"Cover that up lass, those eiders mean to have our catch."

Jessie threw a handful into the basket and closed the top. She hiked up her skirt and lifted the creel onto her back. "God help me, this is heavy. Let's find the lads."

They waded through the flats, watching kittiwakes corkscrew on sea updrafts. A family of oystercatchers preened in the sun, each bird mirrored on the glistening mud.

"Do ye want me to take a turn? In my day, I carried many a basket of bait."

"Nay. Don't mind my complaining. Keep those wee monsters busy on the way home and I'll be grateful." She shaded her eyes. "Alex loves those lads more than life. He calls Ian his little fisherman, telling him stories of the sea. Dughall he clings to as though he might lose him."

"Did ye tell him about Dughall's birth?"

Jessie burned with shame. "Nay. I'd been barren so long. When he said that I'd given him two sons, I couldn't deny it. It's been seven years and no one has claimed the boy. With the way his mother was beaten, it was a blessing that he came to us."

Maggie nodded. "Her ring is in a crock on my shelf. Without that, no one can identify him."

"Thank God. We love him as our own. Alex would die if we lost him."

"Don't fret about the lads," Maggie said. "Alex loves them and he loves ye too, with a rare passion. As God-fearing as he is, you could worship the devil and he would stay with ye."

"He would not!" She shifted the creel on her back and scanned the riverbank. Fear gripped her. "They've run off again. Where are those lads?"

***

Red and black and brown. These were the colors Ian saw as he searched for hermit crabs in the rock pool. Red stones sat among black stones, covered with brownish-green patches of kelp. Gobies darted in the water, hiding among weeds and sea squirts.

Ian turned over a water-covered stone. A hermit crab left its hiding place and scampered across a large rock. "There's one! Behind ye, a crab."

Dughall spun around and grabbed the creature's shell, holding it up. "I got him!" He opened the basket and tossed the crab in. "That makes six crabs, ten worms, seven starfish and a pile of rocks and shells."

Ian splashed water at his head, soaking his curls. "Let's get more."

"Hey!" Dughall cried, as he hurled a piece of kelp. A green streak slid down Ian's shirt.

Dughall's eyes widened. "Ooops... Nay, no more." He cocked his head and looked around. "We better head back. Mother is looking for us. Do ye not hear her thinking about us?"

Ian stroked his stained shirt. "Aye, I do. Our clothes are dirty and our shoes are soaked. She'll not be pleased."

Dughall giggled. "Aunt Maggie will threaten to switch us!"

Ian made a face. "Oh, that. Ha!" He saw a spiral pattern in the mud and dug down to catch a lugworm, pulling it out of a hole. "Let's tie this to a length of twine and dangle it in front of that crab. We'll bring it home, so Mother can make soup."

"She won't be mad if we bring her supper."

The worm wriggled as they tied the twine around its middle. Ian wrapped the end of the string around his hand. They lay down in the wet sand and lowered the worm to the bottom. Ian pulled the twine to make the worm dance in front of the crab's cavern.

He frowned. "It won't come out. We're in trouble now."

Dughall smiled. "Nay, Brother. If we think hard and ask the crab to come out, it will."

"You're daft!"

"Nay. It worked on Sunday with the hen."

Ian laughed. "Was that you? The minister didn't like it."

"Come on, let's do it."

They stared into the pool and pulled on the twine. Dughall hummed.

Ian rubbed his forehead. "Ach! My head hurts."

"Shhh... Look, Brother."

The crab peeked out and scuttled sideways after the worm, tearing it apart. Dughall squealed as Ian tangled its leg and wound up the cord. The crab came to the surface, sprouting beady eyes and fierce claws.

Ian gasped. "You made it mad. It means to pinch me! Open the basket."

The crab rested on its haunches and snapped its pincers.

Dughall opened the basket. A hermit crab jumped out and scurried into the rocks. "Hurry brother, they're escaping."

Ian pulled up the crab and swung it into the basket, closing the top.

Dughall smiled. "Let's bring it to Mother. She's really getting mad."

✳✳✳

Jessie laid down her creel. "Rest under the tree, Maggie. I'll find them."

Maggie sat under the willow tree and pulled her gray hair off her neck. "Thank ye, lass." She closed her eyes.

Jessie hurried toward the weed banks. "Ian, Dughall! Where are ye?" She stopped at a small rock pool and stared. The young woman searched the straw-colored rushes and nearby creek bed, finding no trace of them. Her heart pounded as she ran along the riverbank.

"Where can they be? They've never gone this far." Anger gripped her. "I'll beat them myself! Ian, Dughall! Where are ye lads?"

A flock of golden plovers erupted from the trees, wings flapping wildly, followed by two boys struggling with a basket between them. They smiled and put it down.

Ian wiped his nose on his sleeve. "Mother. We caught a crab."

"You can make soup!" Dughall cried.

Jessie ran her hands up and down their wet clothes. "Where have ye been, lads? Look at ye, you're filthy as a clout."

"Shoes are soaked, too," Ian said.

Jessie stiffened. "Ach! Why can ye not listen? I asked ye to stay at the small pool."

Dughall rolled his eyes. "I told ye she was mad. I heard her thinking about us."

Ian held a finger to his lips. "Shhh. We mustn't talk about how we know things."

"So you knew I was looking for ye! Reading my thoughts and driving me daft. Ian is right; you must not say such things."

Dughall kissed her cheek. "Forgive me, Mother."

Jessie softened. "Oh God. I couldn't bear to lose ye. Come on, let's get back to Maggie."

"But the crab..."

"Show me later."

Jessie's head ached as they walked along the river, the boys struggling with the heavy basket. Her blouse was soaked with perspiration. "Mercy. What have you got in there, lads?"

"Stones and shells and starfish!"

"Crabs and worms!"

"Oh, worms." They hiked past the weed banks.

"I'm hungry!" Dughall whined.

"I have a bit of bread and cheese in Maggie's sack. If you hadn't gone so far, we would have eaten."

"Look, there's Auntie." The boys put down the basket and exchanged a knowing look.

"Lads, don't bother her."

They ran to the old woman and kissed her cheeks. "Wake up!"

Maggie woke with a start and drew them close. "Are ye hungry?"

"Starved!"

Maggie gave her pack to Jessie, and noted the position of the sun. "It's awfully late. Did ye find them where they were supposed to be?"

"Nay. They went too far, scaring me to death."

Maggie looked serious. "Cut me a switch from that willow tree, lass."

Ian took a step back. "Ha! You wouldn't."

"I would."

Dughall put on a sad face. "Don't switch us, Auntie. We won't do it again."

Maggie looked thoughtful. "All right. But next time listen to yer mother."

Dughall rolled his eyes and giggled. Ian held a hand to his mouth to hide a smile.

Jessie fumed as she unpacked the sack. *She's as bad as Alex. They'll never behave.*

Maggie smiled. "Come on lads, let's have a bite." They sat under the tree and ate bread and cheese until there was nothing left.

Jessie's head throbbed as she checked her creel. "Time to go. It's getting late."

"Nay, Mother," Ian said. "You must see the crab. It's a big one, and you can make soup."

Dughall reached into the basket. He pulled out his hand and slammed the top down, a shocked look on his face. "Ouch! It pinched me hard." He shook his hand and cried.

Jessie rushed to his side and held his finger up. A deep pinch mark marred his index finger, cutting the skin on either side. Blood welled up and trickled to his palm.

Dughall sobbed. "Oh God. It's bleeding."

Jessie stroked his finger. "Now, now, it's all right. We'll put a poultice on this when we get back." She tore off a piece of her underskirt and wrapped the finger. "Be a brave lad."

Ian sat on the ground, rocking back and forth. He sucked his index finger and wailed. "Yeow ! My finger hurts too."

Jessie reddened. "There's nothing wrong with your finger. Dughall got pinched, not you."

"It hurts!"

Jessie looked at his finger. It wasn't bleeding, but it was swollen. She tore off a piece of underskirt and wrapped it, shaking her head. The lads sat on the ground comparing their wrappings.

Maggie spoke softly. "How long has this gone on, lass? That one feels what the other feels."

Jessie sighed. "A long time. They speak to each other without words, they each know where the other is, and feel each other's pain and pleasure. Sometimes they say what others are thinking. It scares me that people will find out."

"The Second Sight," Maggie whispered. "But this is more."

"Aye. What must we do?"

"Does Alex know about their abilities?"

"Nay. He's blind when it comes to those lads."

"Good. He might tell the minister. The church would say they had the devil in them and try to cast it out. As wee as they are, they might not survive."

Jessie winced as the pain in her head worsened.

"Don't fret lass. This has nothing to do with the devil. It's a rare gift."

"Help me, Maggie."

"We'll show them the danger and teach them to hide their gift, even from their own father."

FAMILY

WHINNYFOLD
ABERDEENSHIRE
SEPTEMBER 1627
ONE WEEK LATER

Morning light filtered in the window of the stone cottage. Dughall lay in bed, listening to his parents making love. Muffled grunts and moans came from under the covers.

What are they doing? I feel them touching, her skin's as soft as lamb's wool, but I can't see it. Oh, Oh. His whang's like a rock.

His mother opened her legs. His father's heart pounded as he positioned himself above her.

Oh God. What's he doing to her now? Dughall rolled over and tickled his brother's lip. "Wake up."

Ian batted an imaginary bug away. "Hey. Stop that! Go back to sleep."

"Shhhh. Listen. They're doing it again."

"Doing what?"

"You know. Don't ye feel it?"

Their mother's voice was soft. "Alex, the lads."

Blankets rustled. "Do ye not think they know what we do?"

"Aye. They know everything."

"Then lay back."

The bed creaked as they moved in unison, breathing heavily.

"Deeper... Don't stop."

Their father threw back his head and groaned. "God in heaven."

Dughall felt the heat rise in him. No wonder Father liked this. A nervous giggle escaped his lips.

Ian snorted. "Ha! I see what ye mean."

The creaking stopped. "Are you lads awake?"

Ian shut his eyes tightly. "Nay, sir. We're asleep."

Dughall reddened. "Oops. Going to sleep right now."

"Good. Not another word from ye."

"Alex," she whispered.

"It's all right, lass. It's time I had a talk with them." The blankets rustled. "Now, where were we?"

"Mmmm…"

There was a knock.

"Ach! Who's there?"

Maggie's voice came from behind the door. "It's yer Aunt. Come to start the shelling and baiting. Send the lass out."

He threw back the covers. "If it's not the young ones, it's the old."

The boys giggled nervously.

Jessie sighed. "You're their father. Talk to them."

"Hmmphh! I will, lass."

Dughall buried his face in the pillow. *Oh God. We're in for it, now.*

***

Jessie and Maggie sat on stools, shelling mussels and baiting lines. Jessie pried a shell and pulled out the mussel with her fingers. She forced it onto a hook, pulled a length of line from the basket, and grabbed another shell, singing a song.

♩♪♩

Who would be a fisherman's wife?
To go to the mussels with a scrubber and a knife
A dead out fire
And a reveled bed
Away to the mussels in the morning

See the boat come beatin' in
With three reefs to the foresail in
Not a stitch
Upon his back
Away to the mussels in the morning ♩♪♩

Maggie wiped her brow. "D'ye want to stop for a bit of bread, lass?"

Jessie's nose wrinkled at the briny smell of shelled mussels. She unwound strips of sackcloth from her fingers. "Aye. I could use a rest. My fingers are stiff."

Maggie poured water into cups and they drank deeply. She opened a basket and uncovered brown bread and cheese. The women ate, regarding the heap of mussels.

Maggie shook her head. "Hmmm…That pile never seems to get

any smaller."

Jessie loved this old woman like a mother. She took off her scarf and wound her hair into a braid. "The lads should be helping. Where have they gone to?"

"They went to the cliffs, to look at the puffins."

Jessie's fear blossomed. The cliffs were sheer. More than one curious child had been lost over the edge.

"Don't worry, lass. They're lads, and I've never seen any as surefooted. Soon they'll be wandering the woods and sleeping under the stars. There's nary a bee or butterfly they can resist."

"Or crabs, or worms."

"Let them play. They'll be men soon enough. A few more hours, and the baiting will be done. Why don't ye leave the lads with me tonight?"

Jessie's skin flushed. A whole night together, without the lads. No need to hide under blankets or listen for their voices. "We could use time alone. If it's no trouble."

"Trouble they are. But I love to have them."

"Bless ye, Maggie. Alex will be home soon. He went to see John about hemp and tar to fix the hull."

"Knock on wood. They better plug that leak. There wasn't a dry stitch on those men when they came back. Best to tie rowan twigs into the lines for luck." Maggie wiped her hands on her apron. "I'll make oatcakes and tatties and herrin' for supper. My mother used to say that a full belly sets a man jigging. Have we any kale?"

"Aye, in the drying shed." Jessie frowned. "Now, where are those boys?"

"They'll be along when their bellies complain. Let's finish our work. The pile will get no smaller by us looking at it."

***

Dughall stood on the precipice and looked below at the sea cliffs. The wind whipped his dark curls around his face. He ran his fingers through his hair, smoothing it back. Water crashed as the tide surged into rock hollows.

Ian gave him a shove, pushing him closer to the edge.

"Hey, stop it!" Dughall shivered as he studied the sheer drop. His heart pounded like a drum.

"Scared ye, didn't I?"

"You know it!"

A puffin stood on the cliff with its bill full of sand eels. It peered into a burrow and bobbed its head, feeding chicks.

Dughall's heartbeat slowed. "Look. A mother puffin feeding her chicks."

Ian nodded and pointed at the sea, where jagged rocks rose out of the water. "There, on the rocks. Four gray seals."

A speckled male plunged into the water and caught a fish. He lay back and floated, biting off the head. Females lay on the rocks, clapping their flippers.

"Do you think they're silkies?" Dughall asked. "That they come ashore and shed their skins, to sing and dance as lads and lassies? Aunt Maggie says if you steal their skin, they'll stay with ye as husband or wife. Your children will have webbed feet."

Ian rolled his eyes. "Just a story, Brother. Have you seen such children? Do you believe everything Maggie tells ye?"

"Aye." He cocked his head and started to sing.

See the boat come beatin' in
With three reefs to the foresail in
Not a stitch
Upon his back
Away to the mussels in the morning

Ian covered his ears. "Ach! Mother and Maggie have been singing that all morning, driving me daft. Must ye sing it too?"

Dughall laughed. "It's stuck in my head! I wish we couldn't hear them."

"I'm for that! Maggie says we must block their thoughts. Can ye not think of another song?"

"I guess so. Father likes this one." He held out his hands and sang in a voice that could charm the birds.

Twas in the month of August one morning by the sea,
When violets and cowslips they so delighted me.
I met a pretty damsel for an empress she might pass,
And my heart was captivated by the bonnie fisher lass.

Ian punched him. "You're daft!"

Dughall's anger flared. "Stop saying that! I am not." He made a fist, but Ian grabbed it and wrestled him to the ground in a headlock. Stars danced in front of his eyes. "Ach! No more."

Ian pressed harder. "Give up?"

Dughall grunted. "Aye!"

Ian let him go. They stood and gazed toward the town of Peterhead, and exchanged a knowing look.

"Father's coming," Ian said.

"Aye. I hear him thinking about us. If we hurry, we can meet him at the tree."

Ian frowned. "Remember what Maggie said. Don't tell him you were reading his thoughts."

"I don't see the harm in it. It's only Father."

"You believe Maggie about the silkies. Can ye not listen to her about this? She says there are some at church who would hurt us."

Dughall bit his lip gently. "Why? We've done nothing wrong."

"They would think we have the devil in us."

Dughall frowned as he recalled the Sunday sermon, filled with hell and damnation. He spoke softly. "Do ye think that we have the devil in us? Because we know things?"

Ian seemed unconcerned. "Nay. Mother says it's a rare gift."

"Why must we hide it? If my gift was to fiddle, people would love it." Dughall's eyes widened. "Father's at the tree with Uncle Robert."

The boys hurried down the path.

"We can tell him we're having tatties and herrin' for supper," Dughall said. "Maggie said so."

"Ach! She never told ye that. We're not supposed to know yet."

Dughall giggled. "All right." He sensed his brother's anger and took a step back. "You're mad, aren't ye? Don't hurt me, I get it."

Dughall left the path and walked in a field of heather, feeling the soft blades of grass between his toes. He smiled as his fingers brushed the tops of the velvety purple bells. They walked for a mile until they spotted their father sitting under a tree.

"Father!" Ian cried, as he ran into Alex's outstretched arms.

Dughall followed on his heels, knocking him into his father.

"Oof!" Alex said. "My sons. Why are ye not helping with the baiting?"

Dughall blushed as he remembered his words. He'd asked them to help Mother with the shelling.

"Maggie said we could go to the cliffs," Ian said, quickly. "We saw seals on the rocks."

"Silkies they are!"

Alex frowned. "Maggie's been tellin' wild stories again. I'll have a serious talk with that woman."

"Nay bother," Ian said. "We know it's not real. Right?"

Dughall winced. "It's just a story, Father."

Alex smiled. "All right. You must be starved. Shall we see if your mother left us some bread and cheese?"

Ian nodded. "Aye."

"Maggie's making tatties and herrin'," Dughall said. "Ach! I mean I hope she is."

Alex stood and shook hands with Robert. "See ye at church tomorrow. We'll caulk the hull afterwards."

Robert smiled. "Aye. Feed these lads before they get into trouble." He gathered the hemp and tar, and started up the path.

***

Alex and his sons walked the path towards the village. He thought of what had happened that morning and wondered what to say. *They're young, but they seem to know everything.*

When they stopped to relieve themselves behind a tree, their urine streams crossed and puddled at their feet.

Dughall laughed. "Try to get it in that footprint."

Ian turned. "You missed. Ha!"

Alex frowned. "Hold on to that thing. You're getting it all over me."

"Sorry, Father."

He shook off the last drop and fastened his breeks. "Lace up. I need to have a talk with ye."

Dughall and Ian exchanged a worried look.

"I'm not angry. It's time we had a man-to-man talk."

Dughall struggled with his laces. "We're not men, Father."

Ian tucked in his shirt. "Aye. Let's forget about it."

Alex smiled. "You're men enough. Sit with me."

They sat under the tree facing their father. He cleared his throat. "You were listening to your mother and me in bed."

Ian winced. "Nay. That wasn't us."

Alex stared. "All that giggling and snorting? Who was it, then?"

Dughall rolled his eyes. "It was us."

"Good. I'd hate to think you were lying to me."

The lads fidgeted.

"When I was a boy, I wondered what my parents did under the covers. Would ye like to know?"

Ian's eyes widened. "Aye."

Alex considered how much to tell them. *They'll let me know when it's enough.* He clasped his hands. "A man and a woman join in wedlock to have a family."

They nodded.

"You've seen a woman, heavy with child. Did ye wonder how the child got in her belly?"

"Aye, Father."

"To make a child, a man puts his seed in a woman. God blesses them, and it grows there."

"You were planting a seed in Mother?"

"Aye."

Dughall looked worried. "How does a man put a seed in a woman?"

"Hmmphh..." Alex reddened. He hadn't planned on going this far. "You've seen your mother, how she looks different from us down there."

"Aye. She doesn't have a whang."

"When the seed comes, a man's member grows hard and he slips it inside her. They move together, milking the seed out."

"I don't believe it!" Ian cried. "Is that the only way children come?"

Alex stared. "Aye."

"Mother's with child, now?"

"Nay. It doesn't work every time."

"So you keep trying?"

"Aye."

Dughall blushed. "Does it hurt her?"

"Hmmphh... Did it sound like I was hurting her?"

"Nay. It sounded like you were having a good time!" Dughall blurted.

"Shhhh..." Ian hissed. "We weren't listening."

Alex chuckled. "It's all right. We were having a good time. The union of a man and a woman is a pleasurable thing."

"Is that why you do it so much?"

Alex reddened with embarrassment. "Aye."

"But Father. Why..."

"How does a seed..."

Alex rubbed his forehead. "Enough! My head aches from all these questions. Come on, lads."

They stood and walked the path to Whinnyfold.

A HANGING IN NEWBURGH

NEWBURGH ABERDEENSHIRE
JULY 1628
TEN MONTHS LATER

Alex manned the rudder as they sailed into the mouth of the river. The port of Newburgh was ahead, its stone buildings standing against a blue sky. He spotted the flagpole of the boat supply house. *I must have a new sail,* he thought. *I hope that Duncan's willing to bargain.*

Waves lapped against the boat as the channel narrowed. Ian and Dughall leaned over the side, skimming their hands in the water.

The smell of the fish market assaulted his nose. "Get ready to take the rudder, lass. I'll drop the sail."

Jessie nodded.

Maggie sat on a crate, grasping the side of the boat. "Can I help?"

"Keep a hold on those lads; get their hands inside the boat." The harbor appeared, with dozens of masts dotting the horizon.

Dughall jumped up. "Father, look at all the people!"

Ian pointed. "There's a priest and a man in strange black clothes, carrying a rope."

Alex had a disturbing thought. *Looks like a hangman. There's a priest with him. We should leave.*

The shore grew closer. He decided to take her in and get a better look. "Sit down, lads. We're about to dock. Take the rudder, lass."

Jessie sat at the stern and took the rudder. Alex dropped the sail, grabbed a rope, and waited at the bow. She steered the boat until it tapped the dock. He jumped out and held the boat off the pier while securing it to a post.

"You're getting better at this, lass."

"Aye, captain."

Alex scanned the shore. The men in black were gone, but dozens of strangers walked towards the hollow. Bile rose in his throat. "I don't like this, lass. There's an execution today."

Jessie nodded. "Likely a murderer, reaping his due."

"Hmmphh... Murderer or no. I don't want the lads to see it."

"You need a sail, husband. We'll do our trading and stay clear of the hollow."

Alex shook off his wariness. "All right, lass. But keep away from crowds. No one knows us here. It could be risky."

Jessie packed a bag with soap and herbs. "Agreed. Come on, lads. We have trading to do."

Maggie grabbed the mast and pulled herself up, straightening her back.

Alex offered her a hand. "Are ye all right?"

"A bit stiff. These bones aren't used to sitting."

He helped her out of the boat and caught the boys as they were passed up.

Jessie climbed onto the dock and smoothed her skirt. "It must be an important hanging. I've never seen so many people."

Alex shrugged. "I'm heading to Duncan's to see about some sailcloth. I'll ask."

"Maggie and I will take the lads to market, to trade soap for tea."

Dughall whined. "I want to go with Father."

"Your father has business."

"I don't mind if they tag along. They're old enough."

"Come on, lass," Maggie said. "Let them go with their father. Without the lads, we'll drive a hard bargain."

"Meet us at the church when you're done," Alex said.

Ian made a face. "It isn't Sunday. I'm not going to church!"

"Nay, lad. We'll meet in front of the church."

Maggie took Jessie's arm and limped down the pier. Alex felt uneasy as he walked in the opposite direction, towards Duncan's Boat Supply. The boys followed on his heels, imitating his walk.

***

Maggie passed a fishmonger, cutting up bait and tossing it into a barrel. *Stinks like rotten fish brine,* she thought. The wind changed, giving them relief. The trader's tent was ahead, decorated with brightly colored ribbons. "Show yer bonny face, lass," she whispered. "Gain his favor. If he gives ye trouble, leave the trade to me."

Jessie smiled. "Just like last time."

"Remember. Three pounds of tea, no less."

They entered the colorful tent and looked around. Reams of cloth were stacked on a table, and bins of spices lay next to boxes of ribbons, yarn, and buttons. Maggie inhaled. Fragrant smells of cinnamon and nutmeg hung in the air.

The olive-skinned man mopped his forehead. "It's a hot one."

Jessie tossed back her hair. "Aye." She rolled a button between her fingers. "What's it made of?"

"Genuine coral, from the Red Sea. One penny each."

Jessie put it back. "Maybe next year."

"A bonny lass should have a rich husband to buy her things."

Jessie blushed. "I'm rich in other ways." She held out a bag. "I want to trade this soap for tea."

The trader pawed through the bars and lifted the bag out of her hands, weighing it on a small scale. "There's too much soap at the market. I'll offer two pounds of tea."

Maggie felt a glimmer of hope. She might be needed after all.

Jessie frowned. "Perhaps you should deal with my mother."

The man reddened. "Do you want to trade or not?"

Maggie spoke up. "Nay. We've been offered three pounds."

The trader glared at the old woman. "'Haps you should take it."

"We might, lad. Tell ye what, give us three pounds and I'll throw in these healing herbs." She held out a pouch for him to inspect.

He sniffed. "Foul smelling. What is it?"

"Yarrow. Makes a tonic to kill a fever."

"Never heard of it."

Maggie closed the pouch, enjoying the game. "Come on, lass. We'll go back to the other trader."

The man frowned. "Wait. You say three pounds of tea?"

"Time's a wastin'. Make up yer mind."

"All right, it's a bargain." He peered in the bag. "Does yarrow have anything to do with witchcraft? They're hanging a witch in the hollow today."

Maggie's eyes widened. "What did ye say?"

"Are ye deaf, old woman? They're hanging a witch. A healer who did strange things." He handed over the tea. "You're in luck. No one wants to trade today. They're all here for the hanging."

Maggie felt a surge of determination. "We'll see about that."

They left the tent and walked towards the church. Maggie's heart ached as she recalled the day they came for her mother. A priest accused her of witchcraft and dragged her from the arms of husband and child. Days later, they were forced to watch the gruesome execution. She slowed down and clutched her chest. "Ach! I can't bear it."

"Are ye all right?"

"Nay, lass! We can't let them hang her. She's a healer like us."

Jessie blanched. "I promised Alex we wouldn't go near the hollow. He doesn't want the lads to see it."

Maggie flushed with anger. "What kind of people are we if we can't stand up for our own?"

"It's too dangerous. No one knows us here."

"Damn the church!"

Jessie glanced around fearfully. "Hush now. Someone might hear ye. This isn't the place to defy the church. Besides, Alex won't let us go."

The old woman's anger grew. "I'm not his wife. He holds no sway over me." They reached the tree that stood in the churchyard. Maggie waited until Jessie sat, and put down her pack. "Take the lads to the boat. I'm going to the hollow to speak for her."

Jessie stood, clearly alarmed. "Don't go! Alex says we can only get into trouble."

"He's a Christian, or so he claims to be. Would Jesus tell him to run away? He didn't shrink from trouble. Go to the boat! I'll meet ye later." Determination coursing through her veins, she followed the crowd walking in the direction of the hollow.

***

Alex ran the sailcloth through his hands. "It's a fine cloth, Duncan. I need enough to make a sail for my scaffie. How much did ye say?"

Duncan stared. "I don't suppose ye have gold or silver?"

Alex reddened. "Nay. I have two hogs that will be ready soon."

"Hmmphh…"

"I could throw in some plaids and soap that my wife made."

"Nay bother. How about you run some cargo to Aberdeen for me?"

Alex felt hopeful. "One run? My boat?"

"Aye. Do we have a bargain?"

"Aye." There was a bulge in the sailcloth. Ian and Dughall wrestled underneath, laughing like fools. "Forgive me, Duncan. Come out, lads!"

"They're fine sons, Alex. It's good to see ye so happy."

His heart swelled. "Those lads are my life."

"How's the wife? And your aunt?"

"Jessie's well. Maggie's feeling her age. Lads!"

Ian and Dughall crawled out from under the sailcloth and stood. "We couldn't hear you," Ian said.

Dughall whispered. "We could too."

Alex frowned. "Which is it, lads?"

Ian blushed. "Both. I didn't hear ye, he did."

"Hmmphh… My business is finished. Let's find your mother."

They nodded.

Alex felt uneasy. "Duncan, what's going on here today?"

"They're hangin' a witch in the hollow. People came from miles around to see it."

"Who are they hanging?"

"A young woman. Came here years ago to heal the sick and deliver babies. Someone accused her of passing a sickness from a child to its mother. The woman died."

"Dear Jesus." He thought of his women, making their way through the market, and hoped they didn't find out.

"I wonder what they'll do to her daughter."

"What? How old is the child?"

"About the same age as your sons."

Alex glanced at the boys. His heart ached for the poor lass. "Was there a trial?"

Duncan frowned. "If you could call it that. The priest and the constable got a confession from her. Rumor is she was tortured."

"God help us! Killing our healers. Are we losing our minds?" His bowels churned. "I'd better find my wife. It's not something I want the lads to see."

Duncan extended his hand. "I don't blame ye. I'll keep the sailcloth and send word when I need ye to make that run."

Alex shook his hand. "Thank ye, friend."

"Take care of those lads."

Alex and the boys left the supply house. His boots clacked on the wooden pier as they walked towards the church. *A healer like my wife,* he thought. *I'll tell Jessie not to tend to strangers. It's too dangerous.*

Seagulls screamed overhead. "Dead fishermen," Ian said.

"What?"

"The gulls. Aunt Maggie says they carry the souls of dead fishermen."

"Superstition. I'll have to talk to that woman." The church spire was getting closer. Alex's face was grim. "Keep an eye out for your mother."

Dughall pulled on his pant leg. "Father. What's torture?"

Alex got down on one knee and looked into the lad's eyes. *He's just a child. How much should I tell him?*

"Father?"

"Hmmphh… It's an evil thing. They hurt ye so bad that ye confess to a crime, whether ye did it or not."

Dughall bit his lower lip gently. "What do they do to ye?"

Alex reddened. "They beat ye or flog ye. I don't know. Sometimes they burn ye or break your bones."

The lad's eyes widened. "It's wrong."

"I know it." Alex stood and tousled his hair.

Dughall balled his fists in frustration. "Father. Are you going to stop it?"

"I wish I could, Son. It's not that simple."

Ian pointed. "Mother is under the tree."

Alex stared at the churchyard. Jessie's hand was at her brow, anxiously scanning the docks. Maggie wasn't in sight. His fear blossomed. "Come on, lads. Your mother's looking for us. Let's run."

They arrived at the church as the bell tolled. People came out of buildings and headed for the hollow.

Alex had a bad feeling. "Where's Maggie?"

Jessie winced. "She went to the hollow. They're hanging a woman, a healer like me."

"I know, lass. It's more than terrible. What does she mean to do?"

"Speak for her."

He ran his fingers through his hair. "Damn it, wife! It's too dangerous. Why did ye not stop her?"

Jessie reddened. "I tried, but she wouldn't listen. You know how stubborn she is."

"When did she leave?"

"Not long ago."

Alex hesitated, torn between his family and the woman he loved like a mother. "She'll get herself killed! Take the lads to the boat. I'm going after her."

Jessie picked up their packs and gathered the boys. "Be careful, husband." She started walking towards the pier. "Come along, lads." The boys followed close behind.

Alex took a deep breath. "Daft old woman!" He walked towards the hollow, fearful of what he would find.

***

Dughall dawdled on the pier, tossing stones into the water. He spotted his mother and brother, nearing the boat. "Where is Father?" He glanced over his shoulder and saw Alex entering the forest. "He's going to stop the torture. I want to help." The boy took off his shirt and jumped off the dock onto the sandy path. Walking to the woods, he passed two rough-looking men drinking from a flask.

One raised his hand and growled, "Lad, stop!"

Dughall stiffened. *Oh God. Strangers.*

The man's yellow teeth gleamed. "I'll be damned. Look at his birthmark."

"He's the right age. This could be our lucky day."

Dughall's fear blossomed as the men blocked his path. Their intentions were clear. *They mean to take me!* He stepped aside and ran into the woods as fast as his legs could take him.

"Grab him! There's a bag of gold at stake."

Footsteps echoed behind him, getting closer. He smelled the man's stale breath, laced with whisky.

"Don't make me hurt ye, lad!"

"Put the knife away. The Earl wants him alive."

Dughall's heart pounded with fear as he reached the hollow. It was filled with people, gathered around a gallows tree. His voice was shrill. "Father, help me!" He spotted Alex just as they were about to grab his arms.

✳✳✳

The condemned woman kneeled on the ground near the gallows tree. She stared as the executioner rested a ladder against the trunk, climbed to the third rung, and threw a rope over a branch.

Elspeth pondered her fate. *Soon, they will wring the life from me.* She touched a wound on her cheek, where they branded her with a hot iron. *Oh, Kale. I couldn't change their hearts. What will become of our little girl?* The pain in her heart took her breath away. *Dear husband. Tell me that ye wait for me beyond the veil.*

The crowd parted as a priest walked among them, an imposing figure in a flowing black robe. He towed a dark-haired child and set her roughly before Elspeth. His voice was cold. "Say farewell to your mother, lass. Heed that you don't take her path, or you'll share her fate." The child shuddered.

Elspeth clasped her chest. "How can you let my daughter see this?"

"You refused to name others."

The executioner called. "Father Ambrose. I need to talk to ye about the rope."

"I'll give ye a few moments, no more." The priest walked away to see the man in black.

Elspeth's heart ached as she tipped the child's chin. "Keira. Look at me."

The wee lass smiled through tears of sorrow. Wordlessly, she covered the wound on her mother's cheek with the palm of her hand.

Elspeth gasped as the healing energy closed the wound. She held her daughter's hand and pressed it to her lips. "Not here, little one. There is great danger."

"Momma. You won't let them kill ye."

Elspeth spoke softly. "Listen carefully. Remember the stories I told ye about your grandmother?"

Keira nodded.

"Do ye remember what I taught ye about the stars?"

"Tell me again."

"Look to the stars and find the Goddess of the hunt, bow and quiver in hand. True north lies beyond the tip of her arrow."

"Now I remember."

"Find your grandmother. Go northwest, sixteen miles or so through the forest. The village is near some standing stones."

Keira's eyes glistened with tears. "Come with me."

Elspeth's heart ached. "I can't. Remember well what I taught ye."

A tear rolled down her cheek. "Oh Momma. Let me die with you."

"Nay, child! It's not your time." Elspeth brushed her lips against her forehead. "Dinna watch it. When my body drops, run to the forest. The Goddess will protect ye."

Keira took a ragged breath. "I love ye, Momma."

Her voice was soft. "Oh child. I love ye, too."

***

Alex looked around the hollow. A large crowd had gathered, talking and mopping their foreheads. The executioner was near the gallows tree, showing a priest the rope. His heart sank. The condemned woman kneeled on the ground, whispering to her wee daughter. He heard a child screaming behind him.

"Father! Help me!"

Alex turned and saw Dughall running towards him. Two men were about to grab his arms. "Dear God!" He shook with anger as he scooped him up.

The men stopped dead in their tracks and stared. Dughall sobbed against his shoulder.

"What do ye want with my son?"

"Nothing."

"Damn it! You were chasing the child."

"Nay, we were playing with him."

"Hmmphh…"

They circled Alex like a pack of wolves. "The lad is yer son?"

"Aye!"

"Let's see that birthmark on his shoulder."

Alex's anger grew. "Nay!"

The man's eyes were red with bloodshot. A shadow of recognition crept across his face as he spied the birthmark. "Where are ye from?"

Alex shifted Dughall in his arms and made a fist. "It's none of your business! Get away before I lose my temper."

The men exchanged a look and left the hollow, walking towards the church. They appeared to be arguing.

Dughall trembled with fear. "They were after me, Father."

"Shhhh… I won't let them hurt ye. What are ye doing here?"

"I wanted to help ye."

"Help me do what?"

"Stop the torture."

Alex's heart ached. It was too late for that. He heard Jessie's voice behind him, laced with relief.

"Thank God! You've got him."

"Two men were after him, lass. They wanted to see his birthmark.

He's shaking like a leaf."

"Let me put his shirt on."

Alex put him down. "Don't take your eyes off him. Those men might come back."

Jessie slipped the shirt over his head. "You scared me to death, child! Why did ye leave us?" She pulled his arms through the sleeves. Dughall started to cry.

Alex scanned the crowd and spotted the old woman's yellow sweater. "Nay bother, lass. We have to stop Maggie."

***

Maggie's outrage grew as she watched the condemned woman. The lass bore signs of a beating and burn marks on her face. The reunion with her wee daughter was heartbreaking. *How can they do this to a child? Have they no shame?* She gathered her courage and faced the priest. "Who speaks for her?"

His eyes narrowed. "It's too late, old woman. She's confessed to being a witch."

"What did ye do to her to get that confession? Torture her?"

"We have our methods of persuasion. This is none of your business."

"It is my business! I'm a healer." She faced the crowd. "Good people. How can ye allow this? Who will tend wounds, set bones, and deliver the babies? How many will die if ye lose yer healer?"

Father Ambrose reddened. "Silence, old woman! God decides who lives or dies, not this witch. The Bible says that 'thou shalt not suffer a witch to live.'"

"Then the book is wrong. Think, man! Jesus wouldn't want this. He loved all people, saint and sinner alike."

"You question the good book? This is blasphemy!" The crowd murmured its consent.

She felt a familiar hand on her shoulder.

"For God's sake, Maggie. They'll string ye up beside her. Think of the lads."

Maggie stiffened. "Alex, what are ye doing here?" She looked over her shoulder and saw Jessie with the boys. Ian stared at the gallows tree. Dughall clung to his mother's skirts. The priest turned his back on her. "How dare he. I'll give him a piece of my mind!"

"Maggie, please. He's a man of God."

"Torturing a young healer. He's no man of God!"

The priest turned around. "Get your mother out of here or I'll assume she's in league with the witch."

Alex's hand tightened around her arm. "That's enough." He led her to his family.

"But it's wrong…"

"Not another word."

Maggie's emotions were raw. Hot tears burned her eyes and threatened to fall. She felt a tug on her skirt and looked down.

Dughall's face was pale. "Auntie. Are they gonna torture her?"

"Ach! They've already done that. Now they'll hang her."

"Can we stop it?"

"Nay."

"What will happen to her daughter?"

"I don't know, lad."

***

Elspeth felt a ray of hope when the old woman spoke for her. It faded when her son dragged her away. She knew the end was near.

"Hang the damned witch!" a man shouted. "It's a shame that God-fearing people are bothered with witches." The crowd grumbled in agreement.

The executioner stood behind Elspeth, touching her shoulder. "I can't hold them any longer, lass."

The young mother stiffened, and held the child close. "I'll always be with ye daughter, look for the signs."

The executioner pried mother and child apart, and led Elspeth towards the ladder. The sun was in her eyes, sparing her the sight until the last moment. She stumbled as she saw the noose swinging.

He caught her. "Don't go soft on me, lass. It will be over soon."

Elspeth straightened her back and walked to the ladder. He prodded her up to the third rung. The crowd jeered as the noose was set around her neck. He tied her hands with a length of hemp.

Dear Goddess. Help me that I might die quickly. She held her head high and stared at her accusers.

Father Ambrose pointed. "Behold. What more proof do ye need? The witch gives us the evil eye."

Elspeth watched her wee daughter's face. Their eyes locked in sorrow and a word formed on her lips. "Run."

The sentence was pronounced. "Elspeth MacPherson, being accused of the detestable practice of sorcery, you are condemned to die upon the gallows. This is according to the laws of the God-fearing people of Newburgh and the Crown of Scotland. As ye remain unrepentant, may God have mercy on your soul."

The executioner placed his hand on her back. "I'm sorry, lass."

She whispered, "Peace be with ye, Brother."

He pushed her from the ladder, launching her body into the air. The branch dipped and the rope stretched so her toes scraped the ground. Her neck didn't break.

Elspeth felt the rope tighten against her throat and struggled to get her hands free. The bindings held fast and she thrashed in vain. She felt her chest bursting as air tried to explode from her lungs, her tongue swelled, and blood pooled in her face. She forced her mind to focus. *Goddess, protect my daughter.*

Her body convulsed and the noose tightened. Floating towards a comforting light, she felt warmth as her bowels released for the last time.

✳✳✳

Maggie felt helpless as she watched the lass struggle. "Goddess take her," she whispered. "Be merciful."

There was a quivering of the body's hands and a straightening of the limbs. She heard gagging and turned to her family. Ian stroked his throat as he stared at the body. Dughall dropped to his knees and prayed. Alex held Jessie close, shielding her from the sight. The woman's daughter stood nearby, staring at the body in disbelief.

"Poor wee orphan."

Alex squeezed her shoulder. "I'm sorry, Maggie."

She stiffened. "Sorry? Where is your God? Where is God now?"

The rope creaked as the body turned. The executioner felt for a pulse, and pronounced the word. "Dead."

A pitiful wail pierced the air as the child ran to the body and kneeled. "Momma! It can't be. Cut her down and let her live. Momma!"

A man turned on her. "What of the witch's bastard child? Seed of the devil, she's not even got a Christian name." He picked up a rope. "Let's dunk her in water to see if she floats."

Keira screamed. "Nay! Help me!"

Maggie saw herself as that child, watching her mother swing on the gallows. Her memories grew into outrage. She faced the man and grabbed his rope. "Leave the poor child alone!"

"Meddling old witch! I'll see ye dead or in hell."

"Don't let the lads out of your sight!" Alex cried. He sprang to her rescue, confronting the man with his fists.

The man backed off and approached the child with the rope. He grabbed her roughly and tied her hands. The poor little lass was numb.

Hysterical screams rang through the hollow. Dughall pressed his fingers to his temples and wailed. "Nay! Stop the torture!"

Ian trembled. "Brother, stop! Ohhh... I can't bear it." He covered his ears and shrieked like a wounded animal.

Dughall's eyes rolled heavenward and he fell to the ground with limbs twitching. Within moments, Ian sank to his knees and fainted.

Chaos broke out in the crowd. "She cast a spell on those lads!" "They're possessed by the devil." The man with the rope backed away. "We're doomed."

Maggie saw her chance and untied the child's hands. "Run, lassie."

Keira's eyes glistened with tears. "Peace be with ye, kind mother."

"Run, child! Don't look back." Maggie breathed a sigh of relief as she ran into the forest.

The priest stood over the boys and made the sign of the cross. "This is the devil's work indeed. She's bewitched these lads. Let her go."

Murmurs shot through the crowd. Mothers gathered their children and hurried them away. Men avoided the body as they streamed out of the hollow.

***

Alex sat on the ground, his heart full of grief. He cradled Ian and stroked his face until he opened his eyes.

"Father..."

Alex smiled weakly. "I'm here, Son. Jessie, what's wrong with Dughall?"

"He's suffering a fit."

His voice was barely a whisper. "Dear God. Like young Jamie McKay."

"Aye. We can't touch him until he stops twitching." She wiped spittle from his face. "Poor lad."

Father Ambrose stared down at them, fingering the crucifix at his neck. "Bring them to the church. We'll drive the devil out."

Alex despised this man of God. "I'll thank ye to stay away from my sons."

"You'll be back, begging for my help."

"Not today."

The priest walked off in a huff.

Jessie smiled weakly. "Dughall's coming around."

Maggie sighed. "Thank goodness."

Alex clenched his teeth. "Maggie, don't say another word. We're picking up these lads and going to the boat before someone hangs us." He looked around fearfully. "Lass, take Ian. I'll carry Dughall."

Jessie stood and took Ian's hand. "Can ye walk?"

"Is my brother all right?"

"Aye."

Alex picked up Dughall and cradled his head against his shoulder. His heart was heavy as they walked out of the hollow towards the harbor.

Dughall stirred. "Father?"

"Aye."

"Did she get away?"

Alex smiled. "Aye. We stopped the torture."

Dughall sighed. "Thank God."

THREAT

HUNTLY CASTLE
AUGUST 1628
TWO WEEKS LATER

Blackheart's eyes flashed as he stared at his manservant. He dug his fingers into the back of his chair and slammed it into the desk. "Incompetence! They had my son, but they let him slip through their fingers."

Connor flinched. "Aye, m'Lord."

"They had nothing else to say?"

"They asked about the reward."

"Bring Boyd and Malcolm to me! When I'm through with them, they'll beg me for the chance to talk."

Connor swallowed hard. "Forgive me, m'Lord. If ye torture them, people won't tell us of the lad's whereabouts. It took me a year to gain their trust after the innkeeper's death."

Blackheart reddened as he took his seat. "How dare ye insinuate that it was my fault! That old fool tried to protect my wife and died for it, plain and simple." He took out a dirk and ran his thumb along the edge of the blade. His voice was cold and deliberate. "You disappoint me, lad. It's been a long time since you needed a lesson."

Connor paled.

His blood boiled. "Lay your hand on the desk, palm up."

Sweat beaded on Connor's forehead as he brought forth his hand and splayed it on the desk. "Forgive me, m'Lord. I only meant to say…"

"Don't lie to me!" Blackheart grasped the little finger and extended it. "When I studied anatomy in France, they called this a useless digit." He lined the blade up with the first joint.

Connor's eyes widened. "M'Lord, please! I'll never question ye again."

Blackheart watched the man's eyes as he released the finger and dug the tip into the center of his palm. "God damn it! I have a son out there, my own flesh and blood, being raised by an ignorant fisherman.

Is my wife with him?" He pressed harder, drawing blood.

Connor drew a ragged breath. "Uhhhh... Nay, m'Lord. The man's wife is a red-haired lass."

Blackheart withdrew the knife. "Hmmphh... Christal must be dead, or she would have run to her father. That old bastard would have brought a hundred men against me. She could have given birth before she died. How old is this child?"

"Boyd said the lad looked to be eight or nine. Had black curls like yours, and the mark of the stag on his right shoulder."

"Interesting." He took out a kerchief and threw it down. "You're bleeding on my mahogany desk. Where was he spotted?"

Connor pulled back his hand and wrapped it. "Newburgh, m'Lord. It's a seaport at the mouth of the Ythan."

"I know where it is! Tell me. Why did they not abduct the lad?"

"M'Lord. The lad's father threatened the men. They thought they could grab him later, but madness broke out at the hanging."

Blackheart stared. "A hanging? Ignorant commoners! Have they no other entertainment? They took my son to a public hanging?"

Connor nodded. "Aye."

"When I find that fisherman, he'll die a slow and painful death." He ran his thumb along the blade. "No one recognized the lad's parents?"

"Nay. Boyd asked around, but no one seemed to know. They disappeared soon after the woman was hanged. Hundreds of people came to see it, some from as far as Aberdeen."

Blackheart stared. "Bring Boyd and Malcolm to the castle for questioning. Tempt them with the offer of a reward."

Connor nodded. "Aye, m'Lord." His eyes were awash with pain.

Blackheart tossed his curls over his collar. *The man looks like he's about to faint,* he thought. He took the stopper out of a crystal decanter and poured two glasses of whisky. The golden nectar smelled of peat and sea salt. "There can be no pleasure without pain. You handled that well, lad. A lesser man would have cried. Join me."

Connor unwrapped his hand. "Thank ye, m'Lord." He lifted the glass carefully, sipping the precious drink.

Blackheart savored the smoky taste and poured another. "Send Garriock to me with his drawing pad. I'll sit for him while he sketches my birthmark. Better yet, he can use my son Gilbert as a model."

"As you wish."

"Take the sketches to Newburgh and ask questions. Throw some gold around. Someone must know who they are."

Connor took another sip. "And if no one knows?"

Blackheart frowned. "God damn it! Take as many men as ye need and cover the major seaports, as far south as Aberdeen. We must find my son."

Dughall

COMING OF AGE

WHINNYFOLD
MID-OCTOBER 1635
SEVEN YEARS LATER

Dughall struggled with the rudder as they approached the Bay of Whinnyfold. The sea was rough, with broken waves and white foam. His jaw tightened.

God help us. We're coming in too fast.

Wet curls whipped his face, obscuring his vision. His brother sat on a crate, gripping the side of the boat. "Hang on, Ian!"

A wave broke over the bow, jolting the stern upward and soaking them to the skin. Rocks appeared portside, as points rising out of the water.

"Watch out for the Skares!" Ian shouted, as he moved to the stern. "Can ye handle her, Brother?"

Dughall's heart pounded with fear. Their lives were in his hands. "Aye. Trim the mainsail! Slow her down."

The lanky, red-haired lad jumped up and manned the rigging. "Ach! Rope's frayed." Water sloshed across the bottom of the boat as he trimmed the sail.

Dughall's bowels churned. "Will it hold?"

"Aye."

"Thank God! Sit down; I don't want ye tossed in the drink."

Ian complied.

Dughall sailed on a starboard tack close to the wind, avoiding the rocks. Bile rose in his throat as he turned into a port tack. Nearing the shore, Ian stood and dropped the sail. The boat scraped the rocky beach and thudded to a stop.

Dughall breathed a sigh of relief, and spoke his father's words. "Thank God for a safe journey. Pull her higher and tie her off."

They jumped out of the 'Bonnie Fay', secured the sail, and pulled the boat onto the sand. Wind whipped sea spray over their heads.

Ian glanced at the cliff above. "Father's up there, pacing like a madman."

Dughall nodded. "I hear him thinking about us. He's sick with worry."

"We were nearly killed."

"For God's sake, don't tell him that."

They waved until Alex turned and headed for the village.

Dughall ran his fingers through his hair. Wet clothes stuck to his skin, making him shiver. "It's a raw day. Shall we haul the catch up to the cottage?"

Ian warmed his hands under his armpits. "Aye. I don't want Mother down here."

The young men propped a creel against the rock. They reached into the hull and grabbed the slippery fish, loading them into the basket.

Dughall got the last cod, shut the top, and lifted it onto his back. "I'll carry it, Brother. Your hands are frozen."

Ian grunted.

Dughall's stomach growled. "Do ye think the midday meal is ready?"

Ian nodded. "I hope so. Mother was making oatcakes and soup."

Lightning streaked the sky to the mountains at Braemar. They started up the steep path. "Pick up the pace, Brother!" Ian cried. "It's about to break loose."

Dughall's mind wandered as they hiked up the cliff. His heart swelled at the thought of a dark-haired lass, her eyes as green as a peacock's feather. He glanced at his brother. "I dreamed of her again."

Ian smirked. "Have ye bedded her yet?"

Dughall shifted the creel higher on his shoulders. "Nay. Father says we mustn't take advantage of a lass."

Ian frowned. "For God's sake, it's a dream. You can do what ye want. Next time, stick your hand up her skirt. See how far ye can get."

Dughall felt a swelling in his loins. "I only want to kiss her. I swear it! Don't make me think about it."

Ian snorted. "Ha! Look at ye. You're bustin' out of your breeks. Mary might have a cousin for ye. I'll ask."

Dughall burned with shame. "Nay. I want to find this lass. I've known her all my life." A cold wind crossed the path, stealing their breath.

Ian shivered. "Come on. You're almost sixteen and you've never been with a lass."

"I know it. I'll find her."

"Ach! Talk to me later, it's colder than a witch's teat."

"Brother!"

Ian smiled. "Well, it is."

***

The storm had come and gone, leaving the sea calm. Gulls returned to the rocky beach, foraging for fish. The Hay cottage smelled of wet clothes, peat, and cock-a-leekie soup.

Dughall opened the door to let in fresh air. He was worried about old Maggie. "How bad is she, Mother?"

Jessie sighed. "Bad enough. Her joints are swollen and stiff. I made bark tea this mornin', but it barely touched the pain."

Dughall's heart ached. "I'll make a hot poultice of heather tips."

"That didn't help last time. Let her rest. It's the best thing."

Alex stared. "She's eighty, Son. At that age, pain's a constant companion." He flexed his fingers. "My hands are stiff, too." He sat on a stool and pulled on his boots. "Storm's passed. I'm going to check on the boat."

Ian got up from the table. "I'll go with ye."

Jessie wiped her hands on her apron. "Help your father, lads. I'll clean up."

Alex stood and drew her close. "Thank ye, lass. We'll check the rigging. She handled poorly in the bay."

Ian put on his coat and handed him a rope. "Line's tattered. I got another out of the loft."

Alex stared. "Are ye coming, Son?"

Dughall felt uneasy. "Nay, Father. I want to check on Aunt Maggie."

Alex wrapped a scarf around his neck. "Sometimes I think you're more healer than fisherman. That's woman's work."

His father's remark stung like a bee. "I guess I'll come with ye."

Alex threw the rigging line over his shoulder. "Nay bother. Ian and I can manage."

Dughall reddened as they walked out the door. At least he didn't say "without ye".

Jessie's hand rested on his shoulder. "Go with them, Son."

"Nay, Mother. Something bad's afoot."

***

He took the kettle outside and lit the fire with a bundle of peat. The pot smelled rank, like the bottom had caught. Jessie emerged with a stack of plates. Her face was lined with pain and weariness. Dughall felt the stiffness in her fingers, radiating to her wrists.

Mother's hands are botherin' her, yet she never complains. He lifted a bucket. "Sit down, Mother. I'll haul water and wash dishes."

Jessie's eyes filled with gratitude. "Bless ye, Son. You always know when I'm in trouble."

The young man smiled. If the green-eyed lass was as kind as his mother, he'd be a lucky man. Sudden movement to his right caught his attention. Jamie McKay ran towards them, his eye twitching furiously. Dughall put down the bucket. "Jamie's coming up the path. He looks bad."

"Is he about to have a fit?"

Pain cramped his forearm. "I don't think so."

The frightened lad grasped his knees and stuttered. "Bbbrother."

Dughall stared. "What's wrong with Glen's arm?"

"Bbbroke."

Jessie frowned. "How did ye know, Son?"

"I feel it, Mother." He touched his forearm. "It's a stabbing pain right here."

Her eyes widened. "Dear God. Don't show us! Where's your mother, lad?"

"Wwwith him."

"Let's get my healer's bag."

Jessie and Dughall entered the cottage. She took her shawl from a peg and drew it around her shoulders. "I asked ye not to speak of the Sight. It's dangerous."

Dughall frowned. "Jamie won't tell anyone."

"How many times have I told ye to hide your gift? They're hanging healers for praying over a man. Magic words! If they knew ye had the Sight..."

"I'll be careful with strangers."

"Careful? Promise me you won't help them."

Dughall remembered the Sunday sermon. It wasn't the Christian thing to do. "Did Jesus turn strangers away? Or lepers? Or the poor? It's wrong."

She sighed. "He was tortured and nailed to a cross for his trouble. Murdered by his own people. Is that what ye want?"

"Nay."

Tears glistened in her eyes. "Think of your family. I'd die if I lost ye."

"Don't cry, Mother. I can't bear it."

"Promise me you'll stay away from strangers."

"I will."

"Good." She handed him a flat board and flask. "Take these. We may have to splint it."

Dughall rubbed his arm. "I'm sure of it."

They stepped outside and shut the door, pulling it tight. Jamie waited anxiously, clutching his eye. Seeing them, he ran between two cottages. They followed him out of the village and past the cliffs, to a meadow that was thick with sweet grass.

Dughall ran his fingertips through the dried blades. Halfway across the meadow, he sensed the child's location and pointed to a grove of apple trees. The boy sat on the ground, with his mother nearby.

"There's Glen and Claire!" Jessie cried. "My hands are stiff. Your friend can hold him while you splint it."

Jamie's eyes widened. "Nay! I'll get sssick."

"Your brother needs ye, lad."

Jamie grimaced and spit on the ground. "Needs ye, lad!" he cried. "Needs ye!" His head jerked violently. "Oh God. Make it stop."

He'll be cursing soon, Dughall thought. "I can manage alone, Mother. He's not well."

Jamie reddened. "Fffforgive me."

"Go home, friend. Your brother will be all right." Dughall watched as the young man ran for the village. He was torn between helping the child and following his friend. "He's headed for a fit, Mother."

"You could be right."

They hurried to the injured child. Glen sat on the ground, cradling his left arm in his right. She stroked his hair. "Poor laddie. What happened, lass?"

"He fell out of a tree," Claire said. "His arm doesn't look right." Glen whimpered.

Jessie lifted his chin. "Be a brave lad. We're going to fix your arm."

Dughall's wrist throbbed as he knelt and cradled his head. "Lie down, wee one. I feel your pain." With the child on the ground, he slipped the flat board under the limb and extended the hand palm up. His face was a mask of concentration.

Claire's eyes widened. "Dughall's going to set it?"

Jessie nodded. "Aye. He has a way with bones."

"Steady it, Mother."

Jessie knelt behind the child, cradled his elbow, and pressed her thumbs on his forearm to keep it still. Glen hissed. "Easy, lad. Feel for the break, Son."

Dughall grasped the crooked wrist and saw that the skin was unbroken. "Can ye move the fingers?" Glen wiggled his fingers slightly. "Good. The break is at the wrist."

The young man opened the bag and took out comfrey oil, cloth strips, and a leather splint. He opened a flask and soaked the splint until the water ran off. Satisfied, Dughall grasped the child's wrist and pressed his thumbs into the lower arm. He closed his eyes and prodded, sensing a clean break.

Glen sobbed. "You're hurting me."

"I know lad. Be brave and I'll take ye fishing."

"His lips are blue," Claire whispered. "Will it be much longer?"

"Nay. I feel the two edges. Mother, lift the elbow and hold it still."

He pulled the wrist and straightened it, popping the bone into place. The boy took a ragged breath and fainted. Dughall worked quickly, smearing comfrey on the wrist and padding it with cloth strips. "Hurry, I want to get this on before he wakes. Hand me the splint."

"What's the oil for?" Claire asked.

"Stops the swelling and helps the bones to knit." He formed the splint around the wrist, tying it with leather laces.

"Why'd ye soak it?"

"Wet leather shrinks to keep the wrist still." With the splint in place, he patted the child's cheek. "Wake up, laddie."

Glen opened his eyes. "Is it over?"

"Aye." Dughall nestled his arm in a sling and lifted him gently into his arms. "I'll carry him. Let's get him into a warm bed."

Glen sniffled. "You promised to take me fishing?"

"Aye, you're a brave one."

***

Jessie packed the bag and picked up her board. They hiked through the meadow and past the sea cliffs. Jamie was nowhere in sight. As they approached the village, Glen fell asleep.

Dughall passed the child to his mother. "Such a brave lad. Someday, I'll have a son like him."

Claire smiled. "I'm sure you will. How should I care for him?"

"Roll a sock into a ball. Starting tomorrow let him grip it so he won't lose strength. There's willow bark in the shed if there's fever or pain."

"Bless ye lad. You're as gifted as your mother."

They continued walking, nearing the cottages. Dughall's mind wandered to another time and place. In the cemetery, women wailed as men lowered a casket into a grave. Claire stood in a mourning dress, tears streaming down her face, as the minister closed his book. Dughall looked down to see Jamie, wrapped in a burial shroud.

The vision cleared. "Jamie's in trouble."

"How do ye know, lad?"

His heart pounded. "Did ye not see him in the shroud?"

"Nay."

Claire's cottage was a few strides ahead. He ran to the door and opened it wide. Jamie lay unconscious in front of the hearth, his arms and legs twitching. He knelt and felt his neck for a pulse. "Oh God."

Jessie lay Glen on a bed and joined him.

Claire kneeled and touched her son. "You were right, lad. How bad is it?"

Dughall lifted an eyelid. "His eyes are back in his head."

Jessie frowned. "We shouldn't touch him 'til the fit passes."

"I think he's dying, Mother. It feels like something's stuck in his throat." He cradled his head and opened his mouth.

"If he seizes, he'll bite your finger off."

Dughall inserted a finger into his throat to feel for a blockage. He pushed on the tongue and removed a mint leaf. Jamie's limbs relaxed, but his skin turned a dusty blue. They waited, hoping for a first breath. "Come on, friend. Breathe!"

Claire's voice cracked. "Will my son live?"

Jessie listened to his chest. "Nay, lass. God's called him home."

"Lord have mercy."

Dughall brightened. "I know what to do. I'll breathe for him."

"It's not for us to question God's will."

"Mother. God doesn't want him dead. Let me try."

"It's too dangerous. I won't have the church accusing us of witchcraft."

Claire paled. "Let him try, lass. I won't tell a soul."

Jessie hesitated. "Go on, Son."

Dughall tilted Jamie's head back and dropped his jaw forward. He took a deep breath and blew into his mouth, but it whistled out of his nose.

"It's hopeless. You can't get it into his chest."

"Wait, Mother." He pinched the nose and forced two short breaths into his mouth.

Jessie held a hand on his chest, her eyes widening. "Do it again."

Dughall blew two quick breaths into his mouth and watched as the chest rose and fell. He repeated it three times and released his nose. Jamie gasped for air. "Thank God! Mother, do ye see what this means? We can help a man breathe."

Jessie paled. "It seems that way."

"We must tell the others."

"Nay. People will say you brought him back from the dead."

Claire agreed. "She's right, lad. These are strange times, when miracles are seen as blasphemy. They would put you and my son to death as instruments of the devil."

Jamie groaned. "Dddevil? Was I dddead?"

Dughall stroked his forehead. "Nay, friend. You had another fit."

Claire stared. "Tell the truth, lad. You saw my son in a shroud?"

"As plain as day."

"Seein' and hearing the coming o' the doom. You have the Sight, don't ye?"

Jessie blanched. "Don't answer that, Son! He's a fine healer. Don't condemn him."

"Easy, lass. My own dear mother had the Sight. Go home and teach your son to hide his remarkable gift."

***

Dughall lifted Jamie into his arms and placed him in the bed. When the lad fell asleep, they left the cottage. The grass was damp and the wind from the sea was raw.

Jessie drew her wrap tightly around her. "God help us."

Dughall sensed her disapproval. "Forgive me, Mother. I didn't mean to put us in danger."

Her voice was tense. "You risked everyone. Jamie. Ian. Your father and me. Don't you see? You'd be tortured and forced to accuse others."

"I wouldn't do it."

"You would. Remember what Maggie said. After a few days, Arabella named her own daughters."

Dughall reddened. "I remember. They burned them on the hill." He ran his fingers through his hair. "I won't put us in danger again."

Jessie shook her head. "Perhaps you should spend more time with your father. I can handle the needs of the village. Maggie can help."

His head throbbed. "Do ye want me to stop healing?"

Jessie sighed. "Nay. It would be like trying to stop the tides."

Dughall rubbed his temple. "Will Jamie be all right?"

"For now."

"Why does he repeat what we say? He doesn't want to do it. He curses and makes strange noises. I've seen him bark like a dog."

Jessie hesitated. "The minister says it's a spirit possessing his body."

"Could it be true?"

"Nay. I've seen this affliction before. Someday we'll find him dead, choked on his own tongue."

Dughall's throat tightened. "Mother. Ian said that I once had a fit."

Jessie frowned. "Aye. It was after that awful hanging in Newburgh."

"Will I have another?"

"Nay. Eight years have passed. It's a wonder we all didn't have fits, watching that poor woman strangle to death. I've never seen your father so mad at Maggie."

"She did the right thing. The child got away."

"I often wonder what happened to the poor lass. I longed to take her home with us."

"Why didn't we?"

"Your father saved Maggie from an awful man, then you and Ian

DARK BIRTHRIGHT - *JEANNE TREAT*

fainted. People thought you were bewitched. It was all we could do to escape with our lives. I prayed that the lass would find her way."

Dughall felt a chill. "Mother. What did she look like?"

"She resembled her mother, with dark hair and fair skin. Her eyes were strange, as green as a precious stone."

Keira

JANE☆

A GREEN-EYED LASS

LOUDEN WOOD
FOREST OF DEER
ABERDEENSHIRE
MID-OCTOBER 1635

NEXT DAY

Keira MacPherson sat on the rough altar stone watching the eastern sky. A beautiful sunrise always brought her closer to her mother. She closed her eyes and spoke from the heart. "Mother, hear me. Last night I dreamed of a dark-haired lad, kind and gentle and pure of heart. His face eludes me but his voice is as beautiful as a lark's song. The dream darkens and I see you on the gallows, cold and lifeless. I long to share your fate, but strangers rescue me from the crowd. It's been years since I've thought of their kindness. I wish you could tell me what it means."

Love surrounded her, giving her goose bumps. She opened her eyes and sighed. "Thank ye, Mother."

The young lass smiled as she opened a sketchbook. The thin piece of hide, finely tanned and stretched over a hoop, awaited the touch of a quill. "Now I remember." She dipped her pen into a well and drew dark curls and a noble forehead. "The eyes are as blue as a cornflower."

Keira drew the pupils and sketched the brows. She dipped her quill and continued drawing. The eyes were well-shaped, nose straight, and chin strong. She examined her work. The face was of a lad with long dark curls and kind eyes. "At last we meet." Her fingers stroked the page, lingering on his full lips. "Who can he be?" she whispered. "I love him like a friend. And why am I seeing Mother's death?"

She'd risen early with her mind awash in dreams and walked through the forest to the stone circle.

Keira touched his cheek with her forefinger. "Handsome lad. Do you dream of me, too?" She wrapped a plaid tightly around her. "Great Goddess. It's cold out here."

Ancient pine trees ringed the circle, stretching skyward from the mist. She looked around at the eleven granite stones, covered with lichens, and remembered the first time she saw them.

***

After the hanging, she'd wandered the forest seeking the stone circle. She walked by day, avoiding outsiders, and found north by the night sky. Five days passed, and she longed for a crust of bread, a soft bed, and her mother's arms. Had the Goddess failed her? Where were the stones?

A familiar voice whispered in her ear. "Look to the creatures of the forest, my child."

She heard leaves rustling and turned around. A brown hare wrinkled its nose and whirled on hind legs. As night fell, she tracked it into this clearing. In the moonlight the circle of stones was almost magical. An old woman waited on the altar stone, wrapped in a black shawl. She was Isobel Devlin, her grandmother.

***

Keira sighed. "It seems like a lifetime ago." At sixteen her childhood was far away, fraught with bad memories. "Grandmother knew I'd come. Mother told her in a dream, and left a sprig of rosemary as a sign." She sniffled. "I wish there was an herb to heal my heart. Why does love hurt so much?"

Shades of dawn cast purple hues over the Forest of Deer. She watched intently as the sun rose higher, illuminating the woods. It was so peaceful.

Keira slipped off the stone. She touched a spot on the altar with her right hand and placed her left on a moon symbol. Energy ran up her arm and across her shoulders. "Truly a place of power. The ancestors understood."

Time stood still as a family of rabbits hopped into the circle and fed upon sweet grasses. The forest was awakening with birdsong.

Her heart swelled. "All creatures of the Goddess. That's what Mother would say." Keira walked to the center mound and bowed her head in prayer. "Bless the ancestors for this sacred place. May the peace of the Goddess be ever in my heart." She glanced down. A sprig of rosemary grew at her feet, untouched by early frost. It was Mother's favorite. She tucked it in her sketchbook next to the drawing of the dark-haired lad. "Somehow," she mused. "You belong together."

Keira felt her mother's touch as she left the circle and headed for the village. Morning light played off twisted branches, illuminating the forest floor. She bent down and gathered a handful of beechnuts, slipping them into her pocket. "For Grandmother's porridge. She'll be waking soon."

***

Keira got back into bed, snuggling against the soft pillow. Across the room, Isobel snorted and held her breath. She counted silently. Four...five...six... Was she dead?

"Breathe, Grandmother!" The old woman gasped and settled on her back. The snoring resumed. "Thank the Goddess." Under the window, a rooster crowed to announce a new day. Keira frowned. "Shush, Fowler. You'll wake her for sure."

Isobel rolled over and spit into a kerchief. "Daft rooster. It's barely morning."

"Sun's been up a while. I've been to the stones and back."

"Great Goddess! It's cold in here."

Keira hadn't noticed. "I'll tend the fire." She got out of bed, went to the hearth, and picked up a wooden poker.

Isobel groaned as she struggled to turn over. "Ohhh... My poor back."

"Stay in bed, dear one. I'll feed the fire and cook some porridge."

Blankets rustled. "Bless ye, child."

Keira stoked the fire with a bundle of peat and stirred the ashes. When the room warmed she washed her hands and picked up a bucket. "I'll milk the cow." She opened the door and left the cottage. It was a crisp fall morning, with dew on the grass and leaves turning red. She looked around at the place she loved so well.

To the north, three cottages stood in a pine forest. There lived the priestess Regan, dear old Michael, and Kevin and Morgaine. To the west, eight cottages stood among beech trees. Four families with children lived there; the Birnies, Wests, Cummings, and Davies. Nessia Birnie was heavy with child, the birth only days away. Two couples lived there as well, Alistair and Janet Murray and Craig and Jeannie Ross. The McFay youngsters, Torry and George and Aileana, shared a cottage. Since the death of their parents, they fought over who should stoke the fire and cook the meals. Deep in the woods lived the old ones Cawley and Florag. No one alive remembered a time when they looked a day younger. Isobel's cottage stood apart, with a barn that held roots, herbs, grains, and animals. To the east lay fields of thistle and heather, rolling hills, orchards, and the meandering River Ugie. To the south, an old forest and the path to the stones.

Keira entered the barn and allowed her eyes to adjust. The sweet aroma of hay mingled with animal dung. The cow bellowed. "Hold on Bessie." She put a handful of oat straw in the trough. The cow munched lazily.

Keira sat on a stool, slid the bucket under her udder, and patted the shaggy animal, warming her fingers. "A wee bit, for Grandmother." She braced her shoulder, gripped the front teats, and squeezed down. Milk hissed into the bucket, sweetening the air. Squirt, squirt, squirt. She grabbed the back teats, and pressed them against her palms until milk filled the bottom of the pail. The cow snorted.

A hairy tail landed across her eyes. "Ach! I guess you're done. Thank ye, Bessie."

She picked up the bucket and left the barn. As she walked home, her mind wandered to the face in the sketchbook. "Handsome lad. Shall we marry and have wee ones?"

Keira entered the cottage and hung a pot of water over the hearth. As it came to a rolling boil, she added a handful of oats, a pinch of salt, and some beechnuts. "Almost ready, dear one."

Isobel sat up and drew the blanket around her. "I feel poorly, child. These old bones are complaining."

Keira's heart sank. The arthritis was getting worse. "I'll brew some tea." She put on a kettle of willow bark tea, served the porridge, and helped the old woman to the table.

Isobel's stomach growled as she gulped her porridge. "Look at me, child. There are dark circles under yer eyes."

"It's the dreams. They're so strange."

"Dreams can be telling. Do ye want to talk about them?"

"Not yet." She blushed deeply as she thought of the handsome lad.

Isobel patted her hand. "I know what ails ye. It's time that ye take a husband."

"You wouldn't mind?"

"Nay, lass. I can take care of myself. If the Goddess is willing, I'll see great-grandchildren before I die."

"Thank ye, Grandmother. We'll talk about it tomorrow."

Isobel smiled. "This is a small place, lass. I already know. Michael stopped by yesterday and asked me for yer hand."

"Michael?"

"Aye. Who else would it be?"

"What did ye say?"

"I gave him my blessing, of course. He wants to marry ye after the full moon."

Keira paled. "I can't marry him, Grandmother. Don't make me do this."

"Why not? Michael is our priest. Ye couldn't ask for a better man."

"He's old enough to be my father."

Isobel rebuked her. "So he's too old. Is that how ye judge a man?"

Keira burned with shame. "Nay."

"What choice do ye have, lass? There is Michael and Torry, and Torry's heart is set on another. The rest are too young."

Keira poked at the porridge, her stomach in knots. "Don't ask me to do this."

Isobel sighed. "Enough, child. It's been arranged. I thought ye loved Michael."

"He's a dear man, but I love him like a father."

"One kind of love grows into another. Someday, ye'll love him as husband."

Keira could barely breathe. "Nay! I'll marry the man who haunts my dreams. A dark-haired lad with a beautiful voice."

Isobel's face darkened. "There's no such man here."

"I know it."

"Ye can't leave this place, child. Outsiders kill us for our beliefs. Look at what happened to yer mother."

"If I tell them about the Goddess, it will change their hearts."

Isobel groaned. "Ach! Your mother said the same thing." The old woman clasped her chest. "Goddess, take me! I've lost one child to the hangman. Have ye no heart, lass?"

Keira's head ached. It was impossible to argue with the old woman. Her voice was childlike. "Forgive me, Grandmother. I do love ye. Let's not speak of it."

The kettle sputtered as the tea came to a boil. Keira poured the bitter brew and brought cups to the table. They sipped in silence, inhaling the spicy steam.

Isobel sighed. "It's time to tell ye how your father died."

Keira felt a chill and hugged herself. "I don't remember him. What was he like?"

Isobel smiled. "Kale MacPherson was older than yer mother, a grown man of thirty when she was sixteen. He was tall and handsome, with piercing blue eyes. He had a bit of gray at his temples, but that just made him more bonny. Kale could ride a horse and wield a sword as well as any man."

"Was he romantic?"

"Aye. Kale loved Elspeth with a rare passion. I remember the day he knelt before me, promising to love and protect her. From that day they lived as man and wife and accomplished many things."

"What did they do?"

"Kale was our priest, a kind and powerful man. He could summon the energy of the earth and stones. He assisted Elspeth in healings, laying his hands on her shoulders. For years, we saw sickness and wounds cured, pain banished, and babies delivered without mishap."

Keira felt a chill. "Mother told me he died when I was two. What happened to him?"

"Kale was a great hunter, child. He scoured the forest on horseback looking for game, bringing back deer and boar. Sometimes he traveled great distances, when food was scarce."

"Did Mother ride?"

"Aye. They hunted together many times. It happened just after the harvest. The nuts and withered fruits were stored, and the smell of blood was thick as sheep were slain and cured. The caterpillar's coat told us that it would be a long winter, so we agreed to send out a hunting party. Kale and Elspeth offered to go. I felt uneasy, but could not deny them. They dressed warm, packed supplies, and rode south. On the second day they came across a hunter attacked by a boar. Pus seeped from his swollen wounds."

Keira frowned. "Poor man! What did they do?"

"We had an unspoken code among us; that we could not let outsiders near us. They thought that we worshipped a devil and killed us for our healing gifts. Kale and Elspeth said that it must come to an end. The outsiders would see that we meant them no harm if we healed this man. She prepared a poultice and dressed his wounds. When his fever raged, Kale held her shoulders as she sent healing energy into the lad with her touch. The man recovered." Isobel caught her breath. "Many of us were afraid, but Kale assured us that he'd been careful. We struggled through a fierce winter, running low on food and yearning for warmer times. Kale set out to find deer." She grasped her heart. "He never returned to us, child. After two days, Elspeth feared that Kale had come to harm, so Michael and I set out to search for him."

"Did you find him?"

Isobel nodded. "Michael and I rode all morning until we met a traveler. Usually we wouldn't speak to outsiders, but we needed to know if the man had seen Kale. I stayed silent while Michael spoke. To this day, I remember their words."

✳✳✳

Michael said. "Ho! My mother and I seek a hunter. He's tall with black hair, riding a horse with white markings."

"I've seen no hunter," the traveler said. "But I have interesting news. They burned a witch in Newburgh. People came from miles around to see it."

"Mercy on the poor woman's soul."

"This one was a man. They say he worked magic on a hunter, joining with a witch woman to heal his wounds. They flogged him bloody, demanding that he name the witch woman, and condemned him to die at the stake. Men chained him to a post and piled wood at his feet. The priest offered to hang him if he named the woman."

"Did he name her?"

"Nay. The priest lowered the torch and started the fire. The witch suffered in silence until flames crawled up his legs, and the air festered with burning flesh. Finally, he spoke."

***

Isobel hesitated, as if staring at a ghost.

Keira's heart ached. "What did he say, Grandmother?"

"Peace be with ye, Brothers." Isobel sobbed.

"Oh dear Goddess. Are you sure it was Father?"

"Aye, child. Michael and I took a terrible risk. We traveled to Newburgh and stood at the stake, staring at the charred body. I prayed that it wasn't Kale, but Michael reached into the ashes and pulled out his wedding ring." Isobel took a ragged breath.

"Are you all right?"

"Nay, child. I loved Kale as a son. He suffered a terrible death to protect us."

"Did you tell Mother how he died?"

"Elspeth insisted that she know the story; what he suffered, his last moments, and what he said."

"Poor Mother."

"The lass was heartbroken. She didn't sleep or eat, wandering the forest day and night. Then she came to me with this daft idea."

"What did she say?"

"I remember it all too well."

She said, "Mother. This cannot continue, this fear that the outsiders have for us, and we for them. How many more will be burned at the stake? I must prove that we mean no harm. I'll go to Newburgh and live among them, healing their sick. If I teach the women about the Goddess, it will change their hearts."

Keira gasped. "Oh..."

"Ye know the rest, lass. It's foolish to think ye can change their hearts."

Her voice was weak. "Perhaps you're right."

"This old heart can't bear another loss. Promise me ye won't leave this place in my lifetime."

"I won't leave you, dear one. I promise."

***

Michael stood on the doorstep, thinking about what he would say. It was time to take a wife and start a family. Isobel had agreed to the match, but he wouldn't force the young lass. There was, after all, quite an age difference between them. *She's a fine healer like her mother,* he thought. *She could serve the Goddess at my side.*

Michael pushed back his graying hair. "I hope and pray that she thinks fondly of me." He rapped on the door. "Ho! Isobel, are you there?"

An elderly voice spoke from behind the door. "Come in."

Michael entered the cottage. The young lass, bonny as ever, sat at the table with her grandmother. Perhaps she already knew. The old woman looked ill. He kneeled at her side. "May I touch ye, old one?"

Isobel nodded. "Aye."

He placed a hand over her heart. "Ye look poorly today."

The old woman winced. "I'm in pain, but I'll live."

"Your heart force is strong. Do ye wish me to do a healing on ye?"

"Aye."

Michael rested his hands on the crown of her head and prayed. "May the healing energy of the Goddess come through me." He moved his hands, touched her face gently, and rested on her shoulders, lingering there. "Relax, old one." He closed his eyes as he ran a hand along her spine. The body suffered from the ravages of time. "May the Goddess ease your pain. Bless ye, Mother."

"Thank ye, lad."

Michael stood and looked at the young lass. She was regarding him with admiration? Apprehension? Curiosity? Her green eyes sparkled.

Isobel coughed.

"I can see that this may not be the best time, kind Mother. I should come back tomorrow."

"Nay, lad. Take my granddaughter for a walk and ask your question."

Michael stared. "Lass, can we talk outside?"

Keira swallowed hard. "Aye. Will you be all right, Grandmother?"

"I have my bark tea. Go with him."

✳✳✳

They left the cottage and stood outside. Keira's heart pounded as she studied him. His face was wrinkled, but he was still handsome. *He has a compassionate heart. Perhaps I could learn to love him.*

Michael smiled and held out his hands. "The Goddess created this beautiful day, yet it's not as bonny as you, lass."

Keira blushed.

His steel-blue eyes sparkled. "Morgaine told me that you splinted Robbie's arm."

"Aye. It was a clean break. He's a sweet child and brave too."

"You're a natural healer, lass. Someday you must have a child of your own to pass your gift to."

"Grandmother wants me to take a husband."

Michael smiled. "What do you want?"

"I don't know. She could be right."

"Lass. I'm not as handsome as a young lad, but still a man. Marry me, and I'll love and protect ye until my death."

Keira was speechless. She shook her head slightly.

Michael raised his hand. "Let me finish. I'm fond of ye. You're so like your mother that I can hardly bear it. Could ye learn to love me?"

Her lower lip trembled. "Great Goddess. I can't lie. I love ye, but you're like a father to me."

Michael looked stricken. "Your mother married a man fifteen years her senior. Their love was deep and rare."

He's a good man. I'm not worthy of him. She flushed deeply.

"Forgive me, lass. I see that I've embarrassed ye, and myself. Such are the dreams of an old man." He shifted uncomfortably.

Her head ached. "It's not your fault. I've never known a man, yet Grandmother tells me I must marry after the full moon. I don't know what I want."

He looked hopeful. "I only ask that ye consider it. We can wait until summer if you wish. Spend time with me and make your decision."

Keira nodded.

Michael took her hands. "There's something else, lass. Regan grows weaker each day. She can no longer serve as priestess. Samhain will be here in a few weeks. Assist me at the stones, to call the Goddess."

"You want me to serve as priestess? I don't know what to say."

"Say that you will."

"I don't know the words."

Michael smiled. "I'll teach you. Now, let's tell Isobel."

A MAGICAL TIME

WHINNYFOLD
OCTOBER 31 1635
TWO WEEKS LATER

The bay of Whinnyfold glistened in the moonlight. Waves swelled and pounded the sandy shore. Dughall threw a bundle of heather on the fire and watched purple sparks float into the air.

Ian pointed. "Look. The bonfires stretch clear to Collieston."

Dughall warmed his hands in his pockets. "Aye. I love the day of the dead. Aunt Maggie says it's the day when the veil between the living and dead is thinnest."

Ian snorted. "Hmmphhh... We don't know anyone who's dead."

Dughall shivered. "Good thing."

"I liked it better when we went guising, begging for apples and causing mischief."

"Father didn't like it."

"Aye."

The wind whipped hair around their faces. "The fire's dying. Let's place the stones." Dughall was solemn as he took out three flat stones. He crouched and planted one in the ashes. "Father's stone is the largest." He moved around the circle and placed another. "Mother's is the bonny pink one." The third stone was lovingly buried in ashes. "Aunt Maggie's. May we have her with us another year."

"That stone will be gone tomorrow."

"Ian!"

"Well, she's awfully old. She could die."

"Let's hope not."

Ian crouched and planted two red stones next to each other. "You and I. Brothers always."

They stood.

Dughall brushed sand from his breeks. "Let's ask Aunt Maggie to tell the story."

"About the well of the dead?"

"Aye."

"Father won't like it."

"We turned sixteen today. We're grown men. I can tell a story from the truth."

Ian snickered. "Well, it's about time."

***

They stood at Maggie's door and knocked. There was a sound inside, and the door opened slowly. The old woman stood with a basket of apples in her hand.

"Ach! I thought ye were rascals come guising to do mischief."

Dughall smiled. "Nay, Aunt Maggie. We've had the bonfire and placed the stones."

"Ye put one out for me?"

"Aye."

"I guess I can live another year."

Dughall frowned.

Maggie stared. "Don't pout, lad. It's the day of the dead. Ye should be haunting the moors. What do ye want with an old woman?"

Ian took an apple from her basket. "Dughall wants to hear the story again."

"About the well of the dead?"

"Aye."

Maggie grinned. She put down the basket, took her shawl from a peg, and pulled it around her shoulders. She stepped outside and closed the door.

Dughall's eyes shone with anticipation.

Maggie drew the end of her shawl across her face and pointed at the moon. "The night was as black as a raven. It was late October and the moon was full. I don't remember what woke me. It could have been a voice in my head."

Ian shivered.

"Are ye afraid, lad?"

"Nay."

"Ye should be."

Dughall's eyes widened. "Tell us, Aunt Maggie."

"I slipped out of bed quietly, leaving James alone, and dressed warm. Somehow I knew I'd go far that night."

"How old were ye?"

"Seventeen I think, and just married. Let's walk to the point."

They walked the path through a row of cottages and followed a narrow stream. Dried heather and wildflowers rattled in the wind. When they reached the point overlooking the Skares, Maggie gathered her skirts and sat, patting the ground.

"Sit down, lads." They sat on either side of her. "I sat in this place feeling the wind lift my hair, and wondered about the souls of the dead. So many had perished on the rocks that year. Young Ewan Quinlan had been tossed in the drink, only to swim to shore. His father Andrew jumped in after him and was bashed on a rock, leaving his arm useless. He disappeared under the waves. Then six men from Peterhead tried to put ashore in a storm and drowned when their scaffie hit the Skares."

"What about that young mother?"

"I almost forgot. Mary Cormoch threw herself off the point after she lost a baby. I thought of those eight as I stared out to sea." A cloud drifted across the moon, darkening the night sky. The old woman paused to admire it.

"What happened, Aunt Maggie?"

"The sea grass and clover was soft underneath me, and I nearly fell asleep. I closed my eyes, and opened them to a wondrous scene." The cloud drifted past, allowing yellow moonlight to flood the beach. She pointed at the shore. "Near the Caudman I saw a figure crawl out of the water. At first I thought it was a seal, so I stood to get a better look. What looked like fur became a dress, soaked with seaweed. A hand reached out and steadied itself, and a head lifted. It was Mary Cormoch, or at least her spirit. She reached into the water and picked up a bundle, the baby she'd lost. My bones chilled as she stared, her eyes as vacant as a dead man's."

Ian snorted. "Well, she was dead!"

"Aye. Behind her, a man crawled out of the sea and rested on the beach. His long red hair and seaman's coat told me it was Andrew Quinlan. Seaweed and water pooled beneath him as he stood and turned to the sea, calling for Ewan. My heart ached."

Dughall stared. "Did ye tell Ewan this?"

"I never told a soul. Things like this get ye flogged as a witch."

"Oh…"

"Now where were we? The six from Peterhead walked out of the sea, pulling a ghostly scaffie onto the beach. Their blue stockings and jerseys glowed in the moonlight. They scratched their heads and looked up at me."

"Were ye scared?"

"My heart nearly stopped when they started up the path."

Ian stared. "I would have run."

"I wanted to run, but I was frozen. I drew my shawl around me as Mary's head appeared. I was riveted to the sight as she stood on the point, pulling down her dress to nurse the spirit child. Seven ghostly men appeared behind her, water squishing out of their sea boots."

"Oh God."

"They came towards me, chilling my soul to the bone. I cried out, beseeching them to stop, but they didn't hear. I could have been a tree for all they cared. The procession passed right through me and walked along this very stream, heading north."

"Why didn't they just float?" Ian asked.

Maggie smiled. "'Haps they didn't know they were dead, so they followed a path that men made!"

She sniffled. "Soon they reached the footpath to the sands of Cruden. I thought that Mary might seek her cottage. She gazed in that direction, smoothed the baby's hair, and kissed his forehead. The fishermen from Peterhead started down the path. Andrew lifted her chin and pointed to the beach. She covered the child and they followed the men on the sandy footpath."

"What did the ghosts look like?" Ian asked.

"They looked like people, but when the moonlight was strong you could see through them. Their eyes were vacant and ringed with dark circles."

"What about the well?"

"Ach! Be patient, lads. I followed as they tramped across swirling sands until they reached the Hawklaw and turned inward toward the sand hills."

"To Saint Olaf's well," Dughall said, ominously.

"Aye. A haze hung over the land as we neared the well. I heard a thousand ghostly voices whispering around us."

Dughall leaned forward. "I love this part."

"The fishermen went first. They walked widdershins around the well and bowed their heads in prayer. One by one, they lifted their leg over the edge and slipped into the well. Andrew was last. Mary stayed, gazing all around. She passed her baby down the well, grasped my shoulders, and looked in my eyes."

"Oh God."

"My heart pounded until her eyes cleared, and I saw a look of gratitude. Her spirit child cried and she loosened her grip. She turned away, walked around the well, and passed down into the afterlife."

Ian snorted. "She went to hell? The baby too?"

"Nay, lad. They went to the Summerland. That's what the Celts called the afterlife."

"They didn't believe in heaven and hell?"

Maggie looked wistful. "Nay. They believed in a magical and loving Goddess, the mother of all living things. The Summerland is where we go to see old friends, rest, and be reborn."

"Reborn? How?"

"Into a new body, to experience life again."

"We've been here before?"

"Aye. Many times."

Dughall smiled. "I like that idea better."

Maggie nodded. "So do I, lad. Don't tell your father."

LOUDEN WOOD

The stone cottage was drafty. A candle illuminated the room, casting shadows. Keira stood naked in front of the fire. A bowl of water, rosemary and lavender sat on the table. She dipped a wool sponge into the water and ran it down her arm to her fingertips. "As I cleanse this body, I purify this mind so my actions may please the Goddess. So mote it be." She placed the sponge in the bowl and picked up her robe.

"Gaze into the bowl after the purifying ritual," Isobel whispered. "Ye may see the future."

She took the sponge out of the bowl and waited for the ripples to subside. Candlelight danced on the surface, yet she saw it clearly. *Nay, it canna be.*

Keira dressed in a black robe, feeling the soft wool on her skin. She smoothed the sleeves and tied her hair back with a ribbon.

"Ye look beautiful, child."

Keira hugged herself. "I'm nervous. What will happen if I forget the words?"

Isobel smiled. "Ye won't forget. Elspeth spoke the words many times."

"I know. I wish Mother could see me. Sometimes I talk to her, as though she's next to me."

"Perhaps she is. We know that love transcends death."

Keira picked up a black ribbon and tied it around her neck. Her fingers held the sacred charm, a pentacle within a circle. "Great Goddess. I'm not worthy of this."

"It's in yer blood, child."

Keira blushed. "Michael is coming. I must go with him to prepare the sacred space." She slipped on her brogues and felt the fur lining between her toes. "Alistair and Janet will walk with you. Will you be all right? You could stay with Regan."

Isobel's voice quavered. "I wouldn't miss this for the wisdom of the old ones."

Keira hugged her tightly. "I love you."

There was a rap on the door. "Ho!" Michael said. "Are you there?"

Keira drew her breath in sharply. The words would not come out.

Isobel stared. "Come in Michael, she's ready."

Michael entered the cottage, in a long black robe that reached the floor. His eyes swept over Keira, from head to toe. "You look like a true priestess, lass. Are ye nervous?"

She clasped her hands to keep them from shaking. "Aye, a bit. Shall we go? I want you to show me one more time."

He wrapped a cape around her shoulders, and glanced at Isobel. "Will you be all right, Mother?"

Isobel nodded. "Go on, Son. Alistair and Janet will walk with me."

"Have ye the sacred anointing oil?"

Keira reached into her pocket and felt the bottle. "Aye."

"Then let's be on our way." He opened the door and looked back. "Peace be with ye, Mother."

They left the cottage. Michael picked up a basket and handed it to Keira. She pulled back the cover and saw a bowl, an apple, a pouch of salt, a flask, and a knife.

Keira's throat tightened. "I forgot. What do we do with the apple?"

Michael smiled. "Don't worry. I was nervous the first time too." He grasped her hand and sighed. "Let me tell you how I felt. When we realized that Kale wasn't coming back, the responsibility fell to me. Oh I'd seen it done a hundred times, and Kale made it look so easy. But the words! We'd lost him, our friend, our leader, our very heart. And here I was this imposter who struggled with words. Everyone looked to me to heal the wound we'd suffered. Would my crude prayers please the Goddess?"

"Oh, dear. That's how I feel. It comes naturally to ye now. No one would guess that ye struggled."

"It took time and practice. People were patient, as well as the Goddess. Kale was with me in spirit. If you ask, your mother will stand with ye."

Keira pressed his hand to her lips. "Thank ye, friend. You're a dear man."

Michael picked up a leather pack, slinging it over his shoulder. "The stones await us. Do ye not hear them calling?"

Wood smoke drifted in the night air as they turned south towards the old forest. Keira looked back at the village. Familiar faces emerged from the cottages, bundled in warm clothes and carrying torches.

"Don't look back," Michael said. "Think about your sacred duties."

Keira took a breath and looked forward. They walked through the forest in silence. Wood smoke faded, and the smell of pine needles prevailed. Leaves crunched as they followed an overgrown path. A great owl hooted in the distance. She took his hand. "It feels like a place out of time."

"Exactly. You're a quick study, lass." They passed the tree that bore the mark of a pentacle and followed a hidden trail. The standing stones were just ahead.

***

They entered the circle of stones and separated. Wind scattered the fallen leaves. His face was serious as he held out his hands.

She felt his energy as he spiraled it through his body and released it through his fingertips. Did he know that she felt it too? "Mother help me," she whispered.

She looked around the circle at her place of sanctuary and placed the basket on a stone bench. The earth beneath her feet vibrated like the wings of a thousand birds. "Great Goddess. I belong here, as my mother before me." She faced him. The moon was rising, illuminating his face.

Michael smiled. "You feel it too."

"Aye. I'm not afraid anymore."

"Excellent. Our friends are gathering outside the circle. We must prepare ourselves." Michael led her to the stone bench, where they sat on either side of the basket. "Start with me, lass."

Keira opened the basket and took out the bowl. She added sea salt and filled it with water from the flask. Together, they dipped their hands in the bowl.

Michael prayed. "As rain washes the mountains, as oceans wash the beaches, I cleanse this body with water and salt. May it please the Goddess."

"So mote it be."

His fingers brushed hers, and she felt the heat rise in her. For a moment, she forgot what came next.

"The oil, lass."

Keira reached in her pocket and took out a bottle. She opened it, dabbed oil on her forefingers, and drew the sign of the pentacle on his forehead. "How do ye enter this circle, Brother?"

"In perfect love and perfect trust." His eyes searched her face as he dabbed the oil and drew the sacred sign on her forehead. "How do ye enter this circle, Sister?"

"In perfect love and perfect trust." Her heart pounded with anticipation.

"They've arrived," he whispered. "You're my priestess. Anoint them and welcome them in."

Keira looked behind her. Kevin and Morgaine stood with young Robbie, his arm in a sling. John put wee Angus down and tried to fasten Nessia's coat around her pregnant belly. Behind them, the McFay children stamped their feet against the cold. She saw the torches of others entering the clearing.

Michael pressed the bottle into her hand and led her outside the circle. "Your flock awaits ye."

The others had arrived. The Wests, Cummings, Rosses, and Davies stood with their children. Cawley and Florag leaned on each other and Alistair and Janet supported Isobel.

Michael spoke. "Behold your new priestess! Come so that she may anoint ye. You can begin, lass."

Keira waited as her friends gathered. She anointed Kevin and Morgaine and young Robbie.

Morgaine touched the lad's shoulder. "My son has something to tell ye."

Robbie looked up. "Thank ye, priestess, for fixing my arm."

Keira reached out and tousled his hair. "You're welcome, lad."

"I will be calling East," Kevin said. He led his family into the circle, taking a position to the east.

John and Nessia stood before her, holding young Angus. She anointed them and watched them enter the circle. Torry and George and Aileana grinned as she drew the symbol on their foreheads.

"I'm South," Torry said. "I'm so nervous. I hope I remember the words." He grabbed Keira and kissed her cheek. "I can't believe you're priestess."

Aileana slapped him. "Clot head! You're not supposed to kiss the priestess."

Michael's voice was stern. "You're on sacred ground. Enter the circle, young ones." He took her arm and led them to the south end.

Keira anointed the families along with their many children. She was gentle with Cawley and Florag, whose wrinkled faces studied her. "Welcome, old ones."

"I'll be calling West," Florag said, in a shaky voice. Cawley took her arm and they shuffled to the western end of the circle.

At last, Alistair and Janet Murray stood before her, supporting a tired Isobel.

"Are ye all right, Grandmother?"

"Thank the Goddess I lived to see this day."

Keira drew the sacred sign on their foreheads.

Janet whispered. "I'll be calling North. May my actions please the Goddess." They took the northern position.

The ritual was about to begin. Michael and Keira entered the center.

His voice was strong and clear. "Blessed are those who witness this ancient rite. Within these stones, I cast sacred space. We stand in a world between worlds."

Keira smiled. "What is between the worlds can change the worlds."

"So mote it be."

"Friends," Michael said. "We gather to celebrate the harvest. The year ends, fields lay fallow, and beasts sleep. Hearken, for the darkness of winter comes."

"It's a time to honor the wheel of life, the cycle of rebirth," Keira said. "The Goddess opens the gates of Summerland to departed souls."

"The veil between worlds is thinnest," Michael said. "We honor our dead and ancestors by remembering them. Though it is a time of darkness, rejoice! 'Tis one turn upon the wheel, to be followed by rebirth."

"May the shining ones join us in the light," Keira said.

Everyone faced east and held out their hands.

"Spirits of the East," Kevin said. "Element Air. Source of light, wisdom and thought. Winged creatures! Sparrow, eagle, and hawk. Hail and Welcome!"

They faced south.

"Spirits of the South!" Torry cried, his voice shaking. "Element Fire. Source of energy, will, and blood. Um... Creatures! Horse and Leaping Salamandar!" He drew a breath. "Um, I forgot. Hail and Welcome!"

They faced west and held out their hands.

"Spirits of the West," Florag said, in a faltering voice. "Element Water. Source of purification, emotions, and love. Creatures of the sea. Fish, Seals, and Mermaids. Hail and Welcome!"

They faced north.

"Spirits of the North," Janet said. "Element Earth. Source of knowledge, speech, and silence. Creatures of nature great and small. Hail and Welcome."

They turned and faced the center.

"Dear Friends," Michael said. "We welcome Spirit, universal energy. Source of life, death, and rebirth. Creatures Raven and Owl. Hail and Welcome! We thank our ancestors, who built this stone circle with their magic. Ancestors and deceased, stand with us tonight."

Keira smiled. "As we go around the circle, each can name a soul who has gone before us. Torry, you can start."

"Me Father, Alan McFay."

"Mother dearest, Jean McFay," Aileana said.

"Aunt Beathas," George said. "Bring us your gooseberry pie."

And so it went around the circle. "Sean", "Uncle Hamish", "Fia", "Grandmother Bonnie", "Silly Mary", "Little Bryan", "Old John the Tanner", "Father Brodie" ...

Keira reached into her pocket and closed her fingers around a sprig of rosemary. "Father... Mother... Hail and Welcome." For a moment, the voices of the dead whispered around them. Gooseflesh rose on her arms.

"Call the Goddess, lass."

She took a breath and held her hands to the sky. "Great Goddess! Mother of all. Help the souls pass into the Summerland. Stir the cauldron of life. Comfort those waiting to be reborn. Grace our circle and witness our rite. Hail and Welcome!"

Michael kneeled and placed his hands on the ground. They joined him. "Children of the stones, we send healing energy to the earth to benefit all people."

"So mote it be." They all stood.

Michael took the apple out of the basket and held it up in the moonlight. "Behold, the fruit of death!" He handed it to his priestess.

Keira cut the apple crosswise so the seeds formed a pentacle and showed the sacred symbol. "Which is also life! See how it forms the star of rebirth." She sliced the apple and placed a piece on Michael's tongue. "Taste the fruit of rebirth, Brother. Dear friends, share in the miracle of rebirth."

They passed the apple around the circle until each tasted a small piece.

Michael looked up at the full moon. "Friends, the wheel has turned. Return to your homes and light the fires."

Keira smiled. "We thank the shining ones who joined our circle. Goddess! Our Lady. Be with us always."

"Ancestors, beloved deceased," Michael said. "Lend us your strength. Powers of Spirit, Earth, Water, Fire, and Air. We rejoice with you! Hail and Farewell!"

"Friends," Michael said. "May the circle be open but never unbroken."

Keira smiled. "May the peace of the Goddess be ever in our hearts."

"Good night, all."

Keira breathed a sigh of relief. She'd served as priestess and hadn't made a mistake. She watched as parents gathered their children and left the circle, flanked by the old ones. The young lass walked to Alistair and Janet, who stood with a tired Isobel. "Oh, Grandmother. You stayed the whole time."

Isobel hugged her. "I'm so proud of ye."

"I'll be home soon. Michael and I must pack up."

"Take as much time as ye want. He's yer intended, after all. Alistair will help me light the fire." She clasped Janet's hand and left the circle.

At last, it was quiet. Only the sound of the leaves rustling in the trees remained. It was so cold they could see their breath. Michael held her hands, rubbing them to warm them up. He was so close that she felt the brush of his wool robe. She wondered if he could hear her heart beat.

He brought her hand to his lips and kissed her fingers. "You did well, lass. I knew ye would."

She gasped.

He pressed his lips against the hollow of her wrist, and lingered there. "You're beautiful."

A fire burned deep inside of her. *Great Goddess! Is this happening or am I delirious?*

Someone coughed behind them. John stood with wee Angus in his arms. He pointed to his wife, sitting on the ground with her back against a stone. "Nessia says the child is coming fast. We need ye, lass."

Keira was light-headed as she prayed. *Goddess, hear me. I stand in your place of power without my healer's bag. Guide these humble hands.* A feeling of calm washed over her. "Take wee Angus to Craig and Jeannie.

Get my healer's bag, some blankets, and a flask of water. Michael and I will attend to Nessia."

John shifted the child onto his shoulders, and sprinted towards the village.

Michael frowned. "I know nothing of birthing a child, lass. Best I follow and get the women folk."

"There's no time, friend. I need your help."

"Goddess help us!"

They hurried to Nessia, who sat on the ground leaning against a stone. Her face was pale and sweaty. Keira kneeled and stroked her hair. "When did the pains start?"

Nessia groaned. "After supper. I thought it was the apple biscuits. My water broke when we tried to walk back." She buried her fingers in her thighs and pushed. "The pains are strong."

"Don't push! I need to see how far ye are. Press your back against the stone. That's it. Hold your knees and take small breaths."

Keira reached in her pocket, took out the bottle of sacred oil, and spread some on her right hand. Michael raised his eyebrows.

She smiled. "The Goddess understands. Bring the flask and something to put under her."

Michael set about his task, returning with a flask and the wool lining to his pack.

Keira held a hand on Nessia's belly, reached between her legs and massaged the perineum, stretching it. She felt the pressure of the child against it. "Hold back, lass. I don't want you to tear." She massaged it further until the opening widened.

Nessia's legs trembled. "I need to push."

Keira felt the head crown. Her arm tingled to her elbow. "I feel the head, so it's not breech." She touched her fingertips to the creamy scalp and felt a heartbeat that spoke of life. "The child's force is strong. Pull your knees to you, and push."

Keira crouched and joined her hands with the baby's head, waiting for a contraction. At last, Nessia groaned and pushed down. Slowly, the baby's face crept out from its mother's skin. Her fingers eased along the cheeks and slid beneath the chin. Nessia pushed again. Fingers guided the baby's progress. A quarter turn and the shoulders were out; a moment later and the body floated into her hands.

Michael was riveted by the sight. "It's a miracle."

Keira cleared his mouth and nose with her fingers. The baby cried and kicked his tiny feet. She heard someone cough behind her.

John put down her healer's bag. "Is that my son, wee Duncan?"

Keira wrapped the child loosely. "Aye. Comfort your wife while I cut the cord. Michael, open my bag and find the deer sinew."

He searched the bag and pulled out the thread, handing it to her. Keira tied the cord close to the baby and cut it. She cleaned his face and passed him to his father.

"Lass, can I get you on your knees? We need to get the afterbirth out."

"I can't."

"You must. Michael, get on the other side of her. We'll hold her under the arms. Come now. I need ye."

As the young mother rocked forward onto her knees, a narrow rush of blood came out. They supported each arm as the afterbirth followed, steaming in the cold air.

"Good, it's out." Keira wrapped it and spread a blanket on the ground. She helped Nessia sit and placed a sponge between her legs to catch bleeding. "John, give your wife her son. Keep his head covered, he must stay warm."

John placed the boy in Nessia's arms and covered them with a blanket. He watched in awe as the lad found her nipple and began to suck.

"Oh!" Nessia cried. "He's not shy about takin' the nipple."

Keira washed blood from her hands and watched the young mother nurse. *Will I ever look into the face of my newborn child? Who will the father be?*

She yawned and saw her breath in the night air. "Michael. We can't move her until morning. Can you build a fire?"

"Aye, lass. I'll fetch some wood and get the torch."

They built a bonfire and settled down for the night. John cradled his wife and child against the cold. Michael and Keira sat near the fire on a log. He wrapped his cape around them, his arm around her shoulders. The perfume of wood smoke mingled with the earthy smells of birth.

She rested her head on his chest, and listened to his heartbeat. "Born today, among the stones. This child will have the Sight."

Michael nodded. "Truly a gift from the Goddess."

"Aye, he is." She drifted off to sleep.

Michael stroked her hair. "You are the gift, lass."

Ian

RITES OF PASSAGE *

TEN MILES SOUTH OF LOUDEN WOOD
AUGUST 1636

TEN MONTHS LATER

It was nightfall deep in the forest. The moon was new, forming a crescent in the sky, and there were many stars. Leaves rustled in the breeze, tree frogs croaked, and a great owl hooted.

Keira's belly rumbled with hunger, distracting her from meditation. Seeking a vision, she'd fasted for days, taking nothing to eat or drink. She closed her eyes and connected to a dear one. "Mother, hear me. Soon I must take a husband and choose my magical name. Grandmother wants me to join with Michael, but a voice whispers that it's not to be. I will marry a stranger, know the miracle of creation, and look upon the face of our newborn son. Where is the one who will be my mate? In my dreams, he is light of heart and pure of spirit, a singer of songs, a man of peace and power."

Ghostly fingers touched her face, warming her heart. Her path was clear. Under an oak tree, she traced a circle with stones and called in the power of the four directions.

She faced the East and held out her hands. "Spirits of Air, thou gentle sprites and airy sylphs, soaring eagle and sweet butterfly. Protect this circle in the dark of night." She faced the South and bowed her head, folding her arms over her chest. "Spirits of Fire, thou leaping salamanders and fiery ones, roaring lion and galloping horse. Protect this circle and shine your warmth upon me." She faced the West and smiled. "Spirits of Water, thou mermaids and mermen, fish and sea birds. Protect this circle and cleanse my thoughts." She faced the North with a serious expression on her face. "Spirits of Earth, thou gnomes and dwarfs, bull and stag and snake. Protect this sacred space in the safe womb of night."

Keira lay down in the center, wrapped in a plaid, feeling safe in this doorway between worlds. Hunger gnawed at her belly as she drifted into fitful sleep. As morning approached, her dreams deepened. Dark eyes watched her from a nearby tree. A peregrine falcon opened its beak and spread wings to take flight. *Looks like a large female,* she thought.

With a piercing cry it took to the air, soaring through the forest canopy to the sky beyond. Keira gasped as she found herself on the bird's back, watching the ground disappear. As her heartbeat soared, she shifted and became one with the falcon. Wind bathed her face as she flexed talons and expanded her wings. "Great Goddess. I'm flying!"

The forest disappeared, giving way to meadows and moors alive with thistle and heather. Her keen eyes scanned the earth for prey. Driven by intense hunger, she flew east until a seacoast appeared, dotted with cliffs and villages. Two young men walked a beach, one with red hair, and the other with long dark curls. They looked up and pointed.

"There he is. My future husband. What can it mean?" Keira woke from the dream with a start. In the morning light, she dug fingers into her arms to ground herself. "Reagan said the falcon soars above the land, seeing all truth." She shivered with knowingness. "I've chosen my magical name. Falconess." She opened her pack and took out some bread, breaking her fast. "Now I must take a husband."

They'd never met, but she knew his voice, his poetry, and his songs. She remembered a dream. He walked through the heather with his hands skimming the purple bells. "A handsome fisherman with a voice like a songbird. I could learn to fish."

A squirrel darted in front of her and chattered. In a blink of the eye, it scurried away through a patch of spotted orchids. Tree creepers searched for insects in the bark of a pine tree. "All creatures of the Goddess. That's what Mother would say."

She made up her mind. "One more night. I will gather herbs and think about what to tell Michael. Tomorrow I'll go home and wait for my fisherman to find me."

WHINNYFOLD

It was early morning in Whinnyfold. Ian watched as Jessie packed bread and dried cod into a sack. "Don't worry, Mother. We'll be back in a few days."

She handed it to him and frowned. "Be careful out there."

Ian smiled. "What will you have to fret about when we're no longer lads? We're nearly seventeen."

Jessie touched his arm. "Never mind that. You both have your plaids? Knives and a bow? Your packs?"

Ian nodded. "Don't worry."

Jessie softened. "I do worry about ye. Where are you going this time?"

"Dughall wants to look for healing plants. I want to hunt, bring back a hare or two, or a pheasant."

"You will watch out for your brother? He gets lost in the things he loves. I swear he has no common sense."

Ian rolled his eyes. "I know it. He drives me daft sometimes."

"Remember well what I taught ye about strangers."

Ian tried to hide a smile. Mother just couldn't help it.

"Now, listen to me," she said, sternly. "You must hide your gift. It wouldn't do to have ye branded a witch. Maggie says they flogged a woman in Aberdeen because she 'knew things' that others thought. Her neighbor accused her of sorcery."

Ian frowned. "Hmmphh… We won't talk to strangers. I'll make sure that Dughall keeps quiet if we come upon anyone." He cocked his head and listened. "Tell him yourself. He's coming up the path from the beach. He just picked a violet for ye."

"Ian! That's exactly the kind of thing ye must not say in front of strangers."

He laughed. "I know it, Mother. I'm just teasin' ye."

Dughall ducked his head, entered the cottage, and held out a bouquet of flowers. "Mother, I picked violets for ye." He ran his fingers through his dark curls and smiled.

Jessie sighed. "Bless ye, Son. Maggie's fingers are swollen and stiff. Can you bring back some willow bark?"

Dughall nodded. "Aye. We have a wee bit left in the drying shed. I'll make her some tea before we leave."

"I hope she'll be all right. Your father's in Peterhead and I'll be gone 'til nightfall peddling fish to the farms. We need cheese and barley meal."

"Maggie's a tough one," Ian said. 'She'll likely outlast all of us."

"I'd best be going." She stood on her toes to kiss them on the cheek. "My creel waits outside. Remember what I told ye about strangers."

Ian nodded. Jessie smiled and walked out the door.

Dughall rolled his eyes. "The strangers speech, again."

"Aye, this time she spoke of a witch who was flogged in Aberdeen."

"A woman?"

"Aye, Brother."

"That's awful. Was it a witch or a person who knows things like us?"

Ian shrugged. "She said it was a woman who knew things that others thought."

Dughall made the sign of the cross. "Mercy! Do ye remember the man they flogged in Peterhead?"

"The thief ye mean?"

"Aye, it was terrible. His cries pierced me to the heart."

"You didn't even watch it. Your back was to him the whole time."

Dughall winced. "I couldn't bear it. The man was demented and barely knew what was happenin'. I had black dreams for days."

"He was a thief, Brother. Perhaps he deserved it. Must ye always feel what others feel? Isn't it bad enough we feel each other's pain?"

"I'm glad that we're one. Do ye wish it wasn't so?"

"Sometimes I like bein' close to ye, and sometimes I hate it. I'd give anything to be separate."

Dughall looked wounded. "Oh. Well, I couldn't bear to see ye flogged. Do ye think it's too dangerous to go?"

"Nay. Aberdeen is a long way off."

They shouldered their packs and left the cottage. Dughall gazed up at the sky. "Did ye see that falcon this morning? It came so close."

"Aye. Daft bird. Do we look like field mice?"

"Nay. Falcons are spiritual creatures. I wonder if it means something."

Ian snorted. "Ach! Maggie's stories again. Will ye ever grow up?"

"Ian!"

"Mother thinks you're a child. She asked me to look after ye."

"Oh."

"She's right ye know. We mustn't talk to strangers."

"We won't. Let's get Maggie her tea and be on our way. I want to make the forest by midday."

Ian smirked. "You get the tea. There's a lass waitin' for me on the cliffs."

"Mary McFarlein? The yellow-haired lass with the big breasts?"

"Aye. She's a bonny one, with the voice of an angel. I'll marry her next year if she'll have me."

Dughall smiled. "I'll get Maggie's tea and meet you on the cliffs. Give the young lass a kiss for me."

Ian snorted. "I won't have to. You feel what I feel. Do ye want me to ask if she has a cousin?"

Dughall gazed dreamily into the distance. "Nay. When I meet the lass of my dreams, I'll know it. She waits for me in the heather."

Ian shook his head in disbelief. *You're daft, Brother. She better not be a silkie.*

***

Dughall opened the drying shed and found a bag of willow bark hanging from a rafter. He closed the shed, took the bag to Maggie's cottage, and knocked on the door.

"Who's there?" the old woman asked, in a weak voice.

"It's Dughall. I brought ye some willow bark for tea."

"Oh, bless ye. Come in, lad."

Dughall entered the cottage. The old woman sat at the table, wringing her hands. Maggie's white hair was disheveled and pain was etched on her face. She pressed her hands on the table to get up.

Dughall's heart ached. "Aunt Maggie, don't get up. I'll make the tea and help you clean up. You look poorly."

Her gnarled hands shook. "I'm better than most my age. I would like to have ye stay a while, though."

Dughall thought of Ian on the cliffs. His skin flushed as he felt his brother kiss the girl, his tongue circling her lips, his hand upon her breast. He pulled on his collar. *Whew! Ah well, he'll be glad for some time alone with the lass.*

Dughall filled the kettle with water, added bark, and hung it over the fire to boil. He sprinkled sand on the dirt floor and swept it, opening the door to push the mess out.

Maggie's face looked haggard in the morning light.

I must tell Mother how bad off she is. Dughall took the pot off the rack, poured a cup of tea, and placed it on the table. He sat and took her hands, examining the fingers and joints. "They're verra swollen but the tea will help. Ian and I are going to the forest. I'll bring back more bark."

Maggie pulled back her hands. "Thank ye, lad. It seems ye're takin' care of me now. I hate being a burden."

Dughall smiled broadly. "I love ye Aunt Maggie. I don't mind caring for ye."

"My goodness, lad. With a smile like that, ye'll be breaking the lassies hearts before we know it. You're as handsome as a prince."

"Aunt Maggie!"

"Are ye goin' near Aberdeen?"

"Nay. Mother told us about the woman who was flogged."

Maggie sipped her tea. "There's terrible things happenin' to healers. They've tortured and hung so many, all in the name of God! I'm no holy man, but I think God is appalled."

Dughall frowned. "The woman who was flogged. Do ye think she was a witch?"

"Nay. She knew things that others thought and healed the sick with herbs. She's an old woman like me."

"Mercy! Do ye think that any of them are witches?"

Maggie touched his hand. "Perhaps a few. But what does it matter?

They're people like us. They heal our sick and tend our wounds. Should we kill them because they're different?"

He squeezed her hand gently. "Nay. It's wrong."

Maggie warmed her hands around the cup.

Dughall felt his skin flush with pleasure and pulled at his collar. Images of Ian flooded his senses. His shirt was off and his heart pounded as his hand slid under Mary's petticoat. Fingers trembled as he traced her knee and moved up to her thigh. He could feel her breath upon his neck and hear her voice.

"Take me Ian," she whispered. "I need ye."

Dughall felt a swelling in his loins and gasped. His heart pounded so hard he could barely think. He stood. "Uh... I have to leave, Aunt Maggie. Right now, before Ian gets himself in trouble with that lass." He embraced her gently. "We'll bring you back some bark."

Maggie sighed. "Bless ye, lad. Be careful."

He opened the door and looked back. "Mother will look in on ye tonight."

Dughall closed the door and leaned against the wall of the cottage, straightening the bulge in the front of his breeks. His face flushed as he ran for the cliffs. He groaned. "Oh God! Ian's gonna be mad. They'll both be mad. Ah, well."

WALK TO THE WESTERN FOREST

Ian trudged ahead of Dughall in stony silence, across a moor that was alive with heather and bog myrtle. Shaking with anger, he let his brother catch up and shoved him hard, knocking his pack to the ground.

"Hey!"

"Damn ye! You couldn't leave us alone and let me take her!"

Dughall frowned. "I had to stop ye. It wouldn't do to get her with child. Father says that it's wrong to take advantage of a lass."

Ian flushed with anger. "Mary asked me to. She begged me! She unbuttoned my breeks and held it in her hand. I wanted her so bad. Oh, God, my head hurts just thinkin' about it!"

Dughall rolled his eyes and suppressed a laugh.

Ian made a fist. "I should punch ye in the head! You think it's funny?"

"Nay, but if you could have seen your bare arse stickin' up in the sunlight, you'd laugh too."

Ian's eyes grew wide. He snorted. "I guess it would be funny. Just wait brother, until you get a lass. I'll not give ye any peace. You embarrassed her, ye know. She ran off with tears in her eyes."

"I'm sorry for that. Do ye think you'll see her again?"

"She'll be back. I promised to take her to the gathering in Peterhead next month."

Dughall picked up his pack and they continued across the windswept moorland. "Good. So you're not mad at me anymore?"

Ian groaned. "Nay, though God knows I should be. Must ye tune in to everything that's happenin' to me? Can ye not turn it off?"

"I've tried. I can block Mother's thoughts and Maggie's songs, but you're part of me. Your thoughts and feelings are strong."

Ian frowned. "I know it. Sometimes I feel like I'm living inside of your head, as daft as ye are."

"But Ian…"

"I'm tellin' ye now, leave Mary and me alone! Push my thoughts from your mind."

They left the moor and climbed a modest hill, stopping at the top to drink from their flasks. Clumps of orange-yellow ragwort grew among the rocks. They climbed down the other side and walked through a meadow, spread with sweet smelling grasses. Wild barley, ripe for harvest, rustled in a soft breeze. They reached the edge of the forest at midday and walked among trees, picking Foxglove that grew amidst roots of gnarled bark.

"What's this plant for?" Ian asked.

"It's good for a bad heart, though ye have to be careful. Too much can kill ye."

"Hmmphh…"

The forest hummed with insects and birdcalls. Dughall held his hands out to the earth. "Forgive me, Brother. A poem, for your lass."

"I am the forest,
My heart and soul are trees around me.
My arms are branches etched against the sky.
My blood flows as wind through the trees.
My tears are drops of rain falling from leaves.
My laughter is like birdsong.
From my roots new life springs.
I am the forest."

TEN MILES SOUTH OF LOUDEN WOOD

Yellow flowers sat upon stalks, blossoms open to the sun. Keira stood in a patch of calendula, pinching heads from the stems and pulling off petals. She dropped the flowers in a basket at her feet and drank from her flask.

"I'll dry the flowers and infuse them in beeswax. We'll make enough healing salve to last the winter." She held a handful of petals to her nose, inhaling their sweet scent. "Truly a gift from the Goddess."

Keira looked beyond the meadow at a patch of willow trees. Their bark was dark brown, perfect for harvesting. She thought of her grandmother, racked with arthritis. "I must get some bark, for Grandmother's pain."

The noontime sun warmed her face. "How can I tell her about Michael? If she had one wish, it would be that I marry him." She reached in her pocket and closed her fingers around a sprig of rosemary. "Tell me, Mother. What should I do?"

"Daughter," a voice whispered. "The one you seek. He's coming."

***

Dughall watched his brother lay his pack down under an oak tree. The red-haired lad slipped a bow and quiver off his shoulder and put them on the ground. He took out three feather-tipped arrows, and ran his fingers along the tips.

"Where are ye going?"

"Hunting. I don't suppose ye want to come."

Dughall shuddered. "Nay. I couldn't bear to kill something."

Ian smiled. "I thought so. We'll bed down here tonight. If it rains we'll have cover."

"It won't rain. There's not a cloud in the sky." He laid down his pack at the base of the tree.

Ian packed the arrows and hiked the quiver onto his shoulder. "Look for some onions or wild carrots. I'll see if I can take down a hare for supper."

Dughall winced. "Do ye have your dirk? You must grant it a merciful death."

Ian touched the knife at his belt. "Aye. Stop fretting about the little woodland creatures. That's why I'm here, so ye don't starve to death. Where will ye be?"

"I saw a patch of willow near the meadow. I'll cut and strip some bark for Maggie."

"All right. We'll meet up later. If you come upon anyone, remember what Mother said."

"I won't talk to strangers."

He watched Ian walk through a stand of pine trees. Dughall hiked his pack over his shoulder and walked through the forest. Soon he emerged at the edge of a meadow, ablaze with wildflowers and heather. The willow trees were on the other side, about a quarter mile away. He walked through the meadow in a daze, running his fingers across the tops of the heather, and broke into song.

Twas in the month of August one morning by the sea,
When violets and cowslips they so delighted me.
I met a pretty damsel for an empress she might pass,
And my heart was captivated by the bonnie fisher lass.

Her petticoats she wore so short, they came below her knee.
Her handsome leg and ankle, they so delighted me.
Her rosy cheeks her yellow hair, for an empress she might pass,
And wi' her creel she daily toiled, the bonnie fisher lass.

In the distance, he saw a slender young woman standing under a rowan tree. Long dark hair fell to her shoulders, curling on the bodice of her dress, and a petticoat showed below her skirt. She held a willow rod in her hand and stripped bark into a basket. He continued to sing.

I stepped up beside her and to her I did say
Why are you out so early? Why are you going this way?
She said I'm going to look for bait, now allow me for to pass.
For our lines we must get ready said the bonnie fisher lass.

Her petticoats she wore so short, they came below her knee.
Her handsome leg and ankle, they so delighted me.
Her rosy cheeks her yellow hair, for an empress she might pass,
And wi' her creel she daily toiled, the bonnie fisher lass.

As Dughall drew close, the girl looked up and regarded him with startling green eyes. *It's a vision,* he thought. *She's the lass I dreamed about.*

She put down her knife and spoke in a soft voice. "Hello, lad. You can come closer."

"It can't be," he whispered. "I've heard that voice in a dream."

Dughall looked into the basket. It was full of calendula flowers and willow bark. "You're a healer. I must be dreaming."

Her green eyes widened as she touched her heart. "You're not dreaming."

"I won't hurt ye, lass. I'm here to gather willow bark for old Aunt Maggie. Her hands are swollen and stiff."

"You're a healer?"

"Aye. Mother taught me the healing ways of plants. I've treated sores and fevers, and set broken bones. I even birthed a few babies, though the womenfolk don't like it much." He smelled lavender in her hair.

She touched his cheek. "I heard ye singing. You have a beautiful voice."

Dughall blushed and grasped her hand, taking it from his cheek. Closing his hand around hers, he felt her heart beat. *She's verra nervous. Her heart is pounding like a drum.*

"What's your name, lass? Where do ye come from?"

"My name is Keira MacPherson. I live in a forest village north of here. And you lad?"

"Dughall Hay," he stammered. "I come from a fishing village on the coast. Whinnyfold. I'm with my brother, Ian. He's hunting."

She released his hand and smiled. "Well, Dughall Hay. I have enough willow bark. Let me help you strip some for Aunt Maggie."

Dughall's heart pounded with anticipation. His imagination ran wild. *Oh God... Ian will never believe this.*

***

Miles away, Ian drew back his bow and let the arrow fly. It streaked through the air, striking a hare in the chest. The beast squealed and struggled as it dropped to its side. Ian drew his dirk and walked to the fallen creature, slitting its throat. It trembled for a moment, then closed its eyes and lay still.

"It's a good thing you're not here, Brother." He wiped the blood and fur from his knife. His thoughts connected to Dughall and his pounding heart.

What are you up to, Brother? Willow bark givin' ye a hard time? He pushed his thoughts away and turned to the hare.

Ian opened his pack, found a length of twine, and wrapped it around the hind legs. He threw the rope over a pine branch, suspending the hare, and ran his fingers over the soft pelt. "I can use this for mittens." The lad took out his knife and cut off the head, allowing the blood to drip out. He sliced off the forefeet and cut the skin around the hock joints of the back legs, making a final cut between them. He removed the tail and pulled the skin down over the body, then cut the carcass from belly to ribs and eased out the innards. Ian cut off the rear feet at the hock joint, and cut down the carcass. He wrapped it in skin and stuffed it in his pack, then washed his hands with his flask.

"We'll have roasted hare tonight." He hiked his bow and quiver over one shoulder and slung his pack over the other. The forest was still as he hiked towards their encampment. Walking through a clearing, Ian heard a loud squeal coming from a thicket. Something thrashed in the bushes, and he heard the telltale huff-huff of a boar that had been disturbed.

"God, help me!" He looked around for a tree to climb. Ian's muscles clenched as the boar burst through the brush, tusks aiming for his legs. He ran to a stand of pine trees, slammed his shoulder into a branch, and groaned as he pulled himself up. The boar snorted below, butting the tree with its head. After a while, it lost interest and lumbered off into the forest.

Ian winced as he took off his pack and hung it from the tree. Sweating, he cradled his shoulder and rocked in pain. "Ach! I'm seeing stars. I'll never make it back." He reached out to his brother. "Dughall! I didn't mean it when I told ye to block me. Hear me!"

***

Dughall and Keira sat on the ground, stripping willow bark into a pile.

"Tell me about Aunt Maggie."

Dughall smiled. "Maggie was our healer for a long time and she taught me many things. I love that old woman dearly. When we were children she told stories about mermaids and silkies and creatures of the forest. She loves to sing; has a song for everything, even shellin' and baitin' the mussels."

Keira smiled. "We learn so much from the old ones. My grandmother taught me about healing plants, and showed me how to dress wounds and set broken bones. It's been a hard year. Grandmother's bent with pain and longs to join my mother in the spirit world."

Dughall felt a chill. "Your mother's dead?"

"Aye." She clasped her hands to stop them from shaking.

Her eyes are as green as a precious stone. Just like Mother said. Could it be? He saw that she was upset. "Forgive me, lass. I didn't mean to trouble ye."

Keira sighed. "Some things are painful, even after many years."

Dughall picked up a rod and stripped bark into the basket. "I'm sorry about your mother."

"She's been dead a long time, since I was eight. I watched her die in an awful way, thinking there was something I could do to stop it."

Dughall felt her heart ache and struggled with his emotions. "Tell me about her. What was she like?"

A tear spilled down her cheek. "She was beautiful and kind, and braver than I can hope to be."

He reached out and wiped the tear away, not knowing the words to say. Images of a child filled his mind, kneeling at her mother's body. It was hanging from a gallows tree. Dughall shook off the vision. His heart swelled as he touched her hand. What could he say? "Where's your father, lass?"

"My father's dead, too."

For a moment he was without words. "I can't imagine growing up without parents. I've been blessed."

She smiled through tears. "Can I sit next to ye, lad?"

"Aye."

She moved next to him, her arm lightly brushing his.

The scent of her hair made him smile. *She smells like lavender,* he thought. *Just like Mother.* He put his arm around her.

Keira snuggled closer. "Tell me about your parents."

Dughall smiled. "My mother has red hair, eyes as blue as the sea, and a smile that melts your heart. She's stronger than any woman I've known; carries a hundred weight creel for miles. Oh, and she loves violets. I pick them for her all the time. Father loves her madly."

"Is your father romantic?"

"Nay. Father's a hard workin' fisherman who loves his wife more than life. He's always holding her close and saying that he loves her."

"Does she love him?"

"Aye. When Father's on a rough sea, she frets until he returns, afraid that the sea will claim him. Many a day has she spent on the rocks, looking for his boat."

"Is your father good to you?"

"Aye. He taught us to be men, to fish the seas and protect our home. Of course he's not afraid to teach us right from wrong. It can be unpleasant when he has a talk with ye. He's never raised a belt to us, though God knows we've given him reason. He's the best father a man could have."

"You are truly blessed, Dughall."

"When I marry, I can only hope to be the man he is."

"I think you already are."

Dughall stiffened. Deep within, he heard his brother's cry and felt an intense pain in his shoulder. His heartbeat raced. "I'm coming," he whispered.

"What's wrong, lad? You're shaking like a leaf."

"My brother's hurt. I have to go to him." Dughall stood and massaged his shoulder. "Mercy, that hurts like the devil!"

"But how do ye know?"

He winced in pain. "Don't ask me, lass. I'm not allowed to talk about it."

"I know. The Second Sight." Her face brightened.

Dughall was shocked, but he took her hand and helped her up. "Aye. Ach! I'm not supposed to tell anyone." He cocked his head and listened. "Ian's in the forest a few miles north. A boar nearly gored him. He can't get out of a tree." He clutched his shoulder and drew his breath in sharply. "The pain is awful."

Dughall turned north and walked through the meadow, taking long strides.

Keira struggled to keep up. "Why must ye hide the Sight? Where I come from it's a gift."

"Aunt Maggie says it's a gift, too. But the church would say we had the devil in us." He swallowed hard. "They kill people like me."

Keira reddened. "I'm afraid that your aunt is right."

"You say it's a gift, lass. Most would think me strange. You're not afraid of me?"

"I will never fear you." They entered the forest and stood among pine trees, feeling relief from the sun. Swallows darted overhead, catching insects. "Which way, lad?"

Dughall held out his palms and pointed east. "Over there. Do ye not hear him?"

"Nay, but you do."

They hiked through dense forest until they emerged in a clearing. Ian was sitting in a pine tree, cradling his shoulder and looking miserable. Dughall ran ahead and stood at the tree.

Ian groaned. "Thank God, you came. The pain's so bad I'm seeing stars. I thought you were blocking me."

Dughall smiled. "I thought you wanted to be rid of me."

"Not yet! This doesn't mean you can bother Mary and me." He grasped his shoulder and winced. "Oof!"

Dughall flinched. "Looks like that boar got the best of ye, Brother."

Ian's eyes widened. "I must be seeing things. Who's the bonny lass?"

"Her name is Keira. Nay bother. Let's get you down." He untied the pack from the branch and caught the bow and quiver. Dughall supported his brother and lowered him to the ground.

Ian clutched his arm. "That hurts like the devil! What's wrong with my shoulder? It doesn't look right."

Keira kneeled and looked at the misshapen shoulder. She ran her fingers around the joint and upper arm. "I've seen this before. It's out of joint."

Ian groaned. "I don't believe it."

"Show me, lass."

Keira took Dughall's hand and showed him where the bone of the upper arm had slipped out. "We have to pop it back in before the swelling starts. I'm afraid this will be painful."

Sweat beaded on Ian's forehead. "She's not touching me! Take me home and Mother will mend it."

Dughall spoke softly. "It's a long way home, and us without a horse. You can't walk that far in pain. She's a healer. I'll help her."

"Can ye, Dughall?" she asked. "With your Sight, this will hurt ye."

"I'll feel it whether I help or not."

Ian glared. "Damn it! What else does she know?"

Dughall rolled his eyes. "It's all right. Where she comes from, the Sight's a gift."

Ian frowned. "Gift or not, she knows about us. A bad thing, Brother." He clenched his teeth and hissed. "Oh God. Do what ye must, I can't bear it any longer."

"Lay him on the ground." Keira reached under her dress, unfastened her petticoat, and stepped out of it.

They stared. *I could learn to like her,* Ian thought.

"Brother!" Dughall cradled his shoulders and helped him to lay flat.

Ian groaned. "Does she know what she's doing?"

"I think so."

Ian frowned.

Keira tore off a length of petticoat, rolled it into a ball, and placed it in Ian's armpit. She ripped the seams from the rest and fashioned it into a crude sling. They watched as she took off her brogues and grasped Ian's wrist with both hands.

"Cry if you must, lad. I won't think less of ye." She placed her foot in his armpit against the cloth ball and pushed as she pulled on his wrist, extending his arm.

Ian hissed. "Damn it!"

"Be a brave lad."

Tears ran down his cheeks.

"It's free. Keep his shoulder still while I turn the arm."

Dughall kneeled and cradled the shoulder. Sympathetic pain shot up his arms. "I feel your pain, Brother. We are one."

Keira eased her foot out of his armpit and kneeled. She laid his arm flat, and then bent the elbow, supporting it with one hand. Her other hand held his wrist up. She turned the upper arm, seeking the angle to push the bone back in. In a swift movement, she pressed the ball of the upper arm back into the socket. Ian cursed and fainted.

Dughall released the shoulder and sank to the ground. "Dear God!"

Keira examined the joint. "It's back in place. Are you all right?"

"I'm alive and whole."

"Thank the Goddess."

His brother was sprawled on the ground, as pale as a ghost. "Is he dead?"

"Nay. Just fainted. Let's get a sling on before he wakes up."

✳✳✳

Dughall hiked to the meadow to pick up the baskets of bark and calendula. He found her campsite and packed up her things. "What's a lass doing so far from home? I thought only lads roamed the forest in a plaid."

He took their belongings and returned to the forest clearing where Ian lay sleeping. "My brother looks pale."

Keira spoke softly. "The lad's going to be all right. He woke, but there was so much pain that he fell asleep. There's swelling around his shoulder."

Dughall nodded. "I'll gather wood and light a fire. I saw that ye have a pot. We can make some willow bark tea."

"He told me he snared and dressed a hare. It's in his pack." She pointed to a pile of tubers on the ground. "I found some parsnips. We can make supper."

Dughall's belly rumbled. "I'm so hungry, I could eat pine needles. I'll get the fire going."

He gathered firewood and built a fire in the clearing. When it grew hot, Keira boiled the bark and strained it through cloth. As she waited for Ian to wake, she cut the hare into strips and roasted it on sticks. The parsnips were wrapped in leaves and baked at the edge of the fire.

Ian woke and used his good arm to sit up. "Mercy! It still hurts, but not like before."

Keira frowned. "Is that a thank you?"

Dughall touched a hand to his brow to hide a smile.

Ian stared. "I guess so, lass. Is that roasted hare I smell?"

"You can't be bad off if your belly's complaining." She handed him a cup of willow bark tea. "Drink this. It will help the pain."

Ian made a face as he gulped the bitter liquid. "Thank ye, lass."

She took the cup and handed him a stick with a chunk of roasted hare. "Can ye manage that?"

His hand shook as he held the stick to his mouth. "Aye, I'm starved."

She kneeled and unwrapped the parsnips, allowing them to cool.

Dughall took two sticks from the fire and handed one to her. "Eat, lass."

They sat around the fire, eating roasted hare and parsnips until there was none left. Ian wiped his hand on his breeks. "Where did ye learn that trick with your foot, while pullin' on my arm?"

"A lad in our village throws his shoulder out every harvesting season. I've healed him more than once." Keira offered him another cup of tea. "Drink this, it will ease the pain." She leaned over and spoke softly. "Will ye be all right for a while? I need to talk to Dughall alone."

Ian snorted. "Take care of the lass, Brother. Show her how grateful we are."

***

They left Ian and walked through the woods to a nearby oak tree. Dughall's heart raced as she moved closer. He reached down to pick a violet, and presented it to her.

"Sweet Lass...
Bonny as a flower.
Strong as the wind in winter.
Wise as an ancient healer.
Steady as my pounding heart.
That is what you are."

Keira took his hand and squeezed it. "Poetry. You don't seem like brothers. You're so different."

Dughall reddened. "I'm sorry for what my brother said, lass. I'll not take advantage of ye."

Keira's dress brushed his breeks. She touched his cheek and parted his lips with a finger. "It doesn't matter what he thinks."

Dughall's skin flushed. His heart beat so hard that he could barely think. She put her arms on his shoulders, pursed her lips, and waited.

***

Ian's heart pounded with anticipation as he reached out to his brother. Images of Dughall and the lass flooded his mind. She was pressed against him, asking for it. "All right, Brother!"

He heard her whisper. "It doesn't matter what he thinks."

For once, he liked being connected. "Kiss her!"

Soft lips invited him. She sighed.

Ian's frustration peaked. "Dughall, lad! For God's sake, kiss her. Touch her breast! Must I tell ye everything?"

***

Dughall pushed his brother's thoughts away and trembled as he kissed her lightly. Her lips were soft and moist, and suddenly they were open. He took a breath and shuddered. Her tongue found his and he responded, kissing her passionately. He was light-headed as her fingers caressed his back. Keira sat on the ground and pulled him down beside her.

He was breathless as he leaned forward to touch her face. "Are ye sure, lass?"

She placed his hand on her bodice. "Aye."

The curve of her breast was soft. He reached down and ran his fingers under her skirt, tracing her knee.

The lass shuddered. "It's meant to be," she whispered, as she unlaced his breeks. "Take me right here."

Dughall felt a swelling in his loins. "Oh God. I can't control it."

***

Ian was racked with sensation. He felt his hand upon her breast, her hand upon his swollen member. A sharp pain in his shoulder made him squirm.

Her voice was soft. "Take me."

"Ach! Do it, Brother. Take her! For God's sake, you're killing me."

***

Dughall took her hands and struggled to control himself. His heart thundered in his ears. "No more lass. Father says it's wrong." Somewhere in his head he heard Ian groan.

Keira trembled. "Great Goddess! Where I come from, it's never wrong. When a man and a woman feel connected, it's sacred."

"Sacred? We're not married. What if I get ye with child?"

"Then the child is meant to be. I've dreamed of ye, lad and our newborn son."

Dughall raised his eyebrows. "Then the dreams are stronger than both of us. Time and again, I've come to ye in the heather."

Her green eyes misted. "Aye. Singing and caressing the purple bells. How can it be? It seems I've known ye all my life."

He had to tell her. "In a sense, we have known each other."

"How?"

"Your mother died in Newburgh, on the gallows?"

She looked stricken. "You were there?"

"Aye."

Her green eyes filled with tears.

"Don't cry, lass. I didn't condemn her. I was the lad who fainted."

She touched her heart. "Oh. And the woman who saved me?"

"Aunt Maggie."

"Is this a cruel joke?"

"Nay. For some reason, our paths have crossed again."

Her lip trembled. "I worship the Goddess, like my mother. You won't condemn me?"

"Nay. It seems I'm meant to take care of ye."

She snuggled close. "What will we do?"

"We'll have to keep quiet. With my gift and your religion, it could be dangerous. We can talk tomorrow."

"There's no time left. Grandmother needs me. I must leave at first light."

Dughall touched her cheek. "Go home and wait for me, lass. I'll find a way to make ye my wife, and come for ye in spring."

She smiled. "Husband and wife. I'll wait forever."

He felt lightheaded. "How will I find ye?"

"The village is ten miles north in the Forest of Deer, near the banks of the Ugie. There's a stone circle nearby."

He kissed her hand. "Ten miles north."

"Don't forget me, lad."

"You haunt my dreams. How can I forget?"

***

They returned to the clearing and laid their plaids on the ground to spend the night. The forest hummed with crickets and leaves rustled in the trees.

Dughall tended to his brother, noting that he barely spoke. "Don't be mad," he whispered.

Ian glared. "Are ye daft? She wanted it as badly as you did."

"So ye felt it?"

Ian nodded. "It was awesome. How could ye stop it?"

Dughall sighed. "It was the hardest thing I've ever done. I felt like I was going to burst."

"Ha! At last ye understand. When we get home, I'll ask Mary if she has a cousin for ye."

"Nay, Brother. I plan to marry this lass."

Night approached. Dughall stoked the fire and watched the flame grow. He sat next to Keira and held her hand, admiring her slender fingers. As the moon rose, they heard the sound of hooves and a horse snorting. A rider on a black stallion entered the clearing.

"Ho!" Michael said. "Is that you, lass?"

She let go of Dughall's hand. "Aye, Michael."

Dughall watched the man as he approached the fire. He was tall and stately, reminding him of the minister at church. His face was wrinkled and his hair was gray.

"You're not alone." His voice was judgmental.

Keira stood. "It's all right Michael, they're friends. The lads needed a healer."

"We don't help outsiders."

Dughall wanted to protect her, but had second thoughts. *He's really angry. The man's too old to be her lover, yet there's something between them.*

Keira's voice was childlike. "I'm a healer, Michael. I had to help them."

Michael stared. "We'll discuss that later. Pack your things, lass. Your grandmother's dying."

Michael

CHANGES

SOUTH OF LOUDEN WOOD
AUGUST 1636
ONE HOUR LATER

They rode in silence through the forest, on Michael's horse Black Shadow. Keira sat on the saddle in front, and his arms encircled her as he held the reins. She felt him tremble. *He's angry,* she thought. *I can feel it in my bones.*

Michael pulled back slightly on the reins. "Whoa, Shadow." The horse snorted, took a few steps backward and stopped. He dismounted and patted the animal's face. "Good boy. We'll rest here a while. You've had a long night."

Michael barely looked at her. "Stay here with Shadow." He helped her dismount and handed her the reins. "I'll make sure we haven't been followed." Before she could reply, he walked in the direction they came from and disappeared into a stand of trees.

Keira tied the reins to a tree and stroked the horse's face, making soothing noises. Her thighs ached from the tension of the long ride. "We both need a rest, don't we? At least you're not angry with me." Wind rustled leaves in the trees, making her shiver. She sat on the ground and drew her wrap around her. "Oh, Grandmother. I love you so. Please hang on until I get there."

Michael walked out of the woods and sat on the ground across from her. "No one followed." He placed his hands on his knees and took a deep breath, fixing his stare on the ground between them.

Keira felt an explosive energy coming from him. She wanted to ask what was wrong but didn't dare to speak.

He raised his head and stared. "Outsiders! You brought outsiders to us! You of all people should realize the threat that they pose."

She'd never seen him this angry. "They needed a healer. A boar attacked the lad. His shoulder was out of joint."

His eyes narrowed. "Your father died because he healed an outsider! You've heard the story many times. How could ye do it?"

"They're simple people like us. I can't ignore a man who needs help because he's an outsider!"

Michael grasped her hand tightly. "I stood in front of your father's body. What was left of it! Shackled to a post on Agony Hill. He'd been burned alive because he wouldn't tell them where your mother was. The traveler said that he'd been tortured, flogged until his back was bloody! This is what outsiders do to us. It didn't matter that he healed one of them."

Keira trembled, as much from anger as fear. "How can you say this to me? I know how he died and Mother as well. I know what they died for! Did ye not understand their message?" She pulled her hand away. "Ten years have passed. Can we not try to get along with outsiders? If they see that we mean them no harm, they won't hurt us."

Michael clenched his jaw. "That is exactly what your mother said when she left us to live among them. Great Goddess, child! Do ye not remember what ye saw that day, when they hung her before your eyes?"

He called me a child, she thought. *It's over between us.* She clutched her heart and looked into his eyes.

He stared, waiting for her answer.

Images of the gallows filled her mind and brought back the heartache. The pain almost took her breath away. "I remember her death all too well. It was more than terrible. But I don't believe those lads will hurt us."

Michael clenched his fists and shuddered. "Did you tell them where you came from? Do they know where our village is?"

Her face flushed as she decided to lie. "Nay. They said that they come from a fishing village on the coast. But all I said was that I lived far away."

"Thank the Goddess!"

"They won't bring us harm. They know what it's like to be fearful of others. Dughall has the gift of the Sight."

"The Second Sight? Goddess protect us! It doesn't matter that you didn't tell them where you live. Deep inside, he knows. We may be doomed."

Keira felt the power of his agony. "That's enough! I did what was right. Did ye not see that they were grateful? They won't hurt us."

Michael rubbed his temples. "Lass, will you not be satisfied until you stand before my burnt body? Or that of young Torry?"

Keira felt like she'd been slapped. Her face burned with shame. "Nay. Not my friends. I would rather die."

"You may! Do ye not know that there's a price on your head? A bag of gold to anyone who captures the witch's child. Will they keep quiet if there's gold to be had?"

Fear rose in the back of her throat. Then she remembered Dughall's touch, filled with love and compassion. Could the dreams be wrong? "Dughall will not harm me." She stood and walked to Shadow. Her hands shook as she untied the reins. "Can we leave now? I want to see Grandmother before she passes."

Michael stood and nodded. His face was ashen as he spoke. "There's no need to tell Isobel, but we will not marry. It's clear to me now. The only lady I will serve is the Goddess."

Keira swallowed against a lump in her throat. "I understand." Hot tears threatened to fall.

He helped her up on the saddle and mounted in back. She snuggled against him and felt him stiffen. A tear slid down her cheek as she reached into her pocket and clasped her fingers around the sprig of rosemary.

"Peace be with you daughter," a voice whispered.

With heavy hearts, they rode through the forest towards the village.

✼✼✼

They reached the outskirts of the village just before dawn. As they approached, Keira saw Janet outside of Isobel's cottage, sitting on a bench and wringing her hands. She dismounted.

Janet sniffled. "Thank the Goddess you're here. Her pain is great and she's barely breathing. She sees Elspeth in the room."

"Thank ye friend, for all you've done." Keira squeezed her shoulder and entered the cottage.

Michael and Janet followed her through the door. Isobel lay on the bed, her shaking hands grasping the blanket. Her breath was short.

Keira struggled to hold back tears. *Her lips are so blue,* she thought. *The end is near.*

"Oh Elspeth," Isobel whispered. "My beloved daughter. Have ye come for me at last?"

Keira sat on the bed and touched her clammy hand. "Grandmother. I've come back from the forest. I love you so much. Don't leave me."

Isobel's hand lifted and touched her cheek. Her eyes widened with recognition and she smiled through the pain. "I love ye child. It's been a blessing to see ye grow into a young lass."

Keira's heart ached. "Grandmother, let me do a healing on you." Tears flowed freely down her face.

"Nay, child. I'm weary of this life. This old body is spent. It's time for me to join my daughter in the Summerland."

"Please, dear one."

"Michael will care for ye now."

Keira glanced at Michael. Tears streamed down his cheeks, but he wouldn't look at her. Isobel's hand dropped to her chest. She closed her eyes and her mouth fell open. A trickle of drool ran to her chin as her breathing grew shallow.

"I love you, Grandmother."

Isobel nodded slightly and stopped breathing. The candle in the room flickered, the flame rising then falling suddenly. Janet sobbed openly.

Keira was numb as she picked up Isobel's hand and held a finger against the wrist. No heartbeat, not even a flutter. She laid the hand on the bed and stood. "I'm all alone in the world now."

Michael kneeled at Isobel's side. He drew the sacred sign on her forehead and offered a prayer of passage.

"Oh Goddess
There is great sorrow
A cherished one has gone
Friend, Mother, Grandmother
Passed into the Summerland
Usher her spirit with your soft embrace
May we find comfort; dry the tears from my face
Warmed by your love
Our hearts and minds are one
The wheel of life turns
The cycle of rebirth goes on
Peace be with you, Mother"

Keira felt a hand on her shoulder and turned to embrace Janet. Michael stood and opened his arms as well. As she hugged him, she felt him suppress a sob. *He loved Grandmother as I did. He's a good man. What have I done?*

Together, they left the cottage and watched in silence as the sun came up. Dawn broke to the east, promising a beautiful summer day. Keira smiled sadly. "The Goddess grants us a piece of the Summerland."

Michael embraced her. "I'll return later to bury her. Peace be with you, dear sister."

Keira watched as he walked towards his cottage.

"Would ye like to get some sleep at my place?" Janet asked, softly. "You must be exhausted from your long ride."

It was true, every muscle in her body ached. "Nay. I can't sleep. I want to sit on this bench and pray to the Goddess."

Janet hugged her. "All right. If there's anything I can do, just ask." She suppressed a yawn and headed down the path to her cottage.

Keira sat on the wooden bench and prayed. She waited for Grandmother to come out and sit with her, for the Goddess to comfort her, for tears that didn't come. She nearly fell asleep and was startled when the wind whipped up, rustling the trees. Before her eyes, hundreds of hares scampered into the clearing, regarded her curiously, and loped into the forest. A feeling of peace and everlasting love washed over her, and she wept until she could cry no more.

RETURNING HOME

SOUTH OF LOUDEN WOOD
AUGUST 1636
THE NEXT DAY

Morning sunlight filtered through the canopy of trees, warming the forest floor. Dughall scattered dirt on the fire, smothering the embers. He stooped to pick up a yellow flower, lying where her basket had been, and sighed. "We never said goodbye, lass." He tucked the blossom into his pocket.

Ian adjusted his sling, resting the knot behind his neck, and groaned. "Mercy, that hurts. Are we ready?"

Dughall crouched on the ground. "Can ye walk? I can carry our packs and your bow and quiver, but I may not be able to support ye."

Ian winced. "I want to go home. One more night on this hard ground and you'll have to carry me. Mother must look at my shoulder. It hurts like the devil."

"I looked at it this morning. There's bruising, but the joint is in place. The lass knew what she was doing."

Ian stood. "Hmmphh... That remains to be seen. We'd best get started."

Dughall walked around the campsite, slinging the bow and quiver over his shoulder and picking up both packs. He glanced at his brother and felt the pain that was etched in his face. "We'll hike to the base of the hill. Then we'll rest awhile."

They walked through the forest until they emerged into the meadow. A flock of birds traced a lazy arc in the sky. Sunshine beat down on them, making them sweat. They turned east towards the hill, walking in silence.

Ian snorted. "You almost had her brother. That's the kind of lass I like. She's not afraid to show ye what she wants."

"Brother, don't. It's not like that. She's the lass of my dreams."

"I can't believe she grabbed ye down there. Not even Mary was that forward at first. You nearly killed me when you stopped."

Dughall blushed. "It's not like that, I tell ye. Where she comes from, when a man and a woman feel connected, it's sacred."

"Ha! Sacred! I'm for that. Are there more like her?"

"I don't know."

"Do ye know where she lives?"

"Sort of."

"And she expects ye to marry her?"

"Aye."

"No wonder ye like her. She's as daft as you are."

Dughall felt the anger rise in him. "Stop it!"

"Sacred?" Ian teased. "Did it feel sacred when you had your hand upon her breast? Or your tongue in her mouth? Oooh, sacred. You should have pulled her dress up and taken her."

Dughall made a fist. "Stop talkin' about her that way! If ye didn't have your arm in a sling I'd punch ye."

Ian raised his eyebrows. "She's just a lass. Why are you mad?"

"I mean to make her my wife."

"Marry her? She's not a fisher lass. I can't see her carryin' a hundred weight creel on her back. She couldn't bear the life. Father will tell you so."

"I know what Father says, but I'm meant to have her. We dreamed of each other."

"It will never work."

Dughall frowned. "Let's not talk of it anymore. You're driving me mad." They continued on in silence, walking until they reached the base of the hill. He put down the packs and ran his fingers through his dark hair. "Let's rest a while."

They sat on the ground under a small pine tree. Dughall pulled out his flask and took a drink, then passed it to Ian.

"You're not mad anymore," Ian said. "I can feel it."

"Aye."

"That man who came for the lass, what did ye think of him?"

Dughall frowned. "He's too old to be her lover, yet I sensed a tension between them. He was verra angry. I wanted to stop her from leaving with him."

"I felt it too. You couldn't have stopped her. Her grandmother was dying."

"I know it."

"Was he her father?"

"Nay. Her father and mother are dead."

"An uncle, then?"

"I don't know. I hope he doesn't beat her."

"Well, she didn't seem afraid of him."

Dughall reached in his pack and took out some dried cod. "Eat this. It will give ye strength. You look poorly."

Ian made a face as he chewed the salty strip. He swallowed hard, then leaned against the tree and closed his eyes, cradling his arm. "My shoulder hurts like hell."

"Sleep. I'll wake ye when the sun is overhead."

Ian nodded and drifted off.

Dughall reached into his pocket and closed his fingers around the yellow flower. "Where are ye, lass? I promise I'll find a way to marry ye."

Whinnyfold

It was late morning in Whinnyfold. The sky was clear and a light sea breeze blew in from the southeast. Maggie and Jessie stood outside, around a boiling pot of water and pig's lard. Steam rose from the pot, making them sweat. Jessie wiped her brow and tucked a strand of hair under her cap.

"Let me stir for a while," Maggie said.

Jessie was worried about the old woman. "Are ye feeling better?"

Maggie's white hair blew about her face. Her gnarled fingers struggled to tie a scarf behind her head. "I can't stop living because I'm old. Maybe it will help to get these hands moving."

I should help her, Jessie thought. *But she's proud.* She stirred the pot and waited.

At last the scarf was tied and Maggie tucked her hair away. "Let me stir, lass."

Jessie handed the pot stick to Maggie, and wiped her hands on her apron. "It's almost ready. Soon we'll skim it and add the ash water. Then there's the stirrin' for a day or two. Effie and Nora will take their turn." She watched as Maggie stirred the pot, making the lard float to the top. "God, it smells awful!"

Maggie wrinkled her nose. "Phew! Thank goodness there's a breeze. When the lassies get here, we'll put in some lavender. It won't smell so bad then."

"I want to add goat's milk, right at the end. For your dry skin."

"Bless ye, child."

Jessie gazed at the cliffs, watching the gulls and kittiwakes. "I have a bad feeling about the lads. Ian's voice plays in my mind, crying out to me."

"Don't fret, lass. They've only been gone a few days. When they were lads, yer husband and Robert roamed the woods for a week before we worried. Ian and Dughall are resourceful young men. If they get into trouble, they'll know what to do."

Jessie smiled. "You're right. They're likely having a good time, hunting and gatherin' herbs. Ian promised to stay away from strangers."

"The lads are nearly seventeen. They'll be grown men before ye know it, with wives and children of their own."

"Oh Maggie, I love them so much. It will be a bittersweet day when they leave to start families."

"They'll always be close. Besides, do ye not want some time alone with that dear husband of yours?"

Jessie blushed. "Aye. It was wonderful last night. Alex was just as he was on our wedding night. The man leaves me breathless."

Maggie gave her a knowing look. "No need to worry. The lads will be back before you know it." She flexed her hands. "I hope Dughall brings willow bark."

APPROACHING WHINNYFOLD

Dughall touched his brother's leg and shook it gently. "Wake up. The sun is overhead."

Ian opened his eyes and drew his breath in sharply. He clutched his arm and groaned. "I'm hurting all over and I feel hot."

Dughall felt his forehead. "You might have a fever, or it could be the sun." He pulled out the flask and offered a drink of water.

Ian's hand shook as he drank from the flask.

Dughall frowned. "You look pale, Brother. Do ye want to stay here tonight?"

"Nay. I want to go home. Help me to stand."

Dughall grabbed his brother under his good arm and lifted him. He leaned him against the tree and picked up the bow and quiver and their packs.

Ian straightened himself and stood on his own. "All right, let's go." They climbed the hill to the top and rested a while. The sun beat down on them as they sat on the rocks. Ian's shirt was soaked with sweat.

Dughall studied him. "You look better, Brother. Do ye think ye can make it through the moor?"

"Aye. Have ye thought about what to tell Mother?"

"What do ye mean?"

Ian wiped sweat from his face. "Do ye think we should tell her about the lass? You know what she thinks about strangers."

"I guess she'll be mad," Dughall said, ominously. "We'll get the speech again. Even so, I don't want to lie to her."

"We won't lie. We just won't tell the whole truth. You helped the lass. Can ye not say that ye set my shoulder yourself?"

Dughall winced. "I don't know. What about the trick the lass did with her foot in your armpit? Mother knows I've never done that before."

"Tell her you got lucky. You knew what to do. God helped ye."

Dughall frowned. It was beginning to sound like a lie.

Ian reddened. "Don't tell her everything. She'll be mad and I can't bear it. Promise me!"

"All right. But I don't like it." He picked up their packs and gazed at the sky. "If we mean to get home by supper, we'd best be going."

Ian's belly rumbled as he got to his feet. "Supper. I'm so hungry I could eat stale bread. I hope Maggie makes tatties and herrin'."

They climbed down the hill. Dughall stayed close to Ian, ready to throw down their gear and support him. They walked across the moor, through heather and bog myrtle, avoiding the ruts. Soon they emerged into a meadow that was ripe with sweet grasses. In the distance, they saw the tree that marked the path to Peterhead.

Ian staggered as they reached the tree. "I can't take another step."

Dughall lay down their packs and sat his brother on them. "Stay here. I'll get Father." He sprinted past the cliffs and came upon Whinnyfold. Near his cottage, he saw Maggie and Mother making soap with Effie and Nora.

Jessie looked up. "Dear God! Where is Ian?"

Dughall stopped to catch his breath, resting his hands on his knees. "By the path to Peterhead. He's been hurt. Where's Father?"

Effie wiped her hands on her apron. "I'll get Alex. He's on the beach." She walked to the cliff and headed down the path.

Jessie placed a hand on his shoulder. "What happened, Son? Is it bad?"

"Nay. His shoulder was out of joint but we popped it back in. He's in pain and can't take another step."

Alex appeared with a worried look on his face and ran his fingers through his hair. "Take me to your brother."

"Follow me, Father." Dughall ran for the cliffs, with Alex and Jessie on his heels. "He's near the big tree by the path."

When they came upon Ian he was sitting on the packs with eyes closed. Alex stood back as Jessie felt his arm and shoulder. Ian moaned as she ran her hands under the sling.

She placed a hand on his forehead. "He's got a fever. Let's get him to bed."

Ian groaned. "Nay. I want some supper."

"That's a good sign," Alex said. "He can't be too bad off if he wants food. I'll carry him back." He lifted Ian into his arms and walked towards the village, with Jessie at his side.

Dughall grabbed the packs and followed.

Whinnyfold

Later that evening, Ian sat up in bed drinking a cup of willow bark tea. An empty plate lay at his side. He'd filled his belly with tatties and herrin'. Alex and Jessie sat at the table across from Dughall.

"You've told us about the boar, and how ye hurt your shoulder," Alex said.

"There's some bruising," she said. "But it's set back in place. How did ye do it, Son?"

Dughall felt uneasy. Above all things, he hated to lie.

"Dughall did it all by himself," Ian said. "He knew what to do. It was painful but he popped it back in."

Alex stared. "Is that the truth, Son?"

Dughall reddened and shifted in his seat. Perhaps if he didn't speak, it wouldn't be a lie.

"It's true," Ian said. "He's embarrassed to tell ye. Only God helped him."

Jessie glanced at Alex and raised her eyebrows. Alex clasped his hands and fixed his stare on Dughall. "Tell me the truth, Son."

Dughall looked at his brother with a pained expression. He glanced at his parents. They didn't look mad, but they were waiting. "A lass did it. I helped her."

Ian groaned. "Ach! How did ye know?"

Jessie smiled. "Well for one thing, your sling was made from a lass' petticoat."

Dughall rolled his eyes. "Ha! See brother, we don't have to lie. They're not mad."

Ian gave him a withering look.

"Tell us about her," Jessie said.

"Oh God," Ian groaned.

"She's a healer like me. The young lass took off her petticoat and tore it up, making a ball and a sling. She put the ball in Ian's armpit and pressed her foot against it. Then she pulled on his arm until it straightened."

"I thought she was trying to kill me."

"Then I helped her hold his shoulder, while she turned his arm and popped it back in. Ian fainted."

"I did not! That's enough, Brother."

Alex brought a hand to his mouth to hide a smile. "Quite a story, but something says there's more to tell." He squeezed Dughall's shoulder. "Thanks for telling the truth, Son." He spoke to Ian in a stern voice. "Tomorrow, you and I will talk about bein' truthful."

Ian's face fell. "Forgive me, Father."

Alex stood. "Save it for tomorrow, Son. I'll be back later. I must check on Maggie before it gets dark. She's worried about ye." He walked to the door, ducked his head, and went outside.

Jessie frowned. "The lass is a stranger. Were ye careful about what ye said?"

Dughall sensed her fear. "You don't have to worry, Mother. Where she comes from the Sight is a gift."

Ian rubbed his forehead and moaned.

"Dear God! She knows that ye have the Second Sight? How did she find out?"

"I was strippin' willow bark with her when Ian got hurt far away. In my mind I heard him cry out and felt pain in my shoulder. I told her that he was hurt and I had to go to him. She guessed that I had the Sight."

Jessie gasped. "You said it was so?"

"Aye, Mother. I couldn't lie."

Jessie paled. "Does she know where ye live?"

"Aye, I told her. Don't worry. I mean to make her my wife."

Jesse shook her head. "Heaven help us."

Ian snorted. "I can't believe it. Dughall's in love."

TALKING SENSE

WHINNYFOLD
AUGUST 1636
One Day Later

It was daybreak in Whinnyfold. Sunlight streamed through a crack in the door, casting a glow on the wall. Jessie smiled drowsily, content in the warmth of the bed and the man beside her. She snuggled next to his body. "It's morning, love."

Alex rolled gently and wrapped his arms around her. "Thank God, the lads are safe."

"I was thinking the same thing."

On the other side of the cottage, the lads snored. Alex frowned. "They must be worn out. I'll have to talk to Ian today."

"Go easy on him, husband. His shoulder is bruised and painful."

"He's lucky I won't bruise his backside. That's the one thing I can't stand, not telling the truth."

"Why do ye suppose he did it?"

"I don't know, but he tried to get Dughall to go along. That lad couldn't tell a lie if his life was at stake."

Outside, they heard sounds of the village waking. Over the noise of sea birds, Maggie talked to Effie Deans.

Jessie sat up. "Maggie must be outside. We must finish the soap-making."

"Aye, ye must go."

Jessie threw back the blanket and got out of bed. Maggie would be wondering where she was. She pulled the nightshirt over her head, slipped on a dress, and took a moment to look at her sons. Dughall's face was peaceful as he hugged his pillow. Ian lay on his back snoring with the sling on his chest. Her heart swelled with gratitude.

I would die without them, she thought. Jessie opened the door and walked into the morning sunlight. She heard water breaking on the rocks and smelled salty air.

Maggie stood at the iron pot with Effie and Nora, holding up a pail. "The goat's milk. She wasn't pleased with my cold hands."

Effie stared with tired eyes. "Are ye sure ye can finish it, lass? We heard about Ian."

"He's alive and whole. He had a fever but it's gone now. Dughall took care of him and got him home."

"That lad is a Godsend," Nora said.

Jessie nodded. "You've been stirrin' all night. Go home to bed. Maggie and I will finish the soap."

Effie passed the pot stick and wiped her hands on a grain sack. "Thank ye, lass." She pointed to a basket of lavender. "We added brine this morning. Now ye must stir in the herbs."

Nora yawned as she took off her apron. "I've laid the settin' troughs on the ground and the pouring ladles beside them. I could sleep like the dead."

Maggie waved her hand. "Be off with ye then. Work well done. There's enough soap to last the winter."

Effie and Nora headed down the path to their cottages.

Maggie smiled as she flexed her hands. "Bless that lad, for bringin' me willow bark. This is my first morning without pain."

Jessie looked into the pot. The mixture was thick, ready for pouring. She put down the pot stick and picked up the basket, sprinkling lavender buds in the soap. "It looks good. Add the goat's milk slowly." She picked up the pot stick and stirred as the old woman poured from the pail. "Enough. Get the ladles ready."

Maggie picked up the ladles, smeared grease on the bowls, and handed one to Jessie. They scooped the soap mixture into the greased troughs until the pot was empty. Maggie wiped her face. "Phew! Glad that's done for another season."

"Aye, I'm for that."

"Alex said that a young lass set Ian's shoulder."

"Aye, well there's a story."

"Your husband was angry. He said that Ian lied to him."

Jessie sighed. "I don't know why. It's not like he beats them. Dughall told the truth, though."

"What will Alex do?"

"He told Ian that he means to have a talk with him about bein' truthful. The lad wasn't happy about it. Sometimes it's worse waitin' for him to talk to ye."

"Even so, the lad's lucky. I saw his shoulder. The lass knew what she was doing."

"Maggie, there's a problem. She knows that they have the Sight."

"What? How did she know?"

"She was with Dughall when Ian got hurt far away. He felt Ian's pain and insisted that his brother was in trouble. She guessed that he had the Sight."

"Did he admit that it was true?"

"Aye. He said he wouldn't lie."

"She could bring ruin upon us! Does she know where we live?"

"He told her."

Maggie groaned. "Sometimes that lad has no common sense."

"She said that where she comes from the Sight is a gift."

"A gift? Where does she come from?"

"I haven't asked Dughall. He says that he intends to make her his wife."

Maggie raised her eyebrows. "His wife? Why, the lad's never shown interest in lassies. Somethin' says there's more to tell."

"He looked so dreamy when he said it. Maggie, can ye talk to the lad? You seem to have a way with him."

Maggie took off her apron. "Send him to me this afternoon. Tell him his old Aunt needs help. I'll do my best."

***

Ian sat at the table, cradling his arm. His sling was off and the throbbing was constant. "I hope Father leaves me alone. I can't bear it."

Alex poked his head into the cottage. His voice was stern. "Ian. Come outside and sit with me at the worktable. I need to have a talk with ye."

"God help me." Ian stood and supported his arm, and walked outside into the sunlight. His father was seated at the table, tanning the hide of the hare he'd killed. Ian sat opposite him, resting his arm on the table. The pain was terrible, but the anticipation was worse.

Alex ran his fingers through his hair and cleared his throat. He lay the skin flat with the fur side down, picked up his knife, and scraped away the loose bits of flesh. He stopped and stared. "You lied to me."

Ian's heart pounded with fear. "I'm sorry, Father. I thought Mother would be mad if we told her we talked to a stranger. I can't bear it when she's mad."

"I don't like it when she's mad either. But I wouldn't lie to her. It's against all we believe in."

"But Father…"

"There's no excuse for lying to your parents, Son. What ye did was wrong." He took his knife and trimmed the ragged edges of the hide.

Ian didn't dare to speak.

Alex put down the knife and gripped the table. "So, what should I do with ye?"

Ian's eyes grew wide. "Did ye never get into trouble? What would your father have done?"

Alex clenched his jaw. "My father would have stripped off my shirt and breeks and beaten me with a belt 'til I couldn't breathe."

Ian flinched. "He did that to ye?"

"Aye, many times."

Ian saw the anger in his eyes and panicked. "You've never taken a belt to us!"

"Not yet."

His fear blossomed. "Father, please! Don't hurt me."

Alex softened his stare. "I won't do that to ye, Son. It was bad enough my old man did it to me."

Ian took a ragged breath.

"So tell me, what should I do with ye?"

Ian reddened with shame. "Forgive me for what I did. I'll never lie again."

Alex hesitated. He sprinkled brine on the pelt and rubbed it into every crack and wrinkle. "I forgive ye." He stood and walked to the edge of the cliff, leaving Ian to contemplate his words.

***

Maggie sat outside on a wooden stool, with a fishing net stretched across her lap. Her head was down as her fingers worked the wooden needles, repairing the net with rough twine. Her singing voice was thin and high from old age.

> *O weel may the boatie row,*
> *and better she may speed;*
> *O weel may the boatie row,*
> *That brings the bairns' breid.*

A deeper voice joined in. She looked up and saw Dughall standing there.

> *The boatie rows, the boatie rows,*
> *The boatie rows full well;*
> *And muckle good before the drag,*
> *The marline and the creel.*

She smiled. "Ye have a beautiful voice, lad."

Dughall pointed to the wooden needles. "Can I help ye with that?"

Maggie shook her head. "Nay. I'm feelin' better now. All that trouble and ye still brought me the willow bark. Bless your heart."

"Can I sit with ye awhile? I need to talk."

Maggie searched his face. "Why, of course lad." His eyes were as blue as a flower. *He's so handsome,* she thought. *No wonder the lassies are after him.*

Dughall sat cross-legged on the ground across from her. He ran his fingers through his hair and cleared his throat.

Just like Alex, when he has somethin' to say.

Dughall smiled. "I'm glad you're better. I love ye and I missed your singing."

Maggie gave him a knowing look. "I'm an old woman, with a voice not worth hearing. But ye can say that ye love me anytime." She put down her needles. "Tell me about the lass."

Dughall reddened. "Mother told ye?"

"She didn't say much. Only that ye mean to make her your wife. Ye were only gone two days. How did it happen?"

Dughall placed his hands on his thighs and bit his lip gently. "Well, there's a story here."

Maggie glanced at the sky. "There's plenty of time before supper."

"I hope ye don't think me daft. Have ye ever dreamed of someone who ye didn't know? A dream so strong that it seemed real?"

"Aye. I dreamed of my husband James, long before I met him. He walked with me on the beach and spoke of the life we would have. I nearly fainted when I met him."

Dughall's eyes widened. "That's how it was with her. I dreamed of a lass with dark hair and green eyes who waited for me in the heather. She said hello, and I knew her voice. She smelled of lavender, just like Mother. We belonged together."

"Hmmm... This was the lass you met in the forest?"

"Aye. Ian went hunting. I took my pack and walked through a meadow filled with heather, singing and touching the purple bells. I came to a stand of willow trees and saw her strippin' bark. I thought she was a vision."

"Did she seem to know ye?"

"Aye. She said that she'd dreamed of me."

Just like James and me, Maggie thought. "What was she doing there?"

"Gatherin' healing plants. I told her about ye and she helped me strip bark. We talked about our villages and families. She lives with her grandmother because her parents are dead."

"Poor lass."

"Then Ian got hurt. I cried out and grabbed my shoulder because it hurt like the devil."

Maggie blanched. "Is that how she knew ye had the Sight?"

"Oh God. Mother told ye."

"Aye."

He winced. "I wasn't careful about what I said. Ian called me daft."

"Does she know where ye live?"

"Before Ian got hurt, I told her. Mother must be mad."

Maggie touched his hand. "She's not mad, just worried about ye. The lass could bring disaster upon us."

"Don't worry. Where she comes from the Sight is a gift. She asked me why I tried to hide it."

"I've never heard of such a place. Where does she come from?"

He shrugged his shoulders. "A village near the Ugie River."

"Hmmphh… Does it have a name?"

"I couldn't ask her. A man came and took her away because her grandmother was dying."

"Oh dear. The poor child. What makes ye think ye can marry her? Is she attracted to ye?"

Dughall blushed. "Aye. After she healed Ian, we went into the woods and kissed for a long time. I thought I would die of pleasure." He looked down at his hands.

Maggie tried to hide a smile. "Tell me, lad. I've lived a long time and seen many things."

Dughall looked up. "She said that she dreamed of me and our newborn son. We belonged together. Then she placed my hand on her breast and her hand on my… Ach! I can't say these things!"

"Did ye get her with child, lad?"

"Nay. She said that where she came from it was sacred. But I couldn't take her. Father says it's wrong to take advantage of a lass."

Maggie frowned. *Sacred? Where do you come from, lass?* "Can ye tell me anything about her that was strange?"

Dughall thought for a moment. "Well Aunt Maggie, ye know how we say things like 'Oh God' and 'Thank God'?"

"Aye."

"She said Goddess."

Maggie was rendered speechless. For years, she'd worshipped the Goddess in private, hiding it from the eyes of the Christian church. Her mother was hung as a witch. The color drained slowly from her face. "Can it be?" she whispered.

Dughall shook her gently. "Are ye all right, Auntie? I can't explain it, but I love her. We belong together."

Maggie swallowed hard. "I believe ye, lad. Maybe we're both daft." She glanced at the sky. "Time for supper. We made biscuits and soup."

Dughall grasped her gnarled hands and helped her up. "Thanks Aunt Maggie. I love ye."

"I love ye too." Maggie didn't know if she should be happy or afraid for the lad. *It's meant to be,* she thought. *How can I tell Jessie?*

They walked towards his cottage, watching gulls soar overhead. Dughall smiled. "They carry the souls of dead fishermen. Someday, I'll fly with them."

Mary

THE GATHERING

WHINNYFOLD
SEPTEMBER 1636
TWO WEEKS LATER

It was late afternoon in Whinnyfold. A southeast wind blew across the waves, peaking them in whitecaps. Water crashed on the rocky shore, scattering hundreds of tiny hermit crabs. Ian and Dughall stood on the beach, hurling stones into the water. Kittiwakes and gulls dove into the surf, breaking the surface with a beak full of cod.

Dughall took a deep breath, feeling the power of the wind and sea. "I could never live inland. I love the sea."

"Aye. Days like this are the best." Ian picked up a rock, weighing it in his hand. "My arm is almost as good as new. But I won't be throwin' the caber tomorrow." He leaned back and tossed it into the sea.

"Keira said ye must be careful or it will pop out."

Ian snorted. "You're still thinkin' about her, aren't ye? Let me find ye a lass for the gathering. Mary has a cousin who's been askin' after ye."

"Nay. I don't think so."

"Are ye sure? Her cousin Jane's a fine lookin' lass. Wears her petticoat shorter than Mary. Her lips are like cherries and her breasts are..."

Dughall reddened. "Stop it!"

"Maybe she'll think it's sacred too! It could be those dark curls of yours makin' them say that. Look at ye, your loins are swellin' just thinkin' about it."

Dughall looked down and blushed. He straightened the bulge in the front of his breeks. "I don't want anyone else."

"Well, it's a shame. Jane could show ye a thing or two. Think of it as practice for when you see your lass again."

Dughall frowned. "Is that what we do as men? Practice? What do you think Father would say about that?"

Ian glared. "For God's sake, don't tell him. I can't bear it when he has a serious talk with me. I'm just teasin' ye."

"All right."

Ian eyed him suspiciously. He sat on the ground and drew a circle in the sand with his finger.

Dughall dropped down next to him. He felt waves of anger coming from his brother. "You're mad that I told them the truth. I can feel it."

Ian picked up a stone and threw it into the sea. "I didn't tell ye this, because I was ashamed. Father was verra angry that I lied to him. I thought that he meant to beat me."

Dughall's eyes grew wide. "Did he bring a strap?"

"Nay. It wasn't like that. I should have apologized, but I argued instead. He said that there was no excuse, what I did was wrong. Then he asked what he should do with me."

"Oh God. What did you say?"

"I was mad! I said 'Did ye never get into trouble? What would your father have done?'"

Dughall rolled his eyes. "Do ye not know when to keep your mouth shut?"

"I guess not. He said that his father would have stripped him naked and beaten him with a belt 'til he couldn't breathe."

"His father did that?"

Ian stared at his hands. "Many times, he said."

"But he's never taken a belt to us."

"That's what I said, though I was bein' real respectful. I was sittin' there holding my shoulder, thinkin' he meant to beat me. My heart pounded so hard I thought I'd die."

"Did he hit ye?"

"Nay. He said he wouldn't do what his father did."

"Thank God."

"I begged him to forgive me and promised I would never lie again."

"Well, at last ye showed some sense."

Ian flushed with shame. "Aye. I should apologize to Mother as well."

Dughall nodded.

"Promise me you'll not tell Father what I said. He's not too pleased with me."

"All right. But you must not bother me about the lass."

Ian sniffled. "I'll be glad when I'm a man and won't have to worry about these things."

They looked out to sea and saw a scaffie sailing north to Peterhead. Ian grunted. "John Galt and his son Grady."

"Grady will be in the stone's throw."

"Aye, Brother. He's a tough one to beat."

Dughall sensed someone watching and looked up at the cliff to see Maggie waving, snow-white hair blowing about her face. He stood and brushed sand from his breeks, and signaled to her. "Maggie's up there. It must be time for supper." He extended a hand to his brother.

Ian took his hand and pulled himself up. They walked across the beach to the cliff side path.

Dughall stopped at the hollow of a sand hill to pick violets, and handed them to Ian. "For Mother. Best they should come from you."

***

Maggie's breath was short as she entered the cottage. "The sea is rough. I hope it calms down tomorrow."

Jessie wiped her hands on her apron. "What about the lads?"

"They're coming. I found them on the beach."

Jessie put the oatcakes on the table. "Good. Supper is almost ready." She picked up the ladle and stirred the pot of soup.

Maggie sniffed. "It smells good, lass. The leeks are strong and verra tasty. Makes even the cod taste better. Will Alex be home for supper?"

"Nay. He's in Peterhead helping them set up tents for the gathering."

Maggie tied her hair back. "Are the lads joining the games? Ian shouldn't with his shoulder on the mend."

"I told him I didn't want him in the games. He wasn't happy about it. He wanted to impress that lass he's been seeing."

"Mary McFarlein?"

"Aye."

Maggie loved matchmaking more than anything else. "She's from a good family in Peterhead. Her father's a fisherman and her sisters have many children. It's not a bad match for him."

"Aye. Alex knows her father, Andrew. They've talked about the match and would like to see it soon. The lad and the lass are strong-headed and they don't want to see them get into trouble."

Jessie took the pot off the fire and placed it on the hearth. "Andrew is willing to give Ian a share in a boat when they marry."

Maggie raised her eyebrows. "A generous offer. Does Ian know?"

"Nay. Andrew plans to talk with him at the gathering."

"Changes in the wind. Has Dughall mentioned his lass again?"

"Nay. It makes me nervous. Ian says she's not a fisher lass. Did Dughall tell ye anything about her?"

The old woman hesitated. "Aye. I don't know what to say about it. Ye'll think me daft."

"Maggie, please."

"All right. Do ye remember what I told ye about my husband James? How I dreamed of him even though we'd never met? In my dream, we walked the beach hand in hand and spoke of the life we would have together."

Jessie smiled. "I remember."

"When I met him in Peterhead, I nearly fainted. He said that he'd dreamed of me, too. We fit together as hand and glove, and married within the month."

"A romantic story."

"Aye. Dughall said that he dreamed of a lass who waited in the heather. He knew what she looked like, the sound of her voice, and her scent. This was the lass he met in the forest. She said that she dreamed of him too."

"Dear God."

"The lad was embarrassed to tell me, but they went into the forest and were passionate with one another."

Jessie stared. "Dughall? I can't believe it. He didn't get her with child?"

"Nay. He stopped short of it."

"Thank God."

"He's sure that they belong together. Dreams are never wrong. I believe him."

Jessie was quiet for a moment. "Perhaps Alex can talk to her father."

"Her parents are dead. She lives with her grandmother, but Dughall said the old woman was dying."

"Poor little orphan." Jessie ladled soup into bowls. "She's not a fisher lass, but we could use another healer. Dughall could spend more time fishing with his father."

Maggie brightened. The match was almost made. "Aye. We can teach her about shelling and baiting."

"When Ian's betrothal is settled, we'll think about it. Where does she live?"

Maggie bit her lower lip gently. "Some village on the Ugie River. But there's more to tell." She pondered her suspicions.

A breeze blew across the hearth as the door opened and the lads came in. Jessie held a finger to her lips, silencing the old woman.

Ian held out the violets to Jessie. "Forgive me, Mother. I'll never lie again."

WHINNYFOLD NEXT DAY

It was early morning in the cliff-top village. The door to the cottage was open, letting in fresh sea air. Alex tucked in his shirt and adjusted the strap of his sporran so the tail hung no further than the bottom of his kilt. It had been years since he'd worn it.

Jessie smiled. "Your best kilt. I forgot how handsome ye are in it." She slipped on a flowing skirt over a saffron-dyed blouse and petticoat.

Alex's heart swelled. "A fine skirt, with stripes the color of blooming heather. But not as bonny as you, lass." He placed his hands on her hips and drew her close. The lavender in her hair made him smile. "Where are the lads?"

"They started out at dawn. Ian was eager to see where the games were being held. Dughall wanted to practice the stone's throw."

He kissed her forehead. "Mmm... He's a strong lad. He might have a chance against Grady Galt. Did ye tell Ian not to play?"

"Aye. He wasn't too pleased. I think he wanted to impress young Mary McFarlein."

Alex smiled. "He'll impress her all right. Andrew plans to talk with him about marrying his daughter. He's going to offer him a share in a boat and one of his cottages. The lad would be daft to turn him down."

Jessie snuggled against him. "If all goes well, we'll have a spring wedding. Are we set to sail?"

"Aye. The 'Bonnie Fay' is rigged and ready. Maggie is waiting on the beach. I packed up the plaids and soap that ye have for sale. It's time to go."

Alex took a cloak off a peg and wrapped it around her shoulders. He could tell that she wanted to ask something by the way the tips of her ears reddened. "What is it, love?"

"Should I bring my harp? Maggie wants to hear me play."

He kissed her palm and lingered there. "She's not the only one. It would give me pleasure to hear ye play."

Jessie shivered. "I love ye, husband."

He felt his loins swell. "Ach! I can't control it."

Jessie smiled. "I don't want ye to control it. Oh Alex. Lads or no, we'll finish this tonight."

Reluctantly, he released her.

She handed him the lunch basket and picked up the sheepskin bag holding her harp. "Maggie must be wondering where we are." They went through the door, secured the latch, and headed down the cliff side path to the beach.

PETERHEAD

Ian and Dughall stood on the soggy playing field. Insects buzzed about their heads as the flattened grass steamed in the morning air.

"It rained last night," Dughall said. "I hope the sun dries up the field."

"Aye. Wet grass is bad for the stone's throw."

They looked around the field and saw the caber, the stone, and the hammer lying on the ground. "This looks like where the games will be held."

On the edge of the field were canvas tents, with bright ribbons streaming from them. The clans would meet in these tents, take their meals, and display their wares. Several large cooking pots stood ready over peat and wood bundles.

Dughall's heart raced. "I'm so excited I can barely stand it. There'll be drumming and piping and storytelling. Do ye think that Mother will play her harp?"

"She hasn't played in a verra long time."

"I hope she will. Father loves it."

They shaded their eyes and looked past the field at the town of Peterhead, where dozens of people scurried about, preparing for the gathering. Dughall could hardly believe it. "The town is filled with people. Are they here for the gatherin' or the healing well?"

Ian shrugged. Tall buildings lined the main street and a church with a spire rang its bell. The south pier lay beyond, where scaffies and rowboats arrived steadily. "I've never seen so many sails. You can hear them in the wind."

"Aye. Fluttering like the wings of a white butterfly."

"You have a way with words, Brother. No wonder the lassies like ye."

Dughall picked up the heavy round stone, and held it at his shoulder. He grunted. "It's verra heavy. But I think I can do it."

"See how far ye can throw it."

He nested the stone in the crook of his neck and cocked his arm. His expression was serious as he tossed the stone as far as he could.

"Not bad! Better than last year. See if ye can throw it farther."

Dughall raised his eyebrows. "Look behind ye, Brother. It's Mary's father."

Ian turned and saw Andrew McFarlein, dressed in his best kilt and sporran, with a dirk in his sock. There was a determined look on his weathered face, as he stopped in front of them.

Andrew's red hair glinted in the sunlight. "Do ye know who I am?"

Ian extended a hand. "Aye. You're Mary's father."

Andrew smiled broadly. "That I am! I'm Andrew McFarlein." He took Ian's hand, shook it vigorously, and turned to Dughall. "A fine throw, Dughall Hay. Ye may have a chance against Grady Galt."

Dughall brightened. "Do ye think so?"

Andrew clapped him on the back. "Aye. Work at it, Son. Can I take your brother for a while? I need to have a serious talk with him."

Dughall smiled as his brother squirmed. "Go with him, Brother. I need to practice for a while."

***

Ian felt Andrew's large hand on his shoulder. *Oh God*, he thought. *Not another serious talk.* They walked off the field towards the main street in Peterhead.

"I hear ye hurt your shoulder, lad."

Ian grunted. "Aye. It could have been worse. A boar nearly gored me."

"How's it feel now?"

"Hurts a bit, but not like before."

"A good stiff drink will take care of that."

Ian stared. Barren heather land and peat bogs lay to the west. They walked in silence along King's Common Gate, passing stone cottages and tenements.

Andrew cleared his throat. "See those cottages, lad?"

Ian nodded.

"Those four belong to my family, as well as the land clear to Bankhead Road. There's room for one more."

Ian swallowed hard. The man was smiling. How much had Mary told him?

"The Earl built a bulwark in the harbor. That's a good thing! This burgh will grow to twice its size in a few years."

They continued on past the fish-house tenement and Walker's place, until they came to a road that led to Keith Inch. A two-storied tavern stood against the harbor, built of timber with a covered veranda on the south side. On the front of the building, an inscription was cut. 'The Crack. She wrecked on Keith Inch in 1588.' Bolted to the wall was the figurehead from the bow of the ill-fated ship, a mermaid with red hair, a green dress, and bare breasts. Someone had nailed a wooden pint into her hand.

Ian stared. "Dear God." Those nipples looked real. "Why do they call it The Crack?"

"That's a corruption of a Dutch word, kraecke. It's a three-masted trading vessel, deep and round-built. Ever seen one in the harbor?"

"Nay."

"Next time one arrives, I'll send for ye." Andrew started up the wooden steps. "My friend Klaas runs this place. He's a Dutchman. Come on, lad."

Ian hesitated. "They serve spirits here. Father will kill me."

Andrew chuckled. "It's all right, lad. Alex knows that I'm takin' ye here." He climbed the steps to the upper story.

Ian followed. Andrew opened the heavy door and ushered him in. Faces regarded them warily as they walked past the long bar and seated themselves at a table in the back. Ian looked around. He'd never been in such a place before. The light was dim and it smelled of meat pies and stale tobacco. The man at the next table was motionless, head resting on his arms, his hand locked around a pint. Six empty glasses and a half-eaten meat pie stood on the bench next to him.

"Don't touch that man," Andrew said. "If ye wake him, he'll cut your throat." He went to the bar and came back with two glasses of whisky, setting them on the table. "Drink with me."

Father will kill me, Ian thought. He barely croaked, "I've never had a whisky before."

"Just one. You're a man now, or at least that's what I'm told."

Oh God. Here it comes. He lifted his glass and sipped the whisky. The golden liquid burned his throat and warmed him down to his belly.

Andrew gulped his whisky, slammed down the glass, and looked Ian directly in the eyes. "I'm not a man to waste time. I understand that ye are interested in my daughter Mary."

Ian's heart thumped in his chest. He swallowed hard. "Aye."

Andrew pounded his fist on the table. "Good! She likes ye too. I'm here to make ye an offer."

Ian took a sip of his whisky and felt emboldened by its warmth. "An offer?"

"Aye. I'm a man of means, Son. I own a few fishing boats and a tract of land in Peterhead. My daughter is determined to take ye as husband. Marry her and I'll give ye a half share in a fishin' boat and a cottage. So what say ye, lad?"

Ian's eyes widened. He imagined a life of his own, with a cottage, a boat, and the big-breasted lass as his wife. No more lectures from Father or lookin' out for Dughall. He lifted his glass and belted his whisky. "I'll marry her."

Andrew tipped his glass and downed the rest of his whisky. He pounded the table, making the glasses jump. "Good! Then it's settled. We'll announce your engagement today. You'll wed in the spring." He stood and slapped Ian on the back. "I like your attitude and your red hair. Let's get back to the gathering, Son."

Ian stood and steadied himself against the table. He was dizzy, but he felt like a man. He followed Andrew out of the tavern and walked down the main street. Ahead, he saw Mary in a white frilly dress, running towards them. Her yellow hair was tied with blue ribbons, and flowed behind her in the breeze.

Mary stopped in front of them and clasped her hands. She glanced at Ian, then at her father. "Did ye ask him, Father?"

Andrew held his arms out to her. "Aye, lass. He's agreed to be your husband."

"Oh thank ye, Father." She kissed him on the cheek.

Andrew smiled. "My bonny little lass."

She stood back and reddened. "Leave us alone, Father. I need to talk to Ian."

Andrew grinned. "I guess you're a woman now. I'll go tell your mother." He turned and walked away.

Mary grasped both of Ian's hands. "Oh, Ian. Please don't be mad. I love ye so much I can't think of anything else. I promise this will be a good thing."

Ian saw that her father had turned the corner and was out of sight. Her breasts struggled against the bodice of her dress. As he wrapped his hands around her waist, she put her arms on his shoulders and parted her lips. Still dizzy from the liquor, he kissed her deeply until he felt her sigh.

She slipped off a shoe and ran her foot up his leg. "You taste like whisky."

WHINNYFOLD

Alex hoisted the mainsail and guided the boat out of the harbor, past the Skares, and north for Peterhead. He was grateful that the sea was calm today.

Maggie sat on a wooden crate, grasping the side of the boat. The sleeves of her sweater came past her wrists, and the bottom of her striped skirt rested atop her shoes. Her brow wrinkled as she smiled.

He tightened the jib. "The sea is calm today."

Maggie spit into the water. "Good thing. The lads should have helped ye sail."

Jessie gave her a warning look. "It's all right. I can help Alex."

Waves lapped peacefully against the sides of the wooden boat. "There's no need," Alex said. "I'll stay close to shore, where it's calm. The lads can help me sail back."

Jessie looked at the cargo, three wooden crates of plaids and soap. "We did well, Maggie. We have a lot of goods to trade."

"Aye. We need barrel stays and wooden spoons and hemp for repairin' nets. I'll think of the rest."

Alex nodded. "I heard that a cooper would be there. Name of McLennan. The man should have barrels and stays for trade."

Jessie looked thoughtful. "I checked the larder. We need tea and honey."

Alex guided the boat seaward as they approached Slains Castle. The fortress stood tall and foreboding against the landscape, with smoke drifting up from its chimneys. The gardens were a riot of color. "I wonder if the Earl of Erroll will come to the gathering?"

"He hasn't come the last two years," Maggie said harshly, as she closed her eyes.

Alex reddened. The old woman invited trouble with her opinions. "Now, Maggie. It would be foolish to speak ill of the Earl. We'd best keep our thoughts to ourselves."

Maggie frowned. "Hmmph... Every other generation they get themselves allied with the wrong sort, and we pay the price. My grandfather died at the battle of Flodden. Years later, my brothers died when the trouble with the Spaniards came. I don't understand it."

"Well. We won't speak of it today. We've had peace for nearly forty years."

She opened her eyes and stared. "It's been two generations. Think of the lads."

They passed the castle and Alex steered the boat closer to shore. The waves calmed. He glanced at Maggie, dozing in the sun, and spoke quietly. "She's asleep. Tough old woman. Tell me about the lass Dughall met in the forest."

Jessie's ears reddened. "Dughall admires her because she's a healer. Honestly, she has healing skills that I've never heard of. We could learn a thing or two from her."

Alex wiped his brow. "I've never seen him with a lass. Is he serious about her?"

"Aye. He told Maggie he was passionate with her."

"What! Dughall? If that lad took advantage of her and got her with child..."

"Nay. It wasn't like that. He stopped short of it."

"Thank God. I'll have a serious talk with him. Ian says the girl is not a fisher lass. Dughall should make another choice."

Jessie winced. "He loves her, husband. Dughall told Maggie he's determined to marry her. She has no family to keep her inland. I could teach her what she needs to know."

"Hmmphh..."

"With another healer, Dughall could spend more time fishing."

Alex didn't like it, but the look on his wife's face melted his heart. "It's hard to deny ye, as bonny as ye are. An orphan, then. Let me think on it. I'll talk to our son at the gathering."

Jessie squeezed his arm. "Thanks, love."

They sailed in silence along the coastline, past rocky cliffs and dense pine forests. The small town of Longhaven appeared; it's harbor nearly empty. "Look, lass. They've all sailed for Peterhead." He took the boat seaward and felt the wind in his face. Just before the port of Boddam, a stone cottage stood alone on the cliff. "John Galt's cottage."

Jessie nodded. A few more miles and the granite walls of Boddam castle appeared on the shore. "Oh Alex. The pink castle always takes my breath away. Do ye think the Earl of Marischal will be there today?"

Alex grunted. "Nay. He's likely off on the King's business."

Maggie stirred, as the sea grew choppy. She opened her eyes and stared at the horizon. Alex wondered how he would keep her quiet.

PETERHEAD

The burgh of Peterhead loomed on the horizon. Dozens of sails dotted Port Henry harbor and many rowboats as well. The approaching pier was busy with activity. Alex felt grateful. The sea was an unpredictable force. "Thank God for a safe journey. I never tire of sailing into this port."

Jessie stood and gripped the masthead. "I'm so excited! Look at how many boats are here."

Alex held a wooden pole against the pier to stop the boat and handed it to Jessie to keep it steady. He jumped off the 'Bonnie Fay' with a rope and tied her to a post on the pier. The old woman stood. "Stay there, Maggie! I'll help ye after I unload."

Alex boarded the boat, uncovered their cargo, and picked up a wooden crate. He stepped onto the pier and set the box down, then helped Maggie and Jessie off. As they walked along the pier, they passed old fishermen on benches, tidying their lines. Womenfolk sat nearby, some watching, and some knitting and having a chat. Alex led them off the pier onto a path. They walked for a half-mile in the sun until they saw the field with brightly decorated tents upon it.

Jessie smiled. "The ribbons are beautiful. It will be wonderful to see everyone again."

"Aye. Our tent is just ahead." Alex saw that Maggie was failing and put down the crate he was carrying. He held her arm and led her to the tent, sitting her on a wooden bench. His heart ached for the old woman. "Stay here, Maggie. Jessie and I will set up the goods." Her eyes were already closed.

Alex made several trips to the boat, until all of their goods were in the tent. He took a drink from his flask and sat down for a moment. He looked at Jessie, admiring her womanly form. She was bending over, setting up the cooking pot for fish stew. A yellow petticoat showed below her skirt. He walked to her and patted her backside.

Jessie blushed.

Alex smiled. "I'm going to look for Dughall."

✳✳✳

Alex came upon his son on the game field and watched with pride as he threw the heavy stone. "A good throw, lad. You're a match for Grady Galt."

Dughall glanced at his father. "I've been practicin' all morning."

Alex beamed. "That ye have. I'm proud of ye."

Dughall rubbed sand between his hands and wiped them on his breeks.

Alex looked around the playing field. "Where's Ian?"

Dughall rolled his eyes. "He left with Andrew McFarlein. The man wanted to have a serious talk with him."

Alex tried to hide a smile. "He did, did he? We'll have to see what comes of it."

"Ian was nervous."

Alex smiled. "I would be."

Dughall picked up his shirt off the ground and slipped it on. "Where is Mother?"

"Your mother and Maggie are with the womenfolk, helping them with the feast. I need to have a talk with ye. Leave the stone and walk with me."

Dughall tucked his shirt into his breeks. "All right."

They walked off the field and followed the path towards the south pier. Gulls screamed overhead as sails flapped in the wind. Alex led him to the 'Bonnie Fay', moored at the far end of the pier. They boarded her and Alex searched for the sheepskin bag holding Jessie's harp. He found it near the mast and handed it to his son. "Take this."

"Mother's playing?"

"Aye. I told her it would give me pleasure to hear her play."

Dughall smiled. "She really loves ye. I want to marry a lass just like her."

Alex cleared his throat and ran his fingers through his hair. "That's what I need to talk to ye about. You're nearly seventeen. I've never seen ye with a lass. Have ye thought about marrying, Son?"

"I think about it every day."

Alex searched for the right words. "The lass you met in the forest. Are ye serious about her?"

"Aye. I want to make her my wife. Her skin is soft and she smells of lavender just like Mother. She's a bonny healer; knows things about healing that I've never seen. When I'm with her my heart pounds like a great drum."

Alex raised his eyebrows. "Did ye take advantage of her?"

"Nay! We kissed for a verra long time, and I thought I would die of pleasure. But we stopped before it went too far."

Alex wiped his hands on his breeks. "Thank God. Ian says she's not a fisher lass, is that true?"

Dughall winced. "Aye, but she's a fine healer. Mother can teach her about shelling and baiting and cleaning the fish. Please, Father! We belong together."

Alex had never seen him so desperate. "Hmmphh… Do ye think that she'd be willin' to live here? Your mother says she's an orphan."

Dughall smiled. "I'm hopin' she will. I love her."

Alex saw the dreamy look in his son's eyes. *Dear God. He's so tender hearted. I hope she cares about him.* He stepped off the boat onto the pier and checked the ropes. "We'll talk again after the games. Let's find your brother and see what news he has for us."

Dughall stepped onto the pier with Jesse's harp under his arm, and they walked along the shore until they reached the path. In the distance, competing bands of pipers practiced in the shade. The ear-piercing tenor and bass drones of the bagpipe sounded above the flapping sails. Aromas of fish stew and fresh bread made their bellies grumble and drew them to the womenfolk.

***

John Barrie and Cheney Morris stood on the south pier, looking out to sea. "It's a bad day to be lookin' for a boat coming in from Aberdeen," John said, as he shaded his eyes.

Cheney wiped his face with a soiled kerchief. "Aye. Look at all the boats. Must be some kind of clan gatherin'. Strange people these fisher folk, but the women are bonny." He spit a yellow hocker on the ground through a hole in his front teeth.

John gagged. "Jesus Christ, Cheney! The 'Speedwell' was due to arrive yesterday. I heard that the skipper ran into trouble with a storm. Blackheart will be mad if his cargo was lost."

Cheney wiped his nose and sniffled. "I dinna wanna think about it. Let's go to The Crack for a pint and a meat-pie. There's games this afternoon on the field outside of town. We could watch and check the harbor later."

John took a last look out to sea. "All right. I hope that boat comes in. I'd hate to be the one to tell him." He picked up a bag off the ground and wrinkled his nose as he handed it to Cheney. "Old man, you stink like a polecat. Can ye not bathe once in a while?"

Cheney frowned. "I bathed last month, what more do ye want? I even used soap!" His lips slid back over yellow teeth as he sneered. "Besides, it's unhealthy to bathe."

John cringed. "I'll need more than a pint to stand ye for another day." They turned and headed along the pier towards the path. John walked behind the old man, staying upwind of him.

***

Maggie and Jessie stood at the cooking pot with Effie and Nora, watching the fish stew. Maggie added a basket of haddock to the steaming mixture of onions, carrots, and tatties. As Effie stirred, Nora threw in a handful of parsley and tarragon, and a cup of mustard seed.

Maggie beamed. "Ian and his lass are coming. Mary looks like she's about to burst with joy. He has his arm around her." She wiped her hands on a sack.

Jessie watched the approaching couple. "He must have accepted Andrew's offer." She handed her apron to Effie.

"I'll watch the stew," Effie said.

The young couple came closer and stood before them. Mary raised her eyebrows. "Tell her, Ian."

Ian reddened. "Ummm... Mother. We have something to tell ye."

"Good news, I hope."

"Aye."

Maggie held up a hand. "Your father and brother are walking across the field. Ye can tell us all."

They waited for Alex and Dughall to join them. Jessie held a finger to her lips and smiled at her husband.

"Mother, is that fish stew I smell?" Dughall asked. "I'm starving."

Jessie nodded. "Aye, but first your brother has news for us."

Ian put his arm around the lass. "Mary and I plan to wed in the spring. Her father offered me a share in a boat and a cottage in Peterhead. I hope this pleases you."

Jessie hugged the young girl, and turned to Ian. "I can't speak for your father, but it pleases me. I'm ready for grandchildren."

Alex had a serious look on his face. "Hmmm... A generous offer, not to be denied. You're a man, now. See that ye act like one. I'm pleased."

Ian breathed a sigh of relief. "Thank God."

Dughall smiled. "I'm happy for ye."

"It's wonderful news," Maggie said, "I might get to see some precious little ones before I die."

"Come, now," Jessie said. "There's fish stew and fresh bread. Nora made apple biscuits. We'll eat our fill and watch Dughall in the games."

***

It was early afternoon on the playing field. After the caber toss, the crowd gathered to see the throwing of the heavy stone. Men stood together, discussing the game with passion, as women fanned themselves in the hot sun. Alex looked around. "Most of Peterhead must be here."

"Aye," Jessie said. "All our friends and even some strangers."

Alex watched his son on the field, sizing up his competition. "I hope that Dughall does well."

Andrew McFarlein chuckled. "If he keeps the form I saw this morning, he'll do fine. He's a strong lad. I wish I had another daughter for him."

Dughall stood on the edge of the field, watching Grady glide forward and throw the heavy stone. Grady grunted and placed his hands on his knees as Hugh MacNeil walked the field and measured the throw.

"A good throw!" Hugh cried. "Little better than thirty feet." He marked the location with a flat marker, picked up the heavy stone, and brought it to Dughall. "Your turn, lad."

***

John Barrie and Cheney Morris stood in the crowd, watching the young man holding the stone. Cheney poked John in the ribs. "I must be dreaming. Who does he look like?"

John stared. "Blackheart's son, Gilbert. Actually, he looks just like Blackheart when he was young. What do ye make of it?"

"I don't know." Cheney cleared his throat and spit on the ground.

***

The sun beat down on the field, making them sweat. Dughall put down the stone and took off his shirt, laying it on the ground. The muscles in his back tightened as he picked up the stone and stood in back of the marker stick. Dughall nested the stone in the crook of his neck, cocking his arm. He concentrated and glided forward, tossing the stone as far as he could. The crowd buzzed with speculation. Dughall placed his hands on his knees and took a breath. He massaged his arm to stop the muscle from twitching.

It was too close to call from a distance. The crowd was silent as Hugh walked the field and measured the throw against the first marker. "Thirty one feet. Dughall Hay takes the contest!"

Dughall shook Grady's hand. "A good match, friend."

"Aye. We'll play again soon."

Dughall picked up his shirt and laid it over his arm. He walked off the field to his family and embraced his smiling parents.

"I'm proud of ye, lad," Alex said. "Today, my sons became men."

Dughall smiled broadly. The crowd gathered around and congratulated him, patting him on the back.

***

John and Cheney blanched and looked at each other. "He bears the mark of the stag on his shoulder," Cheney said. "The birthmark of the Gordon clan."

"Aye. I saw it clear as day. How can it be?"

"The son that Blackheart lost. Christal's child. How old would he be?"

John thought for a moment. "Gilbert was seven when Christal ran away. He's twenty-four now. If she bore that child, he'd be seventeen. The lad looks to be about that age." They shuddered as the lad with dark curls broke into a familiar smile. John shook his head. "Jesus Christ! It must be him."

"Aye. Find out where he comes from. Blackheart may have lost his cargo, but I think we found his son."

John watched as the lad embraced his family. "Poor bastard."

ABDUCTION

WHINNYFOLD
OCTOBER 1636
FOUR WEEKS LATER

It was a cold October morning in Whinnyfold. A southeast gale roiled the sea, sending streaks of foam into the air. There wasn't a boat on the sea, and gulls flew landward. Jessie shivered as she pulled a wool sweater around her shoulders. "Take your coats, lads. The wind is strong and the air is cold. It feels like winter."

Ian argued. "We don't need them yet."

Dughall silenced him with a stare. He took their coats from a peg and handed one to his brother. "We'll take them, Mother. Don't fret." He hugged her close.

Jessie felt the warmth of his embrace and melted. *He's so tall,* she thought. *I barely come to his shoulder.*

Her uneasiness returned. "My mother used to say that days like these never bring good. Where are ye going? With your father?"

"Nay. We're going to the meadow. I want to gather dried heather to brighten the cottage. It may be our last chance before the snow flies."

Jessie smiled. *Always thinking of flowers. It will be a lucky lass who marries him.*

Ian slipped on his coat and kissed her absently on the cheek. "We'll be back by mid-day. Don't fret. We're men now. Father said so." He opened the door wide, letting in a gust of cold air. "Come on, Brother."

Dughall frowned. "I'll be along. Close the door behind ye. Mother is shivering." Ian went through the door and closed it. Dughall held her close and kissed her cheek. "Goodbye, Mother. I love ye."

Jessie's heart swelled.

***

Maggie groaned as she threw back the blanket and sat up. She gritted her teeth as she straightened her spine. "Great Goddess! How much pain can a body bear?" She swung her legs off the bed and slipped her feet into her brogues. "There's no sense layin' in bed when there's work to be done."

Her breath hung in the cold air. "It's like winter." She threw a shawl around her shoulders and hobbled to the hearth. A few embers sparkled among the ashes. "Thank goodness, it's not dead out." She tossed a bundle of peat on the dying embers and poked them until the peat caught. Before long, the cottage warmed.

Maggie washed her face in a bowl and tied back her hair with a ribbon. She put on a pot of water for tea and sat at the table, examining her gnarled hands. "Won't be long now. Nothing works like it did."

There was a rap on the door. Alex would be coming to check on her as he always did. Maggie straightened her gown, stood, and unlatched the door. The door to the cottage creaked, and then flew open. Two men burst into the room and shut the door.

Maggie retreated behind the table and picked up a candlestick. "What is this? Get out of my home!"

One man held the door shut and one stood before her. The man at the door was a commoner, wearing breeks, a leather shirt and crude shoes. He nervously fingered the knife at his side. The man before her wore a kilt of blue and green, woven with gold thread. A silk shirt and a wool cape topped his broad shoulders. He was over six feet tall, easily towering over her.

Maggie's eyes grew wide. On his cape he wore the brooch of the Gordon clan. The man looked oddly familiar. Her heart pounded in her throat.

"Do ye know who I am, old woman?"

"Nay, my Lord."

"I'm the Earl of Huntly." Dark hair fell to his shoulders in curls and his blue eyes narrowed in anger.

Maggie's thoughts ran wild. *He looks just like Dughall. Goddess help me, it's his father!*

The Earl drew his dirk and ran the blade against his thumb.

She recalled what he did to his pregnant wife. "Don't hurt me!" A trickle of cold sweat ran down her back.

His voice was deep and deliberate. "Hold the door, Connor. See that no one interrupts us." He fingered the sharp edge of his knife and stared. "Old midwife, we're going to talk. You know who I am, don't ye? I'm told that the lad looks just like me."

Maggie felt her heart stop. She put down the candlestick and gripped the table. "My Lord. I don't know what ye're talking about."

His expression hardened. He reached up to a shelf and knocked a pitcher to the floor, breaking it to pieces. A small crock sat on the shelf alone.

Maggie gasped. *He mustn't find the ring!*

The Earl stared. "You were the midwife who delivered my son, seventeen years ago. Don't deny it."

"Nay!"

He made a fist and backhanded her across the face, splitting her lip. "Don't lie to me!"

Maggie swooned and caught herself on the edge of the table. She held a shaking hand to her mouth and whimpered. "Have mercy, my Lord."

He flexed his hand, making a fist. Maggie braced herself for another blow.

He grunted. "Hmmphh. So you won't cooperate. Perhaps I should interrogate the young midwife with the red hair. A bonny lass, I'm told. When I'm through, I'll have my way with her."

Maggie's fear blossomed. "Nay! She knows nothing. Don't hurt her!"

He reached up and knocked the crock off the shelf, shattering it. A gold ring clattered across the floor and rested at his feet. Maggie's heart sank.

The man picked up the ring and rolled it in his fingers, reading the inscription. "Christal's wedding ring. I need no further proof. They stole my son and raised him as an ignorant fisherman! I'll kill them for this."

Maggie's heart told her what to do. *I've lived long enough...* She kneeled on the floor, closed her eyes, and prayed. *James, dear husband. Tell me that ye wait for me beyond the veil.* She swallowed hard and stared at the man. "My Lord. It's my fault alone. I delivered yer wife's child and she died. Then I delivered another. The father was at sea and the mother was delirious. I put yer child in the cradle with hers and told her she had twins. They think that the lad is their own." Maggie steeled herself. Had she fooled him?

The Earl's eyes narrowed. "A serious complication."

"Your wife was dead and the child was hungry. He would have perished within days. I did what I thought was best. Do with me what ye will, but don't hurt them."

The man smiled, reminding her of Dughall. But this smile was cold and threatening. He reached out with his left hand, locked fingers in her hair, and pulled up until her neck stretched. "I believe ye." He drew his dirk and pressed the blade against her throat. Blood trickled down her neck onto her gown.

Maggie closed her eyes and saw the faces of her family. Ian and Dughall eating biscuits. Jessie hiking a creel onto her back. Alex raising the sail in his boat.

The Earl tensed. With a quick motion, he pressed the tip deeper and drew his dirk across her throat. Maggie's eyes widened with shock, and a blood bubble formed on her lips. He threw her body face down onto the floor. "Old witch. May you rot in hell with my traitorous wife!"

He rolled the ring between his fingers and threw it in a pool of blood.

As Maggie's world faded, she saw a familiar face. *Oh James. Ye waited for me.*

***

Dughall fell to his knees in the tall meadow grass. "Maggie's in trouble!" He grasped his throat and coughed, spitting violently on the ground. "I must go to her."

"Breathe, Brother!" Ian pounded him on the back. "How do ye know?"

Dughall retched. "Oh God. I taste blood. They've cut her throat!"

"Who would do such a thing?"

Frightening images flooded his mind. "Two men. Mercy! I think she's dead. I don't feel her anymore." He made the sign of the cross.

Ian's eyes widened. "You can pray later. We must go home. Mother may be in trouble."

Dughall got off his knees and ran through the meadow, following his brother. "Oh Maggie," he whispered, as tears welled in his eyes. "My heart is broken."

***

Leaving the meadow, they sprinted towards the path to Peterhead. Breathing heavily, they reached the old tree as a group of strangers appeared on horseback. The men dismounted quickly and surrounded Ian and Dughall, some drawing their dirks.

"Hold them!" a man cried. "It's Blackheart's son."

Ian studied the six men. Five were dressed in breeks and cloth shirts, like commoners. One looked like a young nobleman, no older than twenty-five. He wore a kilt of blue and green, a silk shirt, and polished black boots. Strangely enough, the man resembled Dughall. Ian saw that their dirks were drawn. *We're unarmed. They can take us easily.* He noted the only way out, between the young Lord and an old man.

Dughall rested his hands on his knees and held up a hand. "We mean you no harm. I must warn my mother." His hand went to his throat. "My old Aunt was murdered. Someone cut her throat."

The men paled. Ian winced. "Keep quiet, Dughall."

A pimply young man stepped back in fear. "How does he know about that?"

"He has the Sight, like his mother." The older man shook his head. "You'd best hide it, my Lord. Blackheart hates the third eye." He squeezed Dughall's arm and nodded towards the horses. "You'll come with us, now."

Dughall shook off his grip. "I'm not your Lord."

"You are, lad. You're ignorant of who you are."

"Why must I come with ye?"

"My Lord. We've come to bring ye back to your true family." He signaled to his men and pointed at Ian. "Kill that one. We don't need him."

Three men were on Ian in a flash. One punched him in the belly as another held his hands behind his back. The third man pressed a blade against his neck. Ian blanched as a stream of blood trickled down his neck. The point of the knife dug deeper. *I'm a dead man,* he thought.

The man grabbed his hair and stretched his neck. "Say your prayers, lad."

Dughall shuddered. "God help ye, Ian."

For God's sake! Ian cried silently. *If they think you're a Lord, you can stop it.*

Dughall heard his brother and acted. "Stop it, I say!" His eyes narrowed as he balled his fists. "If you kill him, you'll answer to me!"

The man let his knife drop. "As you wish, my Lord."

Everyone looked to the young Lord in the blue and green kilt. He was admiring the fingernails on his hand and smiling. The young man had been standing on the sidelines, watching Dughall carefully. He was tall with dark curls that fell to his shoulders. The lad came forward and stood before Dughall, touching his hair. "Amazing. Threatening them already. You're as bad as Father."

Dughall frowned. "Who are ye?"

"Your half-brother, Gilbert."

"You're not my brother."

Gilbert smiled. "Wait 'til you see Father. You look more like him than I do."

"I already have a father. This is a terrible mistake." He pointed at Ian. "I'll go with ye, but you must let him go."

Gilbert snapped his fingers. "Let his friend go, he's not important."

The man holding Ian released him and grumbled. "Lucky lad."

Ian grasped his throat and looked at his hand. Seeing only a little blood, he breathed a sigh of relief.

The boys began their silent communication. Dughall raised his eyebrows. *Run, Brother.*

Ian shook his head slightly. *I won't leave ye.*

You must. They'll kill ye! I'll find a way back.

Ian nodded. They meant to let him go, so he turned and ran towards the cliffs. When he was far enough away, he looked back to see Dughall mount a horse and ride off with the strangers. He ran for home with his heart pounding in his chest.

A BAD DAY

WHINNYFOLD
OCTOBER 1636
SAME DAY

Alex stood at the water's edge. The sea was rough, with whitecaps as far as the eye could see. On days like these, he felt close to the ancients who fished these shores. "By God's grace I'll die here." Waves crashed on the beach, sending spray into the air. "No fishing today. What a difference a day makes."

Yesterday, he'd walked among rock pools, spotting sea stars and anemones. They'd taken the boat as far as Cruden, where small lines netted cod and ling. Today the pools were gone, covered by rising tide, and the air smelled of brine and ash. Alex threw the heavy fishing net over his shoulder and walked the beach to the cliff side path. The wind was strong with a cold bite. He stopped and fastened the top button of his jacket. "My God. It feels raw today." He shifted the net to his other shoulder and started the steep climb.

For some reason, Maggie appeared in his thoughts. Her face beckoned to him with love and gratitude, smiling through pain. "Cold weather's taking a toll on her." When he'd checked on her yesterday, she hadn't left her bed. He remembered how frail she felt in his arms. Jessie would know what to do.

Alex reached the top and shifted the net to the other shoulder. He walked the path to his cottage, laid the net down, and opened the door. Inside, the warmth of the fire made his muscles ache. He hung up his coat and looked around the room. His wife kneeled at the hearth, brewing tea. She was bundled in a heavy sweater. He coughed. "It's a bitter day. Where are the lads?"

Jessie came to him. "They hiked to the meadow. I can't keep them inside, even on a day like this." She put her arms around his chest and shivered. "You're like ice."

He grunted. "I need to talk. Have you got some tea?"

Jessie went to the hearth and looked in the pot. "It's ready." She poured two cups of tea and put them on the table. They sat down opposite each other.

Alex studied her as he warmed his hands around the cup. *My bonny wife,* he thought. *My heart, my soul, and my life.*

Jessie smiled. "What is it, husband?"

He sighed. "It's Maggie. When I checked on her yesterday, she hadn't left her bed. I don't think she could, her back was paining her so bad. I had to help her up. Something must be done about it."

Jessie looked thoughtful. "There's not much to do. Her arthritis is getting worse. The bark tea helps a wee bit. Maybe Dughall's lass will know something."

Alex's heart ached. "Even if the lass agrees to come here, it won't be until spring. I'm worried that Maggie will fall and break a bone. Can we bring her to live with us? The lads could stay in her cottage."

Jessie took his hands. "Listen to me, husband. Your heart is in the right place. I love her like my own mother. But Maggie will never leave her home. She says the spirit of her husband lingers there."

He stiffened. "The church doesn't like superstition. The minister calls it blasphemy."

Jessie frowned. "There are things in life that we don't understand. It doesn't mean they can't be. When two people love each other, it goes beyond death." She gazed into his eyes. "We love each other deeply. Don't you hope it's so?"

His heart melted. "Aye, lass. But we'd best not say it at church."

Jessie stood and took her coat from a peg. "Let's ask Maggie if she wants to spend the winter with us."

Alex felt hopeful. "Thank ye, wife. She's a stubborn old woman, but I love her dearly."

***

Jessie held his arm as they walked the path to Maggie's cottage. The wind blew their hair about them and tugged at their clothes. As they approached the cottage, they saw that the door was open.

Alex stiffened. "How strange."

Jessie felt uneasy. "Maggie must be up and about."

"Something's wrong, lass. She would never leave it open on a day like this."

They entered the cottage and were struck by a coppery smell of blood. The candle was out and the fire in the hearth had turned to embers. Maggie's limp body lay face down on the floor in a pool of blood. Alex made the sign of the cross. "God in heaven. Is she alive?"

Jessie knew that she was dead. There was too much blood around the body. She swallowed against a lump in her throat. "I don't think so."

"How did it happen?"

Jessie steeled herself and crouched next to the body. Against all reason, she touched Maggie's neck and felt for a heartbeat. There was none. As she took her hand away, she saw that it was bloody. "Help me turn her over."

Alex kneeled and rolled Maggie onto her back. Their eyes widened at the sight of a gaping slash across her throat.

Jessie gasped. "She's been murdered! Oh, Maggie. "

Alex flushed with anger. "Who would do this to an old woman?"

"I can't imagine." She saw the broken crockery on the floor. "They were looking for something." With tears in her eyes, she searched through the broken pieces. In a pool of blood, she found the wedding ring of Dughall's mother. Fear gripped her heart as she stuffed the bloody ring into a pocket. "The lads! Oh, dear God. Where are they? Ian! Dughall!"

Alex held her tight. "Calm down, lass. You said they hiked to the meadow. This has nothing to do with them."

The tips of her ears reddened. "Forgive me, husband."

He stroked her hair. "Shhhh… There's nothing to forgive." Tears rolled down her cheeks. Alex stared at the body. "You didna deserve this, old woman." He stroked her white hair. "She was as precious to me as my own mother. I'll find who did this and bring them to justice."

Jessie washed blood from her hands and dried them on her skirt. She feared the worst. "My sons…"

"What's wrong with ye, lass? The boys are fine." He folded Maggie's arms over her chest and covered her with a blanket.

Jessie struggled with her coat. Her hands shook so badly that she couldn't fasten the buttons.

Alex helped her. "Calm down, wife. There's nothing to fear. I'll protect ye."

"The lads…"

"All right. Let's find them." They left the cottage and latched the door. Alex looked around for signs of intruders. "The door's intact. She must have let them in." He winced. "Ach! She probably thought it was me, coming to check on her."

"Poor Maggie."

"Let's find the lads, and then I'll go to the castle and report the murder."

Jessie's heart sank. Would the truth come out?

***

Alex spotted Ian as he entered the backside of the village. "Dughall's not with him, lass." Ian ran to them and tried to catch his breath. "Where's your brother?"

The lad coughed violently and spit on the ground. The wound on his neck was exposed.

Jessie blanched. "Someone tried to cut his throat!"

"Let's get him home." Alex took his arm, walked him to the cottage, and unlatched the door. Inside, he seated the boy at the table, stripped off his coat, and pulled back his collar.

Jessie searched frantically through her healer's bag.

"Nay bother, lass. It's a flesh wound." Alex sat opposite the lad. "Well?"

Ian's eyes widened. "Maggie's dead, isn't she?"

"Aye. How did ye know?"

Ian rolled his eyes. "Dughall knew it. He grasped his throat, saying she'd been murdered. A man slit her throat."

Alex frowned. "God help us. Where is your brother?"

Ian reddened. "We were worried about Mother and hurried back. Six men on horseback stopped us at the old tree. They drew their dirks and held me at knifepoint."

Jessie paled. "What happened to Dughall?"

"They didn't hurt him. The men called him my Lord! They were there to take him back to his true family."

Her hands shook. "Oh my God."

Ian pulled back his collar and showed them the wound. "They were going to slit my throat, and they nearly did. Dughall said that if he was their Lord, they must let me go. He agreed to leave with them if they set me free."

Alex reddened. "You left him there?"

"Aye, Father. They would have killed me. Dughall told me he would find a way back."

"How could he tell ye that, with them standing there?"

Ian looked at his mother. Jessie shuddered. "They can speak to each other without words. I've known it for some time."

Alex massaged his brow. "What! They have the Sight? Why has no one told me?"

"Husband, please…"

He pounded his fist on the table. "We'll talk about that later! Why would they take him? He's not a Lord, he's our son."

Ian flinched. "One of the men was a Lord, wearing a kilt of green and blue. Dughall looks just like him. The man said he was his half-brother."

Jessie cried softly, wiping her eyes with a kerchief. Ian shivered.

"Get him some tea, lass."

Jessie stood and went to the hearth. She stifled sobs as she poured the tea and set the cup on the table. Ian sipped the strong brew.

Alex struggled to control his anger. "So they took him."

"Aye, on horseback. About an hour ago."

"Which way did they go?"

"Northwest."

Alex felt a surge of determination. "We'll never catch them on foot. Kidnapping is a capital offence. The Earl of Erroll will help us to get him back." He squeezed his wife's shoulder. "Stay here, lass. I'll send the MacNeils to help with Maggie. Ian and I will go to the Earl."

Jessie sobbed uncontrollably. "You can't go to the Earl."

Alex drew her close. "Settle down, lass. We'll get him back. I promise."

"Oh husband. Don't hate me!"

Alex stared. "What's wrong with ye, lass? I don't want to leave ye like this, but I must see the Earl. They murdered Maggie and stole our son." He stood up to go.

"Wait! I have something I must tell ye."

He stared.

Jessie trembled with fear. "I should have told ye years ago. On the day that Ian was born, a young noblewoman rode into town. She was heavy with child and in labor. She wore a gold ring, this one." Jessie put the bloody ring on the table. "Maggie took her in and made ready for the birth."

Alex's face was ashen.

"The woman had been beaten and wouldn't say who she was. She never spoke, until the child was born. Maggie said she held the child and whispered 'Poor little one, your father must never find ye.' Then she bled to death."

Ian snorted. "The child was Dughall? He really is a Lord?"

Alex held up his hand. "Silence, lad." His world was falling apart.

Jessie blew her nose. "Maggie brought the child here and asked me to take him. I was the only one nursing a bairnie."

Alex's voice was hoarse. "You're telling me I'm not his father. Why did ye not say this from the beginning?"

"I was barren for so long. You were proud that I gave ye two sons. I couldn't tell ye otherwise."

Alex put on his coat, methodically fastening the buttons.

Jessie flushed with fear. "Don't hate me. I beg ye to forgive me."

Alex shook his head in disbelief. "You and Maggie. Both of you lied to me." Pain etched his face as he put on his hat and gloves. Without looking back, he opened the door and left the cottage.

He stood outside in the bitter cold, feeling angry and confused. "Where can I go?" His heart was breaking. "I can't see the Earl. It was their right to claim him. He's not my son." His eyes filled with hot tears. Alex held a hand to his mouth to stifle a sob. "My son! Oh God, Dughall. It doesn't matter. I love ye so much. You're still my son."

THE FOREST, ABERDEENSHIRE

Seven men traveled on horseback until the sun was high, on trails that led northwest through dense forest. Dughall rode with three men in front and three in back, who were preventing his escape. He noted trees along the trail and memorized rock formations. *I'll get away. I must remember the way back.*

They entered a clearing in the forest and dismounted. "Tie off the horses," Gilbert ordered. "Build a fire and make some tea. Father will meet us here."

Two of the men busied themselves collecting wood and building a small fire. Dughall sat on the ground and watched as they unpacked an iron pot and a flask of water and made tea. His belly rumbled. "Oh God. I'm hungry."

An old man with a hole in his teeth pulled a flask of whisky out of his saddlebag. "Here's to a successful day. Blackheart will be pleased." He took a drink and passed the flask to a young man.

The lad wrinkled his nose in disgust. "You stink, old man." He threw back his head and drank his share, then tipped the flask over the old man's head and poured. "'Haps you should bathe in it."

The old man gasped. "Bastard! You're wasting good whisky." He grabbed the flask and drank again. "You'll get no more from me."

Gilbert joined Dughall, threw a plaid on the ground, and sat next to him. "Put the flask away, Cheney. Father will be mad if he finds you blootered again. It's been a while since you tasted his whip, it could be entertaining."

The old man stuffed the flask into his saddlebag. "As you wish, my Lord."

Gilbert wrinkled his nose. "I can smell you from here. You'll bathe when we get back or I'll see that they take the scrub brush to you."

The old man winced. "Aye, my Lord."

"Who is Blackheart?" Dughall asked.

Gilbert regarded him with disdain. "Have you lived in a cave all your life? They're talking about our father. The Earl of Huntly."

"Hmmmph... Why do they call him that?"

"You'll find out soon enough. Father has a terrible temper. Take care not to get him mad."

Dughall frowned.

"They say your name is Dughall."

"Aye. My name is Dughall Hay."

Gilbert raised his eyebrows. "He might let you keep your given name, though it was to be George William. But you're not a Hay; you're a Gordon."

"I'm not your brother. This is a mistake."

"Father will be here soon. He'll talk about what happened to you. I wouldn't argue or you'll suffer terribly." Gilbert stood and brushed off his kilt. "I'll say this once. When he beats you, take it like a man. Don't struggle or cry out. If you do, he won't stop."

Dughall's eyes widened. "He means to beat me? He doesn't even know me."

Gilbert chuckled. "That's never stopped him before." He walked to the fire and spoke to the young man tending it.

The lad poured a cup of tea and handed it to him. Then he poured another and brought it to Dughall. "For you, my Lord."

A man walked into the clearing, held two fingers to his mouth, and whistled. "It's Blackheart and Connor. I climbed the hill and saw them coming." The men grew silent and packed their saddlebags, preparing to leave. They stood at their horses staring at the ground.

Gilbert walked to Dughall. "Stand up, lad. Father will be here in a moment. Show him respect. You know what that is, don't you?"

Dughall stood. "Aye." He kept his eyes on the path at the end of the clearing. Hooves struck the ground and a horse squealed as a whip cracked its backside. Two men on horseback entered the clearing, their horses sweating with exertion. The man on the chestnut mare was a commoner, wearing plain breeks and a shirt. The other man was a Lord, wearing a kilt of blue and green and a wool cape. His black stallion snorted and pawed the ground. Dughall felt a wave of nervousness coming from the men.

The Lord dismounted and gazed in his direction. He walked to Gilbert and Dughall and stood before them. He was powerfully built and over six feet tall. His blue eyes flashed as he touched Dughall's curls. "Take off your shirt, lad."

Dughall unfastened the buttons of his shirt and took it off, holding it in one hand.

Blackheart grabbed his right arm and touched his birthmark, stretching it to make sure it was real. He smiled and dropped the arm. "Ha! He bears the birthmark of the Gordon clan. Look at his face. He looks just like me. The lad is my son and you will honor him as such."

The response was unanimous. "Aye, my Lord."

This is a mistake. He looks like me, but he's not my father. Dughall gasped as the man turned his head to talk to a servant. His profile was too familiar. *He killed Maggie.* He slipped on his shirt and fastened the buttons.

"Bring us some whisky," Blackheart demanded.

A man scrambled to get a silver flask out of Blackheart's saddlebag and handed it to him. "As you wish my Lord."

Blackheart sat on the ground and drank from the flask. "There's nothing like twenty-year-old whisky, made from the finest barley. Sit with me, my sons. I have something to say."

Dughall eyed him warily as he sat opposite him on the plaid. He noted that Gilbert's face was solemn as he sat next to his father. Blackheart offered Gilbert the flask. The lad took it and poured whisky into his tea until it filled the cup.

"Enough." Blackheart snatched the flask and offered it to Dughall. "Have a drink with me, Son?"

"Nay. I've never had a whisky. It's the devil's drink."

Blackheart frowned.

Dughall swallowed hard. "This is a mistake. I'm not your son."

Gilbert raised his eyebrows in alarm. He tipped his cup and belted the drink.

Blackheart's eyes narrowed with anger. He held up his hand. "Don't say a word until I'm finished. You're ignorant of this, but you are my son. Seventeen years ago, my wife left me. She was heavy with child when she disappeared. I searched for both of ye for years. Weeks ago, I learned that she'd traveled to Whinnyfold and died after giving birth. The midwife gave the child to a couple who had just birthed a son. The old witch didn't want to admit it, but I found my wife's wedding ring in her cottage."

Dughall's heart sank. *It can't be. Maggie died because of me.*

Blackheart drank from the flask. "What say ye lad? You just learned you're the son of an Earl. Think of what this could mean. Cat got your tongue?"

"I'm not your son. I have a family. I don't want to be the son of an Earl."

Gilbert paled and rubbed his temple.

"My son was raised as an ignorant fisherman!" Blackheart cried, angrily. "He wallows in his ignorance like a pig in the mud."

Dughall flinched. "I'm not ignorant. I can read."

"Ha! Can ye now? So what have ye read?"

"The Bible. They taught us at church."

"So you've read the Bible, have ye?" Blackheart said. "No wonder you can't think!"

He's a madman! His heart thumped as he looked for an escape route.

Blackheart's voice was as cold as ice. "Don't run, lad. Don't make me hurt ye."

"You're not my father. I already have a father. I don't want to be your son." He searched the depths of his soul for courage. "You can't keep me here. I'm not a child, I'm a man."

Blackheart rose to his feet. His face flushed with anger as he flexed his hand, making a fist. Dughall glanced at the men. No one would look at him. Even Gilbert avoided him, gazing at his fingernails. Blackheart walked to his horse and searched through his saddlebag, extracting some leather thongs and a three tailed strap. He took off his cape and laid it over the saddle, unbuttoned his cuffs, and rolled up his sleeves.

Dughall paled. "Oh, God."

"Remember what I told you," Gilbert whispered. "Don't struggle or cry out."

Blackheart turned to two of his men and pointed to the ground before his feet. "Bring him here." The men walked behind Dughall and grabbed him under the arms. They pulled him to a standing position and led him to Blackheart, throwing him on his knees.

Dughall's heart thumped as he kneeled on the cold ground.

Blackheart cleared his throat and spoke in a threatening tone. "It doesn't matter what you think. You're my son. I'm your father. You don't have to like me, but you do have to respect me. If you tell me one more time that I'm not your father, I'll kill the fisherman you call Father."

Dughall shuddered. The man really meant it.

Blackheart watched him squirm. "You will stay with me from now on. If you go back there, I'll make ye watch while I slit their throats." His eyes flashed as he played with the strap. "Do you understand?"

"Aye."

"I'm going to give you a beating," Blackheart said as he ran his fingers through the leather tails. "You say you're a man. We shall see. My father told me that a man must bear his punishment in silence and nay struggle nor cry out."

Dughall lowered his head and whispered, "Ian help me."

"Stop mumbling! Stand up and take off your shirt."

Dughall stood and removed his shirt, dropping it to the ground. He waited with his head down.

Blackheart threw the leather thongs to his foreman. "Murdock! Bind him to that oak tree."

The tall man caught the thongs in one hand. He took Dughall by the arm and led him to the tree. "Hug the tree, lad."

Dughall's stomach churned as he wrapped his arms around the trunk.

The man tied each wrist and placed his foot on the trunk. He pulled hard on the leather strips, drew the lad's chest against the tree, and tied them in a knot. He whispered in Dughall's ear. "Best that ye don't struggle. Forgive me, my Lord."

Dughall burned with embarrassment.

Murdock spoke in low tones. "We've all been in your place. First chance ye get, tell him what he wants to hear. Spare your backside."

Dughall gritted his teeth. "I can't lie."

"Trust me, ye will."

Dughall tested his bonds and found that he couldn't move. His hands barely touched and his wrists tingled. He felt rough bark against his bare chest and cold air on his back. Gooseflesh rose on his arms. *Dear God, let me go home!* His flesh crawled as Blackheart touched him.

The man ran a hand across his naked back. "He's been raised as a lass. There's not a mark on him. Didn't that fisherman beat ye, lad?"

Dughall stiffened under his touch. "Nay!"

Blackheart chuckled. "Well, then. There's a first time for everything. I'll try to do ye justice." He laid into him with the strap, striking him hard across the shoulders and blistering his back.

Dughall flinched as pain flooded his senses. Thwack! He grunted as a sharp blow struck him in the lower back. He wanted to scream but caught himself. *Don't struggle or cry out...* Sweat beaded on his forehead as he waited for the next blow. He gasped as the strap bit into his blistered shoulders, drawing blood.

Dear God! Tears burned in his eyes and threatened to fall. *Don't cry.* He blinked them away and chewed on his lip until he tasted blood. The strap whistled through the air and met his flesh again and again.

Blackheart gave him ten blows, watching him flinch as the skin blistered and bruised. "The lad's as strong as an ox," he announced. "He refuses to cry."

Dughall pressed his forehead against the tree and forced himself to think of home. *It's a bad dream. I'll wake up and see them soon. Father, Mother, Ian, and Maggie.* He felt Ian reaching out to him, holding his face, saying something. *Do what ye must to stay alive.* Three brutal strokes across the mid-back knocked the wind out of him. He tried to get a grip on the fear surging through his body. *No more! I'll go mad.*

Blackheart growled in Dughall's ear, "Shall I continue? Or have ye had enough?"

"Enough. I'll do what ye want."

"Tell me who I am."

Dughall's heart sank. He couldn't tell a lie. Ian's words echoed in his head. *Do what ye must to stay alive. Father says so.*

Blackheart raked a sharp fingernail across a welt in his back. "I've gone easy on ye so far. I can make this last a long time. Don't make me hurt ye. Tell me who I am."

Dughall's skin crawled. "You're my father!"

Blackheart threw the strap on the ground. "That I am. Glad we settled it. See, I'm a reasonable man." He rolled down his sleeves and buttoned his cuffs. "You did well, Son. A lesser man would have begged or cried." He signaled to his foreman. "Release him."

As Murdock untied him from the tree, Dughall shook with relief. The tall, rangy man with straight brown hair and hazel eyes reminded him of Uncle Robert.

The muscles in his arms bulged as he worked on the bindings. "Are ye all right, m'Lord?"

"I can't feel my hands."

Murdock sat him on the ground and massaged his wrists and hands. "Settle down lad. It's over."

Dughall winced as the feeling came back, like the sting of a thousand ants.

Murdock stopped. "Am I hurtin' ye, m'Lord?"

Dughall grunted. "Nay. The feeling's back." Murdock brought his shirt and held it out behind him. His shoulders burned as he slipped his arms into the sleeves.

He handed him a flask of whisky. "Take a drink, my Lord."

"Nay. Whisky is the devil's drink."

"Consider it a medicinal tonic, for the pain. It's a long ride home, and your backside will sting like the devil. I remember it well."

Dughall accepted the flask and took a drink. It burned his throat and warmed him to his belly. He breathed easier as the pain subsided. He drank from the flask again and gave it back. "Thank ye for your kindness, sir."

The foreman smiled. "We'll talk later, m'Lord."

***

Blackheart glanced at them as he spoke to Gilbert. "Will you look at that? Murdock seems to have a way with him. It could be useful."

"Aye, Father."

The Earl smiled as he pulled on his riding gloves. "When we get home, send for my tailor. Get him some proper highland clothes. He looks like a commoner. Tomorrow, we'll start his lessons. Call the schoolmaster, take him to the library, and see that he doesn't read the Bible." He mounted his horse and tightened the reins. "I don't care how long it takes; I want to get home tonight. Fresh horses are waiting for us at Duff's farm."

WHINNYFOLD

Alex sat on the beach throwing rocks into the sea. A fierce wind roiled the sea and chilled him to the bone. His thoughts returned to his childhood, right after his mother died. He'd sat on the point watching the tides, feeling lost and alone. He felt that way now. A wave scattered the tiny crabs and soaked his shoes. "At least the tides still come and go." Alex sniffled as he wiped a tear from his eye. His throat burned with sorrow. "I can't bear it."

Gulls screamed as he stood and brushed sand from his breeks. He could barely feel his fingers. With a heavy heart, Alex climbed the cliff side path to the village. He walked through the rows and saw Ian sitting outside at the worktable. Guilt stabbed at his heart. "It's not his fault. The lad nearly lost his life. I was wrong to show my anger." He stiffened as Ian flinched and grasped the edge of the table.

Alex ran to his son.

***

Ian felt rough tree bark against his bare chest. He flinched as the strap blistered his brother's back, drawing blood. Ian cried out where

Dughall could not, and bit into his lip.

Alex squeezed his shoulder. "What's wrong? Are ye sick?"

Ian took a ragged breath. "It's Dughall. A man's flogging him."

Alex pounded his fist on the table. A bone in his wrist cracked. "He's a Lord! Why would they do such a thing?"

Ian's eyes clouded as the strap fell again. "Dughall won't call him Father."

Alex groaned as he cradled his wrist in pain. "God in heaven! It's against all I believe in." He grasped his son's face and looked into his eyes. "Can ye reach him?"

"Aye."

"Tell him to do whatever it takes to stay alive."

Ian nodded and closed his eyes, feeling the comfort of hands on his face. His body flinched as the beating continued. After a while, he calmed and opened his eyes.

Alex ran a finger across his mouth, wiping away a trace of blood. "Are ye all right?"

"Aye," Ian said, weakly. "It's over. He called him Father."

Alex cradled his wrist. "I swear on my mother's grave, I'll bring him back."

Ian rubbed his wrists. "God help ye, Dughall."

Murdock

RECONCILIATIONS

WHINNYFOLD
OCTOBER 1636
NEXT DAY

Alex struggled with emotion as he stood in the church cemetery. Maggie had been like a mother to him. The thought of lowering her into the ground tore his heart to pieces.

The minister closed his book and made the sign of the cross. "So we bury our sister in Christ. Maggie McLeod. Beloved aunt, healer, and friend to many. In the name of the Father, Son, and Holy Spirit. Amen."

"Amen," the family murmured.

The minister shook Alex's hand and started his long walk back to Boddam. The black mortcloth was placed over the body, a plank put in place, and the rough pine box lowered into the ground. Robert and Hugh MacNeil shoveled earth until the coffin was covered, and marked the grave with a granite stone.

Robert wiped his hands on his breeks. "I'm sorry, Alex. We all loved her. Someday we'll find out who did this."

Alex stifled a sob. "My life is over. Nothing will ever be the same."

Robert embraced him. "Go to your wife, man. Don't let this come between ye. It will eat ye alive."

Alex stiffened.

Robert shook his head. "Ah well, you're a stubborn one. We'll be on our way. If you need anything, ask."

"Thank ye, friend." Alex kneeled at the gravesite, bowed his head, and made the sign of the cross. "Goodbye Maggie. I forgive ye." He looked back at his family and sighed. Guilt stabbed him as Ian stood with Jessie, offering her a kerchief. Tears streamed down her face. He stared at the gravesite. "Dughall should be here. He loved her more than anyone." Alex walked to his wife and son. "Take care of your mother. I'll be heading home now." He left them standing at the gravesite, and walked the path alone towards Whinnyfold.

***

It was late morning when he reached the cottage. Alex wanted to sail away, but the sea was too rough. He crawled into bed and slept for hours, waking to a throbbing wrist. "Oh God," he groaned.

Jessie's voice was timid. "I made tea, husband. There's a cup for ye on the table."

"Hmmphh…" He got out of bed and sat at the table, cradling his hand. "Where's Ian?"

"He's gone off with Mary for a while. I think it will do him good." Jessie put her healer's bag on the table and sat opposite him. "Ian said that ye hurt your wrist." She reached out and took his hand.

Alex winced.

"Let me see it. You won't be able to fish if it heals wrong." She turned it over and looked at the swelling, then felt the bones in the hand and wrist.

Alex flinched as a sharp pain shot up his arm.

Jessie felt the bone again. "You've broken it. Not badly, just a small crack. Let me wrap it for ye."

Alex pulled his hand away. "Nay, it's only pain. I can bear it."

Jessie's face was solemn. She got up, took something from behind the door, and placed a stinging nettle branch on the table.

His eyes widened with shock. She couldn't mean it.

"Beat me, Alex. I can't bear your silence any longer. You didn't even sleep with me last night; you slept in Dughall's bed."

"Oh God." He swallowed against a growing lump in his throat. "Nay, lass."

Tears welled in her eyes and threatened to fall. She pushed the branch closer. "Beat me, husband. I deserve it. I lied to ye and ye can't forgive me. Hurt me as much as ye want, then take me back to your bed."

Alex's heart ached as he grasped her hand and held it tight. "Don't do this. I can't beat ye."

She sobbed openly. "Then forgive me, damn it. I'm so sorry! I can't bear this pain alone. Maggie was like a mother to me, and Dughall is my son. I don't care what they say. He suckled at my breast. He is my son!"

His heart was breaking to pieces. "Jessie…"

"Do ye know what he said yesterday before they left? 'Goodbye, Mother. I love ye.'"

Alex's face fell. He walked around the table and embraced her. They cried together, his sobs matching hers. He took her face in his hands. "Shhhhhh… I forgive ye."

She clung to him with all her might. "I'll never keep anything from ye again."

Alex stroked her hair. "It's all right."

"I love our son. Tell me we haven't lost him."

His head ached. "We'll get him back. I'll go to Peterhead tomorrow to make inquiries. Someone will have noticed a lord with a blue and green kilt. Ian said his name was Gilbert."

"How will he survive? He's got no common sense and doesn't know enough to hide the Sight."

Alex rubbed his temple. "Ian will know if he's in trouble." He made the sign of the cross as if to ward off evil. "Thank God, Ian will know."

HUNTLY CASTLE - HIGHLANDS

Dawn broke over Huntly Castle, after a calm cloudless night. Dughall woke in a large feather bed that was covered with cream silk sheets. He sat up and tried to shake the sleep from his eyes. "Oh God. Tell me it was a bad dream." He ran the soft sheets between his hands and knew it was real.

They'd arrived after midnight at the castle; its massive walls overshadowing the land. A frightened servant ushered them through the gate, genuflecting to the Earl. Murdock walked him to the bedroom wing and showed him his room. It was larger than the stone cottage, with a fireplace and massive furniture. The servant built a fire in the hearth, warmed the room, and helped him undress. Dughall had fallen asleep immediately, exhausted from the ride.

He got out of bed and walked over to a long mirror. He'd never seen himself in a looking glass, only in a reflection from the water. It seemed like the face of the Earl stared back at him. "I do look like him."

Dughall flexed his shoulders and winced. His backside burned as he twisted. He remembered the brutal beating. "Mercy!" He looked in the mirror and shuddered. Bruises and welts covered his back, some purple and some starting to yellow. His skin was cut at the shoulders and just above the waist. "He's a madman. The wounds could fester. I'll ask Murdock for some salve."

He felt an urge to relieve himself and looked around the room. A fancy flowered chamber pot sat in a corner. Dughall snorted. "Such a fine thing to pee in? I hope it's a chamber pot." He peed in the pot until the bottom was covered, and then looked around. "Now, where are my clothes?"

Dughall scanned the room and spotted them on a chair. He remembered that Murdock had carefully folded them and placed them there last night. He dressed, tucked his shirt in, and brushed dirt from his breeks. He put on his socks and shoes and wrinkled his nose. "I smell like horse dung."

Dughall noticed a fine pitcher and bowl, and poured water to wash his face and hands. "Mother should see these fine things." His heart ached as her face came to mind. "I want to go home." There were long barred windows on the outer wall. He looked out onto a courtyard, alive with morning activity. Birds flew overhead as servants scurried about, carrying eggs and loaves of bread, and emptying chamber pots. A man led a horse across the courtyard towards what looked like stables. Several large hunting dogs followed obediently, their tails wagging in anticipation. An old woman lifted her skirts and walked towards the castle, followed by a small boy carrying a crate. She struck him on the ear when he failed to keep up.

Dughall smiled. "This is verra entertaining. But I don't belong here." He looked beyond the courtyard at the forest that lay to the north. It was a riot of color, brown and gold and red. His stomach growled. "I'm starving." There was a knock on the door and Dughall opened it.

Murdock stood in the hallway, his clothes changed and hair carefully combed. His face was solemn. "I've come for ye, my Lord. The Earl wishes to see ye for breakfast."

The mention of food made his stomach growl. "I'm for that." He stepped into the hall and hesitated. "Should I bring the chamber pot?"

Murdock brought a hand to his mouth to hide a smile. "Nay, my Lord. You needn't lift a finger. From now on, your needs will be attended to by servants." The man closed the door and led him down a long hallway. The walls of the corridor were twice as high as a man and the floors were made of granite. Paintings of the Earl and other lords hung on the walls.

A red-haired lass scurried out of a bedroom carrying a chamber pot and stopped before them. Her eyes grew wide with fear. "Forgive me, m'Lord." Her eyes focused on the floor as they passed by.

Murdock touched his shoulder, leading him down the hallway.

"Why is she afraid of me?"

"This mornin' the Earl lined up the help and told them his son had returned. He said that they must honor and obey ye or suffer the consequences."

"I don't like it. They shouldn't be afraid of me."

Murdock frowned. "My Lord. It doesn't matter what you say to me, but you must be careful about what you say to the Earl. Keep your opinions to yourself. Remember what happened to ye yesterday."

Dughall grimaced. "Thanks Murdock. Kick me if I say the wrong thing."

"I won't be kickin' ye any time soon, my Lord."

"I looked at my back this morning. There are wounds that could fester. Can ye bring me some calendula salve?"

Murdock looked surprised. "Aye, my Lord. What do ye know about such things?"

Dughall smiled. "I'm a healer. I've treated wounds and fevers and broken bones. I've even birthed a few babies."

"I'll get the salve. But keep that to yourself. There's no need to do what ye did before, be it healing or fishing. Your calling is to be a Lord. The Earl's sons must be ready to take his place upon his death."

"I don't know how to be an Earl."

"Your training starts today." They reached the door to the dining room and stopped. Murdock touched his shoulder. "Remember what I told ye. Don't argue with him. I don't wish to see ye beaten again."

They entered the dining room. Dughall looked at the long polished table, surrounded by twenty chairs. The room was well lit, with lamps on the walls. At one end of the table sat Blackheart and Gilbert. They stopped talking and looked in his direction. Blackheart pointed at the chair next to him. Murdock led Dughall to the chair and held it while he sat down.

Blackheart grunted. "Leave us, Murdock. I'll send for ye later."

"Aye, my Lord." The servant bowed and left the room.

A young girl placed a steaming plate in front of Dughall. It was filled with eggs and ham and sweet cakes. She poured a cup of tea and bowed as she backed away. "Pleased to serve ye, my Lord."

Before Dughall could answer, she hurried out of the room. The aroma of ham and eggs made his stomach growl. He wanted to grab the food and stuff it into his mouth. Blackheart and Gilbert watched him.

They think I'm ignorant. I know what to do. He picked up a fork from the side of his plate.

Blackheart smiled. "Ha! I see you're not totally ignorant." He leaned over and sniffed. "You smell like horse dung, lad. So do I. Gilbert had a bath this morning. I'll have them pour us a bath and we can talk." He picked up a brass bell and rang it.

An older woman entered the room and bowed her head. "M'Lord."

"Marcia. Pour us two hot baths. My son and I will bathe after breakfast. Send the Murray lasses to us once we've started."

"Right away, m'Lord." She hurried out of the room.

Dughall set about devouring his breakfast. The ham and eggs warmed his belly. He smiled when he tasted the sweet cakes. They were better than Maggie's apple biscuits.

Blackheart spoke to Gilbert. "Did ye get the tailor?"

Gilbert blanched. "I tried Father, but he's gone to the next village. I sent Atkinson to tell him to come right away."

Blackheart frowned and rubbed his hands together. "I'll expect him tomorrow at the latest. When will you see the schoolmaster?"

Gilbert stood. "I'm leaving now, Father. I'll make sure that he comes tomorrow as well."

"Good. Your brother can use my clothes for a few weeks, but I'll not be pleased if it goes beyond that. Tell the tailor what I said. Now be off with ye."

Gilbert nodded to Dughall. "Brother." He bowed to his father and left the room.

"Come on lad," Blackheart said, clapping Dughall on the back. The lad flinched. "Sorry son, I forgot. You're as strong as an ox. You won't feel it in a few days." He wiped his mouth on a silk napkin, threw it on the table, and pushed back his chair to stand up.

Dughall stood to join Blackheart and followed him out of the dining room. They walked the long hallway in silence and entered another wing of the castle. *This place never ends.* They turned a corner and walked down another corridor. "Where are we going?"

"To the bath chamber. You do bathe, don't ye?"

"Aye. Most times in the sea."

Blackheart shook his head. "I can see that we have a long way to go, Son. It's all right. I'm a patient man."

Patient? You almost beat me to death. Dughall remembered Murdock's advice and kept quiet.

They reached the bath chamber and opened the door. Two copper bathtubs stood side by side about three feet apart. Lavender-scented steam hung in the air. A servant emptied a bucket of hot water into one of the tubs and turned to them. "My Lords. Your baths are ready."

"Adieson," Blackheart said. "This is my son. He hasn't got any proper clothes. Wait until the lasses are done with us, and then bring us two sets of clothes from my wardrobe."

Adieson bowed. "Aye, my Lord." He placed two towels and two bars of soap nearby and left the chamber.

Dughall watched as Blackheart sat and took off his shoes and socks. He stood and stripped off his shirt, showing a chest that rippled with muscles.

"Come on lad, undress."

Dughall slipped off his shoes and socks and pulled his shirt over his head. He gasped as Blackheart took off his kilt and stood naked before him.

"It's all right, lad. We're family."

Dughall pulled down his breeks and stepped out of them. He looked up to see the man staring at his groin.

"Hung like a horse. I see you're a Gordon in every way." He stepped into the tub and sat down.

Dughall stepped in his tub and drew his breath in sharply. He sat down slowly and frowned.

"What's wrong, lad?"

"It's hot."

Blackheart smiled. "Here we don't bathe in the sea. We bathe in hot water brought by our servants. You'll get used to it. Now lather up."

Dughall took a bar of soap and rolled it between his hands. He lathered his thighs and legs, and washed his feet.

"I've decided to let ye keep your given name. Dughall it is?"

"Aye."

"I planned to name ye George, but Dughall is a strong name and it has a history in my family. I'll let ye keep it."

"Thanks. I like my name."

Blackheart studied him. "Good. I'll call ye Dughall and you'll call me Father."

Dughall nodded. *We settled that yesterday with your strap,* he thought.

"They told me you're nearly seventeen. What day were ye born on?"

"The last day of October."

Blackheart frowned. "Hmmmph... All Saints Eve. An ominous day to be born on." He rolled the soap between his hands. "So tomorrow you turn seventeen."

Dughall nodded. "Aye. I was to be married soon after."

"I don't suppose she was a daughter of a Lord."

"Nay."

"Forget about her. We don't marry commoners. Someday, you'll marry a lass of your standing."

Dughall's heart ached, but he held his tongue.

Blackheart's expression hardened. "I've been married twice. Gilbert's mother was a cousin of mine. Died in childbirth. I swore I would never marry again, but I changed my mind. The last time was for political advantage, to your mother." He snorted. "What do ye want to marry for? Women are only good for two things, for us to take our pleasure and bear our sons. We don't need marriage for that!"

Dughall flushed deeply and stared into the water.

Blackheart chuckled. "It seems I've upset ye. I know what ye need. I remember what it was like to be seventeen. If I didn't have a lass in my bed every night, I'd go mad. You needn't suffer. Choose from any of the young lasses here; they'll be happy to accommodate ye."

Dughall raised his eyebrows. "They will?"

"They will if they don't want their backsides beaten." There was a timid knock on the door, followed by muted whispers. "Two of them are coming to wash us now."

Two young lasses entered the chamber, carrying baskets of fragrant oils and perfumes. They bowed. "M'Lords." The older one kneeled at Blackheart's side and proceeded to wash his arms and chest. She opened a bottle, poured oil on her hands, and reached into the water. The younger kneeled at Dughall's tub and picked up the soap, rolling it between her hands. She was no more than fifteen, with yellow ringlets and deep blue eyes.

She looks like Mary, he thought. Dughall held his breath when she touched him.

She lathered his arms and chest and giggled under her breath when he reddened. The soap slipped into the water and she reached down, brushing her hand against his thigh. It slipped again and she found it in his lap, against his swollen loins. She smiled and wrapped her hand around his member.

Dughall grasped her hand and held it to his chest. "Nay, lass."

She looked at him fearfully. "Forgive me, m'Lord. I only wished to please ye."

Dughall held her hand tightly. "Not today," he whispered. "You needn't be afraid of me." He released her hand and she proceeded to wash his hair. When she was done, she opened a bottle of oil and spread it on her hands. She massaged his arms and rubbed the silky oil into each of his fingers.

She batted her eyelashes and smiled. "My Lord. I'd be pleased to give ye a manicure later."

Dughall heard Blackheart groan loudly and saw him lean back in the tub. *Mercy! I know what that is.*

Blackheart touched his lass on the face. "Thank ye, Bridget. Leave us now."

The lasses stood and gathered their baskets. They bowed respectfully, and took their leave.

They were alone again. Dughall didn't know what to say. He lay back in the tub and rinsed soap from his ears. *Is this what it means to be an Earl?* He held his tongue.

Blackheart rinsed his chest in the water. "You act like you've never been with a lass."

I can't lie... Dughall hung his head. "Aye, it's true. I was to be married. It's a serious commitment."

Blackheart shook water from his dark hair. "No son of mine remains a virgin at seventeen. You're about to have one hell of a birthday, lad."

***

It was late afternoon in the servant's quarters. Bridget Murray sat at the dressing table and stared into the mirror. She ran a silver-handled brush through her hair and rolled it into a French twist. *A plain face has its advantages,* she mused.

Her yellow-haired sister primped in the mirror and squealed with excitement. "He's so handsome! He looks just like the Earl."

Bridget frowned. "Don't ye be doin' anything foolish. He's a lord."

Julianna held a hand to her heart. "But sister, he's not like the Earl. He blushed when I took him in my hand."

Bridget adjusted her earring and stared. "That's not for us to be sayin' to anyone. When we're called to their chambers, it's a private matter."

Julianna wrinkled her nose. "I won't tell anyone."

Bridget wagged a finger at her. "You just told me. Do I need to remind ye about what happened when ye bragged about Lord Gilbert?"

Julianna rubbed her backside and flushed deeply. "Nay. I remember it well."

Bridget softened. "You heard it this morning. The Earl said that we must honor and obey his son or suffer the consequences."

"I'll obey him in bed! I'll do whatever he wants."

"You're incorrigible. Whatever you do, keep your mouth shut. There'll be no paddling this time. You're old enough that the Earl will beat ye with the strap. It's best you stay away from the lad."

Julianna stamped her foot. "I won't stay away! I must have him. He's not like the Earl. I just know it."

Bridget sighed. "That may be true. But it won't be long before the young Lord is just like his father. The apple never falls far from the tree."

Julianna sulked. "That's your best dress. Where are ye going tonight?"

Bridget shook her head. "I'll never tell."

***

That evening, Dughall had supper with Blackheart and Gilbert in the dining room. Serving lasses brought steaming platters of roast lamb, potatoes, and vegetables. Cutting boards with breads and sweet butters and dessert cakes stood on the table. It had been a busy day. The Earl left him with Murdock, who took him on a tour of the castle. By the time they were done, he was starved.

Dughall gorged himself until he could eat no more. He pushed his chair back from the table and stifled a burp.

Blackheart smiled. "You eat like a horse, lad." He helped himself to another sweet cake. "I remember what it was like to be seventeen. I played hard and was hungry all the time. The kitchen couldn't keep up."

Gilbert changed the subject. "Tomorrow, the tailor comes in the morning. He'll fit you for some new clothes. They should be ready in few days."

Dughall nodded. "Thank ye, Gilbert."

"The tutor will start your lessons the day after next. Tomorrow he'll visit the library and discuss your training with Father."

Blackheart nodded. "Dughall, seeing as it's your birthday tomorrow I've decided to throw a party. I've invited nobles from the nearby village. We'll have food and drink and a swordplay contest. Do ye like music?"

"Aye. I like the fiddle and the harp." He felt a pang of homesickness as he thought of his mother.

Blackheart slapped his hand on the table. "The harp it is. Bring on the minstrels! Take care of it Gilbert." He pushed back his chair and stood up. "Well lads, I have important business to take care of. Meet me here for breakfast."

Gilbert nodded. "Good night, Father." He glanced at Dughall and raised his eyebrows.

Dughall understood all too well. "Good night, Father."

Blackheart smiled broadly as he left the room.

Gilbert pushed back his chair and stood to leave. "A wise move. Calling him Father."

Dughall threw his napkin on the table and joined him. "We settled that yesterday. I don't wish to be at the takin' end of his strap."

"At least you're not stupid. If you want to avoid a beating, let him have his way. Don't interfere with what he does and do what he tells ye."

Dughall nodded.

They walked out of the dining room into the hallway. Murdock was waiting, leaning against the wall. He straightened up and bowed. "My Lords."

"Murdock will see to your needs," Gilbert said. "I have an engagement with Bridget Murray. A plain lass, but verra talented in bed." He smiled as he straightened his shirt, then turned and walked down the corridor.

***

The air was cool as Blackheart mounted his favorite stallion and rode to the northern part of his estate. Following a path through the woods, his thoughts were on his youngest son. It had been a good day and they'd settled some things. "He's a strong lad. It's only a matter of time before I win him over." The Earl dismounted and tied his horse to a post in front of a stone cottage. He patted the horse tenderly on the nose. "Good boy, Demon. Rest here awhile. I won't be long."

The horse nickered, nuzzling his arm. He straightened his cape and knocked.

153

Blackheart smiled as the door opened. "Hello Kate…"

She was dressed in an indigo robe with satin slippers, a gift that he'd given her. Thick chestnut hair cascaded about her shoulders in a tangle of curls, and she smelled of lavender. Kate touched his face, running her soft fingers along his jaw. "My Lord. I heard that you were back." She turned away and glanced over her shoulder with a seductive smile. "It's been far too long. Take me to bed and command me."

He walked past her and closed the door. The cottage was small, but it was furnished with the finest things from foreign shores. China and porcelain dolls brightened the room. A four-poster bed stood in the corner, draped in the purest cream silk. The fire in the hearth burned brightly, warming the room.

Normally they would get right down to it, shedding clothes and inhibitions with equal abandon. But tonight he had an agenda. He took off his cape and hung it on a peg. "Have they cared for ye properly while I was away?"

Her cheeks flushed as she reached inside her robe and touched her breast. "I can't imagine needing anything else. Only you."

He felt a stirring in his groin and struggled to control himself. He had a favor to ask. Her scent overpowered him.

She smiled. "I heard that you found your son. They say that he looks just like ye."

Blackheart moved closer and gazed into her hazel eyes. "Aye. He's the mirror image of me. We got off to a bad start, but today was a better day. I have plans for him." He noted her fine features and touched her face, running his thumb across perfect lips. "You look like a goddess, lass."

She took his thumb into her mouth, sucked it, and let go.

"You missed me." He unbuttoned his shirt and laid it across the table, then stripped off his shoes and socks and stepped out of his kilt. He looked up to see her open the robe and drop it to the floor. Her slender body stood before him, breasts brazenly exposed, rose-tipped nipples tempting him. His agenda would have to wait. Blackheart pulled her close and kissed her deeply. He felt her tremble, lifted her in his arms, and took her to bed.

***

Their passion quenched, he lay beside her. She curled against him, her backside to his body, and slept. He lost himself in the silkiness of her skin.

Blackheart woke her gently and turned her, so she lay flat on the sheets. His expression was serious as he stroked her chestnut hair. "I have a favor to ask."

"Anything m'Lord."

He ran a finger along her lips. "My son turns seventeen tomorrow.

He's never been with a lass."

She raised her eyebrows. "Not like you, m'Lord."

"I'd like you to be the one. I thought of sending that little harlot Julianna, but she can't keep her mouth shut. He needs a real woman to be patient and show him what to do."

Kate bowed her head. "M'Lord."

He stroked her hair. "You're the only one I can trust to be discreet."

"I would do anything for ye."

"I know ye would. Dughall's his name. Tomorrow we'll have a birthday celebration. Stay out of sight. After he retires, enter his bedchamber, let him take ye, and show him how to please a woman."

"Aye, m'Lord."

He ran a finger across her nipple, feeling her tremble. "Teach him well. I promise I'll be grateful."

Kate

NOT ALL BAD

WHINNYFOLD
OCTOBER 31 1636
THE NEXT DAY

Alex ran his fingers through his hair. He pulled the boat onto the beach, lowered the sails, and stowed them in the hull. His face was grim. "A discouraging day. I'm glad she didn't come with me."

Alex crossed the beach and climbed the path to the village. He couldn't face his wife just yet. He walked out to the point, lost in thought. The wind was raw. "How can I tell her? It seems hopeless."

Dark clouds gathered overhead, promising a storm. How could they get him back? His mind searched for possibilities, finding none. At last, he bowed his head in prayer. "Dear God. My son is lost to a cruel and ruthless man. Show me a way to get him back." For a moment, the sun peeked out from behind a cloud. His heart lightened. "Dughall, my son! Hang on. God will help us."

It was time to face his wife. Alex tucked frozen hands into his pockets, walked to the stone cottage, and went inside. His wife kneeled at the hearth, cooking the evening meal. He hung up his jacket and went to her.

Jessie stood and wrapped her arms around his chest. "Oh, Alex.

You're frozen through."

Guilt stabbed him. *Thank God she still loves me,* he thought. *At least we have each other.* He led her to the table, where they sat across from each other.

"How's your wrist, husband?"

"Throbbing. I guess it was too soon to sail."

Her expression was hopeful. "What did ye find out?"

"I sailed into Peterhead and scoured the taverns and inns. I talked to shopkeepers and fishermen and anyone who would listen. I saw Andrew McFarlein and the harbormaster Angus Phinnie. I asked if they saw a lord in a blue and green kilt who came to town days ago."

Jessie raised her eyebrows.

"Some didn't know but those who did agree. The lord's name was Gilbert and he traveled with a party of seven men. One of them was his father, the Earl of Huntly."

Jessie shuddered. "Lord Gordon? The one they call Blackheart? Dughall is his son?"

Alex shared her fear. His bowels churned. "Aye. He's a powerful man with a reputation for cruelty. It's a wonder that we're not all dead."

"Oh. Maggie accepted sole responsibility."

His throat burned. "I know it. And Dughall spared Ian's life."

"It's been seventeen years. How did they find him?"

Alex rubbed his temple. "A tavern lass heard them talking about a lad who bore the birthmark of their clan on his shoulder. One of them saw Dughall at the gathering and noticed the resemblance, as well as the mark."

"He took his shirt off for the stone's throw."

"Aye. The lass said they asked about Whinnyfold and who was the midwife seventeen years ago."

Jessie's face darkened. "Is it lost, then?"

Alex felt her heartbreak. Against all he believed in, he told a half-truth. "Nay, lass. There's always hope."

"Can we talk to the Earl of Erroll?"

"Nay. He and Lord Gordon are allies. He might say that Maggie got what she deserved." His head ached as he told her the rest. "Dughall's been taken to Huntly Castle, about 35 miles from here. We can't walk in there. The Earl would be in his rights to have us killed. The lad's a man now; they can't keep him against his will. We must pray that he finds his way back."

Tears streamed down her face. "Is that all we can do?"

Alex squeezed her hand. "Pray, lass. If it's meant to be, God will help us."

Huntly Castle

Dughall stood in front of a long mirror in the sewing room. He was naked but for a cloth that he held around his middle. The tailor had arrived that morning to measure him for a set of clothes. Sean Fittie was a bent old man with bad teeth. He fluttered around the young lord; afraid he would incur the wrath of the Earl. He was a day late.

Dughall wrinkled his nose. *The man smells of body odor and perfume.*

Fittie used a tape to measure Dughall around the waist, across the shoulders, and under the arms to his middle. He recorded the measurements in a book and continued, measuring his hips, thighs and inseam.

Dughall fidgeted. "How many ways can ye measure a man? I've lost count."

The tailor wrote in his book. "Forgive me, my Lord. Only a few more measurements are needed. Stand as straight as ye can."

Dughall nodded. He drew the cloth tighter around his middle and straightened his back. His shoulders burned.

Gilbert stood by. "Hurry up man! The Earl wants four sets of clothes, some formal in the style of our clan, and some casual. Silk shirts as well as linen. Kilts. Breeks. A wool cape. Oh and don't forget the riding clothes, we start his lessons next week."

The old tailor frowned. "Aye, my Lord."

Gilbert's expression hardened. "Knit him some socks and tell the shoemaker to make two pairs of shoes and some riding boots."

The tailor's hands shook as he measured the lad, from the nape of the neck to his waist. He ran the tape from shoulder to hand, and measured the upper arm and wrist. Fittie recorded the measurements in his book, next to the others. He bowed deeply. "I have all that I need." He reached for the cloth around Dughall's waist. "Allow me to help ye get dressed."

Dughall gripped the cloth. "Nay. I'll do it myself!"

The old tailor was shocked. "Forgive me my Lord. I did not mean to offend ye."

Gilbert looked at a clock and frowned. "Get out of here old man. You have work to do and you're already a day late."

The tailor bowed, with a panicked look on his face. "My Lord. I'll have these for you as soon as I can."

Gilbert smirked. "You'll have them in three weeks, or suffer the consequences. Perhaps you'd rather speak to the Earl. He's with his mistress, but I'm sure we can interrupt him."

"Nay my Lord! Dinna disturb him. It will be as you wish. My people will work day and night if necessary." He trembled as he packed his things into a bag and genuflected. "My Lords."

Gilbert waved his hand, dismissing him. The little man cowered as he backed out of the room.

Dughall was silent as he tucked his shirt into his kilt.

Gilbert chuckled. "He very nearly wet his pants."

Dughall nodded. "Aye."

"I hope you were listening," Gilbert said. "This is how an Earl deals with a tradesman who displeases him."

Dughall sighed as he pulled up his socks.

***

The schoolmaster sat at the library desk across from the Earl. The large room was well lit with standing oil lamps. Massive shelves stood on each wall, filled with books from many disciplines. Logan Crombie pushed up the spectacles on his nose as he regarded the shelves of books. He had never seen such a collection of Greek literature. "An impressive library, m'Lord. Where should we start with the young Lord's education?"

Blackheart slapped his hand on the desk. "Well, he says he can read. We shall see about that."

The schoolmaster blanched and took a breath. "Shall we start with language and literature, then?"

Blackheart stared. "Aye. That's a good place to start. Make him read aloud, until you're sure he understands. Tell me what you find."

Crombie pulled out a leather book and opened it. He poised his pen to write and raised his eyebrows. "He's had no formal education?"

Blackheart narrowed his eyes. "How dare ye imply that he's stupid!"

Crombie's heart thumped. He closed his book and swallowed hard. "Forgive me, m'Lord. I apologize for my poor choice of words. I did not mean to imply anything about the young Lord."

Blackheart stared until he squirmed. "I leave this in your hands. A Lord must be schooled in the traditions of the world. It will be up to you to show him literature, history, and mathematics. You will teach him and speak to no one of his progress or abilities. If you do, you will answer to me. Is that understood?"

Crombie's fingers shook as he clutched his book. This task could be a death sentence. "As you wish, m'Lord. I will be discreet."

Blackheart smiled in a manner that was cold and threatening. "Start his lessons tomorrow, and report back to me each week."

Crombie nodded. "Aye, m'Lord." The grandfather clock chimed eleven times, drawing their attention.

Blackheart waved his hand, dismissing the man. "Now be off with ye. I grow tired of this conversation."

The schoolmaster stood and carefully slipped the book and pen into his coat pocket. He didn't dare to voice his concerns.

Blackheart held up his hand. "One more thing. Keep him away

from the Bible. He already has the morals of a peasant."

Crombie stared. "As you wish, m'Lord."

***

Dughall followed Gilbert out of the sewing room into the hallway. Maids and serving lasses passed them by, bowing their heads and paying respect.

Blackheart emerged from the library and joined them. He studied Dughall, who was wearing one of his best kilts. "Hmmphh… I trust that you handled the tailor."

Gilbert paled. "Aye, Father. We just finished with him in the sewing room. He's a sniveling little man, but he promised to have the clothes in three weeks."

Blackheart's eyes grew wide. "All of them?"

"Aye. I said that he must or suffer the consequences."

"Ha! Then I leave it to you to decide what those consequences will be. He will never get it done on time."

Gilbert looked out a window to the courtyard below. "Something public, in the courtyard. It could be entertaining."

"Take care not to kill him. He's the only decent tailor around here."

Dughall cringed. *I will never be like them,* he thought.

Gilbert cleared his throat. "Father, I have a favor to ask. I've been spending time with Bridget Murray. I wish to take her as my personal servant."

Blackheart smiled. "A plain but talented lass. Provide her with jewelry and dresses and she'll open her legs every night. All right son, she belongs to you. It's time you take a mistress. That makes six servants who are under your care."

Dughall frowned. "What do ye mean?"

"Those six answer to Gilbert alone, grant his requests, and accept his discipline when they displease him."

Dughall was shocked, but stayed silent.

"Murdock belongs to you, lad. He's willing to lay down his life for you and will do whatever you wish. You must punish him if he displeases you."

"Murdock agrees to this?" Dughall asked.

Gilbert chuckled. Blackheart silenced him with a stare. "Aye, he agrees. We provide for all his needs. You're his Lord. I'm the only one who can change it."

Dughall was quiet for a moment as he thought about this. *Murdock would be safe with me.* "All right, Father. I accept him as my servant."

Blackheart smiled broadly. "I'm beginning to enjoy your company, lad." In the hallway beyond, Murdock walked towards them. "Your servant is coming, Son. Stay with him and act like a Lord. Gilbert and

I must attend to the particulars of tonight's party."

Dughall watched as the men departed towards the Grand Hall, leaving him in Murdock's company. The young Lord looked down at his silk shirt and fine kilt. He fingered the tail of his sporran so that it lay straight.

"My Lord," Murdock said. "You look handsome in those clothes. Like a true Lord."

"They're not mine. They belong to the Earl."

Murdock paled. "My Lord, it would be wise to call him Father."

"I'll try to remember. Can we walk outside? I hate being inside so much."

"As you wish. We'll go to the courtyard."

Dughall smiled at the man who reminded him of Uncle Robert. "Good. I need to talk to ye."

They walked in silence down a long corridor until they reached a door that entered into the courtyard. Murdock drew a cape around Dughall's shoulders, grabbed a wrap for himself, and they went outside. The wind was raw and the air was laced with moisture, promising an early snow. Autumn leaves blew across fieldstones and settled at their feet. Dughall breathed deeply and shivered.

"Is it too cold out here for your Lordship?"

Dughall sat on a bench and motioned for Murdock join him. "Nay, it makes me feel alive."

The man looked around uneasily. He sat on the end of the bench and made himself look smaller than the young Lord.

Dughall leaned forward and clasped his hands. "Murdock, are ye kin to the Earl. I mean Father?"

"Nay, m'Lord."

"Are ye indentured, then?"

"Nay."

Dughall considered his next words carefully. "Why do ye stay? He's a brutal man and you said he flogged ye."

"I don't think about it, m'Lord. I have a warm place to sleep and food in my belly. The Earl hasn't whipped me in years. I know what to do to avoid his anger. Sometimes I think he's the devil himself, and sometimes I think he's a man doin' what he has to do." Murdock looked thoughtful. "He's a fierce warrior and a true swordsman. I've fought beside him and he leaves no living man behind. He came back for me on the battlefield when I was wounded. It's verra confusing."

Dughall sighed. "Aye, I guess."

"My Lord? Has he told you that I'm your personal servant?"

Dughall stared. "He just did."

Murdock got down on one knee and took his hand. "My Lord. I pledge my loyalty, my service, and my very breath to ye. You may do with me as you wish. My life is in your hands."

Dughall burned with embarrassment. *I must act like a Lord.* "You have nothing to fear from me. I will treat ye well. Get off your knees and sit with me."

Murdock got up and sat beside him. "You're troubled. What do you wish to know?"

"How long have ye been with the Earl?"

"Twenty eight years, since I was a lad of ten."

"Then you would have known my mother."

Murdock paled. "Aye. Shouldn't ye ask the Earl about her?"

"I'm asking you. Tell me about her." Dughall tasted the man's fear. "I won't tell anyone about this."

Murdock swallowed hard. "My Lady was a bonny lass, nineteen when she married the Earl. She had clouds of dark hair, deep blue eyes, and a smile that melted your heart."

Dughall raised his eyebrows.

"Forgive me, m'Lord. I shouldn't talk about my Lady that way. I was a fool of twenty-one and that's what I saw."

"It's all right."

"She was the daughter of Lord Drake, the Duke of Seaford. He sent her with wagons of fine things and her own maidservant. They said it was a marriage of convenience, to bind the clans together. A male child of that union would have been a powerful symbol of their alliance."

"Why did she leave him?"

Murdock picked at his fingernails. "The Earl hated her. She had a strange gift, she knew things that others did and thought. My Lady knew when he'd been with his mistress and what they'd done, right down to the smallest act. Their arguments echoed through the castle, sending us scurrying for cover."

Dughall sighed. "She must be my mother. I have that same gift."

"You must hide it."

"It's a hard thing to hide, when something is happening to one ye love. Continue, Murdock."

"The Earl called her a witch! She tried to leave him more than once, to run to the Duke, but didn't get far. Each time, the Earl brought her back and beat her mercilessly. You know what a temper he has."

Dughall frowned. "How did I come to be born in a fishing village?"

Murdock looked around fearfully. "The last time my Lady ran she was pregnant, almost to term. She told her maid that she didn't want the Earl near her baby. The unfortunate lass couldn't keep her mouth shut. The Earl found out and went to her chambers, to find that she'd run again." Murdock took a breath.

"Go on."

"I was with Blackheart that night. Six of us followed the tracks that she and her servant made. It wasn't long before we found them." He frowned. "The Earl searched through his saddlebag, took out a rope with a noose, and ordered Fang Adams to string up her maid. My Lady fell to her knees. She pleaded and cried, but it did no good. I knew the lass they hung that night. At least he didn't ask me to hang her."

"What happened to my mother?"

"The Earl was verra angry with her. He slapped her face when she refused to get up. Then he forced her onto the horse in front of him and took her home."

Dughall leaned forward. Curls fell around his face, hiding tears in his eyes.

"That night, he beat her senseless. Her screams frightened us all. We prayed that he wouldn't hurt the child."

Dughall shuddered and drew his cape around him. His heart was breaking for a woman he never knew.

"Are ye all right, m'Lord?"

His voice was hoarse. "Did she run again?"

"She got out of bed and disappeared the next day. We searched for her in the forest, thinking she would go to her father. He never found her."

Dughall took a ragged breath. Tears slid down his cheeks.

"Are ye all right, m'Lord?"

"Aye."

"The old midwife told the Earl that his wife died in childbirth. She gave the baby to a couple who had just birthed a son."

Dughall sighed. "That would be my brother Ian."

"The red-haired lad we let go?"

"Aye."

The servant handed him a kerchief. "I'm glad we didn't kill him."

Dughall wiped his face. "I'm a good man, Murdock. I don't want to be like the Earl. I must run away." He glanced at his servant and saw fear in his face.

"You mustn't leave my Lord! No matter what happens. He'll hunt you down and punish you severely."

Dughall swallowed his fear. "I've been on the takin' end of his strap. I know the risk."

"Nay. He was just playin' with ye. I've seen him flog a man until blood ran to his heels. It didn't matter that he begged for mercy."

Dughall stared. "Father expects me to do that. He says I must punish you when you displease me."

"Aye. You must."

Dughall frowned.

"I'll try not to displease ye, m'Lord. But to be honest, I'd rather it be you than the Earl."

"Murdock, I can't stay here."

"Please, lad! We need a Lord who's a good man. It could change

163

things. You don't have to be like him."

Dughall sniffled. "Do ye think I could make a difference?"

"Aye, my Lord. I don't think he'll kill ye. You're the grandson of the Duke. Gain your father's respect and he may listen to ye."

Dughall felt hopeful. "I'll consider what you said. I'll gain his favor before I challenge him."

"My Lord. He's a powerful man. Choose your battles carefully."

"I can stand his beatings. I lived through it once and I can bear it again. But if he means to turn me into a beast I'll go."

"Where would ye go? To the Duke?"

Dughall smiled. "There's a lass I care about. We were to be married. I'll find her."

Murdock groaned. "You're the son of an Earl and the grandson of a Duke. You would deny your destiny for a lass?"

"It would be better than losing my soul. You're my servant. Will ye come with me?"

"My Lord. You're so young! You don't understand what he'll do to us."

"I asked ye a question. Will ye come?"

Murdock brought a hand to his neck and swallowed hard. He was as pale as a ghost. "Aye. I promised to serve ye and I will."

***

That evening, the courtyard was filled with people. Nobles and their wives donned fine clothes and joined the Earl in celebrating his son's birthday. Dughall memorized the names of people who were presented to him. He followed Gilbert's lead, offering his hand and nodding his head when appropriate.

As they waited for dinner, a swordplay competition ensued between Blackheart and one of the nobles, Angus MacVey. People gathered around as the two men skillfully exchanged deadly blows. Dughall and Gilbert stood on the sidelines with their manservants, watching the fight.

A chill ran up Dughall's spine as his father wielded the heavy broadsword. "He's an awesome fighter!"

Murdock smiled. "Aye, that he is."

"I want to learn how to do that!"

"Good, lad. It's my job to teach ye."

Dughall flinched as the swords clanged. Angus' sword nicked the Earl's arm, drawing blood. The Earl glanced at his stained shirt and reddened with anger. Women gasped and men fingered their knives nervously.

Dughall felt the tension in the air. "Do they mean to kill each other?"

"Nay, m'Lord. Though the victor does have the option of taking the loser's life."

Dughall frowned, yet he was riveted to the action.

Blackheart raised his sword to stop a blow and used his strength to push. Angus' sword flew from his hand and the large man fell backwards onto the flagstones.

A woman cried out, "Angus! Dear God."

The crowd was silent as MacVey lay sweating on the ground. His sword was out of reach and his expression was desperate. Blackheart held the tip of his blade against the man's throat and pressed harder. A small stream of blood trickled down his neck.

The crier called out. "The contest is won. The Earl is the victor!"

The fallen man groaned. "Mercy!"

Dughall held his breath. He'd never seen a man killed right before his eyes.

Blackheart turned to him. "What say ye, Son? It's your birthday. You decide."

Dughall's eyes widened. "Decide what?"

Gilbert sneered. "Whether he lives or dies. It's up to you." Somewhere in the crowd, Anna MacVey sobbed. The man on the ground trembled.

Dughall's stomach churned. *I must act like a Lord to gain his respect.* He scanned the crowd and saw that all eyes were on him. *Oh God.* The lad stood tall and cleared his throat. "It's my birthday. I'm feeling generous today. Angus was a worthy opponent. I say that he lives."

Blackheart drew back his sword and stepped away from the quivering man. "A wise choice, my son. It would have been messy to say the least. Let nothing spoil tonight's celebration."

"Thank ye, Father."

Murdock's hand rested on his arm. "Impressive, my Lord."

Blackheart stripped off his bloody shirt, threw it aside, and pressed a cloth against the cut on his arm.

A lady in the crowd gasped. "Look at the muscles in his chest. Now there's a man!"

The Earl slipped on a clean shirt and fastened his cufflinks. He pulled on a blue dining jacket piped with gold buttons, and joined his sons. "Gentlemen and ladies. Today my son turns seventeen. Join us in the Grand Hall for a feast and celebration."

***

The Grand Hall was larger than any place Dughall had ever seen. Dinner seating for forty people dominated the eastern side of the room. The western side had a theatre, complete with an elevated stage and an area for minstrels. Iron chandeliers and wall sconces provided soft candlelight. Boughs of fragrant pine decorated each table. Portraits of Lords and Ladies hung on the walls, as well as ancient swords and elaborately decorated dirks.

Dughall sat with his father and brother at the head of the first table. As he looked around the room, he couldn't help thinking about his family. It was Ian's birthday too, and he would give anything to be home again. The meal was beyond his wildest dreams. Beef and fowl were served with potatoes and vegetables and freshly baked breads. Whisky and wine flowed freely, though Dughall wouldn't touch it.

During dinner, a white-haired woman in a velvet dress sat onstage, playing the dulcimer. With great skill, she plucked the strings and worked the frets, playing an old ballad. The sweet melodic sound made him smile.

"Enjoying yourself, Son?"

"Aye. I love music."

The ballad ended and the old woman stood. As she gathered her sheet music from the stand, the audience clapped. Blackheart leaned over and spoke in his ear. "That's Donella Geddes, the wife of the cooper. Would ye like to hear the harp?"

Dughall smiled. "Aye."

Blackheart nodded to a servant. The young woman left the room and returned with the harpist, leading her to the stage. A lad followed her, carrying a gilded harp. The harpist was a bonny lass with long red hair and clear blue eyes. She wore a green and red tartan skirt, and a blouse with ruffled sleeves. She lifted her skirt slightly as she took the stairs, revealing a lace petticoat. The young woman scanned the crowd for the Earl, and smiled when she saw him. She straightened her skirt and lifted the bustle as she sat.

Dughall's eyes grew wide. "She's bonny."

"Flora Laing." Blackheart whispered. "A talented lass, in more ways than one."

The crowd quieted. She straightened her back and ran her slender fingers over the strings of the harp. Her eyes were downcast as she played, weaving a magical tale of love and honor.

Dughall was entranced. "She plays like she loves it."

Soft light reflected off her red hair. He smiled sadly. *Mother played like that,* he thought. *I miss her terribly.*

The notes rolled off her fingers, casting a magical spell. With a flourish, she ran her fingers across the strings one last time, and the ballad was done. Flora stood and bowed slightly. The crowd clapped as she left the stage.

Blackheart smiled. "Bring more wine and whisky. The minstrels are here. It's time to get bawdy."

A serving lass came to their table and poured a glass of wine for each person.

"Nay, lass," Dughall said. "I don't drink."

"Leave it here!" Blackheart growled. "It's your birthday, Son. The day you become a man. Have just one."

Gilbert raised his eyebrows. Dughall lifted his glass and sipped slowly. "All right. But only one." The burgundy wine was sweet and rich, nothing like the mulled wine he'd tasted at gatherings.

On stage, minstrels set up their stools and instruments. A middle-aged man with leather breeks and a linen shirt took a fiddle out of a case. He tied his long hair back in a ribbon and tried the strings. A young lad opened his pack and took out a wooden flute. They played a lively tune that promised a night of fun. The man came to the front of the stage. "Lords and Ladies! I trust that that yer well tonight."

The crowd roared. "Aye!"

"I see that ye have enough to drink."

"Aye!"

"Then let's get on with it! I present to ye from the grand city of Edinburgh, Loony Lucy."

A young woman entered holding a basket of laundry on her hip. Her hips swayed as she strutted back and forth on the stage. She was dressed in rags and a feather hat, and was barefooted. She held a hand to her brow and looked into the audience. "Aaaaooooowww! Loony Lucy I am. Aren't I lovely? Where's the birthday lad?"

Gilbert nudged Dughall. He stood, facing the stage.

Lucy grinned, showing her missing front teeth. "Ach! He's a handsome one, too." She pushed her blouse off her shoulders. "My Lord, I'm an expert with sheets and what happens between 'em. Are ye sure ye don't need a laundress?" The crowd roared.

Dughall shook his head and smiled. He took a sip of wine and sat down.

Lucy pouted. "Well isn't it always like that. The handsome ones are shy. Sing with me, now." As the fiddle and flute played, she put down her basket and belted out a song.

I have seen the lark soar high at morn
Heard his song up in the blue
I have heard the blackbird pipe his note
The thrush and linnet too.
But none of them can sing so sweet
My singing bird as you!
Ah..........................
My singing bird as you!

If I could lure my singing bird
From his own cosy nest
If I could catch my singing bird
I would warm him on my breast!

Lucy held the bodice of her blouse and batted her eyelashes.

♩ ♪ ♩

> *Oh I will climb a high high tree*
> *And I'll rob a wild bird's nest*
> *And I'll bring back my singing bird*
> *To the arms that I love best!* ♩ ♪ ♩

Lucy pointed to a bonny lass at a nearby table. "My fair Lady, your fortune. A handsome lad with a beautiful voice will woo ye."

Her husband pouted.

Lucy curtsied. "My Lady, pardon me but what are ye doin' here with your father? Forgive me m'Lord! I am loony."

Dughall clapped his hands and laughed. A moment later, he was distracted by an angry voice.

The Earl's hands were pressed against the table. His manservant Connor was whispering in his ear. "The Duke!" Blackheart cried. "Who let him in here?"

Connor cringed. "I don't know m'Lord, but I'll find out. The Duke is in the hall. What do you wish me to do?"

Blackheart pounded his fist on the table. The room grew quiet. He sat back in his chair and thought for a moment, then looked at Dughall. "It seems that your grandfather is here, lad."

Dughall remained silent.

"Ah well. It would have come to this sooner or later." Blackheart motioned to Connor. "See him in."

"My Lord," Connor said, nervously. "He's here with six armed men."

Blackheart frowned. "Tell the Duke that he may bring one of his men inside. This is a birthday celebration; his man must leave his sword."

"As you wish, m'Lord." Connor bowed and took his leave.

"Clear two places at this table for the Duke and his man." Blackheart demanded. He pointed at a noble and his wife, who stood and took their leave.

Arguing was heard from outside the door, then it opened and two men walked in. Both were tall and dressed formally in the blue and red kilts of their clan. The young man was powerfully built, and his dark eyes scanned the room as a hand rested on his dirk. The older man carried a cane that was topped with a golden lion's head.

Blackheart's expression hardened as the men approached the table. "Sit down." They took their places opposite him.

Dughall studied the older Lord. The Duke was an old man with gray hair and startling blue eyes. His clothes were made of silk and wool, and a silver brooch decorated his cape. He glared at the Earl through gold-rimmed spectacles.

His face is wrinkled. Dughall observed. *He must be as old as Maggie.* He glanced at his father and back to the Duke. *They hate each other. I feel the anger.*

"James," Blackheart growled.

The Duke stiffened. "Robert."

Blackheart's eyes narrowed. "I had hoped never to see ye again."

"And I as well. I understand that you have my grandson here."

Blackheart smiled coldly. "I do." He examined the nails on his left hand and fingered a gold ring. "Who's your man?"

The Duke struggled to control his anger. "This is my servant Jamison."

"Where's your son Andrew? He's always at your side."

His shoulders dropped. "Andrew is dead. He was killed in a hunting accident weeks ago."

Blackheart raised his eyebrows. "He left no heir?"

"Nay."

The Earl leaned back in his chair and folded his arms across his chest. "Well, isn't this interesting? This makes my son heir to your estate and title."

The older man reddened. "Aye, it does."

Oh my God. Dughall cringed.

Blackheart clapped his hands, calling for wine and whisky. "We have two things to celebrate tonight. My son's seventeenth birthday and a new alliance between our clans. Is it agreed?"

The Duke closed his eyes, and then slowly opened them. "Aye, it's agreed. I want to see my grandson."

Blackheart pointed. "He's right here, next to me. Do ye not see the resemblance? Dughall, meet your grandfather, the Duke of Seaford."

Dughall's heart pounded as the man looked him over. Slowly, the anger in his face softened and changed to recognition. He bowed his head respectfully. "Grandfather."

"I wish to speak to my grandson."

Blackheart waved his hand. "Talk to him."

"I wish to speak to him alone. You can send his manservant with him."

"All right." The Earl snapped his fingers and gave Connor an order. "Send for Murdock." He leaned forward. "Take care that you don't abscond with the lad. I have more armed men than you do. You and I will talk about our new arrangement at a later date. I want your word on this. "

The Duke's eyes narrowed. "You have my word."

Murdock appeared behind the young Lord.

"Murdock. The Duke wishes to speak with his grandson. Go with them to the dining hall and stay with them at all times. See that my son returns to the party when you're done."

"As you wish, m'Lord." Murdock touched Dughall's shoulder and spoke softly. "My Lord. Allow me to pull out your chair."

Dughall placed his napkin on the table. His heart was in his throat as he stood and followed his servant to the exit.

Murdock allowed the Duke and his man to leave the room. "My Lord," he whispered. "Lord Drake is a powerful man. Show him respect and speak only when you are spoken to. He hates the Earl. It would be bad if you told him about his daughter."

"Thank ye, Murdock."

They left the Hall and joined the Duke and his manservant. Following behind, they walked the stone corridor, its walls lined with gilded tapestries. Dughall watched the old lord's shoulders shake with anger and felt his frustration. "He's angry. What does he want?" he whispered.

Murdock's hand rested on his arm, reassuring him. "He's not mad at you, m'Lord. You'll be fine."

They turned down a corridor and arrived at the dining hall.

***

Blackheart called his manservant. "Take six armed men to each exit. Make sure that the Duke leaves alone with his men. Take care that my son is not with them."

Connor nodded. "Aye, my Lord."

"There is a traitor amongst us. Find out who told the Duke that I found my son. I'll deal with them tomorrow. "

***

Dughall held his breath as they entered the dining hall and walked past a line of chairs to the head of the table. The only light in the room was from a candle and shadows loomed on the wall. Murdock picked up a taper and held it in the fire until it caught. He walked around the room, lighting sconces.

The Duke held a kerchief to his mouth and coughed uncontrollably.

Jamison appeared at his side. "Are ye all right m'Lord?"

The Duke nodded. He raised his hand and spoke to the servants. "Jamison, Murdock. Wait for us at the end of the table. Give us some privacy."

"Aye, m'Lord."

The Duke sat in an ornate chair and motioned for Dughall to sit beside him. "Speak softly, lad. I don't want the servants to hear us."

Dughall pulled out a chair and sat down. He clasped his hands and waited for the man to speak. *Is he a madman like the Earl?*

The Duke raised his eyebrows. "There's no need for you to fear me.

I'm angry at the Earl, not at you."

Dughall rolled his eyes. "Thank God."

"Do you believe in God, lad?"

"Aye."

"So do I. How long have you been here?"

"A few days."

"How did they find you?"

Dughall thought for a moment. "I went to a gathering in Peterhead with my family and took off my shirt for the stone's throw. Murdock said they saw the birthmark and my resemblance to the Earl. I was taken from my home a few days ago."

"Let's see the birthmark."

Dughall unbuttoned his shirt and slipped it over his head. He twisted his arm to show the mark on his shoulder.

The Duke grabbed his arm and examined the mark, stretching it. "It's the mark of the Gordon clan."

Dughall flinched.

The Duke pushed his chair out to look at his backside. The old man ran a finger across a welt. "Damn him! Has he beaten you already?"

Dughall was ashamed. "Aye, just once."

"How did he do this?"

"Oh God. He tied me to a tree and beat me with his strap."

"This is no way to treat a young Lord! He whipped you like a common servant. I won't stand for it! Put your shirt on, lad."

Dughall slipped his shirt over his head and tucked it loosely into his kilt. "I can bear it. I can take it again if I have to. I won't let him change me."

The Duke studied him. "You have a lot of courage. Few men would stand up to him. Where do you come from?"

Dughall winced as he thought of his family. *Can I trust him? Will he kill them?*

The Duke raised his eyebrows. "I won't hurt your people. I must find out what happened to my daughter. If she's dead, I must bring her remains home. I'll take them a message from you."

Dughall bit his lip gently. "I'm a good man, Grandfather. A simple man, not a lord. I was born in Whinnyfold, a village on the North Sea. I've had no schooling, but I'm not ignorant. The church taught me to read the Bible." The old man smiled. Dughall held out palms. "Look at these hands. They're rough and calloused. I fished the seas with my father and brother, chopped wood, and hauled peat. I was the one who emptied the chamber pot." He sighed. "Now they tell me I'm the son of an Earl and the grandson of a Duke. This is verra confusing. My bedroom is larger than my cottage. I want to go home."

The Duke pushed his spectacles up higher on his nose. "Who raised you, lad?"

"Alex and Jessie Hay."

"Who was the midwife when you were born? I must talk to her."

Dughall's heart ached. "Aunt Maggie's dead. The Earl slit her throat on the day that they took me."

The Duke raised his eyebrows. "He killed her in front of you?"

"Nay."

"Someone told you this?"

"Nay."

The man sighed. "You saw it some other way, then."

I can't lie to my own grandfather.

"Tell the truth, lad. I won't condemn you."

"Oh God. I shouldn't tell ye this, but I know things that others see and feel. I don't know why, but she was calm as he slit her throat. I fell to my knees and choked on her blood."

The Duke paled. "There's no doubt that you're Christal's son. You have her strange gift. Take care that your father doesn't find out."

Dughall nodded. "Grandfather. When you see my family, say that I love them. I think of them every day."

"I will. Lad, did you understand what I said to the Earl?"

"Aye. I'm sorry about your son."

The Duke wiped his eyes. "Do you know what it means? My children are dead, and you're my only living heir. My estate and title will belong to you someday. I don't trust the Earl. I know in my heart that he caused my daughter's death. But I will deal with him for your sake." He stood up to leave. "I must go."

Dughall joined him. "Will I see you again?"

"Soon."

"Will I ever see my home?"

The Duke picked up his cane. "You say you believe in God."

"Aye."

"God has chosen you for greater things. He had a reason when he took you from us. You've grown up as a good man. God returned you to us for a purpose."

Dughall frowned. Why would God do this? Could it be true?

"Think lad. As Duke, you can help your people in countless ways. They'll never have to suffer through a hard winter. I promise that someday you'll visit them." He spoke softly. "Tell the Earl that I demanded to see your birthmark, to verify your parentage. Say nothing about your people; it would put them in danger. It's a wonder that he didn't kill them." He put his cane down and embraced the lad.

Dughall felt the warmth of the love he had for his daughter. He saw a bonny child with clouds of black hair and clear blue eyes, calling to her father. He stepped back and smiled. "She couldn't say Papa. She called you Poppy."

The Duke nodded. With tears in his eyes, he motioned for his servant. "I must go. I'll find a way to protect you. There's a man in the castle who is loyal to me. He'll tell me if you're in trouble. In the meantime, be careful, lad."

***

Dughall and Murdock watched as the Duke and his man disappeared down the corridor toward the Grand Hall.

Murdock straightened Dughall's shirt and buttoned his cuffs. "The Duke wanted to see your birthmark."

"Aye. He had to be sure. It seems that I'm his only heir."

Murdock stared. "What about his son, Andrew?"

"He was killed in a hunting accident."

Murdock's hands trembled as he adjusted the strap of Dughall's sporran. "My Lord. Do ye know what this means?"

"Aye. Someday I will bear his title. My head aches just thinkin' about it."

"Dear God. We must get back to the party." They started walking the long hallway towards the Grand Hall.

"Murdock, will ye help me? I have much to learn about being a Lord."

"We'll start tomorrow, m'Lord. You must learn to ride and to handle a sword and dirk."

They entered the Grand Hall in time to see heated words being exchanged between the Earl and the Duke. They were standing close and shouting.

"I will raise my son as I see fit, and that includes disciplining him!"

"See that my grandson does not disappear like my daughter did, or you'll answer to me!"

Dughall flushed with embarrassment. They were fighting over him. The Earl rested his hand on the handle of his dirk. The Duke pressed a button on his cane and a blade popped out. Jamison and Connor drew knives from their socks.

"They mean to kill each other!" Dughall cried, as he started towards them.

"M'Lord, stay here!"

Dughall hurried to the two men. He held them apart, his hands on their chests. "Father. Grandfather. Please! I will honor you both and do what's expected of me."

At first, they were speechless. Blackheart waved his hand. "Stand down, Connor."

The Duke nodded. "Stand down, Jamison. I'll take my leave, now." He retracted the blade in his cane, glanced at his grandson, and left the room. Jamison followed on his heels.

Blackheart wiped his brow. "As you were, good people. It was a simple misunderstanding. Drink up!" He smiled as he poured two whiskies and set them on the table. "It's been an interesting evening, Son. You're either foolish or you have a lot of courage. It's dangerous to come between men about to draw their knives." Blackheart pointed to a chair. "Sit down and have a whisky with me."

Dughall paled.

"Come now, it's what I expect. You have an eventful night ahead of you."

***

The celebration was over and the castle was quiet. Servants scurried about, tending to fireplaces and cleaning up the Hall. Murdock walked Dughall to his bedchamber and went inside. He poured water into a bowl and hovered as the young Lord washed his face and hands. *The lad's tipsy,* he thought. *It wouldn't do to have the next Duke of Seaford fall down and hurt himself.*

Dughall smoothed back his hair and looked in the long mirror. "I hardly recognize myself in these clothes."

"You've had quite a day."

The lad steadied himself against the armoire. "I'm dizzy from that whisky."

"You'll be fine, m'Lord. You only had two."

"I think it was three. Father expected it of me."

Murdock took his arm and led him to the bed. "Sit down, m'Lord. Let me take care of ye." The servant took off his shoes and socks, and removed his sporran. He unpinned his kilt and lifted it over his head.

Dughall smiled. "I'll never get used to this."

"To what, m'Lord?" He unbuttoned his cuffs and stripped off his silk shirt.

Dughall yawned. "You tend to my every need."

"That's what I'm meant to do."

Murdock threw back the covers and top sheet and tucked him in. He stoked the fire with apple wood and laid out his clothes for the next day.

Dughall ran his hands across the soft pillowcase. "They changed the sheets again." He closed his eyes. "I never used to sleep naked. Goodnight, Murdock."

"I'll take my leave now. Good night, m'Lord."

Murdock walked to the door and opened it. His eyes widened as he saw the Earl's mistress, Kate standing in the hall. She held a finger to her lips and motioned for him to come out. Murdock walked into the corridor and closed the door. He kept his head low, not wishing to offend her. She was dressed in a scanty blue robe with satin slippers.

"My Lady. Are ye lost? The Earl's chambers are over there."

Kate smiled. "The Earl sent me to teach his son. A birthday gift for a lad who's never been with a lass. Is he within?"

"The young Lord is in bed."

Kate touched his arm. "That's just where I want him. Murdock, speak to no one about this. The Earl insists that this be discreet."

"Aye, m'Lady."

She untied her long braid and let her chestnut hair fall around her shoulders. "What's his name?"

Murdock was stunned by her beauty. "Dughall," he stammered.

Kate smiled. "A strong name, worthy of a Lord. Leave us now. The lad and I have a long night ahead of us."

He walked the hallway, glancing back as she placed her hand on the door and slipped into the bedchamber. Murdock took a kerchief from his pocket and wiped his face. "The Earl must admire the lad. No one touches Kate, not even Gilbert." As he walked towards the servant's quarters, Murdock reflected on the day. "Fortunate lad. Lucky that I was chosen to serve him."

***

The fire in the hearth softly illuminated the bedchamber. Dughall ran his fingers under the silk pillow, trying to ground himself. "Oh God. The room is spinning." He closed his eyes and drifted. In the back of his mind, he heard the door creak open. "Murdock, did ye forget something?"

A soft female voice answered. "The Earl is right. You're the mirror image of him."

Dughall opened his eyes and rolled to face her. "You're not Murdock."

"Nay, lad." The bonny lass loosened the belt of her robe. She grabbed the top blanket and pulled it off the bed, leaving it in a heap on the floor.

His eyes grew wide.

She smiled. "My Lord, my name is Kate. The Earl sent me to teach ye how to take your pleasure. He said that it's expected of ye."

Dughall sat up, holding the sheet around his waist. Kate opened her robe slowly and teased him with a glimpse of her breasts.

He stared. "I'm dreaming. It must be the whisky."

She stripped for him, pushing one sleeve off her shoulder, then the other. The robe slipped off and she held it in front of her, barely covering her private parts. She dropped it to the ground.

Dughall shook his head to break the dream. The vision moved closer, sitting next to him on the bed. She was naked but for a gold chain around her neck. He was stunned by her lavender perfume. "In my dreams I can do what I want. I don't want to wake up." He ran a finger along her cheekbone and parted her lips. She took his finger into her mouth and sucked it gently.

"You're real, lass!"

"Aye." Her tongue found the inside of his hand and traveled to his wrist.

Dughall felt the heat rise in him. "Oh God. You don't have to do this, lass."

Kate pulled the sheet away from his thighs and saw that he was aroused. She ran her fingers through the hair on his chest. "I want to do it. You have a beautiful body. I'm honored to be your first."

Dughall's heart pounded as he kneeled and held her shoulders. "It's wrong. We're not married. What if I get ye with child?"

"Ye can't. I'm barren. A lord shouldn't worry about such things."

He frowned, but his body flushed with desire. Her hands were so soft. He opened his mouth to speak.

Kate put her hands around his neck. "Shhhhhhhh... It's never wrong when a man and a woman want each other. I want you. Am I not pleasing to ye?"

"Aye, but..."

Kate kissed him and welcomed his tongue into her mouth.

The whisky softened his inhibitions. He cradled her head and kissed her back, feeding from the sweetness of her mouth. She pulled him closer. Her scent drove him mad. Dughall laid her on the pillow, searched her hazel eyes, and knew she was willing. He lay beside her, placed his hand on her breast, and caressed her nipple. "I've never been with a lass."

"I know." Her hand reached down to his manhood and stroked it gently.

He closed his eyes and shivered, his breath coming in short gasps. She tightened her grip and continued. His body tensed. Dughall could bear no more. He opened his eyes and groaned. "I can't control it, lass."

She took his hand and placed it between her legs, opening for him. "I'm ready for ye."

Dear God! She's so wet. What should I do? Stolen glimpses of his parents guided him. He rose to his knees, straddled her and held her arms above her head.

Kate flushed. "Aye, hold me down! Like that. Lie atop me with your body against mine and tease me."

His Second Sight guided him. "I know what ye want, lass. I can feel it." Dughall's heart raced as his body molded to hers, feeling her silky skin. He kissed her neck and ran his tongue along the inside of her arm. He lingered at the curve of her elbow until her back arched. "Easy, lass." He buried his face in her neck, kissing her behind the ear. His tongue lingered there as she struggled.

Kate gasped and cried out, "Ohhh... Take me now, my Lord!"

He released her arms and steadied his hands against the sheets. Kate's legs opened and he buried himself inside of her, joining his body to hers. *Can a man die of pleasure?*

She directed him. "That's it. Thrust inside of me, slowly, slowly. Don't release it yet. Make it last a long time."

He held his breath and rode the waves of pleasure, again and again, making it last like she asked. Dughall tensed. He stopped and threw his head back, drops of sweat falling from his forehead onto her face. His eyes reflected pain and pleasure. "Please, lass."

She placed her hand on his chest. "Your heart beats like a stallion's. Don't stop, my Lord. Take your pleasure."

He kissed her neck and ran his tongue up to her mouth, silencing her. He pumped slowly at first, increasing the rhythm until she shuddered. His control was lost and he exploded inside of her.

Dughall trembled as his breathing slowed. He lay at her side, tracing the contours of her face. She was flushed and her breathing was shallow. He watched her. "Are ye all right?"

"Aye. There's no doubt. You are your father's son."

"Will ye be leaving now, Kate?"

"Nay, we have some time. I want to teach ye how to please a woman."

"There's more?"

She smiled. "There are as many ways as lovers in this world. Let me show you what they do in France."

WHINNYFOLD

Ian lay in bed, staring into the darkness. It had been a bittersweet day. His parents had presented him with a dirk, a kilt, and a sporran of his own. Alex had a man-to-man talk with him about the commitment of marriage, and Jessie prepared a special meal. Solemnly, they knelt and prayed for Dughall, asking God to bring him home.

Ian hadn't felt his brother since the flogging. All his life, he wanted to be separate. Now Dughall was gone, and it felt lonely. *Are ye too far away or dead?*

He was fast asleep when the visions came, stronger than ever. In his dream, Dughall lay beside a bonny lass, his tongue circling her mouth, his hand touching her breast. She was naked but for a gold neck chain and a patch of hair between her legs.

Ian's skin flushed as the scent of lavender filled the room. Her soft lips tasted like mulled wine. Silky fingers stroked his manhood, gently at first, then insistently. His heart pounded with anticipation. He gasped as the lass took Dughall's hand and placed it between her legs, opening for him.

Ian felt a stirring in his loins. She was hot and wet like Mary.

Her voice echoed in his ear. "I'm ready for ye."

"Dughall, for God's sake! You're killing me."

He felt his brother rise to his knees, straddle her, and hold her arms down. He held his breath as Dughall lay on top of her and kissed her body.

Her voice was desperate. "Now, my Lord!"

Ian threw off his covers and sat up in bed. He stroked himself and felt the ache of frustration. "All right, Brother," he whispered. "Do it now."

Flashes of thrusting made him squirm, her warm silkiness overwhelming his senses. Ian gasped as the lovers shuddered with pleasure. His body flushed and sweat beaded on his forehead. The lass kneeled and ran her wet tongue along his brother's thigh. She wanted to do it again.

"Ohhhhh...." Ian groaned. "Not again. I can't bear it!"

His cry woke Alex and Jessie. They jumped out of bed and fumbled around trying to light a candle.

Alex tried to calm him. "Is it Dughall?"

Ian nodded, with a wild look in his eyes.

"Are they hurtin' him?"

"Nay."

"Is he all right?"

Ian groaned. "Aye, he's better than all right."

Jessie held the candle and pointed to Ian's groin. "Husband, look."

Ian grabbed a blanket and covered himself.

Alex brought a hand to his mouth to hide a smile. "It's all right. Our son became a man tonight. Let's go back to bed."

As Ian settled into bed, his thoughts were with his brother. After a while, he closed his eyes and drifted. "Well brother, I guess it's not all bad."

Gilbert Gordon

LESSONS

HUNTLY CASTLE
NOVEMBER 1 1636
THE NEXT DAY 3AM

Kate lay next to the sleeping young Lord. She curled against him, her backside to his warm body. *I don't want to leave him.*

The air cooled as the hearth fire waned. She sat up and let her eyes adjust to the darkness. Kate slipped out of bed, pulled on her robe, and tied the belt loosely in front. *How does he know what I want?* She slid her feet into slippers and arranged her hair.

Kate leaned over and kissed his temple. The young Lord's lips moved slightly as he slept. "It's been a pleasure, lad. You'll see me again; whether he sends me or not." She ran her fingers lightly along his jaw, feeling the prickle of stubble. "He's innocent, yet he knows what to do. It's as though he can read my desires."

Dughall stretched his body on the silk sheets.

"How can two men look so alike, yet have such different hearts?" She sighed. "Don't even think it, Kate. You know who you belong to." She walked to the window and looked out into the night. Thin wisps of fog floated through the courtyard, illuminated by a waxing moon. In a few hours dawn would break. "This is madness. I must return to my quarters before the Earl wakes."

Kate crossed the room, opened the door, and stepped into the hallway. She closed the door and was startled by a figure leaning against the wall.

Blackheart stepped out of the shadows. "Enjoy yourself, Kate?"

His tone frightened her. "My Lord, I did what ye asked."

The Earl stroked her hair. "I like it when you wear it down."

She drew a breath. *He reeks of whisky. Dear God! He's been waiting all night.*

Blackheart untied the belt of her robe and let it fall open. His eyes were on the patch between her legs. "Kate, Kate. It's not fair to tease ye with that young lad. You need a real man."

Her heart pounded erratically. "Aye my Lord. Let's go to your bedchamber."

"That we will." He cupped her breasts and kissed her roughly.

The taste of whisky overpowered her.

"Sweet lass, you're as bonny as you were ten years ago. I'm sure that the lad was taken with ye." He released her and stared, his eyes narrowing with suspicion.

She hugged herself to stop shaking. To show fear would be a dreadful mistake.

Blackheart growled, "We're going to my bed and you'll tell me everything that ye did during these last four hours."

She avoided his eyes. "He's just a lad. I let him take me, and then we fell asleep."

He tipped her chin. "Don't lie to me. Don't make me hurt ye."

Kate struggled to hold back tears. "Forgive me, my Lord. I did what ye asked."

He picked her up in his arms, his fingers digging into soft flesh.

She saw anger flickering in his eyes. "You said you'd be grateful."

His tone was hard. "You'll tell me the truth and I'll show you how grateful I am."

"Don't hurt me!" she sobbed. Her tears betrayed her.

Blackheart smiled. "Now Kate, you know I never do anything to ye that ye don't want."

***

Morning light filtered into Dughall's bedchamber. He woke suddenly, wondering if Kate was next to him. The young Lord rolled over and saw that she was gone. He ran a hand across the sheet where she'd rested her body and lingered on a wet spot. "Oh God. Was it a dream?" He caught a whiff of lavender, and picked a long strand of chestnut hair from the pillow. "She *was* here."

He sat up in bed and brought a hand to his temple. His head throbbed painfully and his mouth was dry. "Ach! It must be the whisky."

There was a knock on the door and Murdock entered. He walked to the bedside and held out a silver goblet. "My Lord. Water with a pinch of willow bark. Just what ye need when you've had a bit of whisky the night before."

Dughall took the cup and drank it down, wincing at the bitter taste. "Thank ye, friend. That's the last time I drink whisky."

Murdock smiled. "We shall see, my Lord." He walked to the hearth and stoked the fire with apple wood, poking the ashes until the embers caught. "Did ye sleep well, lad?"

"I didna get much sleep. Father sent a lass to my bedchamber."

Murdock came to the bedside. "I don't wish to pry into your private matters, but if ye need to talk I'm here."

Dughall rolled his eyes. "She was bonny!" He held up the strand of hair. "Long hair and deep green eyes. Her body smelled like lavender. I thought it was the whisky until she took my finger in her mouth and sucked it."

Murdock raised his eyebrows.

"I'd never been with a lass before. She showed me what to do and drove me mad with pleasure. I didn't know there were so many ways to make love to a woman. You should see what they do in France!"

Murdock smiled. "You've had quite a night, m'Lord."

"Aye."

The servant hesitated. "M'Lord. You mustn't speak to anyone about this."

"Why? Her name was Kate. I want to see her again."

"Do ye know who she is?"

"Nay."

"Kate is the Earl's mistress. No one touches her but the Earl. We don't even dare to look her in the face. If he sent her to ye, it was a gift. Only he can send her again."

Dughall frowned. "She belongs to him?"

"Aye."

His head throbbed. "Why would he send her to another man? Why does he not marry her?"

"All good questions."

Dughall rubbed his temples. "I don't understand it! He won't let me marry the lass I love. Then he sends me one I can't have."

"M'Lord. It's getting late. Gilbert requests your presence in the dining room. You start your lessons today with the old schoolmaster."

Dughall groaned. "Oh no. Not with this headache."

Murdock smiled. "It will be gone before ye know it. Let's get ye dressed and down to breakfast."

***

Gilbert stood in the dining hall, listening to his father rant. His stomach churned as the man belted his whisky and smashed the glass in the fireplace. *What's wrong with him? I think he's lost his mind.*

Blackheart's tone was threatening. "God damn it! Are ye listening, lad?"

"Aye."

"I'm going for a bath. See that your brother starts his lessons with the schoolmaster after breakfast. It's best that I don't see him this morning."

Gilbert's nerves were raw. "As you wish, Father."

"We have a traitor among us. Someone told the Duke that his grandson was here. The peasants didn't know 'til the day of the party. It has to be someone close, who knew we were returning with him."

"How will we find the traitor?"

"I talked to Connor last night. He found out who asked questions and who left the castle after we returned. We narrowed it down to two men. I had them taken below." Blackheart stared. "You'd better get ready, one of them was yours."

The young Lord swallowed hard. "Who was it?"

Blackheart flexed his hand, making a fist. "Mills."

Gilbert's head ached. Mills was a trusted servant who'd been with him since childhood. Could it be him? He'd told the man about finding a lad with the clan's birthmark. Mills asked questions, but it hadn't seemed suspicious. His mind raced. *Damn it! He disappeared for a day after we returned, saying his mother was sick.* Another glass broke in the fireplace, sending shards all over the floor.

Blackheart stared. "Did ye hear me, lad? Mills could be the traitor."

Gilbert paled. "Aye. What do you want me to do?"

"Nothing for now. Fang will find out who the guilty party is. Take care of your brother. I'll send for ye later."

"Aye, Father."

As the Earl left the dining room, Gilbert held his stomach. *I pray it isn't you, old friend. I'll have to hang you.*

***

In the bowels of Huntly Castle lay a catacomb of ancient punishment cells. The rooms were dim, with a dirt floor and manacles on the wall. Doors were heavy and mold covered, with small barred windows.

Bruce Mills sat on the floor of a cell and hugged his knees. His shirt was gone and his back bore bloody stripes that Fang had given him that morning. He wiped his nose and sniffled. "God help me. I'm so afraid."

The servant heard the door to a nearby cell creak open and muffled conversation. He recognized the voice of Patrick Duff as he argued and cried. Fang's voice boomed, threatening him with torture. Bruce shivered as he heard the sound of manacles snapping around the lad's wrists. *God in heaven.* He heard Fang laugh, then the sound of the whip striking the lad's flesh. He counted the strokes, ten, then twenty, and covered his ears as the lad screamed. Fang demanded a confession.

Bruce shook with fear, yet guilt gnawed at him. *I can't let a man suffer because of me.* He stood and walked to the door, and listened to Fang railing at the lad.

"I don't know the Duke!" Patrick cried.

Bruce's eyes were vacant. *I'm a dead man.*

The beating resumed. His mind counted strokes, first thirty then forty. Bruce retched as Patrick begged for mercy, his voice growing weak. He pounded on the door and yelled out. "For God's sake, stop it! I confess. Let the lad go."

Sweat dripped from his forehead as the beating stopped. He heard the click of manacles unlocking and a thud as the lad dropped to the ground. Bruce leaned against the wall and hugged himself. His heart squeezed painfully as he thought of his wife and son. *Forgive me Catherine,* he prayed. He blanched as the door opened.

***

Dughall's headache waned as he ate breakfast in the dining hall. He was thirsty, and drank cup after cup of water.

Gilbert was in a foul mood. He brooded and snapped at the serving lass as she brought another plate of cakes. "Leave us alone, wench. We're done."

Dughall looked up. "Brother, are ye all right?"

"Nay, lad. I have dirty business to attend to. Are you done eating?"

Dughall pushed back his plate. "Aye. I'm feeling better now."

"Well, I'm glad someone is. Father's in a foul mood." He stood and knocked over a cup, flooding the table. "Damn it! Can nothing go right today?"

Dughall joined him. "The lass will clean it up. Is the schoolmaster here yet?"

"Aye, he's in the library. Father says that he'll start with literature. You can read, can't you?"

Dughall reddened. "I'm not ignorant. I can read the Bible."

Gilbert shook his head. They left the dining room and walked down a corridor towards the library. Gilbert hesitated as they stopped in front of an ornate door. "Behave yourself today. I have a mess on my hands and won't have time for you. I'll tell Murdock to pick you up after your lessons."

Dughall nodded. "All right."

"Take a bath and put on fresh clothes. Formal ones. There may be an execution in the courtyard tonight." He pushed the door open and led him into the library.

Logan Crombie stood behind the desk, thumbing through a book on Greek literature. He pushed the spectacles up on his nose, bowing his head. "My Lords."

Gilbert addressed him with impatience. "Crombie, this is my brother Dughall. I must be on my way. See that you teach him well."

Crombie picked up a book and motioned for Dughall to sit opposite him.

"As you wish my Lord."

***

Blackheart sat in the copper tub, soaking his body. He lay back, allowing the hot water to surround his neck, and reviewed events in his mind. "Barrie and Morris told me about the lad when they returned from Peterhead. They were told to keep quiet, or suffer a whipping. Only Gilbert and I knew about it. Someone close betrayed us." He flushed with anger. "It has to be Mills! Gilbert can't keep his mouth shut."

Blackheart rolled the soap between his hands and lathered his groin. The thought of Kate moving her soft lips along the lad's naked body disturbed him. "She taught him the French practice! Has the whole world gone mad?"

Connor entered the chamber with a set of towels and the Earl's formal clothes. He hung them up and laid the towels on the washstand. "M'Lord. Would you like me to send the Murray lass to ye?"

Blackheart frowned. "Nay, keep her away. I'm not fit for female company today."

"As you wish, m'Lord."

There was a timid knock on the door. Blackheart stared. "God damn it! Get out of here and see who it is."

***

Connor opened the door and saw a young lad standing outside. He walked into the hallway and closed the door quietly behind him. "What is it, Rabbie?"

The boy took a breath. "I ran all the way. Fang sent me. He found the traitor!"

Connor paled. "Who is it, lad?"

His eyes grew wide. "Bruce Mills. Will there be an execution?"

Connor glared, silencing him. "It's not up to me, lad. What about the other man? Patrick Duff?"

"He's in rough shape. Fang gave him forty lashes."

"Tell Fang to bring Patrick to my quarters and lay him on my bed. Face down, mind ye. I'll send for a healer. Do ye understand?"

"Aye."

"Be off with ye. You don't want to be near the Earl when I tell him." The lad took his leave, turning on his heels and running down the hallway.

Connor straightened his shirt. "The Earl's in a foul mood. I hope he doesn't kill the messenger."

***

Blackheart sat up in the tub and glared. "What is it now?"

Connor handed him a towel. "M'Lord. I talked to a messenger from Fang. He got a confession from one of the men."

"Excellent. Who is it?"

"Gilbert's servant, Bruce Mills."

Blackheart's anger exploded. "Damn him to hell! I thought so. The Duke couldn't get a man close to me, so he planted one with my son." He stood and let the soapy water drip off. "Gilbert can be an idiot, sometimes. He talks too much."

Connor averted his eyes and handed him a towel.

Blackheart's mind raced as he dried himself. "Tell Murdock to stay with Dughall. Keep him out of my sight! Then find Gilbert and tell him to meet me in my study."

"Aye, m'Lord."

Blackheart slipped on a silk shirt and stepped into his kilt. Connor was almost to the door. "Wait. Have the carpenter prepare the gallows in the courtyard. Spread the word that we're executing a traitor tonight. Everyone is to be present. See that Mills' wife and son are kept under guard."

"As you wish, m'Lord."

"When I get through with him, no one will dare betray us."

***

The study was a solemn room, dimly lit with wall sconces. Curtains masked tall windows and overstuffed chairs filled the room. Gilbert entered the room with trepidation. As his eyes adjusted to the light, he saw his father in a chair, sipping whisky. His stomach churned. *How can he drink that in the morning?*

Blackheart's eyes narrowed. "Sit, Gilbert. We're going to have a talk."

Gilbert sat in a chair opposite his father. *He's in a foul mood. I'd best keep quiet.*

Blackheart filled his glass from the decanter, poured another whisky, and handed it to him. "Drink this. You're going to need it."

Gilbert held up the glass and stared at the amber liquid. He took a breath and belted down a swallow. His throat was on fire.

Blackheart watched him intently. "Tell me about Bruce Mills."

Gilbert paled and took another swallow.

"Don't lie to me! What did he know about Dughall?"

Gilbert gripped the glass, afraid that his hand would shake. "Forgive me, Father. I told him that we found my brother. He asked me when we were going to get him. Mills has been with me since I was a lad. I didn't think he'd betray me."

Blackheart scowled. "I thought so."

Gilbert's fear blossomed. "He's the traitor, then?"

Blackheart belted his whisky. "Aye. Fang got a confession out of him this morning."

"Damn!"

"We have to decide his fate. He's your servant. What do you propose we do with him?"

"I don't know."

"Come on, lad! Act like an Earl."

Gilbert searched his mind for an appropriate punishment. "I trusted him and he betrayed us. We have to hang him."

"Good. You've learned your lessons well. It's the only thing that can be done. We can't let the help think that it's acceptable to be loyal to outsiders." Blackheart took out a pipe and filled it with tobacco. He lit it with a taper and inhaled deeply.

Gilbert held his breath. The rank smell assaulted his senses.

The Earl exhaled, filling the air between them with smoke. "We'll make a spectacle of it. Haul him up there with his shirt off. Turn him around so the help can see his stripes. Put the fear of God in them all."

Gilbert winced. "I'm sure Fang made a mess of him. What about his wife and son?"

"Catherine and your little friend Charles? Make them watch. There's nothing like a wailing woman to drive a point home. You can do what you want with them after he's dead."

"I'll think of something."

Blackheart handed him the pipe. "Take a puff or two. You need to dull your sense of smell so you can stand where we're going."

Gilbert took the stem into his mouth and inhaled the smoke. He coughed.

Blackheart smiled. "Let's visit Fang and get the whole story. It's time you saw what happens to men who are taken below."

***

Murdock knocked on the door of the library. It was late morning, and the young Lord's lesson was nearly over. He opened the heavy door and slipped inside.

Logan Crombie picked a piece of lint off his green sweater. He acknowledged the servant and showed him a seat.

Dughall sat in a chair with a book across his lap, reading aloud. He came to the end of a chapter and looked up. "Murdock."

"Aye, m'Lord."

"This book is about lords and ladies, and what they did on a hunting trip. I don't know all the words, but I will soon."

"My Lord," Crombie said. "You're an apt and willing pupil. It will be a pleasure to teach ye."

Dughall smiled. "I want to learn about other places and times. I want to read about France." He held out his hands. "Look at all the books."

Murdock was glad. Perhaps the lad would want to stay after all. "The Earl has quite a library."

"Teacher, are we done for today?"

"Aye, my Lord. We will meet again tomorrow morning."

"Can I take this book with me?"

"It would please me if you did."

Dughall stood and stretched. He tucked the book under his arm and walked to the door with his servant. He turned and faced Crombie. "Thank ye, teacher."

"You're welcome, my Lord."

Murdock opened the door and guided him into the hallway.

***

The stairway to the catacombs was narrow. Gilbert followed his father as they descended into the lower levels, taking the granite steps one by one. The smell of urine and feces assaulted him. He took a white kerchief from his pocket and cupped his nose. "Father. This is disgusting!" He ran his hand along the wall and stared at his mold covered fingers.

Blackheart chuckled. "It's as close to Hell as it can get."

"Fang lives down here?"

"Aye. He likes it that way. No one bothers him. The man's an animal but he's useful."

They reached the bottom of the stairs and walked a corridor that was dimly lit by wall torches. Gilbert gagged as he pushed aside a cobweb. "Dear God. How much farther?"

"Fang's quarters are ahead."

An arch to their right led into a small chamber. They walked into the room and looked around. Crude pine furniture filled one end of the chamber, a bed, washstand, table and chair. The linen on the bed was streaked with reddish-brown stains. A water pitcher sat in a cracked bowl, covered with dust and dead flies.

Gilbert wrinkled his nose. The chamber pot was overflowing. The other end of the chamber had a worktable that was covered with instruments of torture. Ropes and chains sat among thumbscrews, knives, and a board of nails. On the wall hung an assortment of leather whips, some plain and some laced with bits of iron or glass. Several were caked with blood. Bile rose in his throat. "For God's sake, Father. Do we have to stay here?"

Blackheart scowled. "Aye."

Behind them, Fang Adams cleared his throat and spit on the floor.

Gilbert turned to see the man that everyone avoided. He was short but solidly built, with a heavily muscled chest. A long scar ran along his jaw, a souvenir from a knife fight. He clenched his fists, making his forearms bulge.

He reeks of body odor, Gilbert thought. There were lice crawling in the man's hair and fresh blood on his breeks.

"My Lords."

Blackheart nodded. "I hear that ye got a confession."

Fang grinned. "Aye. That bastard Mills."

"What did he say about the Duke?"

"He's been taking gold from the Duke since his daughter disappeared. He notified Lord Drake when ye returned with the young Lord."

Gilbert stiffened. "I want to see Mills."

Blackheart stared. "Why?"

Gilbert took a whip from the wall. "I have a personal score to settle with him."

"We'll see him after we finish with Fang."

"He's my servant. I want to see him alone."

"Very well," Blackheart said. "Take him to Mills. I'll wait here. I need to talk to ye about the execution."

Gilbert's heart pounded as Fang led him down the hallway. He walked far behind the man, avoiding lice jumping off his head. They stopped in front of a heavy door and unlatched it. It creaked open. Gilbert saw a half-naked figure sitting on the ground, chained by the neck to the wall. Mills looked up and met his gaze, with eyes that were glazed with pain.

"I'll put him in manacles for ye, m'Lord. Then you can beat him as much as ye like."

"Nay, leave us! Go back to my father."

Fang checked the prisoner's chains. "He can't hurt ye, m'Lord. He's chained to the wall."

"I said leave us."

"As you wish." Fang pulled the chain taut, choking the man. "Behave for your master, or I'll skin ye alive with a hot knife." He dropped the chain and left the room.

Gilbert listened to Fang's fading footsteps. He crossed the room and examined the prisoner's bloody back. "God in heaven."

Mills' voice was weak. "Does it look as bad as it feels?"

He crouched in front of the prisoner. "Aye."

"Forgive me, m'Lord."

Gilbert's voice was laced with frustration. "You've been with me since I was a lad. I thought you were my friend. Why did you betray us?"

Mills reddened. "It seemed harmless. All I had to do was look out for the Duke's daughter or her child. I never thought they'd return."

"What did he offer you?"

"A few gold coins each month." He took a ragged breath. "I know it was wrong. Forgive me."

Gilbert swallowed hard. His head ached as he thought of what they'd do to the man. "Father intends to hang you tonight."

Mills shuddered. "Fang told me. Oh God. I'm so afraid! M'Lord, send me to the gallows but spare my family. They know nothing of this."

Gilbert squeezed his shoulder. "I'll see what I can do."

Mills sobbed. "Bless ye, m'Lord."

The young Lord stood and looked around the cell. A rat crawled along the wall and disappeared into a hole. He gagged as he moved to the door. "Goodbye old friend," he whispered. "God have mercy on ye."

His heart was heavy as he walked the corridor to Fang's quarters. He entered the chamber and heard his father giving instructions.

"Flog him again before ye bring him up. Take care that ye don't kill him. I'll make an example of him."

Gilbert was appalled. "Isn't it enough, Father? His back is ripped to shreds. Can't we just hang him?"

Blackheart growled, "How dare ye challenge me! He's a traitor and we'll show him no mercy."

"You've tortured him enough."

"Get out of my sight, lad! I'll deal with ye later."

Gilbert fled into the corridor with his heart in his throat. He heard his father giving final instructions. "Use a glass whip on him."

The young Lord held his head in his hands. "Nay! I can't bear it."

Blackheart appeared at his side and scolded him. "An Earl must never show weakness."

"Mills was my friend. I can't do this to him."

"He's a traitor. Let this be a lesson to ye. We don't have friends."

He felt nauseous. "I hate this place. Can we go?"

Blackheart ranted. "Friend? Are ye daft? He's lucky I don't skin him alive."

Gilbert paled. This could get a lot worse. "Father, please. I'm going to be sick. Can we go?"

"No stomach for it? How will ye ever take my place?"

The lad vomited on the floor, and retched until there was no more bile.

Blackheart clucked his disapproval. "God almighty! You're worse than a woman. Are ye done?"

Gilbert nodded weakly.

"Let's go. We have to prepare for tonight."

***

Dughall followed Murdock to the dining room to have his midday meal. Neither the Earl nor Gilbert was there, so the servant lingered, leaning against the wall.

"Murdock, why don't ye sit down and eat with me?"

"It's not proper, m'Lord. There would be hell to pay. You don't want to punish me, do ye?"

"Nay. I'll never do that."

"Don't say that, lad. The day may come when you have to. Then you mustn't think of me."

Dughall frowned. "I don't understand it."

"You will someday."

"Gilbert said that there might be an execution."

"The Earl identified a traitor in our midst. The man confessed this morning. A hanging is in order."

Dughall put down his fork. "A traitor. How interesting. What did he do? Murder someone? Or tell secrets to our enemies?"

"Nay, lad. It seems he was loyal to the Duke. He told him that his grandson had returned."

Dughall paled. He couldn't let Grandfather's man die on his account. He pushed back the plate and threw his napkin aside.

"You haven't finished lunch. Are ye all right, m'Lord?"

"Nay. Do ye know this man?"

Murdock sighed. "I know him well. Bruce Mills, one of Gilbert's servants."

Dughall brightened. "Then Gilbert gets to decide. I can talk to him."

"My Lord, this is not your affair. I've been told to keep ye away from Gilbert and the Earl. They're in foul moods."

Dughall pushed back his chair. "I can't let this happen."

Murdock kneeled and held his shoulders. "Trust me, lad. There's nothing you can do. The Duke wouldn't want you to put yourself in harm's way for any of his men. Promise me that you'll stay out of it."

Dughall's heart sank. It made sense. "I promise. I don't like hangings. Will ye be there tonight?"

"Aye. I won't leave your side."

"Thank ye, Murdock."

"Come along now, they're pouring your bath."

***

The sun went down soon after the evening meal. All able bodied inhabitants of the castle put on their wraps and made their way to the courtyard. Torches illuminated the far end of the square, where a platform holding the gallows had been hastily erected. The carpenter checked the trap door one more time. In a quick movement, the lever triggered the bolt and released the door. Satisfied, he reset the trap and took his place in the crowd.

It was a cold and clear night, with stars visible in the sky above. Snow clouds hovered to the east. Dughall and Murdock stood in the castle hall, near the door to the courtyard.

"Crombie says he'll teach me about the stars and the moon. Did ye know that the earth's not flat?"

Murdock buttoned the young Lord's cape. "Seems flat to me."

"Aye. But it's not."

"You've really taken to your lessons, lad. That's a good thing."

"I didn't know there was so much to learn." He shook with anticipation. "Oh God, I'm so nervous. I fainted at the last hanging."

Murdock raised his eyebrows. "You mustn't do that tonight. The Earl will expect his sons to be strong."

"I wish we could stop it."

"M'Lord. Remember your promise. Stay out of it. You don't want to see either of us hurt."

Dughall nodded. "All right. But I don't have to like it."

Murdock sighed. "It won't give me pleasure to see the man hang. I knew him well. Yesterday you asked me about being a Lord. This is part of it. You must punish a traitor."

Bridget and Julianna passed by, nodding to the young Lord. Bridget donned a wool wrap and bent over to lace up her shoe. Julianna pushed her blouse off her shoulders and licked her lips seductively. Dughall's eyes grew wide.

Murdock touched his shoulder. "Look away!" he whispered. "Don't encourage her."

Dughall averted his eyes.

Murdock cleared his throat. "Bridget, the young Lord has important business tonight. It would be best if you kept your sister away from him."

Bridget noticed her sister's antics and flushed with embarrassment. "Julianna! Have ye no shame? Forgive us, m'Lord." She pinched the girl's ear with her thumb and forefinger and led her to the courtyard door.

Dughall stared. "Ha! What's wrong with her?"

"She wants to bed ye, lad. She does this to all the Lords. Don't let her near ye."

"Why?"

"Julianna can't keep her mouth shut. The Earl calls her the little harlot."

Dughall laughed.

Murdock threw a wrap over his arm. "It won't be long before the snow flies. I'll bring a blanket in case you get cold." The sound of a drum, a large bodhran, echoed from the courtyard. "My Lord, they're calling the crowd to order. They'll bring out the prisoner soon. We must go."

Dughall winced. "Oh God. Do we have to watch it?"

Murdock opened the door. The drumbeat was louder now and more insistent. "Aye, m'Lord. I'll stay at your side."

With a heavy heart, he followed the servant into the courtyard.

***

Bruce Mills kneeled in his cell and prayed for his soul. "I've been foolish, God. Greed has been my downfall. Forgive me." Tears fell as he thought of his wife and son. "Dear Jesus, protect my family. Help the young Lord." The door creaked open and Fang entered. Mills looked up fearfully. "Is it time?"

Fang didn't answer. He unlocked the neck chain, jerked him to a standing position, and struck him hard across the face, splitting his lip. The condemned man stared through a haze of tears. Fang shoved him against the wall, gripped his right hand, and snapped it into a manacle above his head. He grabbed his left hand and locked it in the other manacle.

Mills felt the cold wall against his chest. Blood roared in his ears, fueling his senses. "I've told ye everything. What are ye doing?"

Fang took a whip from his belt and cracked it in the air.

Mills took a ragged breath. "Isn't it enough? You mean to hang me. What do ye want?"

Fang's voice was cold. "I want to hurt ye."

***

The courtyard was full of people. Dozens of men, women, and children stood around the gallows. Some jostled to get a better view, while others stayed their distance. Dughall scanned the courtyard. "The whole castle's here."

"Aye, m'Lord."

The drummer stood at the gallows, holding a large bodhran by its wooden crossbars. He beat the drum, calling the crowd to order.

Dughall took a breath. The drumbeat echoed in the courtyard and vibrated the flagstones beneath his feet. He held a hand to his chest, but all he could feel was the drumbeat.

"Are ye all right, m'Lord?"

Dughall shuddered. "Aye." He stared at the drummer, watching the beater strike the drum. He wrinkled his nose. Some people smelled like urine.

Murdock led him to a guarded area where the Lords would stand. Blackheart and Gilbert were nowhere to be seen. The crowd grew quiet as a matronly woman and her son were forced to stand before the gallows. The woman's eyes searched the crowd frantically. The lad looked to be about fourteen, with fair skin and red hair.

"He looks like my brother Ian."

Murdock nodded as a guard shoved the lad closer to his mother.

Dughall swallowed hard. "Who are they?"

Murdock whispered. "The traitor's wife Catherine and his son Charles."

"They have to watch? That's cruel."

The drum beat faster, announcing the Earl's arrival. Blackheart and Gilbert walked across the courtyard and stood near the platform. Gilbert's face was red. He massaged his temples as the Earl growled at him.

Dughall caught part of their conversation.

"…hate you!"

"Hate me if ye must. You'll understand someday."

"Gilbert doesn't want to hang him." Dughall whispered.

Murdock stiffened. "Let them be, m'Lord. Don't speak unless spoken to."

Dughall nodded. He glanced at his father and felt his fury.

Blackheart glared, and then turned his attention to the gallows.

"Don't look at them." Murdock whispered. "We don't want to draw their anger."

Gilbert paced nervously, his eyes locked on a door at the end of the courtyard. The door opened and three men emerged. Fang and another man held the prisoner under the arms, dragging him forward. The man's hands were bound and he was bare-chested.

Dughall met his eyes for a moment. "God in heaven," he whispered. "He's half dead already."

The crowd murmured as they walked him up the stairs to the platform that supported the gallows. He was met with cries of "Traitor!"

Bruce Mills couldn't stand alone. His legs failed and he sank to his knees.

Fang was at his side. "Stand up bastard, or I'll take ye below again."

The prisoner steadied himself and stood, first with one leg, then the next. Blood trickled from his lip.

Blackheart walked up the stairs and stood next to the condemned man. His presence agitated the crowd. "Tonight we come together to execute a traitor. This man, Bruce Mills, confessed that his loyalties are to the Duke. He dared to spy on us and report back to his master."

A man in the crowd raised his fist. "Hang him."

"Not yet." Blackheart motioned to Fang. "Turn him around."

Fang grabbed Mills by the shoulders and turned him so the crowd could see the stripes on his back. The glass whip had cut him to the bone across his shoulders.

The crowd grew quiet. Some looked away, while others were riveted to the sight.

Catherine Mills sobbed. Her son shook with anger as he held her in his arms.

Blackheart ranted. "This is what will happen to any of ye that betray us! There will be no mercy."

Dughall's heart ached. "They tortured him. God help him."

Murdock whispered. "My Lord. Turn slowly and face your father. He's watching you."

Dughall turned. The Earl's cold rage frightened him.

Blackheart motioned to Fang and descended the stairs, taking his place by Gilbert.

Fang turned Mills, slipped the noose over his neck, and tightened it behind his ear. The prisoner took a ragged breath. His eyes widened at the sight of his wife and son.

Dughall's senses were flooded with the man's love for his family. "Murdock! It's breaking my heart. We can't let this happen."

"It's too late, lad."

Blackheart frowned. "Gilbert! He's your servant. Give the order."

The young Lord's voice was weak. "Hang him."

Fang pulled the lever, releasing the door beneath the prisoner. He grinned as the body dropped, cleanly snapping his neck. The scent of feces laced the air as the dying man evacuated his bowels. The rope creaked as the body turned slowly. Catherine Mills knelt with her son and made the sign of the cross. She didn't wail.

Blackheart stared. "Stupid woman! What will ye do with them?"

Gilbert stepped forward. "Fang, take his wife and son to the main gate and put them out. I wish to never lay eyes on them."

Blackheart stared. "What? You're letting them go?"

"Aye."

"Hmmphh…"

Fang came down from the gallows and took Catherine's arm. The woman shook off his grip and held her head high. She took her son's hand and followed Fang across the courtyard to the main gate. They were turned out into the night with only the clothes on their backs. A light snow started to fall.

Dughall shivered. "They'll freeze to death. It's wrong."

Murdock sighed. "M'Lord. Gilbert granted them a second chance. It would have been worse had they stayed here."

"I don't understand it. Oh God! My head hurts like the devil. Take me to my room."

Murdock frowned. "You do look poorly. I'll say that you're ill. They may let ye go."

Dughall nodded.

"Try to look sick and let me do the talking." They walked over to the Earl, where Murdock bowed respectfully. "My Lord. Your son has taken ill."

Dughall's face was ashen. He really did feel sick. His voice was weak. "Forgive me, Father."

Blackheart's eyes narrowed. "Stay out of my sight, lad. Go to your bedchamber and get some sleep. We'll talk in the morning."

Dughall shuddered.

"As you wish, m'Lord." Murdock led the lad across the courtyard into the castle. They walked the long corridor in silence and turned into another hallway.

"Father hates me. I can feel it."

"He doesn't hate ye."

"I think he's mad about the lass."

"Now, why would he be mad about that? He sent her."

"I don't know, Murdock."

***

They entered his bedchamber and lit a candle. Dughall thought of the woman and her son, trying to keep warm in the forest. There was nothing he could do.

Murdock stoked the fire with apple wood and poured water into the bowl. "Wash up, lad. You should lie in bed in case the Earl visits."

Dughall splashed cold water on his face. "I can't sleep yet."

"My Lord. Would you like your book? I'll light some more candles."

"Aye. Maybe it will take my mind off the hanging."

The servant helped him undress and tucked him into bed. He lit two candles on the table and handed him the book. "I'll return to make sure the candles are out."

Dughall shivered. "Thank ye, friend."

Murdock took his leave and left the room. Dughall opened the book to a new chapter. Words blurred on the page as he tried to focus his eyes. "I should read. There's much I don't understand about being a Lord." He struggled with a few pages and put it aside. His heart throbbed.

Dughall got out of bed and sank to his knees. The floor wasn't as cold as the forest. He made the sign of the cross and folded his hands in prayer. "Dear Jesus, help the woman and her son." He thought of his family, of Alex and Jessie and Ian. He prayed for Aunt Maggie, cold in the ground. His heart swelled as he remembered the lass in the forest. They could never marry. "Life was so simple a few days ago. I knew what was right and wrong. I want to go home."

He crawled into bed and stretched under the sheets, thoroughly exhausted. Dughall closed his eyes and dreamed. He was home on the North Sea. He stood on the cliffs, felt the wind in his hair, and basked in the smell of seaweed and brine. He watched puffins attending their nests, and a gray seal catching fish. "I love the sea. I miss it." Gulls wheeled and shrieked above. They dived into the surf, emerging with beaks of fish. "It was a bad dream. I'll find Maggie at her cottage, singing as she mends nets. Mother and Father and Ian will ask where I've been. We'll laugh when I tell them about the dream. Me, a lord. Ha!"

He walked along the cliff picking violets until he reached the point. Below, the beach was desolate and the harbor empty. A storm rolled in from the southeast, roiling the water and exposing jagged rocks. Lightning flashed as a gaggle of geese glided landward. He recited a rhyme from childhood.

"Wild geese, wild geese, goin' to the sea,
Good weather it will be.
Wild geese, wild geese, goin' to the hill,
The weather it will spill."

"Time to go home."

Dughall looked behind him. The stone cottages were gone, replaced by fields of heather as far as the eye could see; fields that led to the lass in the forest.

Jamison

THE PLOT THICKENS

PETERHEAD
NOVEMBER 2 1636
The Next Day

Jamison was the first to wake, with the smell of burnt peat in his nostrils. The fire in the hearth was out and the room was cold. Last night, he and the Duke rode into Peterhead and secured rooms at the only decent inn, The Crack. A primitive place, certainly not what they were used to. His eyes adjusted to the morning light. He slipped out of bed and gasped as his feet touched the cold floor. Jamison glanced at the window. Light frost coated the panes and obscured the view. "Looks like winter already."

He stood at the chamber pot and relieved himself of the ale he'd indulged in after the Duke went to bed. His head ached from a hangover. "Ach! I should know better."

Jamison stepped into his kilt, pinning it on each side. He tucked in his shirt and pulled on a heavy sweater. His belly rumbled. "These Dutch are strange people. I hope they serve decent food." He poured water into the bowl and washed his face.

"The Duke looked like death when we arrived. Too harsh of a trip for an old man, but I'll not be the one to tell him." Jamison pulled on his boots, slipping a black knife into the right sock. He left the room, walked the narrow hallway, and entered the Duke's room. The old man was in bed, his face racked with pain.

"My Lord, shall I ask the kitchen for hot water? I'll prepare the medicine the healer gave ye."

The Duke's voice was weak. "Aye."

"Perhaps we should rest and visit Whinnyfold tomorrow."

The Duke groaned. "Nay! I must know what happened to my daughter."

Jamison sighed. "All right. I'll get your medicine and tell the kitchen to prepare us breakfast."

"Thank you, lad."

"I'll return soon, my Lord, to assist with your morning ablutions."

***

Breakfast was being served by the time the Duke came downstairs. Jamison helped him to a table and sat across from him. "My Lord. The horses are being groomed and fed. One threw a shoe, so they're taking care of that. We should be ready to go by mid-morning."

The Duke warmed his hands around a cup of tea. His lower lip trembled. "Thank ye, lad."

"Are ye all right my Lord?"

"I'll live. The bark tea will help these old bones."

Jamison raised his eyebrows.

The Duke snorted. "Do you think I don't see it? I'm a fool to make this trip in my state."

"My Lord, I never meant to imply…"

"For God's sake, I'm not angry. I don't have much time left. I must know what happened to Christal."

Jamison's head pounded. *Damn that ale! I can't think straight.*

The innkeeper's wife brought ham and eggs and brown bread. The buxom lass lay plates in front of them and poured water into cups. Jamison wrinkled his nose. The woman smelled of fish and salt.

She wiped her hands on her apron. "Will there be anything else, m'Lords?"

"Aye," the Duke said. "We have business in Whinnyfold with a man named Alex Hay. Is there anyone here who can lead us there? We will pay."

She raised her eyebrows. "My husband Klaas can take ye there. He knows the man."

The Duke coughed. "Good. Tell him to meet us here. As soon as our horses are ready, we'll go."

HUNTLY CASTLE

Dughall's stomach churned as he sat at the breakfast table watching Father and Gilbert fight. He put down his fork and paid attention.

Blackheart drummed his fingers on the table. "You shouldn't have let them go! The woman's not a problem, but the lad will come back to cut your throat in a few years."

Gilbert pouted. "Why would he do that? I gave him his life."

"Well, now. That's not how he would see it. You killed his father. You turned them out into the cold. It was a foolish move."

Gilbert clenched his fists in frustration.

Dughall's mind wandered. He saw the woman and her son walking in the woods, huddled together to keep warm. Connor approached from behind, pulled out a dirk, and slit the lad's throat. The woman screamed. She was next.

"You had them killed." Dughall blurted.

They stopped talking and stared. Blackheart nodded. "Impressive, lad. You're smarter than I thought."

Gilbert blanched. "What? You sent someone after them?"

"Aye. Connor took care of it. Someday you'll thank me, lad."

"Dear God! What did he do to them?"

"They didn't suffer. He slit their throats."

Gilbert gagged. "I'm going to be sick."

Blackheart glared. "No stomach for it? Think long and hard, lad. You'll have to make decisions like this when you're Earl."

Gilbert looked down. "Can I be excused, Father? I need to be alone."

"I'm disappointed in ye, Son! Leave us. We'll discuss it later."

Gilbert pushed back his chair and left the room.

Blackheart studied Dughall. "Perhaps you're better suited to take my place. Did someone tell ye about this?"

"Nay, Father. It was a lucky guess."

"Hmmphh... Somehow, I don't think so. What are ye up to today?"

"I have another lesson with teacher Crombie."

Blackheart nodded. "The schoolmaster says that ye can read."

"Aye. I don't know all the words yet, but I will soon. There are so many books that I want to read."

A silence fell between them. Dughall summoned his courage. "Father, thank ye for sending the lass to my bedchamber. I feel like a man."

Blackheart sat back and blew his breath out slowly.

Dughall read his jealous thoughts. In his mind, Kate's lips moved along his naked thigh and took him in her mouth. *Oh God. She told him.*

The Earl reddened as he flexed his hand open and closed, making a fist.

Dughall's heart pounded. Was he about to take out the strap? "Father, the lass belongs to ye. I will respect that."

The Earl stared. "Hmmphh… I guess it's not your fault. You did what I would have done."

"I apologize if I've made ye angry."

"I accept your apology and your word. Now ye won't blush every time a lass touches ye in the bath."

"Aye. Thank ye, Father."

Blackheart's eyes narrowed. "Seems we have something in common. She's exquisite, isn't she? Do ye like her?"

Dughall nodded.

"I have plans for ye, lad. Please me, and I may send her again."

"For true?"

"Aye. Now be off with ye. Your servant is waiting for ye."

***

Dughall found his servant in the hall and accompanied him to the library.

Murdock stopped outside to straighten the lad's shirt.

"My Lord, how did it go with the Earl this morning?"

Dughall frowned. "Father and Gilbert had words! Father scolded him for letting the woman and her son go. Gilbert argued."

"A bad move. Did you stay out of it?"

"Sort of. Except when I said that he had them killed."

Murdock handed him the book. "What do ye mean, m'Lord?"

"I saw Connor following the woman and her son through the woods. He drew his dirk and slit their throats. First the lad, then the woman! There was blood all over the ground."

"How did ye see this?"

"In my mind."

Murdock stiffened. "My Lord. The Earl hates the Sight! You mustn't tell him what you see."

"Don't worry. He thought that I guessed it."

"So he admitted it. Catherine and Charles are dead."

"Aye. Gilbert was upset. He excused himself, saying he was going to be sick."

"Was the Earl angry at ye?"

"Nay. He said that I was smarter than he thought. Then he got mad."

"Why?"

"I thanked him for sending the lass to my bedchamber. He looked like he was going to beat me."

"What did ye do?"

"I said that she belonged to him, he'd have no trouble from me. Then I apologized for making him angry."

"Good. You're learning."

"I don't understand it. He was furious about the lass. Then he said he would send her again if I pleased him."

"Stay away from her, m'Lord! The Earl gets jealous when a man looks at her."

Dughall rolled his eyes. "But Murdock, she's so bonny."

"Forget her. There's plenty of lasses who'll warm your bed, maybe even that bonny harpist."

"Murdock!"

"Enough lad, time for your lesson."

PETERHEAD

Jamison stood in the barn, talking to the stable hand. "Are the horses ready?"

The young man stammered. "My Lord, I brushed them down this mornin'. Shoed the black one. Watered and fed both. Fine animals."

Jamison took a gold coin out of his sporran and placed it in the lad's hand. "We'll return this evening. I trust that you'll care for them again."

The lad stared at the coin. "Aye."

Jamison secured their leather bags to the saddles and packed two flasks of water.

"Is that the Duke yer with, m'Lord?"

"Aye. Hold the horses here. We will return shortly."

Jamison left the stables and saw the Duke talking to a tall man. He was clad in breeks, a shirt, and a woolen coat. Strange blue stockings topped his boots and blonde hair fell to his shoulders. He appeared to be unarmed. The servant approached them. "My Lord."

The Duke coughed and leaned heavily on his cane. "Jamison, this is Klaas Van Dyck. He's agreed to take us to Whinnyfold."

Jamison nodded. "Klaas, what do you know about Alex Hay?"

The innkeeper shifted uncomfortably. "M'Lords. He's a fisherman, owns a scaffie and runs a fishing crew of four men. An honest man, very religious. Has a wife and two sons." He eyed the Duke suspiciously. "Family's had a lot of grief recently. His old Aunt was murdered; had her throat cut. His son was taken. I'd hate to see anything else happen."

The Duke was somber. "I'm not here to hurt him or his family. I have news of his son Dughall."

Klaas brightened. "He'll be glad to hear that. Let's be on our way."

WHINNYFOLD

Alex secured the 'Bonnie Fay'. The sea was rough, with white-capped waves pounding the shore. Thunderclouds formed to the south, promising rain. He moved a wooden crate in the hull and found a dead pigeon. "Ach! A bad omen." He picked up the bird and buried it in the sand. "No fishing today. The lad and I will stay home and repair nets."

A stormy sea always brought him closer to God. Alex bowed his head and prayed. "Lord, keep my family safe. Bless Jessie and Ian and Dughall, wherever he may be." He threw a net over his shoulder and walked the beach. The wind was fierce and the spray felt like needles piercing his face. He reached the path and cupped his hands, blowing into them to warm his fingers. Alex glanced at the southeastern sky. Somehow, it seemed right. "God wants me home today."

He headed up the cliff side path and approached the four rows of cottages. Maggie's was empty, with no smoke rising out of the chimney. With a heavy heart, he passed it and went home. Alex spread the net on the worktable and entered the cottage. His fingers were stiff and painful, and he struggled with the buttons of his coat.

Jessie stood at the hearth, stoking the fire with a bundle of peat. She hugged him. "Husband. You're as cold as ice."

"Aye. No fishing today. The signs are bad."

"What signs?"

"I found a dead pigeon in the boat."

"Oh dear. That's really bad. What will ye do today?"

"Ian and I can repair nets."

She worked his buttons. "Are your fingers stiff?"

He winced. "Aye. It seems I'm taking Maggie's place. Where's Ian?"

"I sent him to the shed to get tea and willow bark. It will help the swelling in your hands."

He could move his fingers now. "Thank ye, lass."

"Dughall collected plenty of bark, there's a whole bag of it."

Alex's heart ached at the mention of his name. "Oh God, why did this happen? I miss him so much."

Jessie's eyes filled with tears. "Forgive me, husband. I shouldn't have mentioned it."

"We can't be afraid to talk about him, lass. I pray for our son every day."

Ian entered the cottage, carrying two small baskets. He put them on the table and rubbed his hands together. "Tea and bark. Just what ye asked for." He laid his knife on the table. "Are we fishing today?"

Alex shook his head. "Nay. Your mother's making tea. We'll break bread, and then you can climb into the loft and hand me down the worn nets."

Jessie threw a handful of tea leaves into the pot. "Maggie's needles and twine are in the cupboard."

Alex took his son aside. "Have ye felt your brother this morning?"

Ian stiffened. "Nay. You ask me every day."

Alex gazed at the floor. No one understood that the loss of his son was unbearable.

"Father. Dughall's all right. I'll know if something bad or good happens." He smiled broadly. "Maybe that bonny lass will come back."

Alex looked up, reddening slightly. "Can ye tell me about it later?"

Ian nodded. "Aye."

* * *

Jamison's horse trailed the Duke's as they rounded a bend and stopped under a large oak tree.

Klaas pulled back on the reins. "My Lords. Allow me to go on ahead and assess the situation. Wait here. These cliffs can be dangerous."

Jamison nodded. The Dutchman guided his horse close to the cliffs and disappeared from sight. The faithful servant smelled the sea and heard water crashing on the rocks. This was a strange place indeed. He hoped it wouldn't be much farther. The Duke coughed uncontrollably into a kerchief.

"Can I help ye, m'Lord?"

"Nay!"

Jamison sighed. *He's in rough shape today. I hope this doesn't kill him.*

Klaas galloped towards them on his mare. "Whinnyfold is past the cliffs where the sea birds nest. I'll take you to Alex Hay. Shall I wait or can you find your way back?"

Jamison glanced at the Duke and saw his determination. "We might be here all day. Take us as far as the Hay cottage. I can find our way back."

"All right."

"Keep our rooms for us." He reached into his sporran, took out three gold coins, and held them out to the man. "I trust that this will be enough."

Klaas took the coins. "Thank ye, m'Lord. If there's anything else, let me know." He stuffed them into a pocket and tapped the reins. "Whinnyfold is this way."

The horses followed the cliffs and arrived at four rows of stone cottages. The Duke stared. "This is where my grandson grew up?"

"Aye, m'Lord."

"A tiny village. No wonder he feels out of place at Huntly."

They dismounted and led their horses between cottages until the Dutchman stopped at one. The door was closed, but smoke curled out of the chimney. "Wait here a moment." Klaas walked to the edge of the cliff, looked down at the beach, and returned. "Alex's boat is moored below. He should be within."

Jamison smiled. "You're a good man, Klaas. We won't forget this. Leave us now."

* * *

Jessie kneeled at the hearth cooking the midday meal. The smell of oatcakes and cock-a-leekie soup filled the air. Her heart ached for news of her son.

Alex and Ian sat at the table, working on worn nets. Ian pulled the web through his hands looking for bad spots and passed them to his father. Alex worked the long needles. "I really miss Maggie."

"Aye, the old woman took good care of these nets."

"I miss her for other reasons, Son. She was dear to me." There was a knock at the door. Alex looked up. "That could be Robert. I asked him to stop by."

Jessie wiped her hands on her apron, went to the door and opened it. Two men stood outside. The older man appeared to be a Lord. The younger man had a knife in his boot. Her fear blossomed as the thought occurred to her. *This is what happened to poor Maggie!* She tried to shut the door but the young man held it open.

"Lass, please let us in."

"Nay! Help me, husband!"

Alex saw the men in the doorway and rushed to his wife. "What business do ye have here?"

The Duke was solemn. "Are you Alex Hay?"

"Aye."

Ian jumped up and took the knife in his hand. "Mother, Father. Stand back!"

Jamison drew a knife from his sock. "Nay, lad!"

The Duke frowned. "Jamison, stand down." He stared at Ian. "Put the knife down, lad." He leaned on his cane. "I won't hurt you. I have news of your son Dughall."

Alex paled. "Ian. Put the knife down."

"Father! Remember what happened to Maggie."

"I said put it down."

Ian laid the knife on the table and glared at Jamison. Alex took Ian's knife and slipped it into his pocket. "Come into our humble home. News of our son would be welcome." He moved the nets. "Jessie, make some tea. It's a raw day and they look like they've come a long way."

The two men entered the cottage and sat at the table opposite Alex and Ian. Jessie put on a pot of water and added a handful of tea leaves. Burning peat irritated the Duke's throat. He coughed into a kerchief and struggled to catch his breath.

Jessie felt sorry for the old man. "M'Lord. I'm a healer. Shall I put some coltsfoot in the tea? It will help that cough."

The old man smiled. "Aye. Thank you, lass."

Jamison frowned. "My Lord. We don't know these people. It could be dangerous."

"It's all right, lad. I have news of her son. She's not about to poison me." He turned his attention to Alex. "Allow me to introduce myself. I am Lord Drake, Duke of Seaford."

Alex raised his eyebrows. "A duke! How do ye know my son?"

"I am Dughall's grandfather."

"You're the Earl's father?"

"Nay. My daughter Christal married the Earl when she was nineteen. Their marriage was an unhappy one. She was heavy with child when she disappeared seventeen years ago. I've been searching for her ever since."

Jessie brought cups to the table and poured the tea. She sat down and studied the old man. "Your daughter was Dughall's mother?"

"Aye. Do you know what happened to her?"

Jessie hesitated. What would he do when he found out the truth? She wondered if she should lie.

Alex reached out and held her hand. "Tell the truth, lass. The man has a right to know."

Her face flushed. "M'Lord. I can only tell ye what Maggie said. She was midwife."

"Please, lass."

"My son was less than a day old. I was nursing when Maggie came to my door bearing a small bundle. She said that a young noble woman rode in on a fine horse. She was heavy with child and in labor." She reached into her pocket and felt the ring.

"Go on, lass," Jamison said.

She placed the ring on the table. "The lass took off this ring and pressed it into Maggie's hand. Payment offered, I suppose. Maggie put her to bed and made ready for the birth. She saw that the lass had been badly beaten."

"Dear God. Tell me about it."

"Her legs and backside bore welts and her arms were bruised. She'd been bound. Maggie saw rope burns on her wrists."

The Duke rolled the ring between his fingers. "Heaven help us."

"Maggie said that the lass didn't speak 'til the child was born. She held him tenderly and said 'Poor little one, your father must never find ye.' Then she bled to death."

The Duke groaned. "All these years. She was beaten to death by that cruel bastard!"

Jamison frowned. "She didn't tell the midwife who she was?"

"Nay, M'Lord. The child was hungry. I was the only one nursing a bairnie. Maggie gave him to me to raise as my son."

The Duke's voice was hoarse. "By God's grace, he survived. Is my daughter's grave nearby?"

"Aye. It's an unmarked site in the churchyard. Maggie showed it to me once."

"You'll take us there?" Jamison asked.

"Aye." Alex cleared his throat. "First, tell us about Dughall."

"He's alive and well at Huntly Castle, studying to be a Lord. I've only seen him once. He said to tell you that he loves you and thinks of you every day."

Jessie's heart ached. "Will we see him again?"

The Duke touched her hand. "Fair lady, God gave him to you to raise him as a good man. God took him away to serve a higher purpose."

She held back tears. "What do ye mean?"

"I'm an old man and all of my children are dead. Dughall is my only living heir. He will inherit my estate and title soon."

Alex rubbed his temple. "My son will be a duke?"

"Aye."

"My head aches just thinking about it. This means he can never come home."

"I promise you'll see him soon."

"Are they treating him well?"

The Duke shrugged. "The Earl and I haven't been on the best of terms, because of my daughter. I have a man in the castle who will tell me if he's being mistreated."

Ian glared. "Mistreated? They tied him to a tree and flogged him!"

"How do you know that lad?"

Ian frowned. "I can't tell ye."

"We have to trust him, Son."

"Ach! We're not supposed to tell anyone. Dughall and I have the Sight. When something happens to him, I feel it."

The Duke nodded. "My daughter had that strange gift. You two have a connection to each other?"

"Aye."

"This could be useful. Do you know Klaas who runs the tavern?"

"Aye."

"He has horses. I will pay him to come to me if you sense that your brother's in trouble. Don't wait; the Earl's a cruel man."

"I know it."

The Duke stood. "Can you show me where my daughter is buried? I want to take her bones home."

"Aye, m'Lord." Jessie liked this man. She had a feeling that he would bring her family together again.

***

The Duke stood at the gravesite, watching them dig in the hard earth. His emotions were raw and exposed. All these years, he'd hoped to find her alive. Standing at the cottage door, he'd imagined that she'd answer. He grasped his chest and groaned. "I can't bear it."

"Are ye all right, m'Lord?"

"Aye. Keep digging." The pain in his heart took his breath away. *My worst fears have been realized. The dear lass was beaten to death by my mortal enemy.*

Alex and Jamison took off their coats and continued digging. Alex was pale and sweaty.

"Father, let me dig."

"Nay, lad. I need to do this."

Jamison groaned. "We've been digging for hours. Lass, are ye sure this is her gravesite?"

Jessie nodded. "Aye. Maggie showed it to me once."

Alex grasped his chest and took a ragged breath. Ian grabbed the shovel. "You're going to kill yourself, Father. Let me dig." He steadied himself over the hole and thrust the blade deep into the clay. The shovel clanged as it hit something solid.

Ian and Jamison jumped in the hole and dug deeper, exposing a corner of a pine box.

The Duke moved closer. "Looks like a coffin."

Jessie nodded. "Aye."

Jamison and Ian worked steadily, uncovering the box and loosening the dirt around it. When it was free, they lifted it up to the surface. Alex and Jessie grabbed it on both ends and guided it onto the grass. They climbed out of the hole and waited for the old Lord to speak.

The Duke swallowed hard. "I must see her. Open it, lads."

Alex took an iron bar and jammed it under the cover. He pushed down on the rod until the wood creaked and nails loosened. Another push and the cover came free. A tattered mortcloth covered some remains.

Jamison solemnly made the sign of the cross. "Shall I uncover her, m'Lord?"

"Aye."

He pulled back the edge of the cloth, exposing bones and pieces of silk clothing. Jamison sifted through the scraps and found a gold chain with a locket. He handed it to the Duke.

The old man's heart squeezed painfully. "This is her locket. God help me! I loved her more than life."

The men shifted uncomfortably, staring at the ground.

Jessie touched the old man's shoulder. "M'Lord. Maggie said she had a proper Christian burial."

His eyes filled with tears. "Thank ye, lass. I shouldn't cry. I'll be joining her soon."

Jamison laid a velvet cloth on the ground. Gently, he lifted the bones out of the coffin and placed them on it. He covered them with scraps of clothing, then folded the cloth and tied it with thongs. He slipped the precious bundle into a saddlebag.

The Duke held the locket to his heart. His shoulders shook with grief. "I can die in peace now."

Jessie touched his arm. "My Lord. You still have your grandson. Dughall needs ye."

The Duke smiled weakly. "I guess I'll have to live a while longer."

Jamison prepared his horse. "We must go. It will be nightfall before we reach Peterhead."

"Aye. Bring me the gilded box from my saddlebag."

Jamison searched through his saddlebag and took out a small wooden chest. It was made of cherry and had a golden lion's head on top. He handed it to his master.

The Duke placed the box in Alex's hands. "This is a modest gift for you and your family, in gratitude for what you've done."

Alex stared at the fancy box. "I can't accept it, m'Lord. We helped ye because it's the right thing to do."

The Duke smiled. "You're a good man, Alex Hay. Think of it as a gift from your son. I ask only one thing; wait 'til I'm gone before you open it."

"Thank ye, m'Lord. When you see Dughall, tell him we love him. We will count the days until we see him."

Jamison helped the old man mount his horse. He shook Alex's hand and nodded to Ian and Jessie. "Thank ye for helping him bring his daughter home."

Jessie pressed a packet into his hand. "Coltsfoot, for his cough. Make a tea with it."

Jamison smiled as he mounted his horse and tapped the reins. His horse trotted down the path.

The Duke followed close behind. For the first time in years, he was at peace.

***

The Hay family watched in silence as the two men passed the church and took the path north to Peterhead. Soon, they were out of sight.

Jessie sighed. "God answered our prayers. He sent this man to help Dughall."

"Aye, lass. We'll get to see him again."

Ian stared at the box. "Open it, Father. Do ye think it's a dirk?"

"Nay, it's too heavy. I've never seen such a fancy box." He took out a knife and pried at the clasp until it opened. The box was filled with gold coins.

"Oh my God!" Jessie cried.

Ian's eyes grew wide. "How much is there?"

Alex shook his head. "It's more gold than we've seen in many years."

Jessie smiled. "A gift from Dughall. Oh husband. Did I tell ye what Maggie said when she brought the child to me?"

"Nay."

"Sweet lass, he will bring ye luck."

DANGEROUS GAMES

HUNTLY CASTLE
DECEMBER 18 1636
SIX WEEKS LATER

The weapons chamber was a series of rooms in an old wing of the castle. To unlock the massive door, four hands had to touch a series of runic seals. There were no windows, so the only light came from torches that hung on the walls. It was cool in the chamber, the best temperature to preserve the ancient weapons that lay in velvet-lined shelves.

Dughall had been there all afternoon, admiring blades and shields and practicing with short swords. His muscles tensed as he raised his sword to stop a blow. He pushed with all his strength and grunted.

Murdock's eyes widened as he lowered his sword and took a breath. "Excellent my Lord. You handle a sword like you were born to it. The Earl will be pleased."

Sweat trickled down his back. "Oh God. How do we keep from hurting each other?"

"There's the trick, m'Lord. Give it your best; you can't hurt me yet. Try it with the long sword."

Dughall went to the oak table and put down his short sword. A bronze scabbard lay on the table, richly decorated with Celtic symbols. He ran his fingers across the base, admiring the intricately etched designs. "This is beautiful. What does this mean?"

Murdock looked thoughtful. "It's an ancient symbol, a shield knot. Warriors decorated their weapons with it. It offered them protection in battle."

Dughall turned the scabbard over. "Remarkable. What about this one?"

"A trinity knot. It honors Morrigan, the War Goddess. She reigned over the battlefield with her magic. It's said she could shift into a raven or a crow. If you see her washing bloody garments in a river, you're done for!"

"Tell me more."

"I'm not a scholar m'Lord. You might ask your teacher."

Dughall nodded. He picked up the scabbard and unsheathed the sword, laying it on the table. It was cast bronze, with a razor-sharp hammered edge. The leaf shaped blade attached to the bone handle with bronze rivets. "Amazing, Murdock." He picked it up by the hilt and tested its balance. "It's verra heavy."

Murdock smiled. "It takes some getting used to. Your arm will get stronger in time. Try holding it with two hands."

Dughall grasped the hilt with both hands and assumed the correct stance.

"Good, good. Just like I taught ye. That's the middle guard stance. Aim it higher at my chest."

Dughall raised the sword. He closed his eyes and felt the energy of one who came before him, wielding this weapon. Thunder and lightning! A fierce battle on a moor. Blood curdling war cries. Swords clanged and a warrior's head rolled. A word roughly spoken, "Victory!" The smell of fresh blood flooded his senses. Dughall's nostrils flared.

"Are ye all right, m'Lord?"

The young Lord opened his eyes and stared at the sword. "Aye. The weapon has a history. The man's name was Red Conan."

Murdock frowned. "So the old stories tell us. Be careful. You know how the Earl feels about the Sight."

"Aye."

Murdock put down his sword. "Enough for today, my stomach is growling. It must be time for supper."

Dughall laid the sword on the table and stroked the hilt. "Leave this one out. I want to come back to it."

Murdock wrapped the short swords and placed them on a shelf. He sheathed the long sword and left it on the table. They walked across the chamber into a dim hallway, where it was noticeably warmer.

Sweat dried on Dughall's forehead. "I love that sword."

"You can practice with it, but no man can claim it. It's cursed."

"Tell me about it."

"Ask the Earl, he loves to tell the story."

Murdock opened the outer door. They entered the corridor and placed their hands on four of the runic seals. "Press them in reverse order to lock the door; the one on your right first, then the other. Not together, they must be in sequence."

Dughall complied. The servant pressed a seal and rotated another, locking the chamber.

"I want to know what these symbols mean. Tell me about the four we touched."

Murdock pointed to the first seal. "Hmmm... Let me see if I can remember. Uruz stands for physical strength and endurance, important for a warrior. This one next to it is Fehu. The bringer of wealth." He pointed to the third seal. "Teiwaz, the spiritual warrior. It embodies strength, objective judgment and fairness. The last one is Ansuz, bringer of messages from a higher power, inside and outside of yourself."

Dughall smiled. "I like that one." He stood back and looked at the wall. "So many. Do ye know what they mean?"

"Nay m'Lord, but the library has a book on runic symbols." They walked the hallway and entered a corridor that lead to the dining room.

"Murdock, tell me about the Gods and Goddesses of the Celts. It's interesting that they see God as male and female. You know how we always say 'Oh God.' I once knew a lass who said 'Great Goddess.'"

Murdock paled. "Are ye saying she's a witch?"

Dughall hesitated. "Does it matter? I've been studying the Greeks and they had Gods and Goddesses. The Egyptians and the Celts did too. I'm starting to think that it's all the same thing."

"What do ye mean, m'Lord?"

"There's one God. We paint different faces on it, and worship in our own ways. We should respect each other."

"Well! That's a verra different way of looking at it. I wouldn't tell the Earl, and certainly not the priest. The Papists and the Protestants can't even see eye to eye."

"Ah, the church. All my life I hid the Sight, even from my own father. My mother feared that the church would punish my brother and me, maybe even kill us."

"Your brother has the Sight too?"

"Aye. We feel each other when there's trouble, sometimes when good things happen too."

"M'Lord. It doesn't matter what ye say to me, but it would be best if you kept quiet about this. When you're Duke, you can say what ye want."

Dughall smiled. "That's true." The dining room was just ahead. "Murdock. That lass said that where she comes from the Sight is a gift. If my gift was to play the fiddle, people would ask to hear it. I don't understand."

"People fear the Sight, lad. They think you can see into their hearts."

Dughall kept a straight face. "Not all the time."

The servant stared.

The young Lord laughed. "I'm just teasin' ye. I like that story about the War Goddess. Do ye think that it's possible to shift into a crow or a raven?"

Murdock frowned. "I hope not. Ach! My head aches from all these questions." He opened the door and whispered. "Be careful what ye say. I'll see ye after dinner."

"Don't worry, friend. I can take care of myself."

"God help ye, lad. All the Gods you speak of."

***

Dughall sat at the table with Blackheart and Gilbert, enjoying a meal of lamb and potatoes and turnips. He reached for another piece of brown bread.

Blackheart smiled. "That's your third piece of bread. You eat well, lad."

"We were practicing swords all afternoon. It made me hungry."

"Murdock says that you handle a sword like you were born to it. It doesn't surprise me, you're my son."

"Thank ye, Father. Can ye tell me about Red Conan?"

Blackheart's eyes narrowed. "So you've seen the old long sword. That blade is at least a thousand years old. Red Conan was a fierce warrior, protector of a Celtic king. Killed hundreds of men in scores of battles. Fathered thirty children, most of them male. Some think the sword is cursed. Any man who claimed it died before the year was out."

Dughall smiled. "It's beautiful."

Gilbert frowned. "Stay away from that sword, Brother. It's bad luck."

Blackheart stared at his youngest son. "Play with it if ye must, but never claim it."

"All right. I would like to find out about the symbols on the hilt. Murdock says there's a book in the library."

"Crombie says that you're doing well with your studies. I'm pleased, lad."

Dughall took another piece of bread. He picked up a knife and spread apple butter on it.

"Father," Gilbert said. "The old priest was here this afternoon looking for ye. I didn't know what to tell him."

Blackheart was somber. "Christmas is coming, and it seems that we've overlooked something. Your brother must be baptized."

Dughall looked up. "I was baptized when I was a born."

"Not in the true faith. I hadn't realized that you were Protestant. This Sunday the priest will baptize ye. All of the Gordons are Catholic. Have ye got a problem with that, lad?"

Dughall shook his head. "Nay, it's all the same thing."

Blackheart and Gilbert stared. "Hmmph… I can see you'll need some lessons in the Catholic faith."

"Thank ye, Sir. I like learning about things."

Gilbert shook his head in disbelief. "Father. On another subject, what must we do for the Christmas celebration?"

"The dinner menu has been chosen and the guests invited. An intimate group, only twenty-four people. You're in charge of the music and entertainment."

Gilbert nodded. "I'll speak to the minstrels and the woman who plays the dulcimer. Father, can I bring Bridget to the party?"

"Aye, have her fitted for a formal gown. My mistress will be there as well." He stared at Dughall. "Son, I've invited Flora Laing to accompany ye. You remember her, she played the harp."

Dughall smiled. "Aye, she's a bonny lass."

"Before ye lose your heart, remember what I said about what women are good for."

"I won't forget that."

"Good. I'm pleased with ye, lad. What are ye doing this evening?"

Dughall sniffed his shirt. "I need a bath. Murdock will accompany me."

Blackheart pushed his chair back and stood, stretching his back. "I'll be in my study. Meet me here in the morning for breakfast, wearing your riding clothes. We'll take the horses out on the moor. Demon's been restless."

"Can I ride Black Lightning?"

"Aye, Son."

Dughall smiled. He'd spent hours grooming the stallion, whispering in his ear. It was time to become his master.

DRAKE CASTLE

Jamison knocked on the door and entered the Duke's bedchamber. The fire in the hearth crackled, filling the room with the scent of apple wood. The old man had been in bed all day, coughing and running a fever. The servant hesitated. *I hate to give him bad news when he's sick.*

The Duke shivered as he drew his robe around him. "Is it cold in here?"

"Nay, m'Lord. It must be the fever."

Jamison poured a glass of water. The old man's hand quivered as he held the glass and gulped the water. The servant felt his forehead. "My Lord. You look worse. Shall I call the healer?"

"Nay, I can't stand that old woman. She's meaner than a goose. My skin burned for days when she put that mustard plaster on me."

Jamison frowned. "Shall I send McKay to question her?"

"Nay. She wasn't trying to kill me! Stop worrying. What news do you bring of my grandson?"

"Bad news, I'm afraid. Bruce Mills is dead. The Earl had him publicly executed the day after we visited. He said that any man who showed us loyalty would suffer the same fate."

"God in heaven. What happened to his family?"

"No one knows. They were turned out into the night."

The Duke made the sign of the cross. "God help them. We'll send out a search party. What of my grandson?"

"The young Lord is alive and well."

"Good. Who can we get to look after him?"

"No one is willing, for any price. Mills was tortured."

"Damn the Earl! It's only a matter of time before he snaps again. If he hurts that lad, I'll kill him with my bare hands." The excitement was too much. He coughed hard into the kerchief, his chest shaking from the effort.

"My Lord. You can't help your grandson if you die. Get well and we'll visit him. I'll have the scribe write a letter to the Earl on your behalf. Christmas is coming. We can say that we have a gift for the lad."

The Duke's eyes drooped with exhaustion. He lay on the pillow and took a ragged breath. "It's a good idea. I must rest now."

"Is there anything else I can do?"

"Send a courier to the Hays. Tell them that their son is the only connection we have to Dughall. They must notify Klaas immediately if he's in trouble."

Jamison nodded.

"Tell the courier to stop in Peterhead. Instruct Klaas to bring Ian here if my grandson's in dire straits. He can help us find him."

"Aye, m'Lord."

"That kind lass in Whinnyfold. What did she give you for my cough?"

"Coltsfoot. She said to add willow bark for fever. I'll get some from the herbalist and make tea."

The Duke sighed. "Why can't we find a healer like her?"

HUNTLY CASTLE

Murdock helped the young Lord undress and tucked him into bed. He pulled the blanket up to his shoulders. "It's winter, m'Lord. I can get ye a night shirt to wear to bed."

"Nay, I like sleeping naked. The sheets are soft."

"As you wish."

"It was a good day. I studied the Greeks with Crombie and practiced swords in the weapons chamber. Father was nice to me. He said that he was pleased with me."

"You've had quite a day."

"Father invited Flora Laing to accompany me to the Christmas party."

Murdock smiled. "The harpist with the red hair. A bonny lass."

"Aye."

"Crombie will be gone for a few weeks. Do ye have plans for the morning, m'Lord?"

"Aye. After breakfast, we're taking the horses to the moor. Father said I could ride Black Lightning."

"A spirited horse. I'll put out your riding clothes." Murdock walked to the chest and opened a drawer. He took out a heavy shirt, vest, and riding breeks, and laid them on a chair. He opened the wardrobe and chose a pair of boots and woolen socks. "Sleep well, lad. A winter ride can be verra strenuous."

Dughall yawned as he stretched on the silk sheets. "Good night, friend."

"Good night, m'Lord."

✼✼✼

Kate's heart was in her throat as she walked the dark hallway. She had to reach the young Lord's chamber before anyone saw her. *Think lass! What will ye say if the Earl comes out of his bedchamber?* An icy hand gripped her heart as she remembered what he did last time. She glanced at her wrist. *If he binds me again, I'll go mad!*

Kate stood in front of Dughall's bedchamber and looked in both directions. No one was in the hallway. She entered the room and closed the door quietly. *I'm safe for the moment.* The only light in the room was from the hearth. It was stoked with hard wood and burned steadily. Kate removed her coat and scarf, laying them on the chair. She stared at the outline of the young Lord's body as he slept under the covers. "How can two men look so alike, yet be so different?"

She went to the hearth, lit a taper, and walked around the room lighting candles, two on the long table and one on the bedside stand. *I want to see his body, and I want him to see mine.* She slipped off her shoes and socks, and pulled her dress over her head. She was naked underneath. Kate walked to the bed and pulled off the blanket, dropping it on the floor. The young Lord stirred. She grabbed the sheet and stripped it off the bed. He rolled onto his back, still asleep. Her heart pounded with anticipation. *He's like a God!* Kate arranged her hair loosely on her shoulders. She crawled onto the bed, straddled him, and lowered herself until their groins met.

Dughall woke suddenly, with a swelling in his loins. "Oh God. I'm dreaming."

"It's not a dream, m'Lord."

He grasped her arms. "Nay, lass! You belong to my father."

Her eyes narrowed. "Shhhh… It's all right. You've been a good lad. He granted us another night together."

"Father was pleased with me, but I never thought he'd send ye."

She placed her hands on his chest and moved against him, rocking her pelvis. "My Lord. I can't stop thinking about ye. When he touches me, my body aches for ye."

Dughall groaned. "Lass, don't do this. I can't bear it."

Her voice was sultry. "I'll do what ye want. Command me."

"Oh God. I can't think!" He lifted her and laid her on the sheets. "No more."

"My Lord…"

He held a finger to her lips to silence her. "Shhh…"

Kate shuddered. "Don't tease me, m'Lord. I need ye."

"This is what ye came for, lass. I can feel it." Dughall slipped down on the bed and opened the patch between her legs, stroking her. "It's like a flower, so soft. With petals like a rose in summer. I am the hummingbird who will feed from your flower."

Her body flushed with desire. Kate gasped as he bent his head to give her pleasure, just as she'd taught him. *How does he know what I want? How can he possibly know?*

HOURS LATER

The room darkened as the fire waned and candles flickered out in their holders. Dughall's heart fluttered as she curled against him, her warm backside to his body. His lips brushed the back of her head. "Are ye awake, lass?"

"Aye, m'Lord. I don't want to leave."

"Then stay."

Kate nodded. It was getting lighter. In an hour, the sun would rise in the eastern sky. She faced him and placed a hand on his chest. "I must go. It's almost dawn."

Dughall ran a finger across her lips. "You're so bonny. I can't believe he sent you to me again."

"My Lord. You mustn't mention this to the Earl."

"Why not?"

"He didn't send me. I came on my own."

Dughall's heart pounded with fear as he sat up and stared into the darkness. "How could ye do this? He'll kill us."

"Forgive me, my Lord. I needed ye desperately." She took his arm. "We won't tell the Earl. It will be our secret."

"Leave me, lass! How can I lie to my own father? He was furious last time."

Kate smiled. "You won't tell him. Isn't it exciting that we risk everything to be together? Even death?"

Dughall felt nauseous. She must be truly mad. "Oh God… I'm so angry." He gathered the sheet around his waist. "Leave me now! We can't do this anymore."

Kate slipped out of bed and dressed quietly. Her lips brushed his ear. "You'll change your mind."

"Nay, lass. You must stay away."

Her voice was soft. "Think of me, lad. My warm mouth, full breasts, and a willing body. Next time I'll teach ye more about what they do in France."

"Nay, lass!"

"I'll return tomorrow night."

PROTECTION

HUNTLY CASTLE
DECEMBER 19 1636
THAT MORNING

Morning light filtered through the window, heralding the dawn of a new day.

Dughall sat up, rubbed his temple, and got out of bed, groaning as his feet touched the cold floor. "Ach! My poor head." He relieved himself in the chamber pot, his headache worsening as he shook off the last drops. "Oh God. What will I tell my father?"

His hand shook as he poured water from the pitcher into the bowl. He splashed his face and scrubbed his chest, erasing her scent from his body. "I smell like her, of lavender and desire." He rolled his tongue. "It's no use. I can taste her."

Dughall put on a shirt. "What kind of man am I that I can't control myself? How can I keep her away?" He pulled on his riding breeks and sank to his knees. "Dear God, I'm ashamed to tell ye what I've done. Help me to be a good man. I hope it's not too late." His headache flared. "I deserve the pain. Please, Lord. I want to go home! Let me live as a fisherman and marry the lass I love. Look at me! What would my parents think? Would they still love me?" He sobbed until his body shook.

A familiar hand rested on his shoulder. "My Lord, are ye all right?"

Dughall choked back a sob. "Nay. This is misery."

Murdock helped him up and sat him on the bed. He felt his forehead. "You don't have a fever. What's wrong?"

The young Lord reddened. "I need to be married."

Murdock glanced around the room. He saw burnt candles, a woman's scarf, and a long chestnut hair on the pillow. "Kate was here."

"Aye."

"Does the Earl know?"

"Nay, she came on her own. I don't know how to keep her away!

The risk excites her."

"My Lord. This is a serious matter."

"Oh God. I'm so angry with her! She told me that Father sent her, and then she demanded I keep it secret."

"Kate's got a reputation. She's trapped more than one man and thrown him to the wolves. Don't trust her."

Dughall felt nauseous. "Father will kill us."

Murdock flinched. "My Lord. You mustn't tell the Earl about this."

"He's my father. How can I lie to him?"

"You won't lie. You just won't tell him. Are ye so angry that ye wish to see her beaten?"

"Nay."

"The Earl would beat her mercilessly."

"Oh God."

"Do ye wish to take the strap to me?"

"Why would I beat ye?"

"My Lord. It's my duty to protect ye. Obviously, I've failed."

Dughall rubbed his temples. "I can't beat ye for something I've done."

"That's what the Earl will expect."

A bitter taste rose in his throat. "Then I won't tell him. What can I do? Kate will be back tonight."

"You can't send her away?"

The young Lord sniffled. "I can't control it. When I woke she was naked atop me, grinding against my member."

Murdock held up a hand. "Say no more, lad! I'm pledged to protect ye with my body. I'll move my cot in here and sleep in front of the door."

Dughall took a ragged breath. "Thank ye, friend."

"I'll return the scarf and tell her about our new arrangement."

"Tell her to stay away!"

"I will. There's dark circles under your eyes, lad. You haven't slept all night."

"Aye."

"You shouldn't ride today. Shall I tell the Earl that you're ill?"

"Nay, I want to go. I love that horse."

Murdock frowned. "All right. Do ye trust me?"

"Aye."

"Promise me you won't tell him."

"I promise."

"If he asks what's wrong, tell him you have a headache."

"Well, there's truth in that."

"Aye. Let's get ye dressed. I'll hold cold compresses against your eyes to get the swelling down."

Dughall brightened. "You're a true friend, Murdock."

Drake Castle - The Highlands - Scotland

Jamison entered the Duke's bedchamber and carried a cup of tea to the bedside table. The old Lord was asleep, lightly snoring. *This is bad,* he thought. *If he dies before that lad is ready, the Earl of Huntly will control us.* The servant went to the hearth and tossed on a bundle of wood. He stirred the ashes until the flames caught. *Ah well, I've served worse masters.*

The Duke groaned. "Jamison, are you there? I ache all over."

"Aye, m'Lord." He went to the bed and felt the old man's forehead. "Thank God. Your fever's down."

"Aye. Now my arthritis is kicking up. I've been lying in this damn bed too long."

Jamison helped him sit and reached for the cup. "Drink, m'Lord. Coltsfoot and willow bark tea, just like the lass said. It seems to be helping."

The old man sniffled. "Aye, I feel better already. Send that letter to the Earl. I want to see my grandson before Christmas."

"As you wish."

"Now help me out of this damn bed! I'm not dead yet."

The Forest East of Huntly Castle

Smoke drifted in the winter air as they entered the dense forest. Dughall was excited, in spite of his headache. For weeks, he'd longed to leave the castle grounds. This morning, he was riding Black Lightning to the moor.

Blackheart tapped his reins. "Looks like snow, lads. The ground could be icy. Stay alert!"

"Aye, Father."

Gilbert rode along side of his brother. "You're slowing down, lad. Are ye all right?"

"My head hurts like the devil."

"Do ye want to go back?"

"Nay. I'll be all right. I want to see the moor."

The horses snorted as they approached the Deveron and rode along the bank. Weeks of rain had swollen the river to dangerous levels. Dughall's heart raced. "The water moves so fast. How will we get across?"

"Don't worry, lad. There's a bridge ahead." They rounded a bend and spotted a narrow wooden bridge, spanning the river. Water ran swiftly beneath, almost touching the bottom. Blackheart and Gilbert led their horses onto the bridge. The sound of hooves on wooden planks echoed in the air.

Dughall's thighs gripped the horse as he watched the bridge sway.

He patted the stallion's side. "Easy, Lightning." The horse whinnied.

Blackheart looked back. "Lightning knows the way. You're gripping him too tight! Ease off and let him lead."

Dughall loosened the reins and nudged him in the ribs. Lightning stepped onto the bridge and started to cross. The young Lord rubbed his aching temple.

"You look like hell, lad. Are ye all right?"

"Nay, Father. I didn't sleep last night. I have a headache." His horse completed the bridge and stepped onto the path.

Gilbert frowned. "Do you want to go back?"

"Nay, I'll be all right."

"Better now, than when we're on the moor."

Blackheart smiled. "He's fine. You remember what it was like to be seventeen; he probably needs a lass in his bed."

Dughall reddened and coughed into his hand.

Demon was restless, stamping his feet. Blackheart tapped the stallion's reins and guided him towards the moor. Gilbert and Dughall's horses followed close behind.

The wind grew colder as they rode through stands of pine and oak trees. Dughall fastened his coat and put up his collar. They passed a family of white ptarmigans, feeding on frozen heather and blueberry shoots. The male raised his tail and sounded a grating alarm. Dughall shouted, "Look brother, ptarmigans! We must be close to the moor."

Gilbert fell back and rode beside him. "Are you feeling better?"

"Aye. Thank God my headache's gone."

"You should rest this afternoon. I'll engage the minstrels for the party. Is there anything else we want?"

Dughall thought for a moment. "Nay. The harpist will be at our table. Gilbert, can I ask ye a question about women?"

Gilbert looked surprised. "Of course."

"Do ye find them hard to understand?"

Gilbert laughed. "Aye. It's the difference between men and women. Sometimes they drive you mad! Don't worry, Flora is a pleasant enough lass. She won't cause you trouble."

Dughall nodded. "Do ye think that Father's right about women?"

"In what way?"

"That they're only good for two things."

"Nay. Some women are like that, but there's nothing more extraordinary than worshipping a woman who loves you."

"Do ye love your mistress?"

Gilbert chuckled. "Now that I don't have to tell you, Brother."

They caught the force of the wind in their faces as they cleared the shelter of the woods. The spicy smell of heather and bog myrtle told them the moor was ahead. "Can I talk to ye again, Gilbert?"

"Aye. I'm beginning to like you, little brother."

They watched Blackheart as he guided his stallion across the frozen moor. Dried grasses and sedges lay flat against the land. He signaled to them to follow.

Dughall tensed. "Watch out for ruts."

"Lightning knows this place. Give him free rein."

They led their horses around peat bogs, avoiding pits where it had been harvested. Dughall wrinkled his nose. "It reminds me of home."

Gilbert stared. "How so?"

"I played on a moor as a child. When I was older, I cut peat and hauled it to the village."

"How common. Well brother, you should be happy. You'll never have to do that again."

"Aye."

Blackheart galloped towards them. The earth crackled as hooves struck the frozen ground. He dismounted and patted the horse's face. "Good boy. Have ye had enough?" Demon snorted and pawed the ground. Blackheart stared at his youngest son. "You look better, lad."

"My headache is gone."

"Good. Even so, we'll turn back. I don't want ye falling and hurting yourself before Christmas."

"Thank ye, Father."

Blackheart mounted and tapped the reins. Demon whinnied and took the lead. As a light snow fell, they followed him off the moor into the shelter of the woods.

Kate's Cottage, Grounds of Huntly Castle

Murdock broke into a cold sweat as he stood in front of Kate's cottage. He reached into his pocket and fingered her scarf. "God help me." He summoned his courage and knocked.

Kate opened the door and stared. "Murdock. Why don't you come in?"

He averted his eyes. "Nay, m'Lady. It wouldn't be proper. Put on a coat and come out here."

Kate's eyes narrowed. She pulled a shawl around her shoulders and came outside onto the stoop. "Did the Earl send ye?"

"Nay, the young Lord sent me." He reached in his pocket and pulled out the scarf.

Kate reddened. "Murdock, this is none of your affairs. It's between me and the young Lord."

His heart pounded but he stood fast. "'Tis my affair. I'm pledged to protect the young Lord with my life. This will get you both killed."

Anger flickered in her eyes. "We can do what we want. The Earl doesn't have to know."

He pressed the scarf into her hand. "Kate, this must stop now. I want your word that you'll leave him alone or…."

"Or what? You'll tell the Earl? I could say that you threatened me to get into my bed. He'll believe me."

Murdock's fear blossomed. "You could hurt me, it's true. But if you bring this to a head, the young Lord will defend me."

"I don't believe it."

Murdock reddened. "You don't know him verra well. He hates to lie. If the Earl presses him, he'll tell the truth and the truth is on my side."

"You're lying. The young Lord wants me!"

"He said to tell ye to stay away."

Tears welled up in her eyes and threatened to fall. She grabbed his arm in desperation. "Murdock, listen to me. I need him. I'm willing to do anything."

He pulled his arm away. "Don't touch me, lass. From now on I'll sleep in the young Lord's bedchamber. I won't tell the Earl, but if it continues I'll speak to him."

She hugged herself. "The Earl won't hurt me."

"Don't be foolish. I saw what he did to his pregnant wife. It's a miracle that lad survived."

Kate's eyes widened. "All right. I'll stay away."

"Do I have your word?"

"Aye."

Murdock took a deep breath. "Excellent. I'll take my leave now."

She flushed with anger. "Get out of my sight, Murdock!"

"It's been a pleasure, my Lady." He began the long trek back to the castle, hoping that she wouldn't tell the Earl.

HUNTLY CASTLE - THAT EVENING

Murdock helped the young Lord undress and tucked him into bed. "Do ye wish to read, m'Lord? I can light a candle."

"Nay. I'm exhausted after that long ride. I could barely keep my eyes open at dinner."

Murdock smiled. "You must be tired. I've never known ye to lose interest in food." He dragged his cot in front of the door. "This should do it. She won't get past me."

Dughall nodded. "Thank God. Do ye mind going to bed so early?"

"Nay, m'Lord. I'm dead tired. I had a long walk to Kate's cottage and back, and I hauled firewood for the kitchen. Then Hawthorne helped me move my cot in here."

"Was Kate mad?"

"Aye! She argued and threatened me. She even tried tears. I'll never understand women. The bonny ones are the worst."

"She drives me daft."

"I made her promise to stay away. She gave her word."

"Thank God."

"I hope her word is worth something." Murdock took off his shoes and socks. He threw back the blanket on his cot and crawled in. Bed ropes creaked as he tried to get comfortable. He sat up and stripped off his shirt. "It's warm in here, not like the servant's quarters."

"Aye."

"I can see why ye sleep naked."

"Murdock!"

"What?"

"Nay bother. Thank ye for sleeping in my room."

"My Lord. If there's a night you don't want me, I can bed down elsewhere."

"What do ye mean?"

"Hmmmm... How can I say this? If you wish to have privacy after the Christmas party, I'll sleep in the servant's quarters."

"Why would I want privacy?"

"I'm referring to that bonny harpist, lad."

Dughall frowned. "Ach! I'm done bedding lasses for a while. I'll wait 'til I'm married."

The servant smiled. "We shall see about that. Good night, m'Lord."

"Sleep well, Murdock."

***

Dughall closed his eyes and fell into a deep sleep. He dreamed of a meadow ripe with heather and sweet grasses. His feet were bare, and soft blades of grass squeezed between his toes. "God granted my wish. He sent me home." Grasshoppers chirped and blue butterflies mated on ragwort. In a tree, masked meadowlarks sang a jumble of gurgling notes. "I'm dreaming. This is the meadow near the forest. The lass I love waits for me in a patch of willow." He walked through the meadow, singing and skimming the tops of the purple bells. "Lass, I come to ye through the heather in pain and confusion. Help me to be a good man."

Ahead, he saw a slender young woman with long dark hair. She held a willow rod in her hand, stripping bark into a basket. His heart swelled. "My dear Keira. I'll marry her and die a happy man." She motioned to him. "In my dreams, I can do what I want." Dughall walked to her and took her hands, feeling the warmth of her love. Everything was all right. He told her what was in his heart.

"Sweet lass. I love ye more than life itself."

Keira smiled nervously. "You've come at last to make me your wife."

"Aye. My heart yearns for ye."

Her green eyes shined. "Grandmother said that the memory of the heart is better than the memory of the head."

She was kind and beautiful. Why couldn't he marry her? Perhaps she would know a way. "I'm a Lord. Father says I can't marry you."

Her voice filled with sadness. "If you believe that, then it's true."

"I don't want it to be true."

"If we believe we'll marry, it will happen. My people call it magic."

He kissed her gently. "Then magic it will be."

The lass reached in her pocket and took out a small knife. She held his palm, scored it across the lifeline, and offered him her hand.

Dughall pressed his lips to her palm and took the knife. She closed her eyes as he scored her delicate skin. They joined palms and watched as a thin line of blood trickled down her wrist.

She was the first to speak. "Red is the color of courage, strength, and passion."

His heart swelled. "Hand in hand and blood in blood, let this act seal our love. I pledge myself to ye in joy and sadness, wholeness and brokenness, in peace and turmoil, faithfully for all our days. From this moment we are hand fast. We will marry within a year and a day."

"I will wait for ye, Dughall. We'll have children and grow old together."

SOMETIME AFTER MIDNIGHT

The young Lord stretched beneath the sheets. He woke with a start and sat up in bed, staring into the darkness. "She was here!"

Murdock was groggy. "Don't worry, lad. Kate can't get past me."

"I know it."

"Are ye all right?"

"Better than all right. I got hand-fasted to the lass I love."

The servant shook his head. "You've got marriage on your mind, lad. It was only a dream."

Dughall felt the pain of disappointment. "I was so happy. I wish it wasn't a dream."

"Dreams can be verra pleasant. Go back to sleep. You may see her again."

The young Lord hugged his pillow, running his hands underneath. His right hand burned against the sheet. He allowed his eyes to adjust and stared at his palm. It had been scored with a knife and a fine scar ran along his lifeline. "Murdock, wake up. Look at my palm! It wasn't a dream." His voice echoed in the bedchamber, but the servant was fast asleep. His heart soared. "Magic it is, lass. We'll make it happen."

YULE

LOUDEN WOOD
DECEMBER 21 1636
Two Days Later

It was the evening of the winter solstice. A heavy snow had fallen, blanketing the landscape. Keira fastened her white cloak and went outside to gather pine branches for the feast. As she walked in the sparkling forest, she pondered the events of the last few months.

Cawley and Florag died after the first snowfall, wrapped in each other's arms. It was sad to see the old ones go, but she knew in her heart that they wanted it this way. Michael chose young Torry as his apprentice, to follow in his footsteps as priest. She was so proud of him! Best of all, her friends Janet and Alistair expected a child in March.

Her own future was unclear, frightening in some ways. She closed her eyes and offered a prayer. "Goddess, hear me. I promised my love that we shall marry within the year. He is kind and compassionate, with the soul of a poet and a song in his heart. He knows you not, yet his heart is a reflection of your wisdom. Mother whispers that our union is important. Is it the end of the burning times? Will I see the face of my newborn child or shall I suffer her fate?"

A gentle voice whispered through the trees. "Trust me, child."

Keira was overcome with emotion as she held her hands to the sky. "Great Mother. I surrender my fear, my hopes, and my dreams to you. My life is in your hands."

At once, she was filled with a peace so profound that it defied description. Warmth spread throughout her body, as the Goddess' arms encircled her. Her path was clear. The future of her people rested with the handsome fisherman.

Wind whipped snowflakes into the air, stealing her breath, and bringing her back to the moment. "Thank you Mother," she whispered. "For granting me a piece of the Summerland."

Snow buntings twittered in pine trees, ruffling their mottled plumage. "Tirrirriripp..... piu... piu..." Keira reached into her pocket and took out some cranberries, leaving them for the birds. She gathered an armful of pine branches and walked to the barn. Outside, a large cooking pot hung over the fire, filled with lamb stew. Marcia and David West tended the fire and ladled stew into wooden bowls.

Marcia smiled. "Oh, good. You brought more pine branches. They're almost done decorating."

The smell of boiled lamb filled the air. Keira's stomach growled. "I'm starved."

David nodded. "We all are. It won't be long now."

Keira entered the barn and saw that it was decorated with holly and pine boughs. Soft candlelight played on the walls. Fragrant mistletoe, sacred to the Goddess, hung from rafters. She placed her bundle on the table and arranged the branches.

Janet squeezed her shoulder. "Thank ye, lass. Here's a red ribbon to tie it together and cranberries to dress it up."

Keira reached out and touched her swollen belly. "It won't be much longer, friend. Three more moon cycles."

"Aye. What more could I ask for? I have a loving husband, a child on the way, and the best friend in the world. You mean so much to me, lass."

Keira's heart ached. How could she tell Janet that she was leaving? She lowered her head and tied ribbon around the branches.

Torry pulled her close, kissing her on the cheek.

"Torry!"

"I can kiss ye. You're under the mistletoe."

"That I am."

Janet laughed. "If you stand there, chances are you'll be kissed more than once."

It looked like everyone had arrived. David and Marcia brought in bowls of stew and set them on the table. The villagers gathered and bowed their heads in respect.

Michael spoke. "Friends. We gather this solstice night to celebrate Yule. Let us reflect upon the abundance of the harvest and the gift of this wonderful feast. We thank the Goddess for plentiful crops and her profound love and protection."

Keira smiled. "Blessed be."

Michael held out his hands. "Peace be with ye. Let the feast begin."

The villagers gorged themselves on lamb stew and sweetened cakes, filled with nuts and dried fruits from sunnier days. Aileana strummed the harp and George played the Bohdran. They drank mulled wine and apple cider and retired to their homes to get ready for the walk to the stones.

***

Alone in her cottage, Keira stood at the hearth, warming her hands. She took Grandmother's scarf from a peg and held it to her nose. Her heart remembered. "I miss you, dear one." The young lass slipped off her dress and stood naked in front of the fire. She picked up a lamb's wool sponge, dipped it in the purification bowl, and ran it down her arms to her fingertips. "As I cleanse this body, I purify this mind, so that my actions tonight may please the Goddess. So mote it be."

She placed the sponge in the bowl and picked up her robe. Did she want to see the future? "The old ones are dead, gone to the Summerland. We are the old ones now. Tell me what will happen." She took the sponge out of the bowl and waited for the ripples to subside. On the surface of the water, she saw herself nursing a newborn. She stared at the thin scar that ran the length of her lifeline, remembering his words. Her heart soared. "My soul is certain that he is the one."

Keira slipped on the black robe and fastened a chain around her neck, bearing the sacred charm. "Dear Goddess, don't let this be the last time. I pray that my husband will let me keep my ways." The young lass sat on the bed and pulled on her socks and boots. She stood, picked up the bottle of sacred oil and slipped it into her pocket.

There was a rap on the door. "Ho! Are you there?"

"Aye. Come in."

Michael stamped snow from his boots. He was bundled in a wool cape, with a scarf around his neck, and his long black robe reached the floor. "Are ye ready, lass?"

"Aye."

His eyes swept over her, from head to toe. "You're looking better. You've gained some weight. I was worried about ye."

She took his hands and felt the warmth of his friendship. "Dearest Michael. I need to talk to ye."

The corners of his eyes crinkled as he smiled. "What is it, lass?"

"I love this place and my friends. It was a hard decision, but I'll be leaving soon. I promised myself to the man I met in the forest." She felt him stiffen.

"Great Goddess! You would leave this place to live among outsiders? They could torture and kill you! Do you realize the terrible risk you're taking?"

She swallowed hard. "Aye."

"Does he know what you are? That you worship the Goddess?"

"He says it doesn't matter. We are hand fast." She held up her hand and showed him her palm.

His voice was strained. "Does he know where we live?"

"Nay. When the time comes, I'll meet him in the forest. I won't put you in danger."

"Do you love him?"

"More than life itself."

His face fell. "Elspeth said that about Kale. I guess it's meant to be."

"Aye." ·

"How long do we have?"

"Until Spring."

"So soon? Great Goddess! I should choose a new priestess and you must train a healer. Ach! Who will deliver Janet's baby?"

"I may still be here. I'll work with Morgaine and young Aileana. They've always wanted to help me."

He hugged her tightly. "I'm going to miss you. We all will! I'm sorry that it didn't work out between us. Can you forgive me?"

"Michael, please. Don't blame yourself."

"He'd better take care of you!"

"Dughall will protect me. He loves me."

He released her and stared at his feet. A single tear dropped onto the dirt floor.

The roof of the cottage creaked in the wind, accentuating the silence between them.

Her heart was breaking. She never meant to hurt him. "It's time to go, friend. The stones are calling."

He took her cape from a peg and wrapped it around her shoulders. "You've grown up, lass. I guess you're old enough to make decisions. Let nothing spoil our ritual tonight." He held the door and waited for her to pass through.

They walked through the forest in silence. The ground crackled with frost and the wind whistled around them. Michael's lips were blue. "It's a frigid night. Torry and I will build a fire."

She drew her cape around her. "Good idea. We don't have to worry about the old ones, but the children will suffer from the cold."

They passed a flock of wood pigeons, rooting for frozen willow buds and twigs. A gray squirrel chattered and scampered up a pine tree. Keira smiled. "All creatures of the Goddess. I will miss this place."

Michael took her hand. "This place will miss you." He looked behind and saw the villagers following, their torches visible in the distance.

They passed the oak tree that bore the mark of a pentacle and followed the trail behind it. Their breath hung in the cold night air.

They entered the circle of stones and turned to each other.

Keira's face was wet with tears. How could she leave this sacred place? "I'm leaving my friends, my home, and the safety of the stones. Will I serve as priestess for the last time?"

Michael took her hands and smiled. "Dear lass. Wherever you go, the Goddess will be with you."

CHRISTMAS

WHINNYFOLD
DECEMBER 25 1636
FOUR DAYS LATER

Ian stamped snow from his boots and entered the cottage. The walk to the beach had soaked his breeks to the skin. He sat down to take off his boots. "The snow is deep and the cliffs are barely passable. We won't make it to church."

Alex coughed into his hand. "God forgive us. How is the 'Bonnie Fay'?"

Ian took off his coat and breeks and laid them over a chair. The smell of burning peat wrinkled his nose. "I cleared the snow from the hull and checked the rigging. The boat's ready to sail, but the sea's too rough."

"Pray that your brother doesn't need us."

"I don't feel him. He must be all right."

"The Duke said to be ready. How many days have passed since he came?"

Ian stiffened. "Fifty-three. You asked the same thing yesterday." Did father think of nothing else?

Jessie kneeled at the hearth, brewing a pot of tea. She gave him a warning look. "Son…"

Ian sighed. "Father, please. If my brother's in trouble, I'll know it. It doesn't matter how much snow there is. We'll get to Peterhead."

Alex coughed hard, wheezing at the end. "Oh God. My chest hurts."

Jessie stared. "Your cough is worse. Effie says that the grippe is running through Peterhead. Two people have died. I'll put coltsfoot in the tea."

"Thank ye, lass."

She felt his forehead. "You have a fever. Don't go outside today."

"I'm alive and whole. There's work to be done."

Jessie frowned. "Son. Your father needs ye."

Ian felt her anxiety and assumed responsibility. "I'll haul peat and clear a path to Uncle Robert's cottage. Do ye need anything from the shed?"

"Aye. Salted cod and turnips."

He could barely contain his disappointment. "Mother. It's Christmas day."

Jessie dropped a pinch of coltsfoot in the pot. "All right. Bring me some cranberries. I'll use the last of the honey to make sweet biscuits. Ask Robert and Colleen to join us for supper."

Ian grinned as he pulled on dry breeks. "Can I tell them you'll play the harp?"

"I guess so."

Alex was solemn. "We mustn't forget the meaning of this day. Let's pray to God."

They kneeled in a circle on the dirt floor and held hands. Alex bowed his head. "Oh, God. We gather to honor the birth of your son, our savior Jesus Christ. Keep us from harm and help us understand what has happened. Bless Maggie and protect our son Dughall." He made the sign of the cross. "In the name of the Father, the Son, and the Holy Spirit…"

"Amen." They stood and embraced each other.

Ian pulled on his coat and boots. "I'm going to the shed. I can't wait for those sweet biscuits." He wrapped a scarf around his neck and left the cottage, wondering about his brother.

Dughall a lord! You won't be hauling peat today.

***

Jessie brought the pot to the table and poured two cups of tea. They sat across from each other in silence, sipping the bitter brew. *Christmas will never be the same,* she thought. *We might see Dughall again, but Maggie's gone forever.*

Alex sniffled. "I miss Maggie. This is our first Christmas without her."

"I was thinking the same thing."

"I'm such a fool, lass. Last night I stood in her cottage, wishing I could tell her my troubles. She meant so much to me. Did I tell her that?"

"She knew, husband. I think she's watching over us."

Alex nodded.

She poured another cup of tea. They sat with not a word between them, bound by love and common experience. He ran his fingers through his hair.

She smiled. *He has something to say…*

Alex cleared his throat. "Yesterday I walked out to the point and watched the gulls wheeling and diving for fish. I stood in Dughall's favorite spot. Our son must miss the sea."

Her heart ached at the mention of his name. "Aye."

"I feel close to him today, like he's thinking about us."

"Perhaps he's trying to reach ye."

"I want to feel him. What should I do?"

"Open your heart and let him in."

"Someday we'll be together again. God will show us the way." Alex covered his mouth suddenly and coughed until he was short of breath. "Oh God! I have to get better. There's work to be done."

"Not today, husband. Our friends are coming to dinner. They could use some kindness."

"Aye. Robert's had his share of heartache. Their son's been sick, unable to work. They don't know how they'll make it through winter." Alex's eyes widened. He reached under his bed and took out a box, setting it on the table. He opened it and took out a few gold coins. "We'll help them, lass. Dughall wants us to."

Jessie smiled. "I was hoping you'd say that. It's what Christmas is all about." In her heart, she knew that the lad was trying to reach them.

HUNTLY CASTLE

Dughall was silent as he sat at the breakfast table. Father and Gilbert were discussing the chapel service. The Earl poured whisky into a glass and belted it down.

The young Lord's stomach turned. *How can Father drink spirits in the morning?*

Blackheart gripped the table. "I thought that the old priest would never let us go. All this talk about hell and damnation! Who needs that at Christmas Mass?"

Gilbert nodded. "Aye. I thought he'd gone mad."

Dughall put down his fork. This was his chance to get some answers. "Do ye really think that hell exists?"

Blackheart and Gilbert stared.

"I thought God loved us. If we're his creatures, why would he torture us?"

Blackheart frowned. "Hmmmph…. Did ye ask the priest that?"

"Aye. He didn't answer me. He just got mad."

"No wonder we got a lecture."

Dughall continued, oblivious to their shocked expressions. "The way I see it, there is no heaven or hell. We create it right here on earth."

"You think too hard, lad! Keep quiet in front of the priest or he'll have ye saying a hundred prayers a day."

"My knees would wear out."

"Ha!" A serving lass brought a platter of nut breads and hurried out of the room. "Go on, lad. I know ye won't pass that up."

Dughall picked up his knife and a piece of bread. He buttered it and popped it into his mouth. The sweet taste of cranberries made him smile.

Gilbert chuckled. "You never stop eating."

Blackheart drank from his flask. "Were ye pleased with your gifts?"

"Aye. I've always admired Grandfather's pistol," Gilbert said. "I never thought that I'd own it."

"How about you, Son? Black Lightning needed a new owner."

Dughall was truly grateful. "I love that horse. I promise I'll take good care of him."

"Ride him at least twice a week or he'll get restless."

"I will."

Blackheart drummed his fingers on the table. "I have important business to attend to. I won't see ye until the party tonight. Gilbert, amuse the ladies until I get there."

"Aye, Father. When are they arriving?"

"Kate will be here at six. Flora's carriage should arrive shortly after that."

"Bridget will be here as well. I'll see that they're properly entertained."

"Dughall. The Duke is here, with a gift for ye. I met with him this morning about our alliance. I'll allow him a short visit."

"When can I see him?"

"He's waiting in my study with his man Jamison. Murdock will take ye there."

Dughall used his napkin and placed it neatly at the side of his plate. Over the last few months, he'd learned the importance of table manners. He wondered if the Duke had visited Whinnyfold. "I'm done. Can we go now?"

"Aye."

Blackheart stood. "I'll be in the library meeting with the townspeople. It's Christmas and they've come to plead their cases. See you at the party." He walked to the door and left the dining room.

Dughall picked at his nails.

"Are you all right?" Gilbert asked.

"Just a little nervous. I'm going to see the Duke."

"Well, Brother. That would make me nervous. Let's go. Your servant is waiting in the hall."

Dughall followed Gilbert into the corridor.

Murdock straightened up when he saw them. "My Lords."

Gilbert nodded. "Murdock. Stay with my brother in the study. Don't let the Duke order you out."

"Aye, my Lord."

"Keep your eyes open. Father will expect a report. I'm going to the bath chamber. I'll see you later in the Grand Hall."

"My Lord."

Gilbert turned on his heels and walked away.

Murdock brushed crumbs from Dughall's kilt. He pulled up his socks, straightened his shirt, and arranged his hair. "My Lord. You look presentable. The Duke is waiting in the study."

The young Lord trembled with anticipation. "I'm verra nervous. My heart is beating like a drum."

"There's nothing to worry about. I hear that he has a gift for ye."

They walked past portraits of lords, until they came to a set of oak doors. Dughall's heart raced. "I've never been in the study before."

Murdock hesitated. "My Lord. The Duke is a powerful man. Be careful what you say about the Earl and the castle. Be sure to thank him for the gift."

"We can trust him. He wants to help me."

"Aye. But you must walk a fine line between these two powerful men. Do ye understand?"

"I think so."

He opened the door and allowed the young Lord to enter.

Dughall shivered. The study was cool and dimly lit, reminding him of a cave. Curtains masked the windows and tall bookcases cast shadows. "Ach! It smells like whisky and cigar smoke."

A voice spoke from one of the chairs. "Aye, lad. But not from me. I rarely touch the stuff."

Dughall's eyes adjusted to the light. Grandfather sat in a chair, his hand resting on a lion's head cane. The Duke's silver hair was tied back in a thong and he peered through gold-rimmed spectacles.

"Grandfather… It's good to see ye."

"Sit beside me, lad."

Dughall sank into a soft chair. His nostrils flared as the old man leaned closer. He smelled like Maggie, when her health was failing. *He's dying.*

The Duke raised his hand. "Jamison. Murdock. Wait for us by the door. I want some privacy with my grandson."

"Aye, my Lord." The two men moved to the entrance and leaned against the wall.

The Duke coughed as he took Dughall's hand. "Speak softly, lad. I don't want them to hear us. I visited your family."

Dughall's heart soared. "My family? You saw them in Whinnyfold?"

"Aye. I gave them your message. Your mother said that they would count the days until they see you."

Tears sprang to his eyes. "Oh God. Will that ever happen?"

The old man sniffled. "Perhaps when the Earl trusts me enough to let me take you."

"Thank ye, Sir. How are my parents? I would give anything to see them again."

"They're alive and well."

"How will they make it through winter? What will Father do with Maggie and I gone? She baited the lines and I helped with the catch."

"Don't worry, lad. I provided them with a gift from you, a box of gold coins. They won't have to suffer for many years."

"Bless ye, Sir. Did ye find your daughter?"

Pain clouded his ancient eyes. "Aye. The midwife told your mother the story. Christal died in childbirth."

Dughall felt the man's pain. "Oh dear. It was my fault. Forgive me."

"You can't blame yourself for being born."

"I guess not."

The old man stared. "Your eyes are like my daughter's, as blue as the sky. Your family helped me dig up her bones so I could take her home. They're good people."

Dughall nodded.

"Be careful. I no longer have a man in the castle."

"I know. They tortured and hung him. I wanted to stop it, but Murdock made me stay out of it. He said you wouldn't want me to risk it."

"Murdock is a wise man." The old Lord was seized with a coughing spell. His head dropped forward as he struggled for breath.

Dughall slapped his back. "Oh God. Don't die!"

He grasped Dughall's arm and caught his breath. "Easy, lad."

"Grandfather! Are ye all right?"

The old man's voice was weak. "We don't have much time. I know about your brother, that you both have the Sight. I told him to see a man in Peterhead if you're in danger."

"You talked to Ian?"

"Aye, he's a fiery young lad. At the first sign of trouble, do whatever it is you do. Cry out to him. Do you understand?"

Dughall nodded. "Don't worry, Sir. Father hasn't whipped me lately."

"I've asked him not to, but with that man it's only a matter of time. He may do it to spite me." He handed him a gilded box. "The servants are watching us. Open it, lad."

Dughall's eyes widened as he lifted the lid. A rare dirk with a bone handle lay next to a silver sheath. "I've never owned such a knife."

"It belonged to my own dear father."

"I will cherish it always. Thank ye, Sir."

Across the room, a door opened. Connor entered carrying an embossed letter, and approached the Duke. "My Lord. The Earl asked me to give ye this letter. Did you have a good visit?"

The Duke glared. "Can you not leave us alone for a while longer?"

"Forgive me, but the young Lord must prepare for the party."

The old man stood and leaned on his cane. His gnarled hand trembled.

Dughall stood and fought the urge to support him. *He's proud, like Maggie.*

At last, the Duke embraced him. "Merry Christmas, lad."

"Thank ye, Grandfather. You've given me the best gift."

The old man whispered. "Remember well what I told ye."

***

The bath chamber was decked with a small tree, covered with garlands and fragrant candles. Steam hung in the air, spreading the scent of bayberry and pine.

Dughall leaned back in the copper tub, allowing the water to rinse his ears.

Murdock stood at attention, holding a towel. "Can I help ye, my Lord?"

"Nay. Let me soak for a while."

He relaxed in the tub and let his mind wander to last Christmas. He'd trudged through snow to Maggie's cottage, to find her in bed crippled by pain. He remembered how frail she felt in his arms. Father and Mother and Ian waited for him to fetch her. The snow was too deep to go to church, so they knelt in a circle and prayed. Mother played the harp and they sang. He hummed the song, his heart swelling as he remembered each of their voices. *Oh God,* he thought. *I love them so much. I'll never see Maggie again.* He sniffled.

"Are ye all right, my Lord?'

"Aye. I was dreaming about home. I miss my family."

Murdock nodded.

He rinsed his hair and lay back in the tub.

"We have to go, my Lord. The ladies will be arriving soon."

"Not yet." He remembered the box of coins that Grandfather gave his family. *Father can buy a new sail and chickens for Mother in the spring. I hope he helps anyone who needs it.*

"You'll wrinkle if ye stay in there any longer."

"What's the hurry? Gilbert didn't need me in the Grand Hall."

"Nay, my Lord. Conner used that as an excuse. The Earl allowed a short visit, nothing more."

"Grandfather's a sick man. It's Christmas and I'm his only kin. Father could have allowed him a while longer. I don't understand it."

"Those two have hated each other since your mother disappeared. The Earl has an advantage over him now."

"I don't like it. They shouldn't fight over me." He picked up the bar of soap and lathered his chest.

Murdock cleared his throat. "My Lord. About Miss Flora... Should I sleep in the servants' quarters tonight?"

"Nay, friend. I'll not bed any lasses. I promise ye that."

The servant smiled. "The whisky will be flowing. Flora is bonny. You might change your mind."

He glanced at his palm and sighed. "I'll wait 'til I'm married."

"What's wrong, m'Lord? You seem troubled."

"Kate will be there with Father. I don't want her near me. What can I do?"

"Hmmm… It's Christmas so you must be gracious to all the ladies. Show respect, but don't let her drag you off under any pretense."

He stood and let the soapy water drip off. "Can ye stay at my side tonight?"

"Nay, m'Lord. It's a private party. I can wait in the hall."

"Thank ye, Murdock."

The servant averted his eyes and handed him a towel. "I've laid out your formal clothes. It's time to dress and join your brother."

***

Gilbert stood in the Grand Hall, looking over the seating arrangements. Two long tables had been set with red tablecloths and napkins. Centerpieces of pine boughs and holly graced each table. Silver plates and flatware marked each of twenty places. Choice apple wood crackled and popped in the fireplace. A tall pine tree stood against the wall. It was decorated with garlands, bows, and carved ornaments in the shape of hunting horns, horses, and stags. A candle stood on each branch, waiting to be lit.

Gilbert reached in his pocket and fingered a box wrapped in silver paper. It held a gold band with a personal inscription. His heart ached. *I wish I could make her my wife,* he thought. *She'll have to wear it on her right hand.*

A serving lass entered the room and stood before him. Her white apron barely covered her tattered skirt. He remembered that she had a small child.

"My Lord. Lady Bridget is here. Shall I see her in?"

Gilbert smiled. "Aye." He reached in his pocket, took out a coin, and pressed it into her hand. "Merry Christmas, Tavia."

She stared at the coin. "Bless ye, my Lord. Merry Christmas." She hurried out of the room and returned with his mistress.

His heart beat faster at the sight of her. Bridget wore a cream silk gown that was embroidered with thousands of tiny pearls. Her blonde hair was tied back with scrimshaw combs and her face was artfully powdered. He couldn't take his eyes off her.

"Tavia… Bring a mug of ale and a glass of burgundy wine for my Lady."

"Aye, my Lord." She scurried off.

Bridget smiled. "How long do we have before the others arrive?"

"Kate will be here in less than an hour."

"That woman frightens me. She's so cold."

Gilbert agreed. "She's a good match for my father."

"Who will accompany your brother?"

"Flora Laing."

"A kind and bonny lass. Some men would give anything to be with her."

"Not this man. You'll be the most beautiful woman here tonight." Gilbert ran his hands down her arms and felt a spark between them.

She shivered. "Oh Gilbert."

He pulled out a chair. "Sit down, lass. I have a gift for you."

Tavia returned with the drinks, set them on the table, and left the room.

Gilbert pulled out another chair and sat down. He studied her as she held the glass in her delicate hand and sipped the wine. A bead of ruby nectar lingered on her lips. He placed the box in her hand. "A token of my love."

Bridget peeled off the silver paper and opened the lid. She was speechless when she saw the golden band.

Gilbert slid it on the ring finger of her right hand. "There's an inscription inside. 'To my one true love.' I wish that I could make you my wife."

Her voice was soft. "We'll find a way."

His mind whispered that it was impossible, but his heart disagreed. "Aye, lass."

✳✳✳

Kate stood in the powder room, admiring her image in the mirror. She wore an emerald gown of silk and lace that the Earl acquired on a trip abroad. A diamond necklace adorned her delicate neck. She fingered the ruby heart at its center. "Flora Laing is no match for you."

Kate unbraided her chestnut hair and arranged it loosely around her shoulders. She took out a bottle of lavender perfume, dabbed it on her wrists, and pursed her lips. The woman in the mirror looked young, perhaps even innocent. "The young Lord wants me." Her expression hardened. "Murdock had better not be there. I'll throw him to the wolves." She left the powder room, intent on finding Dughall.

✳✳✳

Gilbert stood at the Christmas tree with Bridget, admiring ornaments. His heart was light as he watched her touch a perfectly carved horse.

She smiled. "He looks like Black Lightning."

"Aye. Father gave my brother that horse as a gift. The lad was pleased. It's good to see them getting along after such a bad start."

"You told me about that. How could he flog his own son?"

"I don't know, lass. I'm no stranger to his whip. You've seen the marks."

"It must have been awful for ye."

"I still have nightmares about it. I'll never do that to my sons."

She put her arms around his neck. "I love ye, Gilbert. I would be happy to give ye sons."

Gilbert's heart swelled. "We'll find a way, lass." He stiffened as Kate entered the Grand Hall. Her eyes scanned the room, looking for someone. "Don't look up. Kate just arrived. What in hell is she up to?"

Kate hurried to the tree and stared at the young lovers until they separated. Her eyes grew wide. "Well, if it isn't the bath chamber lass. Bridget?"

Gilbert's blood boiled. "I would ask you to respect my Lady, unless you don't wish it for yourself."

Bridget blushed. "It's all right."

"It's not all right. She's no better than you."

Kate's face hardened. "It's Christmas, my Lord. Can we not pretend to get along?" She looked around the room, clearly searching for someone.

"The Earl is in the library with the villagers. Perhaps you should join him there."

"I'm not looking for him. Where is your brother?"

"Dughall? He's getting dressed. What do you want with him?"

"That's none of your affairs. When will the Earl return?"

"When the party starts, around seven."

"I'm going to the privy, and then I might take a walk. I'll join ye later." She picked up her skirts and left the Hall in a hurry.

Bridget shuddered. "Why must she insult us? Thank God she's gone."

Gilbert felt uneasy. "I don't like her asking about my brother. The lad's so innocent; he could easily be taken by her."

"Your father would kill them."

Gilbert's eyes narrowed. "Aye. I don't trust that woman. I'll talk to my brother tonight."

Tavia entered the room. "My Lord. Miss Flora has arrived for the party. I've taken care of her wrap. Shall I see her in?"

"Aye, lass. Have you seen my brother?"

"Nay, but Marcia drew a bath for him a while ago." She bowed her head and scurried out of the room. A few minutes later, she returned with Flora. "Will there be anything else, my Lord?"

"Bring two glasses of wine for the ladies and two mugs of ale for my brother and me."

Flora stood before them in a blue velvet dress that was trimmed with white lace. Her red hair was tied back in a ribbon and her blue eyes sparkled. "My Lord…"

Gilbert introduced them. "Flora, this is my friend Bridget Murray. Bridget, this is Flora Laing."

Flora embraced her. "We've met before, in the courtyard. You look verra beautiful in that dress, lass."

"Thank ye, Flora."

"The hall looks wonderful. Where is everyone?"

"I suspect that my brother Dughall is on the way. The Earl is in the library speaking with the villagers. He won't arrive until the party starts. Kate is around here somewhere, I think she went to the privy."

"Oh, Kate."

"Do you know her?"

"Aye. I can't say that it's been pleasant."

"Well, lass. You're not the only one to say that."

Tavia returned with their drinks and set them on the table. "I'll be in the kitchen. Ring the bell if ye need me."

"Thank ye, lass."

Gilbert seated the ladies opposite each other. They reached across the table and touched hands.

"Did ye have a good Christmas, Flora?"

"Aye. You may have heard that my father's been ill. It's a miracle that he was able to sit up this morning. The Earl's been kind, sending us food and forgiving our debts. He gave me a Clarsach from Ireland. It has the most haunting sound of any harp I've played. How was your Christmas, lass?"

Bridget nervously fingered the gold band and stretched out her hand. "Gilbert gave me this."

Flora touched the ring and smiled.

Gilbert saw Murdock and Dughall entering the Hall. The young Lord was dressed in a kilt and sporran, a white silk shirt, and a dark blue dinner jacket. "There's my brother!"

Flora looked up. "He looks like the Earl. How old is he?"

"Seventeen. He's still a lad." Gilbert cleared his throat and prepared for a confrontation. "Excuse me, ladies. I must speak to my brother." He stood and walked toward the two men.

***

Dughall looked around the room and breathed a sigh of relief. The Earl's mistress was nowhere to be seen. "Kate's not here, Murdock."

The servant nodded. "Perhaps she's with the Earl. Here comes your brother."

Gilbert arrived and looked around nervously.

Dughall smiled. "It looks wonderful. I see that Bridget and Flora are here."

"Aye. Can I talk to you, Brother?"

"What's wrong?"

"Nothing I hope. Murdock, don't step away. I want you to hear this."

"My Lord."

"Kate was here a while ago. She's in quite a mood. She insulted Bridget and got me angry. That's not what I'm concerned about."

Dughall's fear blossomed. What did his brother know?

"I thought she was looking for Father, so I told her where he was. She said that she wasn't looking for him; she was looking for you brother! I don't like the sound of that. Is there anything going on?"

Murdock paled. "My Lord, don't…"

Dughall's stomach churned. He thought about lying, but he just couldn't do it. "Don't ask me to lie! I have to tell him, he's my brother."

"God in heaven. What is it?"

"Father sent her to me the night of my birthday, to make a man of me. She wouldn't leave me alone after that. I'd wake in the night to find her naked atop me. She said that the risk…"

"…excites her," Gilbert said.

"My Lord. Please don't tell the Earl! I sleep in the young Lord's bedchamber in front of the door. It won't happen again."

Gilbert frowned. "Damn that woman! I thought it was something like that. We've had trouble with her before."

"Did the Earl know about it?" Murdock asked.

"Nay."

"Who was she after?"

Gilbert reddened. "Me. There was a time when Bruce Mills slept in my bedchamber. God rest his soul." He quietly made the sign of the cross. "I won't tell Father, but we must keep her away from you. He'd take the strap to your backside."

Dughall shuddered. "Oh God. I don't want that to happen again. She drives me mad, Brother. Tell me what to do."

"Flora and Bridget are getting along fine. Stay close to us tonight. Don't let Kate drag you off for any reason. If you're in trouble, ask me to step out for a cigar."

"Thank ye Gilbert."

"Murdock. Wait outside, into the wee hours if need be. I'll have the kitchen bring you dinner. I know how insistent she is. He can't be left alone; you must walk him to his bedchamber."

"Thank ye, m'Lord. It's been a terrible secret to bear alone."

Gilbert took out his pocket watch. "The guests are due to arrive. Come on brother."

"Enjoy the party, my Lords."

They left Murdock and entered the Hall. Flora and Bridget looked up and waved.

Gilbert smiled. "You'll like Flora. She's kind and beautiful. Most men would give anything to spend a night with her."

"Not me, Brother. I've given up on bedding lasses. They're nothing but trouble. I'll wait 'til I'm married."

Gilbert chuckled. "If you can do it, you're a better man than I."

***

Kate stood in Dughall's bedchamber, disappointed that she'd missed him. She broke off a strand of her long hair, left it on his pillow, and rubbed her wrist on the silk case, leaving behind her scent. "It's driving me mad. How can ye know what I want?" She walked to Murdock's cot and spit on his pillow. "The hell with ye! I won't let ye come between us."

Kate opened the door and peered in both directions. No one was in the hallway. She entered the corridor and started towards the Grand Hall. As she turned a corner, she ran into the Earl. Her heart pounded erratically. *Think, Kate!*

Blackheart stared. "What are ye doing here, lass? I thought you'd be in the Hall."

"Those women bore me. I grew tired of their useless prattle. I came looking for ye."

"Now Kate, not all women have been blessed with your intellect. It's Christmas. I ask ye to get along with my sons' companions."

"I will try, my Lord."

"Good! I didn't want to leave ye alone, but I've been in the library listening to the townspeople plead their cases. Have they no shame? They think they can ask for anything on Christmas."

She nodded.

"Come with me to my bedchamber, lass. I need my jacket and flask. We must hurry, the guests are arriving."

Kate breathed a sigh of relief. Apparently, he was too distracted to question her further.

***

Dughall sat next to Flora and watched her sip a glass of wine. The bonny lass with the red hair was blushing.

She batted her long eyelashes. "My Lord. Bridget tells me that you're the new owner of Black Lightning."

"Aye. Father gave him to me. I'm lucky to have such a spirited horse. Do you ride, lass?"

"I have a red mare that I care for. There's been no time to ride lately. I have many duties now that Father is sick."

"What's wrong with him, lass?"

"He fell on a peat cutter a month ago, and the blade laid his leg open to the bone. The wounds festered and he's running a terrible fever."

Now, this was a subject he understood. "Are the wounds foul smelling?"

"Nay."

"Good. What did the healer say?"

"When the wounds wouldn't heal, Beathag didn't know what to do. She said he might die."

Dughall touched her hand gently. "I've seen this before. The wound must be cleaned, made free of pus. Then treat it with a poultice of honey and calendula flower. After three days, it should improve. You may need to stitch it with sinew. Willow bark will kill the fever."

Tears came to her eyes. "What do you know of such things, my Lord?"

Gilbert stared.

Dughall felt his disapproval. "I'm a healer, Brother. I could look at his wounds."

"I don't know, lad. Father wouldn't like it."

"It's Christmas. The Bible says that we must help people less fortunate."

Gilbert looked around the table. "All right. But it will be our secret, is it agreed?"

The ladies nodded. Angus and Anna appeared in the entrance to the Hall.

Gilbert straightened his shirt. "The guests are arriving. Let's form a receiving line."

They all stood. The men walked ahead, eager to reach the MacVeys. Flora and Bridget picked up their skirts and followed.

Dughall's mind compiled a list of supplies he would need to work on the injured man. For the first time in months, he felt useful. *By God's grace, we'll heal him.*

***

They stood in a line, receiving and announcing guests. Serving lasses scurried about, lighting candles and pouring drinks. Tavia hung mistletoe from iron brackets and stoked the hearth fire. Donella Geddes sat onstage, playing the dulcimer. The white-haired woman plucked the strings and worked the frets, playing a Christmas ballad.

Dughall's stomach turned when Blackheart and Kate made a grand entrance. Her full skirts swished as they approached the receiving line.

The Earl looked around and embraced his oldest son. "Excellent, lad. It looks like the guests have been seated."

Gilbert bowed his head. "Thank ye, Father."

He moved on to Bridget. "Good evening, Bridget. You look lovely as usual."

"Thank ye, my Lord."

He stood in front of Dughall and Flora. "Son. Flora. You make a handsome couple."

Dughall smiled. "Thank ye, Father."

Kate's expression was cold as she nodded to Gilbert and Bridget. She waited for the Earl to move on and stood in front of Dughall. "Flora Laing. We meet again."

"Aye. Merry Christmas, my Lady."

Kate ignored her. "My Lord. It's a pleasure to see ye. Will ye grant me a dance tonight?"

Dughall's heart pounded. "Nay, lass! You belong to my father."

Kate grasped his arm. "You know what I want. You'll change your mind." She released him and joined the Earl at their table.

Dughall turned a deep shade of red. The lass meant to get them both killed. "God help me."

"What's wrong, m'Lord? Why did she say that?" Flora asked.

Gilbert spoke softly. "She's after my brother. We need your help, lass."

They gathered around Gilbert as he explained. "... no matter what happens, we must keep Kate away from my brother."

Flora took Dughall's hand. "Does the Earl know what's going on?"

"Nay. He doesn't suspect."

"Why don't you tell him?"

"He would beat me mercilessly."

"But it's not your fault."

Gilbert frowned. "That's true, but Kate would tell him otherwise. We must keep her away. Is it agreed?"

"Aye."

"Brother... Don't let her drag you off for any reason. A white lie may be necessary. Tell her I've asked you to step out for a cigar."

"All right."

"Let's seat ourselves. Father is watching."

They walked to the first table and found four empty seats. Gilbert sat on the end, with Bridget next to him. Blackheart sat next to her, with Kate across from him. Kate moistened her lips and patted the seat next to hers.

Dughall's head ached as he read her intentions.

Flora took his arm. "My Lord. Sit across from your brother. I'd like to sit next to Kate so I can talk to the Earl. He's done so much for my father."

Kate glared.

Dughall pulled out a chair and waited for Flora to sit down. He sat across from his brother and rubbed his temples. "Oh God... I need a drink."

Gilbert pointed to a glass of ale. "Go easy on that, Brother. You need your wits about you tonight."

Dughall sipped the ale and nodded.

Blackheart turned to speak to the young lass. "Flora. You look lovely tonight. I remember you as a child, playing at your father's knee. How is James doing?"

Flora sighed. "Poorly, but things are looking up. The healer has some ideas."

"Good. If there's anything we can do, let me know."

"My Lord. We're grateful for the help you've given us. Thank ye for the Clarsach. That harp has the most extraordinary sound."

"You must play it for me sometime."

Flora blushed. "As you wish, my Lord."

Kate's eyes grew wide. "You gave her a gift?"

Blackheart stared. "Aye. Have you got a problem with that, lass?"

"Nay, I guess not."

He laughed. "Well, good! I would hate to think that I had to get your permission. It would be worse than being married."

Kate looked away and drank her wine.

Gilbert spoke softly. "Flora's a brave lass, placing herself between you and Kate. Did you see the look Kate gave her? It wasn't pleasant."

Dughall leaned forward and whispered. "I'm in her debt. Can we see her father tomorrow? If we wait, the flesh will rot."

"I think so. We'll say that we're taking the horses out."

"I'll need whisky to clean the wound and cloth for bandages. Honey in the comb, willow bark, a mortar and pestle, and calendula flower."

"Whisky is easy. The kitchen can get us cloth and honey, but we'll have to see the old healer for the rest."

A sudden movement distracted them. Kate pushed back her chair, picked up her skirts, and left the room in a huff.

"What's wrong with her, Father?" Dughall asked.

Blackheart smiled. "I'd say she was a wee bit jealous."

"Would you like me to follow her?" Bridget asked.

"Nay, lass. Best to leave her alone when she's in a mood."

The conversation continued until Kate returned to the table. She settled into her chair, smoothed her skirts, and smiled sweetly at the Earl.

"Are ye all right, lass?" Blackheart asked.

"Aye. Forgive me, my Lord. Too much wine on an empty stomach."

"I accept your apology. There's no need to be jealous. Each of these ladies has an escort tonight. You'll be coming home with me."

Kate reddened.

Serving lasses brought platters of roast lamb, stuffed fowl, and goose liver with truffles. They carried bowls of roasted potatoes and carrots, and platters of fresh bread and butter. Mugs of ale and glasses of wine were replenished. Everyone waited for the Earl to speak.

Blackheart raised a hand. "Good people. We gather today to celebrate Christmas and thank God for this abundance. May he look upon us favorably in the coming year. I invite you to share in this meal and to stay for the entertainment. Let the feast begin!"

Glasses clinked as toasts were made. "To the Earl and his sons." "To a prosperous new year." "To good health."

Dughall watched as Flora brought the glass to her mouth and sipped the wine. Her red hair made him smile and brought back fond memories. *She reminds me of Mother.* He touched her arm. "Do ye have all that ye need, lass?"

"Aye, my Lord."

He spoke softly. "I talked to Gilbert. We will see your father tomorrow. Tell no one. It must be kept quiet."

She placed a trembling hand over his. "My Lord. I'm truly in your debt. If there's anything ye want from me, just ask."

"I'll not take advantage of ye, lass. Stay by my side tonight."

"As ye wish."

The room filled with the sound of silverware on plates, as the guests ate their supper. Blackheart finished eating and threw down his napkin. "Dughall. I need to talk about your visit with the Duke. Sit next to Kate so we don't have to shout."

Dughall stiffened. Sitting next to that woman was the last thing he wanted.

Gilbert spoke up. "Father. Dughall and I were about to step out for a cigar. Why don't you join us? I'm sure that the ladies would be bored with our conversation."

Blackheart pushed back his chair and stood. "A good idea. I haven't had a fine cigar in days. When did you take up smoking, Son?"

Gilbert smiled. "Not long ago. It's become a wonderful diversion. Come on brother."

"Enjoy yourselves, ladies," Blackheart said. "We will return after dessert."

***

Dughall followed his father and brother to the study. They lit candles and sat in overstuffed chairs. Blackheart opened a mahogany humidor and took out three cigars. He handed one to each of his sons and passed around a lit taper.

"Rich and robust," Gilbert remarked, as he smelled the wrapped tobacco. "Where did these come from?"

"The trader said they came from an island in the Caribbean Sea, called Cuba."

Dughall held the taper to the end of the cigar and inhaled. His throat tightened. *Oh God. At least it tastes better than it smells.*

Blackheart stared. "Tell me what happened with the Duke."

Dughall stifled a cough. "He wished me Merry Christmas and gave me a rare dirk with a bone handle. It's in my bedchamber."

"Show it to me tomorrow. Did he ask about the castle? Or any of us?"

"Nay. Grandfather coughed so hard that he barely got the words out. I thought he might die on the spot."

Blackheart chuckled. "He did look like hell! There might be less time than we think. Are ye ready to take his place, lad?"

"Nay. I have much to learn about being a Lord."

"There have been Lords even younger than you. If he dies, they'll make ye Duke within a week. Your brother and I would advise ye, of course. Think of the lands we would control, the men that would follow us. We would be the most powerful family in Scotland." Blackheart crushed his cigar and stood. "Most interesting. You can show me that dirk tomorrow. Well lads, it's time to return to the party. The ladies must be wondering where we are."

The men left the study and returned to the Grand Hall. As they took their seats, the Earl ordered more ale and wine.

Dughall felt a chill as he looked at the ladies. He was sure that something had happened. Flora's slender fingers clutched a napkin and her neck was flushed. Bridget's hand shook slightly as she grasped Gilbert's arm. Kate seemed unaffected, as cold as an ice storm.

Blackheart smiled. "There's nothing like a fine cigar. Did you ladies have a nice talk while we were gone?"

Kate raised her wine glass. "As usual, my Lord."

Flora reddened. "It was enlightening, to say the least."

Dughall frowned. "Are ye all right, lass?"

"Aye, m'Lord. It was hot in here, but it's cooler now that you've returned."

Donella Geddes picked up her dulcimer and left the stage. A group of minstrels climbed the stairs and began to set up their stools and instruments. A gray-haired man in a kilt and a linen shirt took a violin out of a case. A young lad set up a harp, a guitar, and bagpipes. An old woman in a red dress opened a wooden case and took out a pennywhistle.

Dughall smiled broadly. "I love music." Their music was anything but simple. The sound was an intertwining of light whistle, soft harp, and singing violin. "I could listen to this every day," Dughall said. "I would never tire of it. They play to the very heart of music."

When they broke into a lively piece, people tapped their feet. At last they played a soft song, violin accompanied by harp.

Blackheart walked around the table and led Kate to the dance floor. Gilbert and Bridget joined them, leaving Dughall and Flora alone.

Flora took his hand and held it palm up. "They say that you can tell a lot about a man by the lines in his hand." Her finger caressed the thin scar on his lifeline. "My Lord," she whispered. "You're hand fast."

Dughall blushed. "Aye."

"Do ye love her?"

"With all my heart."

"Then I'll not try to take her place. Do I know her?"

"Nay. I knew her from before."

Her voice was soft. "How can it happen, then?"

"I don't know lass, but it's meant to be. I must stay faithful to her."

The dance ended and the floor cleared. Blackheart and Gilbert returned with the ladies. The steward placed a crystal decanter of whisky and three short glasses on the table.

Blackheart opened it and poured. "Twenty year old whisky; the best in the Highlands. Drink with me, Sons."

Dughall shook his head. "Nay. Last time, it gave me a terrible headache."

Blackheart laughed. "Are ye sure it was the whisky, Son? It was an eventful night for ye in more ways than one."

The young Lord blushed.

"Join us for one, lad."

The glasses were passed and Blackheart offered a toast. "Here's to a prosperous year. May we grow in power and wealth."

Gilbert held up his glass. "May we have good health."

Dughall lifted his, studying the dark nectar. "May we have the wisdom to understand it."

Blackheart laughed. He threw back his head and belted the whisky.

Gilbert sipped it. "It's strong, Brother. Be careful."

Dughall brought the glass to his lips and took a swallow. It was smoky, with a touch of saltiness. Within moments, it warmed his belly and lowered his inhibitions. "Oh God. It's amazing." He took another swallow.

Their attention was drawn to the stage, where Angus MacVey stood talking to the minstrels. The younger man picked up his bagpipes and played a Reel. Angus turned to the crowd and held up a round shield with a sharp spike projecting from the center. He began to tell a story. "Lords and Ladies. A long time ago, a feast was planned. A father sent his son out to kill a deer for supper. The son found the deer, but thought it too beautiful to kill. When he returned home, he couldna find words to tell his father why there was no meat. He danced to tell the story." He laid the shield on the floor.

The Earl stood. "Are ye sure ye want to do this, Angus? You might kill yourself on that spike."

Angus nodded. "My Lord. I'm steady as a rock after all that ale." Laughter filled the hall.

Angus held up his arms and grouped his fingers, forming antlers on his head. He danced, hopping and turning on one foot while passing the other foot in front of and behind the shield. The music stopped and Angus took a bow.

Blackheart smiled. "Wonderful! Next time we do battle, you can lead the victory dance."

Angus picked up the shield and hung it on the wall. "We have many fine voices here tonight. Would anyone like to sing for us?"

Dughall stood and ran his fingers through his hair. "A love song, perhaps?"

Angus nodded. "The young Lord has a love song for us! Come up here."

Gilbert smiled. "Are you sure you haven't had too much whisky, Brother?"

"Nay. I love to sing."

He walked to Angus and spoke to the minstrels. The young man picked up his guitar and strummed.

Dughall explained. "This is a love song called 'Mary's Wedding'. Sing along if ye know the words." He sang in a voice that was clear and steady.

Step we gaily on we go,
Heel for heel and toe for toe,
Arm in arm and row and row,
All for Mary's wedding.

Over hillways up and down,
Myrtle green and the bracken brown,
Past the sheiling through the town,
Is our darling Mary.

Red her cheeks as rowans are.
Bright her eyes as any star,
Fairest o them all by far,
Is our darling Mary.

Plenty herring plenty meal,
Plenty peat tae fill her creel,
Plenty bonnie bairns as weel,
That's the toast for Mary.

He took a bow. The minstrels played a soft ballad as he returned to the table and took his seat.

Blackheart stared at his youngest son. "I didn't know you could sing like that."

"I love to sing. Back home we had songs for everything, for shelling the mussels and baiting the lines, rowing the boat, being in love…"

"Hmmmph … This is your home now."

Dughall reddened. "Forgive me, Father. It must be the whisky."

The Earl belted his drink. "It's Christmas. I can't expect ye to forget your past."

"Thank ye, Father."

Blackheart nodded and turned his attention to Kate, engaging her in a lively conversation.

Flora spoke softly. "My Lord. I don't know quite how to tell ye this. Kate picked a fight with me when you were gone. She told me to leave early. I think she intends to visit your bedchamber." Flora smiled. "She claims that you're twice the man the Earl is."

Dughall froze. "Oh God. She'll get us both killed."

She touched his hand. "Shhh… I have a plan. Let's act like you're taking me to your bedchamber."

"Ach! I don't want to sully your reputation, lass."

"Never mind that. I owe ye a favor. Now stand and take my hand."

Dughall stood and helped her up. Flora melted into his arms and rested her head on his chest.

"Going somewhere, Son?" Blackheart's expression was smug.

The young Lord blushed. "Aye. Lady Flora needs some fresh air. Then we might retire to my bedchamber."

"Ha! What I would give to be seventeen again. I'll excuse ye for the evening."

"Thank ye, Father."

They separated and said goodbye to Gilbert and Bridget. Kate wouldn't even look at them. Dughall took Flora's hand and led her out of the Grand Hall. He felt fortunate to have made such a friend.

***

Dughall and Murdock escorted Flora to her carriage and arrived at the young Lord's bedchamber after midnight. The fire in the hearth was nearly out.

Dughall sat on a chair and took off his shoes and socks. "I can undress myself."

Murdock stoked the fire with a bundle of apple wood. "Nay, my Lord. I'll help ye in a moment." He lit a candle on the bedside table.

The young Lord unbuttoned his shirt. "Don't worry, friend. I'm not blootered."

"I know, lad."

"Kate couldn't get near me. Thank God."

Murdock readied his bed. "It's good to have Gilbert on our side. It doesn't surprise me that he's had trouble with her. You'll sleep well tonight."

"Flora told me that Kate picked a fight with her. Why would she do it?"

"I don't know, m'Lord. I'll never understand women."

The servant helped him undress, taking off his dinner jacket and shirt. He unfastened the sporran and unpinned the kilt. Dughall stood, dropped his kilt on the floor, and crawled under the sheets. He was truly exhausted.

Murdock tucked him in. "Sleep well, m'Lord." The servant pushed his cot in front of the door and threw back the blanket. He kicked off his shoes and crawled in. "Damn her..." he groaned, as he turned over his pillow.

The young Lord lay on his stomach and fluffed his pillow. He caught the scent of lavender and sat up. "Kate was here."

"I know it."

Dughall held up a strand of long hair. "She left a strand of hair on my pillow."

Murdock sighed. "Kate left something on my pillow too."

"What was it?"

"She spit on it."

Flora

HEALING TOUCH

WHINNYFOLD
DECEMBER 26 1636
NEXT DAY

It was early morning in Whinnyfold. A strong wind blew across the point, sculpting knee-deep snowdrifts. Sunrays peeked out from the clouds, promising a break in the weather.

Ian stood on the beach, checking on the 'Bonnie Fay'. He brushed snow from the scaffie's tie-downs and took off his mittens to check the ropes. By the time he was done, his hands were raw. He sniffled. "I miss ye, Dughall. Father's so sick. You always knew what to do."

Ian pulled his mittens on. He followed his footsteps through the snow to the cliff side path and began the long climb. As he reached the top, he steadied himself and walked into the wind towards his cottage.

Jessie met him at the door with a troubled look on her face. She drew her wrap around her shoulders. "I was worried about ye. Your father's worse. I need more water."

"I can't get to the stream, Mother. The snow's deep and it's likely frozen. We'll have to boil snow."

"I was thinking the same thing. Fill the bucket and bring it in." She shivered and closed the door.

Ian grabbed a bucket and found some clean snow. He set it down and used his hands to fill it. His breath hung in the frigid air as he hauled it to the cottage.

Jessie opened the door and helped him bring it to the hearth. She scooped snow into a pot and hung it over the fire.

Ian stripped off his wet mittens, stood in front of the fire, and held out his hands. His fingers burned and tingled. "Oh God. It hurts so much."

Jessie frowned. "Warm them up slowly. Hold them under your arm pits."

Ian held them close to his body and looked down. "Forgive me, Mother. I'm dripping all over the floor."

Jessie hugged him. "It's all right. I know it's hard being the only one."

Ian spoke softly. "I miss Dughall."

"I miss him too. Someday we'll get to see him."

"Let's hope he remembers who we are."

"Ian! Of course he'll remember. He loves us. The Duke said so."

Alex rolled over in bed and coughed hard into a kerchief. He grimaced. "I'm as weak as a newborn bairnie. Is the 'Bonnie Fay' all right?"

"Aye, Father. She's full of snow, but the ropes are tight. At least it stopped snowing."

"Did I hear ye say something about Dughall?"

"Just that I miss him."

Alex sat up and cradled his head in his hands. "Have faith, lad. God will bring us together again."

Ian took off his boots and socks. He peeled off his wet clothes and laid them across a chair to dry. His hands burned as he pulled on a dry pair of breeks and a sweater.

Alex coughed. "Dear God. I ache all over and my head feels awful."

Jessie appeared with a cup of coltsfoot tea, and placed a hand on his forehead. "You have the grippe, husband. Drink the tea and get some rest."

He gulped the bitter brew. "Where will we get water…"

Ian's heart ached. "Lay down, Father. I hauled in snow for water. I'm a man now. I know what to do. You must get well in case Dughall needs us."

Alex lay back exhausted. "You're right. Bless ye, Son." He pulled up his blanket and rolled over.

Ian took his mother's arm and led her to the hearth. The look in her eyes frightened him. He spoke softly. "Is he going to be all right?" They heard him groan.

"I don't know, Son. I'm trying my best. Only God knows."

Huntly Castle

Dughall saddled Black Lightning and stroked the stallion's face. "I love this white streak on his forehead. It looks like a bolt of lightning."

Gilbert smiled. "That's how he got his name."

Dughall felt the horse tremble under his touch. "Easy, Lightning. I'll take ye for a long ride."

"Are you almost ready, Brother?" Gilbert asked, as he saddled his horse.

"Aye." Dughall untangled the reins and checked the stirrups. His thoughts were uneasy. "Do we have everything?"

"The supplies are packed in my saddlebag. We'll see the old healer when we reach the village."

"All right. Come on Lightning." He took the horse's reins and followed Gilbert out of the stable into the courtyard.

Black Lightning snorted and pawed the ground. He tossed his head as snowflakes landed on his face. Dughall held him fast. "Father was right. He gets restless when he hasn't been out for a while."

Gilbert mounted his horse and held the reins. His breath hung like webs in the frigid air. "Let's go, Brother. It's cold out here."

Dughall put his foot in the stirrup and swung his leg over the horse's back. He straightened up and held the reins tightly. Lightning snorted.

"Relax your thighs, little brother," Gilbert said. "The horse can feel it if you're nervous. Lightning needs someone strong to command him."

Dughall took a deep breath and allowed his muscles to relax. Lightning whinnied.

Gilbert's horse led the way as they left the courtyard through the back gate. The path through the forest was snow-covered, unbroken by hoof or footprints.

Dughall's thoughts drifted as he rode through the forest. The horse knew the way and followed Gilbert's horse flawlessly. He saw snow clouds looming to the east. *It's a cold day in Whinnyfold,* he thought. *Ian... Where are ye?* Uneasiness overcame him. A brief connection to Ian told him that Father was sick. His brother was frightened.

Dughall's heart ached. *Oh God... I can't be there. Help my family.*

"The healer's cottage is just ahead." Gilbert announced.

They entered a clearing and saw a stone dwelling with a large woodpile. Smoke drifted upwards from the chimney. They guided their horses closer, dismounted, and tied them to a tree. An old woman sat on a stump, her hands at work stripping bark from a rod. She wore a woolen sweater, a black skirt, and a leather apron. Her white hair was tied in a red scarf, and her face was cragged and weathered.

She peered at them with confusion. "Who goes there?" she cried, in a frail voice.

As they approached her, she stiffened.

"You know me, Beathag. It's Lord Gilbert."

She relaxed and bowed her head. "My Lord... And this other gentleman?"

"My brother, Dughall."

"We were told of his arrival. My Lords. What do ye want with this old woman?"

"We require some herbal supplies. Can we go inside?"

"Aye, m'Lord." Her hands shook as she opened the door and led them inside. She flinched when she realized that they were right behind her.

Dughall touched her face. "You have veils on your eyes, mother. You can't see us verra well."

"Forgive me, my Lord. I see well enough to get around, but I fear that my days as a healer are over. What can I get for ye?"

Gilbert spoke up. "My brother requires a mortar and pestle, willow bark, and calendula flower."

She limped to a small wooden cupboard and opened it. "This is all that I have. 'Haps the young Lord would like to look through my supplies."

Dughall nodded. "Aye. Thank ye, good mother." He searched through the cupboard until he found a mortar and pestle and handed it to Gilbert. Dughall opened a bag of yellow flowers and put it aside. He opened another pack and found what looked like willow bark. He placed a bit on his tongue; it was bitter as expected. "Willow bark."

"Aye, my Lord. How is it that ye understand these things?"

"I was a healer back home," Dughall said, as he handed the supplies to his brother. "Kind mother. You must keep this a secret. My father would not be pleased."

She smiled. "I will keep yer secret."

He touched her face gently. "I wish I could heal your sight, but I've seen this before. There is no cure."

She shook her head. "I know it. The malady comes with old age. I ask that ye find a new healer for the village."

Gilbert nodded. "I promise, old woman, but we must be on our way. Please accept this for your trouble." He pressed a gold coin into her hand.

The old woman felt the surface of the coin and slipped it into her pocket. "Bless ye, my Lords." She led them to the door and hesitated, touching Dughall's cheek. "God go with ye, young Lord. I give ye the healing touch that old Janet gave me, fifty years ago. May God allow the healing to come through ye."

Dughall held her weathered hand. "This is a great honor. Are ye sure I'm the one?"

"Aye. I feel compassion in your touch."

"Thank ye kind mother, for your precious gift. I will visit again. There is much you can teach me." He embraced her and they left the cottage, eager to continue their journey. Flora's place was a few miles ahead.

***

James Laing lay in bed with his leg exposed to the air. His curly red hair was matted with sweat. A sharp smell of body odor lingered in the room.

Flora placed a hand on his forehead. "Your fever is back."

He sighed. "Aye. Let me go, lass. I grow weary of being a burden."

"Father. Beathag doesn't know what to do with your wounds. I've asked another healer to look at ye."

For the first time in days, he felt hopeful. "You know this woman?"

"Aye. But it's not a woman; it's a man. He seems to know a great deal about these things."

"I've never heard of a male healer. How did ye find him?"

"I met him at the Earl's party last night. Young Andrew told me that he saw him go into Beathag's cottage. He'll be here soon."

He held his knee and winced. A bead of yellow pus dripped from the wound. "I would give anything to walk again. Who is he?"

"That's what I must talk to ye about. We have to keep it secret. It's the Earl's son."

James sat up straight. "Lord Gilbert? He's not touching my leg."

"Nay. It's his youngest son, Lord Dughall. They found him in a coastal village near Peterhead. He was a fisherman and a healer."

"Hmmmph... Those fisher folk are known for their strange ways. Perhaps they know more about healing than we do. Why must we keep it secret?"

"The Earl insists that he leave his old life behind. It's not proper for a Lord."

"Why would he help me, then?"

"He said that it's what God would want him to do."

"A Gordon who truly believes in God? I like him already."

Flora smiled. "They'll be here soon."

***

Dughall and Gilbert entered the village and tied their horses to a hitching post in front of the blacksmith's shop. The clang of his anvil sounded musical in the still air. They packed their tools and supplies into a leather bag. The clanging stopped.

A young man came out of the blacksmith's shop and wiped his hands on his leather apron. "My Lords. Shall I care for the horses?"

Dughall smiled. "Aye. Give them some water and a bale of hay." He reached into his pocket, took out a coin, and pressed it into the lad's hand. "I trust that you'll take good care of them."

The lad stared. "Aye, my Lords."

"Can you groom them?"

"Aye."

Dughall reached in his saddlebag, took out a brush and handed it to him. "Brush them down. Be careful with the black stallion. Don't touch his flanks. He's high spirited."

"Aye, m'Lord."

They left him alone and walked to Flora's cottage. A wreath of pine branches and holly hung on the door. They stamped snow from their boots and knocked.

Flora opened the door. "My Lords. I'm pleased that ye came. Father is within."

They entered the stone cottage and took off their coats and scarves, laying them on a chair. Dughall studied her. She looked different in a woolen sweater and skirt, less like a lady and more like the lasses back home. He looked around the room. The cottage was a good size, with a hearth and table on one end, and three beds on the other. The floor was dirt, with hay spread upon it. Dried peat burned in the fireplace, casting a pungent odor. An iron pot hung on a cooking bar that traversed the fire. In front of the hearth, an old collie lay sleeping soundly.

"The dog won't hurt ye, m'Lords. She's twelve years old and nearly deaf."

Dughall watched as Flora lit a candle and carried it to a nightstand by one of the beds. He saw a man laying there with his leg exposed, and sniffed the air. It smelled of sweat, but didn't reek of flesh rot. They joined her at his bedside.

The man sat up and held his knee. "My Lords."

Gilbert spoke. "James. This is my brother Dughall. He tells me that he has some skill with healing wounds. We'll help you, but you must keep it secret. My father must not learn of this."

"Aye, m'Lords. I would be grateful."

Dughall shook his hand. The flesh was feverish, but his grip was strong. He sensed his uneasiness. "Don't be afraid, James. I've treated many wounds. If God is willing, we'll heal ye. Do ye believe in God?"

James grew calm. "Aye."

Dughall grasped his wrist and held his thumb over the large vein, silently counting the pulses. He watched his chest, noting the way that it rose and fell with each breath. "Your heartbeat is strong and your breathing is steady."

"Aye, m'Lord. I was a sturdy man until this happened."

"Good. What I do today will test us both. First, I'll look at your wound. This may hurt a bit."

"All right."

Dughall grasped his ankle and straightened the leg. The upper leg looked ugly. A deep gash from a blade had cut through muscle to the bone. The edges of the wound were red and hot and pus oozed in places. There was a dead flap of skin on one side. It would have to heal some before it could be stitched. He thought for a moment. "Flora. I'll need water and soap to wash my hands. Place a blanket under the leg, to sop up the mess while I clean the wound."

"Aye, m'Lord."

He turned to Gilbert. "Brother... Unpack the whisky and the clean cloth. Set up the rest of the supplies on the table."

Gilbert gagged. "I'm not good at this, lad. I'm having trouble keeping my breakfast down."

"Just unpack it. I'll not ask ye to do any more."

Gilbert nodded and reached for the leather bag.

Flora touched his shoulder. "I'll help ye, m'Lord." She readied the wash water and placed a blanket under the leg.

Dughall scrubbed his hands in the bowl and wiped them dry. "Do ye drink, man?"

James nodded. "Aye."

"Pour him a measure of whisky. This will hurt like the devil."

Flora opened the whisky flask, filled a cup, and gave it to her father.

James bolted it down and closed his eyes. His skin flushed and his body slackened. He opened his eyes and stared. "I'm ready now."

"Pour him another in case he needs it."

Flora filled the cup and placed it on the nightstand. Dughall took his dirk and some clean cloth to the bedside.

James paled when he saw the knife and grabbed the young Lord's arm. "Do what ye must. I'll stand anything to walk again." He released him and looked away.

The young Lord grasped the leg. "Lass. Hold the foot steady."

She complied. He took the flask and tipped it, pouring whisky into the wound. James gasped, but stayed the course. He grasped the blanket and clenched his teeth.

"Hold on friend," Dughall whispered. "Give me time to clean it." He flushed debris from the wound and used a cloth to wipe away pus. He took his dirk and cut back the dead skin. Dughall flushed it again and cleaned the tender area around the wound.

James drew his breath in sharply. His body started to shake. "Dear God! I can't bear it much longer."

Dughall released the leg. "You're a brave one. We're done with this part. Now we must prepare a poultice."

James held his knee and rocked. "Bless ye, m'Lord."

"Lass. Give him more whisky."

Flora held the cup while her father gulped it down. She smoothed his hair back. "I love ye, Father."

"I know, lass," James said. "It's all right. The man knows what he's doing."

Dughall turned away and worked at the table. He used the mortar and pestle to crush the flowers into a fine powder and dumped it into a bowl. He cleaned and sharpened his dirk and pressed honey from the comb, adding it to the poultice. Gilbert and Flora watched intently.

"I could never do this," Gilbert said. "You worked on the man in spite of his agony."

"I don't think of it that way, Brother. I caused him pain, but it's necessary to start the healing. I'm the only hope he has to walk again."

Flora nodded. "That's true. I've never seen a healer use honey."

Dughall smiled broadly. "Aunt Maggie said that bees are remarkable creatures. Honey brings down the swelling and speeds healing. It's the only thing that works on old wounds." He prepared a bandage, spread the poultice on it, and returned to the bedside. Glassy eyes stared up at him.

Dughall touched his arm. "Are ye ready, James? The worst part is over. I'm going to put a healing poultice on it. It should stop the burning."

James nodded. Flora held the leg while Dughall applied the bandage and secured it with strips of cloth.

James sighed. "Thank God. It feels better already."

"I will return in three days to check it. If it improves, I'll stitch it with sinew. Your muscle was torn. You may not get full use of the leg, but at least you'll walk with a cane."

James nodded. "That would be a miracle."

"Aunt Maggie would say that the healing is up to you. You must think of your leg as whole and healed. Promise me that you'll think on it every day."

"I promise. Thank ye, m'Lord."

"Lay back and get some rest. The lass needs to clean ye up."

Flora removed the wet blanket and made him comfortable in bed. James closed his eyes and drifted off. The young Lord returned to the table and scrubbed his hands up to his elbows. He cleaned the mortar and pestle and packed the leather bag.

Flora joined him. "We'd almost lost hope. Beathag didn't know what to do."

"I saw her this morning, lass. Did ye not see the veils on her eyes? She's nearly blind."

"I didna realize. Can ye cure her?"

"There is no cure. It comes with old age. She can't serve as healer anymore, so we'll ask Father to find you a new healer." He handed her a pack of willow bark. "Make a tea of this for pain and fever. Give it to him three times a day. No more whisky. It's only to be used when we work on that leg."

They put on their coats and scarves. Gilbert headed for the blacksmith's shop to check on the horses.

Flora gazed at the young Lord with eyes of gratitude. "Can I touch ye, m'Lord?"

Dughall smiled. "Aye, lass. I'm as human as you are."

She stood on her toes and kissed his cheek. "I will remember what ye did for my father."

He blushed. "It's what a healer does. We'll return in three days. I must get back before my father gets suspicious."

Dughall opened the door and left the cottage. He held a hand to his brow and looked at the position of the sun. "It must be later than I think." In the distance, he saw Gilbert talking to the young man. The lad threw up his hands and went back into his shop. He walked to the horses and helped his brother unhitch them. Black Lightning nickered when he patted him on the face. "Have ye been a good horse?"

Gilbert chuckled. "He nipped the lad when he brushed him."

Dughall smiled. "I guess he earned that coin."

"Aye."

A light snow began to fall as they mounted. Gilbert glanced at his pocket watch. "I'm afraid we've missed our midday meal. You must be starving."

Dughall smiled. "I didn't even notice. It's wonderful to feel useful again."

"I have a new respect for you, little brother. Not many men could do what you did. Let's get under way."

They guided the horses in the direction of Huntly Castle. Gilbert's horse led them through the forest, with Lightning following close behind. It was silent except for the steady clopping of hooves.

Dughall's thoughts wandered. He closed his eyes and saw his father in bed, stricken with fever. He imagined his hands on his body. *Dear God... Today I humbly did your work. I ask ye to heal my father. Send him my love and my healing touch. Amen.*

GIFT OF LIFE

WHINNYFOLD
DECEMBER 29 1636
THREE DAYS LATER

Three long days and nights had passed. A snowstorm blanketed the land, and word came from Peterhead that four people died from the grippe. Jessie attended to Alex, keeping him warm and coaxing him to drink. Coltsfoot helped his cough, but his fever soared. Lost in delirium, he raved that Dughall visited him.

Ian cleared a path to the shed to get food and hauled peat for the fire. He hoped that the boat was secure and worried that they were almost out of water. In the back of his mind, he wondered if Mary was all right. At last the snow stopped, allowing the sun to melt the drifts.

Ian stood in the stream and filled a bucket with water. His heart ached as he held his hands together in prayer. "Dear God. Father's near death and Mother looks awful. We've lost Dughall and Maggie. Isn't it enough?" His stomach churned. "Forgive me, Lord. It's not my place to question ye. I can barely stand, please help us."

The lad lifted the heavy bucket and hauled it towards the cottage. He stopped halfway, put the bucket down, and sniffed his shirt. "Whew… I stink like a polecat." He caught his breath, lifted the bucket, and continued on. He staggered by the time he reached the cottage.

Jessie met him at the door. For the first time in days, she smiled. "His fever broke. He's going to be all right."

Ian breathed a sigh of relief. "Thank God."

She hugged him close. "What would I have done without ye?"

"It's all right, Mother. You might want to step back, I stink."

She hugged him tighter. "I don't care. You smell like a man who's worked hard."

"I hope that Mary's so understanding."

Ian hauled water to the hearth and stoked the fire with a bundle of peat. He noticed that his father's bed was empty.

Alex sat at the table, warming his hands around a cup of tea. His eyes were sunken and his lips were cracked. "Son... Come here."

Ian sat across from him. The man looked like he's seen the fires of hell. "Father. You must be feeling better. You're sitting up."

Alex's voice was weak. "I'm not dead yet. Your mother tells me that ye worked hard."

"Aye."

Alex ran his fingers through his stringy hair. "Thank ye, Son. I'm proud of ye." He coughed into his hand.

"Rest, Father. We can talk later. You've been verra sick."

"This can't wait. I have something to ask ye."

"All right."

Alex reddened. "When Dughall reaches out to ye, what happens? Is it his voice? His touch? Do ye feel it or do ye just know it?"

Ian raised his eyebrows. "All those things and more. Why do ye ask?"

"Oh God. I don't know what to believe. Days ago when I burned with fever, I felt his love. It wasn't words. No voice rang in my ears. He placed his hands on me to heal me. Could it be?"

Ian felt a chill. "It sounds like him."

"I lay in bed feeling his touch, wondering how he knew."

"Dughall never blocked the thoughts of others. He felt the knife on Maggie's throat. He knew you were sick."

"From so far away?"

"Aye. It doesn't seem to matter."

Tears filled his eyes. "Dughall still loves me. I felt it. He must know by now that I'm not his father."

"You'll always be his father. He won't forget us."

Alex smiled. "God will bring us back together. We'll be a family again."

"The Duke said he's destined to take his place. He can't come back."

"Have faith, Son. God will show us the way."

Miles from Huntly Castle - Cottage of Flora Laing Aberdeenshire - Scotland

They stood on Flora's doorstep and stamped snow from their boots. The ride through the forest had taken twice as long.

"Let's hope it stays clear," Dughall said. "We've had more than enough snow."

Gilbert knocked. "It was almost too deep for the horses. Lightning was spooked."

Flora opened the door. "My Lords! You came in spite of the snow."

Dughall studied her face. Her eyes were tired, but a smile lingered about the corners of her mouth. *James must be somewhat better,* he thought with relief.

They entered the cottage and took off their coats. Gilbert unpacked the leather bag and set up the supplies on the table.

Dughall walked to James' bedside. The man was clean and shaven, always a good sign. He sniffed the air. There was no sign of flesh rot. "How are ye feeling, friend?"

James grasped his arm. "My Lord. I'm no healer, but it seems better. The pain is less and my fever is gone. Every day, I've thought of it as whole and healed, like ye asked."

Dughall smiled. "Aunt Maggie was right after all. Lass, hold his leg still while I remove the bandage."

Flora extended the leg and held it firmly.

Dughall untied the bandage and removed the poultice. As it pulled away, a bit of dead flesh came with it. He examined the wound, lightly stretching the skin until he saw that there was no pus. A clear fluid oozed, but that was normal. Deep within, pink flesh grew in bands. He prodded the edges and saw that it was starting to knit. "Good. There's no sign of festering and the flesh is trying to knit. We should stitch it and apply another poultice."

James nodded.

"I'll leave part of it open so the poultice can work and the wound can drain. It will close on its own. Are ye ready?"

"Aye, m'Lord."

"Stitching can be painful, but I promise it won't be as bad as the cleaning. Would ye like some whisky?"

"Nay. I want to watch you work."

Dughall went to the table and washed his hands. He examined a piece of deer sinew, threaded it through a curved needle, and tied the ends in a knot. He returned to the bedside.

Gilbert stared. "I want to see this, lad."

"Are ye sure, Brother? It may get a bit grisly."

"Aye."

Dughall looked at the wound. He decided to start near the knee and work down, leaving it open below.

James clenched his jaw. "Do what ye must, I can bear it."

Dughall glided the needle along the wound edge to the place where he wanted to begin. He rotated his wrist and pressed the needle in, puncturing skin, and pulled the sinew through to the other side. He pierced it and drew the sinew across, pulling the top of the wound together. The first stitch was done.

James shuddered. "It's not so bad. You have skillful hands."

Dughall talked while he stitched. "Back home, I stitched up many wounds. The life of a fisherman is a dangerous one. We work with sharp tools and hooks all the time. Last summer, a young lad sliced open his hand with a rusty dirk. I gave him twenty stitches. It took two men to hold him still." He was halfway done now.

James held his thigh. "Did ye ever cut peat, m'Lord?"

"Aye. Every year we went to the bog and cut for a full day. We spent the next day hauling it."

"I fell on a peat cutter."

"Those blades are sharp and their wounds often fester. It must be something in the peat." Dughall was nearly done. He looked up and saw that Gilbert was pale. He put in the last stitch and tied the sinew in a knot. "All done. I'm leaving a small opening so it can drain. Now we must apply a poultice."

James grasped his knee. "It's a miracle! My leg is whole again. Can I walk?"

Dughall shook his head. "Not yet. Stay off your feet for a week. Then start slowly with a cane." He unwrapped the poultice he'd prepared at the castle, spread it in a clean bandage, and applied it to the wound. "I'm pleased, James. God was on our side."

"My Lord. I will never forget this. You healed me."

Dughall smiled. "Aunt Maggie used to say that we didn't heal people. We allowed God to come through us and provide the healing. I like that better."

"As you wish, my Lord."

Flora smiled. "Aunt Maggie sounds like a wise woman."

"I learned a lot from her. She's dead now, but she was verra special to me." He scrubbed his hands in a bowl of water and packed his supplies in the leather bag. They were ready to leave.

Gilbert spoke. "Promise me that this will be kept secret. My father would be angry if he knew."

James nodded. "I give you my word."

Flora fluffed his pillow. "I promise, m'Lord."

"Good. I've made some inquiries about getting a new healer. There's an apprentice in Old Meldrum who's interested. Name's Marcia MacAdam."

Dughall brightened. "She can understudy Beathag."

"Are you ready to go, Brother? If we don't return by supper, Father will let the dogs loose and come after us."

"Aye, let's go."

They put on their coats and scarves. Gilbert hiked the bag of supplies onto his shoulder and opened the door. "I'll leave the two of you alone for a moment."

Flora waited until he went through the door. "You're a remarkable man, Lord Dughall. Aunt Maggie would be proud."

He smiled. "You were a lot of help, lass. You should consider becoming a healer."

"Perhaps, I will. Can I touch ye, m'Lord? Are ye still human?"

"Aye, more so than ever. Seeing the work of God always makes me feel humble."

Flora took his hand and ran a finger along the scar in his palm.

Dughall read her desires. She wanted him to forget about his promise and take her in his arms. "Nay, lass."

She released his hand. "It seems I've offended ye."

"Nay. I can't give ye what ye want. I'm hand fast."

She blushed furiously. "Am I so obvious?"

"Aye."

Silence hung between them like a veil. Her disappointment was palpable. At last, she spoke. "Your brother's waiting, m'Lord. Thank ye for saving my father."

"You're welcome, lass. I'll return in a week to check on him."

***

Dughall left the cottage and stood on the doorstep. He was elated that James was doing so well. "Thank ye God, for this healing. The man will walk again." He remembered the woman who meant so much to him. "Bless ye Aunt Maggie, for teaching me."

He glanced at his palm and thought of how Flora had caressed it. "Such a bonny lass. Her thoughts were so clear. Sometimes I wish I couldn't read them."

Dughall closed his eyes and remembered the lass he loved.

Her soft voice echoed in his mind. "If we believe we'll marry, we will. Where I come from, we call it magic."

He whispered the vow. "I pledge myself to ye in joy and sadness, wholeness and brokenness, in peace and turmoil, faithfully for all our days." His heart swelled. "Magic it is, lass. Wait for me." He left the doorstep and joined his brother at the hitching post.

***

Flora sat at her father's bedside and absently smoothed his hair. "I'll ask young Andrew to make ye a cane. You'll be walking in a week."

"I won't be a burden anymore. The young Lord has given me back my life."

"Aye."

"Sweet lass. You're taken with him, aren't ye?"

Flora blushed. "He's the most decent man I've ever met."

"There's no need to convince me. You have my blessing to pursue him."

She sighed.

"What's wrong, child?"

"His heart belongs to another."

CRISIS

WHINNYFOLD
FEBRUARY 28 1637
TWO MONTHS LATER

Alex stood on the point and looked out to sea. The 'Bonnie Fay' was ready to sail, but the water was too rough. Heavy snow clouds loomed to the south, threatening bad weather, and waves battered rocks in the harbor. Seagulls screamed like banshees and flew landward.

"That's a bad sign. The gulls know when to take cover." He ran his fingers through his hair and frowned. "It's too dangerous. Better that we walk to Peterhead."

He heard a voice crying his name and looked up. Jessie stood at the cliff's edge, clutching a shawl about her. She reminded him of Maggie. He waved and watched as she went back to the cottage.

His heart ached with the pain of loss. "Dear Maggie. I never said how much ye meant to me. I miss ye, old woman." A lone gull circled overhead, crying as it came closer. It made a final pass and headed towards land. "Dear Jesus. Here I am thinking about the dead. I feel uneasy today. Protect my family."

A sudden wind blew across the point, chilling him to the bone. He shivered and put up his collar. "There's an ill wind. God wants me home today." He fastened his coat and headed for the village.

HUNTLY CASTLE

It was a frigid morning at Huntly Castle. Servants scurried about stoking fireplaces and trying to keep warm. Inhabitants of the castle stayed inside and animals were kept in the barns. The courtyard was deserted. It was too cold to stay outside.

Dughall sat at the breakfast table, finishing his eggs. He pushed away the plate. "Can we take the horses out today?"

Blackheart shook his head. "Nay, Son. It's too damn cold. I told the lad to start the fireplace in the stables."

"Lightning will get restless."

"I can't help that. Didn't ye take him out yesterday?"

"Aye. We ride every day."

Gilbert sipped his tea. "Not today, Brother. The blacksmith must look at my horse. I think a shoe is loose."

His voice was laced with disappointment. "All right. We'll ride tomorrow."

Blackheart drank from his flask. "Murdock says you're progressing with your sword practice. It's time that ye faced me in the weapons chamber."

Dughall swallowed hard. Father had a reputation as a fierce fighter. "Are ye sure I'm ready?"

The Earl stood and flexed his hand around an invisible hilt. "We shall see. Come along now." Gilbert and Dughall pushed back their chairs and joined him. Blackheart stared at his oldest son. "Where will ye be, lad?"

"In the Great Chamber, with Bridget. She's wants to play the harp for me."

"You spend too much time with that lass. She's not of your standing."

"Father. I enjoy her company."

"You enjoy what's between her legs. Just as long as she knows her place."

Gilbert reddened. "She does."

Blackheart smiled. "Good. Your brother and I will be in the weapons chamber. It's time he learned from a master."

They left the dining hall and found Murdock in the corridor. The Earl dismissed him with a wave of his hand. "My son and I will be in the weapons chamber. You can meet up with him later."

"Aye, my Lord." Murdock's face pinched with concern. "Remember what I taught ye, lad."

Blackheart glared. "He doesn't need a reminder. Leave us, Murdock."

The servant bowed nervously, bending like a pine in the wind, and hurried toward the kitchen.

"Good luck, Brother. Father's a fierce warrior."

Dughall winced. *Oh God. I'm not ready.*

Blackheart put an arm around his shoulders. "Never mind what they think. You'll be fine."

***

It was cold in the weapons chamber, due to winds that battered the castle. Dughall could see his breath.

Blackheart walked around the room lighting sconces. "I wish we had a fireplace in here, but it's bad for the weapons. It's colder than a whore's heart."

"We'll warm up once we get moving." The lad took off his sweater and walked to the oak table. His hand stroked the scabbard of the sword of Red Conan.

Blackheart frowned. "Hmmmphh. Is this the sword you've been using?"

Dughall held the scabbard in his left hand and unsheathed the sword. His arm was strong enough to hold it in one hand. "Aye. I love this sword."

Blackheart rolled up his sleeves. "Most men do. It's been known to seduce a man and seal his fate. Any man who claimed it died before the year's end. They say that the sword is waiting for its original owner." He drew his own sword and ran a finger along the blade.

"Father. Do ye think it's cursed?"

"Aye. The last man who claimed it was my Uncle George. He was strong and fast, a true master at swordplay. Within weeks he began to waste away, until he couldn't hold the sword up. Still, he wouldn't renounce it. There wasn't a healer in Scotland who could help him. He died in December of that year, clutching the sword."

"That's terrible."

"It was bad for him, but good for my father. With his brother dead, he became Earl when Grandfather passed."

"Strange how one thing can change so many things."

Blackheart nodded. "Aye. That's what happened to the Duke. That old bastard thought he'd never have to deal with me again. An accident happened, his son died, and you became his only heir."

"How is Grandfather?"

"I don't know, lad. He's alive or they would have come for ye."

Blackheart raised his eyebrows. "You've been holding that sword in one hand. That's quite an accomplishment. It's twice as heavy as any modern sword."

Dughall felt proud. "Aye. It took time to get used to the weight and feel of it. My arm is a lot stronger."

Blackheart took a step back and assumed a defensive stance, holding his sword with two hands. "Come on, lad. Enough talk. Show me what ye can do."

Dughall swallowed hard. He stood with legs apart, one foot slightly in front of the other, and held his sword in both hands.

Blackheart smiled. "First blood?"

"What?"

"We spar until one of us draws blood."

Dughall's heart pounded. "Father... I don't want to hurt ye."

"Ha! So you think you can? Do your damnedest, lad."

"Oh God."

"When you're facing a man's weapon, God has nothing to do with it." He gripped his sword. "Last chance. Strike a blow, lad!"

Dughall remembered what Murdock taught him. He raised his weapon and lashed out in a thrust, slash, and overhead maneuver.

Blackheart raised his sword and warded off the blow. Sparks flew and the sound of metal against metal rang in the air. "Good! You caught me by surprise." He closed in, bringing his sword down in a diagonal strike.

Dughall jumped back and blocked the cut with his sword. The blow sent vibrations down his arms. Fear coursed through his veins.

"Good move, lad! An enemy could have slit ye from shoulder to belly."

They sparred lightly, testing each other; then picked up the pace until they breathed heavily. Blackheart's blade met Dughall's sword with a sharp sound. He bore down until the base of his blade met the crossbar. They were locked.

Mercy! Dughall's muscles screamed with exertion. He pushed with all his strength and grunted.

The Earl pulled back slightly, throwing him off balance, and pulled him to the ground. Dughall's eyes closed as he hit the floor. When he opened them, a blade was at his throat. He glanced at his hand. It held the sword.

Blackheart pressed the sharp tip against his throat. "I win. Drop your weapon." The sword clanged as it hit the floor. The young Lord took a ragged breath. Blackheart frowned. "Gordons don't show fear! Now, for first blood." He withdrew the blade and ran the tip along his shoulder, gashing his upper arm. He reached down, took his hand, and pulled him up.

Dughall felt a fierce sting. He grasped his arm and saw blood welling up on his shirt. He didn't dare to speak.

"It's a flesh wound, lad. You're a worthy opponent, but you'd be dead if this was a real match. Do ye know what ye did wrong?"

Dughall shook his head.

"Sometimes, the strength of a warrior is not enough. You must fight with malice and cunning. I threw ye off balance. Next time, I'll show ye how to avoid that."

"Thank ye, Father." Dughall pulled out a kerchief and pressed it against his wound. Sweat trickled down his back. "It's hot in here."

Blackheart laughed. "Nay, it's as cold as it was. Your blood's a boil. Let's get ourselves cleaned up."

They sheathed their swords and lay them on the oak table. The Earl slapped him on the back. "I'm proud of ye, lad. It will be a pleasure to teach ye."

He had a lot to learn from this man. "Can we spar again soon?"

Blackheart smiled as he buttoned his cuffs. "Aye." They left the weapons chamber and headed for the bath chamber.

***

Kate hurried across the frozen courtyard and entered the castle through the main door. She could see her breath. "It's colder than a witch's teat in here. Where are the servants?" Her cheeks were raw from the frigid air. "I must see the young Lord. Murdock can't keep us apart forever. He wants me. I read it in his face."

Her mind wandered as she took the stairway to the first floor. She remembered the lad as he was on that first night, so innocent and open. A perfect lover. Kate made up her mind. "I'll seduce him and tell him that I carry his child."

She turned a corner and approached the kitchen. A serving lass appeared, carrying a bowl of potato scraps. "Tavia."

The lass bowed her head. "M'Lady."

"Where is the Earl?"

"Ummmm. Rumor has it he faced the young Lord in the weapons chamber this mornin'."

Kate's eyes widened. "Lord Gilbert or Dughall?"

"Lord Dughall, m'Lady."

"Who told ye this?"

Tavia's hand shook as she sorted scraps. "Murdock. He's hauling wood for the kitchen this mornin'."

So Murdock wasn't with him! This was her chance. "I must see the Earl. Where are they now?"

Tavia shrugged. "Don't know. Marcia poured them a bath a while ago."

Kate flushed with anger. "Idiot! You're no help." She picked up her skirts and took the stairway to the main wing.

***

Dughall stood in the bath chamber with a towel around his waist. He held a washcloth against his wound.

The Earl buttoned his cuffs. "Is that still bleeding?"

"It's not so bad." Dughall dropped the towel and stepped into his kilt. "My shirt is bloody. I'll go to my bedchamber and change it."

Blackheart smiled. "Good idea, lad. We wouldn't want the help to think that I tried to kill ye." He slipped on his jacket. "I have to meet with the steward about some whisky. I'll see ye at the midday meal."

Dughall put on his shirt. "Thank ye Father. I hope we can spar again. It's been a good morning."

The Earl nodded. "Aye, Son. That it has." He opened the door and left the chamber.

Dughall picked up the towel and dried his hair. He pulled on his socks and shoes and stopped to check his arm, which was bleeding slightly. "Father can be a good man sometimes. It's hard to understand." He opened the door and walked into the deserted hallway. "Where is Murdock? No matter, I'll catch up with him later." Out of habit, he straightened his shirt and headed for his bedchamber.

***

Kate saw him in the distance, emerging from the bath chamber. She flattened herself against the wall to remain unseen. The young Lord straightened his clothes and headed in the opposite direction, towards the wing that housed the bedchambers.

Fear stopped her from following. Was the Earl nearby? She waited for a moment, staying out of sight. No one else came out of the bath chamber. "Good. He's alone and heading for his bedroom. Just where I want him."

Kate followed, leaving a distance between them. Her skin flushed with anticipation. "I would sell my soul to have him one more time." She turned the corner and saw him enter his chamber.

***

Blackheart sat with the steward in the wine cellar. The white-haired man tapped a cask and poured a glass of red wine. The Earl held the goblet to his nose and inhaled. It was rich and fruity, with a touch of earthiness. He took a sip. "This is excellent. Serve it at dinner tonight."

"As you wish, m'Lord."

"Did ye acquire some of that old whisky?"

The man smiled, revealing a mouthful of yellow teeth. "Aye, m'Lord. Six bottles. I had to promise the distiller more of our business."

The Earl nodded. "Hmmmphh... Not a problem, with the quality of that whisky."

"Is there anything else I can do for ye?"

Blackheart pressed a gold coin into the man's hand. "Nay. Good job, Garrick. I expect that this will take care of ye."

"Bless ye, m'Lord."

The Earl stood and started up the stairs towards the kitchen. At the top, he ran into a serving lass.

Tavia lowered her head. "Forgive me, my Lord. I didn't know ye were coming up those stairs."

"It's all right, lass."

"Are ye looking for m'Lady?"

"Whom are ye referring to?"

Tavia reddened. "Lady Kate."

He was surprised. "Is she here?"

"Aye, m'Lord. I saw her in the hallway a while ago. She asked about ye and the young Lord."

"Which young Lord?"

"Lord Dughall."

He stared as if in deep thought, then frowned. "Thank ye, lass. Go about your chores."

Tavia bowed. "Bless ye, m'Lord."

His suspicion grew as he hurried out of the kitchen.

Blackheart took long strides towards his bedchamber. He couldn't shake the feeling that something was wrong. "Perhaps she's waiting for me in my chamber." The Earl rounded a corner and saw his mistress in the distance. He flattened himself against the wall and watched. Kate glanced in both directions. She untied a ribbon and let down her hair, arranging it around her shoulders. She placed her hand on a door, opened it, and entered.

Blackheart reddened. "That's not my bedchamber." His anger exploded as he ran along the hallway and stopped in front of Dughall's door. "God damn her! She's sleeping with my son. How can they do this to me?" His face flushed with anger. "I'll beat them until they can't breathe!" He stood at the door and waited.

***

Dughall stripped off his shirt and stood in front of the long mirror. He squeezed his arm gently and examined the wound. "Father's right. It's just a flesh wound." He opened a drawer and took out a pot of salve and some cloth strips. As he spread ointment on the cut, he heard a door open. He didn't look back. "Murdock. Where have ye been?"

Kate's voice was sultry. "It's not Murdock. The man's remiss in his duties. We're alone at last."

Dughall's heart pounded with fear. He watched as she took off her coat and shoes. "Nay, lass. You belong to my Father."

She sat on the bed, arranging her hair around her shoulders. "We won't tell him."

Dughall reached to the floor and grabbed his shirt. When he looked up, she was pulling her dress over her head. Her full breasts lay against her naked chest. He rushed to the bed and threw his shirt at her. "Oh God! Cover that up! You must stop, lass."

She grabbed his arm and nuzzled his neck. "Make love to me like ye did before. I'll do whatever ye want."

His stomach churned. "Nay!"

"I'd sell my soul to have a night with ye."

It was all he could do to keep from gagging. "No man is worth that, lass."

He threw off her hand and headed for the door. Opening it, he saw his father, fists poised to strike. Fear gripped his heart. "Father, please. I didn't do anything. Oh God!"

Blackheart saw Kate on the bed, scrambling to cover her nakedness. He pushed the young Lord into the room and grabbed his throat.

Dughall choked. He struggled to pry the hand from his throat, but the man was too strong. Points of light danced in front of his eyes and his arms dropped.

Kate screamed. "Let him go. You're killing him!"

Blackheart released his throat, made a fist, and backhanded him across the face.

Dughall sank to the floor and held his aching jaw. His voice was weak. "Father... please."

The Earl grabbed Kate's hair. "Whore! I give you everything and you seduce my son."

Kate whimpered. "My Lord. It's not my fault. He forced me."

"Don't lie to me, bitch! I saw ye go into his chamber. No one held a knife to your throat." He picked up her clothes and threw them at her. "Wait for me in my bedchamber! You'll be sorry you were born."

"My Lord... Don't hurt me."

"Not another word!" Tears streamed down her face as she gathered her clothes and left the room. Blackheart looked down at Dughall. "We had a good morning together. All the while, you planned to rut with my mistress like an animal."

"Nay, Father. I didn't ask her here."

Blackheart reddened. "God damn it. Don't lie to me!"

"I never lie."

"Stay in your quarters, lad. I'll deal with ye later. You'll be lucky if I don't kill ye."

He was desperate. "Father, please don't do this. I swear I didn't touch her."

"Liar!" The Earl threw up his hands and left the chamber, intent on dealing with his mistress.

***

Dughall sat on the floor massaging his jaw. He noted a swelling and stuck a finger in his mouth to see if his teeth were solid. Several were loose. He heard a woman's scream, followed by pleading. His heart sank. "Dear God. There's nothing I can do." He got to his feet and staggered to the mirror. His vision was blurry and his head ached. There was another scream and an angry voice threatening. "Father's gone mad. He's going to kill us."

Images of Maggie's final moments flooded his mind. Dughall held a hand to his throat and swallowed hard. "I have to get out of here. He means to kill me."

The young Lord rummaged through drawers and took out riding clothes, heavy socks, and a sweater. He tore off his kilt, dressed quickly, and stepped into his boots. His vision was clearing. Fear rose in his throat as he thought of escape and his bowels churned. What if Father was outside the door?

He sank to his knees and prayed. "Dear God. Help me get away. I'm so afraid."

The Duke's warning echoed in his mind. "Ian, hear me! I'm in dire trouble. Send help, Brother." He stood and packed a pair of mittens into his coat and left the chamber. No one was in the hallway.

WHINNYFOLD

Ian sat at the table, discussing the wedding. Since he'd taken her in the shed, Mary had begged him to move up the date. He thought she might be pregnant. "We want to marry sooner."

Alex frowned. "Nay. I spoke with Andrew yesterday. He plans a grand wedding for you and his daughter in May."

Ian swallowed hard. "Two months away. I hope I can wait that long."

"Hmmmphh ... You better, lad."

Jessie kneeled at the hearth, tasting a pot of fish soup. She added a bit of parsley. "Mary's such a sweet lass. I can't wait for grandchildren."

The lad had a strange feeling. *They might come sooner than you think.*

She ladled soup into wooden bowls, brought them to the table, and sat down.

Ian grabbed a spoon. "I'm starved."

Alex clasped his hands. "Wait, lad. We must show gratitude for what God has provided." He bowed his head. "Come Lord Jesus be our guest, let thy gifts to us be blessed. Amen."

"Amen." Ian gulped a spoonful of soup and pushed the bowl away. The fish chowder sat in his stomach like a rock.

"What's wrong, lad? I've never known ye to refuse food."

Ian's eyes widened with panic. "I don't feel well." Raw fear made him dizzy. The Earl was strangling his brother. "Oh God. Not again."

Alex frowned. "Are ye sick?"

Ian grasped his throat and struggled for breath. Stars danced in front of his eyes. He couldn't answer.

"Are ye choking, lad?"

Ian nodded desperately and grunted as his head snapped back.

Alex grabbed his shoulders. "Is it your brother?"

"Aye. The Earl is beating him."

Alex pounded the table. "God in heaven! What can we do? I feel so damn helpless."

Ian massaged his jaw until his vision cleared. "Dughall's on the run. The Earl's going to kill him."

Jessie put a finger in his mouth. "A loose tooth. Maybe two. Does it hurt?"

"Aye. He nearly broke his jaw."

Alex sprang into action. He packed a leather bag with a dirk, a handful of coins, and warm clothes. "Lass, pack some bread and dried fish. Ian and I are off to Peterhead. We might be gone for days."

Jessie went to the cupboard and took out her healer's bag. "I'm going with ye."

Alex paled. "This is no trip for a woman. I want you safe."

"Maggie wasn't safe in her own home."

"For God's sake, Mother. It's too dangerous. We could be killed."

Jessie stared. "Then we'll die together." She packed a bag with bread and fish. "I have to go. Dughall may need a healer."

Alex frowned. "God help us."

Jessie hugged him. "It makes sense, husband. Let's put out the fire and dress warm." She turned to her son. "Find Robert and ask him to watch over the cottage. Tell him we may be gone a while."

Ian left the cottage and stood on the stoop. His mind flooded with Dughall's cry for help. "Hold on, Brother. I'm coming." He lifted his eyes and gazed to the heavens. "Oh God. I put my life in your hands. Do with me what ye will, but spare my family."

PURSUIT AND PUNISHMENT

HUNTLY CASTLE
FEBRUARY 28 1637
MINUTES LATER

Dughall put up his collar and hurried across the deserted courtyard. He thought about taking Murdock, but couldn't find him. He hesitated near the stables. "Should I take Black Lightning?" His heart ached. "Nay. Even though the horse is mine, he'll say that I stole him."

He passed the stables and stopped in the stone brew house to get out of the wind. The warmth of fermenting ale gave him time to think. "I can't go home. Father will kill them if he finds me there. Grandfather's castle is to the northeast. Perhaps Flora will take me in for a night." He left the brew house and walked between outbuildings, towards the back gate. A guard sat in a shack with a pint of ale in his hand. He was sleeping. "God is with me so far."

Dughall unlatched the gate, stepped outside and walked to the wooden bridge that crossed the Deveron. He grasped the guide rope and stared into the fast moving water. "What will he do to my family? It would be best for everyone if I threw myself in." Snow fell as he pondered the icy water. He thought of Alex, Jessie, and Ian receiving the news of his death. His suicide would kill them. "I can't do it. Oh God. Promise me that I'll see them again." He crossed the bridge and walked into the woods, following the path that led to the village.

***

Murdock hurried to Dughall's bedchamber. He'd been hauling wood for the kitchen all morning. "I hope the young Lord hasn't missed me." As he reached the bedchamber, he heard the Earl's angry voice.

Blackheart stood in the hallway, his clothes disheveled and a strap in his hand. He yelled at someone in his bedroom. "Whore! I'm not finished with ye. Don't ye dare leave this chamber."

The servant swallowed hard as the Earl approached.

"Murdock! Have ye been in his chamber?"

"Nay, m'Lord. I was just about to go in."

"Where the hell have ye been?"

Murdock stared at the strap and winced. "Forgive me, m'Lord. They asked me to haul wood for the kitchen."

"I'm not going to beat ye, but I am going to beat my son. I found Kate in there with him."

"You found them in bed together?"

"Nay. But she was undressing."

Murdock paled. "My Lord. This is my fault. I should have been at his side. Let me take his punishment."

Blackheart scowled. "Not this time. I want to see him squirm." He pushed open the door and went inside. "God damn him! I told him to stay here. Where is he?"

Murdock entered the chamber and went to the chest. He saw a kilt on the floor and rummaged through the drawers. His heart sank. "His riding clothes are gone."

Blackheart picked up the kilt. "He ran from me! Just like his mother. He's made it worse."

"He's afraid, m'Lord."

"Gordons face their fear. Get Gilbert and Conner. Seal off the exits and search the castle."

"My Lord. He's your son! Don't beat him."

Blackheart reddened. "Silence Murdock! I didn't ask for your opinion. Do what I told ye."

Murdock turned and ran down the hallway towards the main hall. His heart was beating like a great drum. "God help us."

***

Dughall's hands and feet were frozen as he trudged through the blanketed forest. He glanced behind him to see that snow was covering his tracks. "Good. No footprints to follow." He thought of the tracking dogs his father used to bring down prey. "I hope they can't find men." Dughall stopped for a moment and held his hands under his armpits. "Oh God, Ian. I'm so cold. I hope ye heard me."

Snow fell heavily, obscuring his view of the sky. His stomach grumbled. "It must be midday. I'd better hurry. It's another five miles to Flora's house." He rubbed his hands together and continued walking through the forest.

WHINNYFOLD

Alex stood on the rocky beach and looked out to sea. Heavy waves battered the rocks and splashed into the air. There wasn't a gull in sight. He swallowed his fear. They uncovered the boat, checked the rigging, and pushed the boat towards the water. Alex stopped at the shore and held his knees, breathing heavily.

Ian stared, his eyes wide with anxiety. "Father. Should we walk? You said that we should never sail on a sea like this."

Alex stiffened. "I know what I said. We'd be lucky to walk there by midday. I can sail there in an hour."

"Father. Look at the sea."

"God damn it! I know what it looks like. What shall we do, let your brother die?"

Ian shook his head. "Nay. Mother's coming. She looks like she's scared to death. Must we risk her, too?"

Alex swallowed against a lump in his throat. "I wish I could leave her, but she's right. What if your brother needs a healer?"

Jessie placed her healer's bag in the boat. Her cheeks were red from the wind. "The sea looks rough. Are we ready to go?"

Alex pulled her close. "Aye. God in heaven, I love ye so much. If anything happened to ye, I'd die."

She hugged him tightly.

He suppressed a sob. "Let's pray." They stood in a circle and held hands. "Oh God. We set out upon the water today to help our son. The sea is rough, unfit for man or beast. Protect us and keep us safe. Amen."

Jessie and Alex got into the boat while Ian pushed off, jumping in at the last moment. Alex clenched his jaw as he hoisted the mainsail. Jessie sat on a crate and gripped the side of the boat. Ian worked the rudder, guiding the boat around treacherous rocks into the open sea.

Alex noted some ominous signs. There was a halo around the sun and the swells were higher than the wind justified. A bank of dark clouds loomed to the south. He stationed Ian at the rigging and took the rudder, steering them north towards Peterhead.

He hugged the coast, staying far enough away to avoid the rocks. As they passed Slains Castle, the wind picked up causing great swells.

Ian cried out as the seas leapt short and broke over the boat, coming aboard and cascading off to leeward. He slipped, but caught himself on the mast.

Alex's fear blossomed. "Hold on, lad!" The shock of cold water moved him to action. "Loosen the main sail! Let it fly."

Ian complied and the boat eased forward. He wiped salt water from his eyes. For a few minutes they were stunned by the noise of the wind in the mast and rigging, the hiss of advancing breakers, and the splash of water against the hull.

Alex struggled with the rudder, his face a mask of anxiety.

Jessie gripped the side of the boat, her lips white with fear. She looked to the land and saw a stone cottage standing alone on the cliff. "Thank goodness. It's John Galt's place. We're halfway there."

Alex nodded. A few miles and the granite walls of Boddam castle appeared on the shore. Snow started to fall, obscuring the roiling sea. Time seemed to stand still as they sailed on.

Ian shivered as he checked the rigging. "Oh God. I'm soaked to the skin."

"We all are, lad."

At last, the port of Peterhead loomed on the horizon. Only a few sails dotted the harbor. As they approached the pier, Alex breathed easier. "Thank God."

Ian held a pole against the pier to stop the boat. He jumped off with a rope and tied the boat to a post. Alex helped Jessie onto the pier and handed Ian their bags. He took down the sails, secured the boat, and stepped onto the pier.

Alex hugged his wife and son, unwilling to let them go. Tears clouded his eyes.

"God was with us today. Dughall needs us. Come on, let's find Klaas."

HUNTLY CASTLE

Gilbert's heart was in his throat. A search of the castle found nothing. *Father is livid,* he thought. *We're all in for it, now.*

Blackheart fumed as he paced back and forth in the Grand Hall. "Did ye check the privy?"

"Aye."

"The kitchen and the steward's quarters?"

"Aye. Even the weapons chamber."

"I can't believe he'd leave the castle, it's too damn cold out there. What's wrong with that lad? Why the hell would he rut with my mistress?"

Gilbert swallowed his fear. "It's not Dughall's fault. Kate's been after him."

"How do ye know that?"

He reddened. "Forgive me, Father. She's obsessed with him. Murdock's been sleeping in his room to keep her out."

"God damn it! Why did ye not tell me?"

"I didn't want to make you angry."

"Well, I'm really angry now. Why would he leave?"

"He probably thought you'd beat him."

"I am going to beat him!"

Conner and Murdock entered the hall. "My Lord," Connor said. "It appears that he left through the back gate. It was unlocked. The guard was drunk, out cold."

"Take that man below!"

"Already done, m'Lord."

"Is Lightning gone?"

"Nay. He's in the stables. I looked outside the back gate. The snow covered up the young Lord's footprints."

Blackheart scowled. "Only an idiot would run away on a day like today. Bring my riding clothes and boots. I have his kilt. The dogs will find him."

Connor nodded and hurried out of the room.

"Get out of my way, Son!"

Gilbert stood his ground. "Take me with you."

"Nay. Connor and I will go. Stay here in case he returns and confine him to his quarters."

"Father. Please don't beat him. It's not his fault."

"Silence lad! Don't make me hurt ye." Blackheart pushed him aside and stormed out of the room.

Murdock shuddered. "Dear God. This is my fault."

"What?"

"I failed the young Lord. We should have told the Earl about Kate from the beginning. I talked him out of it."

"Aye, well. It's all water under the bridge. Now we must stop Father from beating him."

Murdock nodded. "They'll come back to the stables. Let's stoke the fire and wait with the horses."

***

Blackheart and Connor saddled their horses and rode to the back gate. Three deerhounds ran at their side, barking and baying with excitement. They left through the gate and dismounted. Blackheart took Dughall's kilt out of his saddlebag and held it to the dogs' noses. "Aye. That's it. Get a nose full. Now, find him!"

The dogs circled around sniffing the ground, their tails wagging furiously. At last, they agreed on a path leading to the bridge that crossed the river Deveron.

"God damn it! He's running to the Duke. I'll kill him with my bare hands." They mounted their horses and followed the dogs into the forest.

***

Dughall staggered through the dense forest. His feet were so cold that he couldn't feel them and he'd lost track of how far he'd come. "What a terrible mistake. I should have taken Lightning. Where am I now?" He trudged through the snow and entered a clearing where a cottage stood. Smoke curled upwards from the chimney. "Old Beathag." He walked to the door and pounded on it. After a few moments, the door opened a crack.

"Who goes there?"

He shivered. "Lord Dughall. Can I come in?"

The door opened. The old woman stared blankly, her eyes completely clouded over. She flinched from the cold.

He took her wrinkled hand and held it to his face. "Forgive me, Beathag. I know I'm cold."

"My Lord. You're like ice. Come in." The old woman limped toward the fireplace.

Dughall crossed the threshold and went to the hearth. He stripped off his mittens and held out his hands. Tingling quickly turned to pain. "It hurts like the devil. I hope I don't have frostbite."

"Don't get too close to the fire. Warm them up slowly."

"Ach! I should know better." He stepped out of his boots and placed them near the fire to dry. "My boots are soaked right through."

"What are ye doing here, lad? It's a day not fit for man or beast."

"I ran away."

Her eyes widened. "Why?"

"Father wants to kill me."

"Have ye been followed?"

He coughed. "I don't think so. The snow covered up my footprints."

"Thank goodness. Well lad, I don't have much but you're welcome to it. Warm up in front of the fire and I'll make soup."

"Thank ye, kind mother. I won't stay long."

"Lay your coat over the chair. The fire will dry it."

Beathag poured water into a pot and hung it over the fire. She added carrots, leeks, and a large soup bone.

Dughall stripped off his wet coat, hung it to dry, and sat in front of the fire. Within minutes, a feeling of uneasiness gripped him, making his skin crawl. Blackheart was nearby, contemplating his punishment. Surely, he would kill the old woman.

He's coming. God help us.

PETERHEAD

Alex stood in the dimly lit bar room, talking to the innkeeper. "My boat's moored in the harbor."

Klaas stared. "You sailed from Whinnyfold today?"

A man at the bar snorted. "The man's daft!"

Klaas frowned. "Keep to yourself, Nicolass. My God, Alex, you're lucky to be alive."

"I know it. Dughall's in danger. The Duke said to see you."

"How do you know he's in trouble?"

Alex was losing his patience. "Never mind that, we know! Will ye help us?"

"I'll saddle two horses," Klaas said. "The Duke said that Ian must come with me."

Alex frowned. "You'll saddle four. We're all going."

Klaas glanced at Jessie. "The woman too? It could be dangerous. She should stay here with my wife."

"That's a generous offer, but she's coming with us. Have ye got a problem with that?"

"Nay, friend. It's a ten-hour ride to Drake Castle over rough ground. For God's sake, change into some dry clothes. Use the room above."

Jessie and Ian headed up the stairs. The innkeeper's plump wife appeared at the door, carrying a tray of mugs. "Will ye stay and eat something?"

"Nay. There's no time to waste. My son's life is at stake."

Klaas sighed. "Maartje, pack us some food and water. I'll saddle the horses. We're leaving for Drake Castle."

"Do you have to go? I need you here."

"I know wife, but this is what the Duke's paid us for these last months."

"What about Mrs. Hay?"

"She's coming with us."

"Poor lass. Is there anything I can do?"

Alex nodded. "Aye. Tell Andrew McFarlein that we'll be gone for a while. I'll talk to him when we get back." He picked up his pack and followed his family upstairs.

FOREST NORTHEAST OF HUNTLY CASTLE

Blackheart's anger grew as he followed the dogs through the woods. He couldn't let the lad reach Drake Castle. He flexed his hand open and closed, making a fist. "How dare he run away! Damn it! I didn't want to break that lad."

"What was that, m'Lord?" Connor asked.

"Never mind." Up ahead, the dogs howled, ran in a circle, and pawed at the ground. Blackheart and Connor dismounted. They walked to the dogs and saw that they'd picked up footprints in the snow. "Excellent! Judging by these prints, he can't be too far."

"Aye, m'Lord."

They mounted their horses and followed the dogs until they emerged in a clearing where a stone cottage stood. The footprints stopped at the door. The Earl reddened. "Stay back, Connor. Tie the horses up here. I don't want to spook him."

Connor tied the horses to a tree and commanded the dogs to stay back. They started towards the stone cottage.

Blackheart growled, "Whose cottage is this?"

"It belongs to the healer, Beathag."

"That old woman? She's half-blind. What does she have to do with my son?"

"Don't know, m'Lord."

Blackheart placed his hand on the door. "We shall see."

***

Dughall sat at the crude wooden table, eating a bowl of hot soup. "I don't wish to put ye in danger. I'll leave after I eat." He shivered and coughed until his face was blue.

Beathag frowned. "Are ye sick, m'Lord? He'll never find ye here. Stay the night and leave in the morning."

"Nay, kind mother. Father is close by, I can feel him."

The door flew open and cold air poured into the room. Blackheart entered, with Connor behind him. His voice was laced with anger. "See that no one interrupts us."

Connor slammed the door and held it. "As you wish, m'Lord."

Dughall stood and looked around the cottage. Fear gripped his heart like an icy hand. There was no way out. "Oh God."

"Don't run, lad. Don't make me hurt ye."

"Father. I didn't bed Kate. Please listen…"

Beathag's voice was thin and frail. "Who's there?"

"It's the Earl of Huntly, old woman. How dare ye harbor my son."

"Forgive me, my Lord. I didn't know he was yer son."

Blackheart grabbed the old woman's arm and twisted. "You filthy old hag! Is this the truth?"

She stared through cloudy eyes. "Aye. I thought he was a lad from the village."

Connor chuckled. "Look at her eyes. She's as blind as a bat. She wouldn't know the young Lord from a lass."

The Earl squeezed her arm tighter, until something popped.

Beathag whimpered. "Ohhh… Dear Jesus."

Dughall knew that his father meant to kill the old woman. After all, he'd shown no mercy to Mills' wife and son. It seemed hopeless, but he had to try to save her. "Let her go! I'll not put up a fight. Do with me as ye will."

Blackheart stared. "I intend to beat ye, lad. Worse than before."

The young Lord resigned himself to a brutal beating. "I'll submit to ye willingly. Let her go."

The Earl let her drop to her knees and smiled.

Will he let her live? Logic said that it was impossible, but his father seemed satisfied. Dughall kneeled and ran his hand along her shoulder, feeling for a break. The joint was out of place. "Forgive me, old mother."

Blackheart grabbed his arm and lifted him up. "Get away from her, lad. Don't make me angrier than I am. Put on your coat and boots."

Conner threw him his coat. He dressed slowly and stepped into his boots. *They're soaked.*

Blackheart placed a hand on the back of his neck and squeezed. "We're going to walk out of here together. You're not to give me trouble or the woman dies. Is that understood?"

Dughall swallowed hard. "Aye, Father." He was getting a really bad feeling.

Blackheart kept a hand at his neck and guided him out the door. As they reached the horses, he turned to Connor. "Slit her throat." The servant turned and headed for the cottage.

"Nay!" Dughall cried. "I'll never run again. I beg ye not to hurt her. Call him back!"

Blackheart grabbed him by the throat and squeezed. "Your actions have consequences. Anyone who helps ye defy me dies." He released him. "Mount that horse. I'll ride behind ye."

Dughall mounted the horse and sat in front of the saddle. Hot tears clouded his eyes. He wiped them away with the heel of his hand. Connor joined them and nodded.

Blackheart mounted behind and took the reins. His voice was ominous. "Gordons don't cry."

Dughall wished he were dead.

HUNTLY CASTLE

Gilbert and Murdock waited in the stables. They stoked the fire in the hearth and sat on bales of hay, sharing some bread and cheese. Murdock wiped his mouth. "I'll offer myself in his place. It's my right as his manservant."

"I've never seen Father this mad. He could kill ye."

"No matter. The young Lord's a good man. I don't wish to see him beaten."

Gilbert sighed. "He is a good man, isn't he? How did that happen in this family?"

Murdock chuckled. "Forgive me, m'Lord. I've never heard ye talk that way."

"All these years, I've looked out for myself. I let Father do what he wanted, just as long as he didn't whip me. God forgive me, I let him torture Mills and put him to death. Then this lad comes along, an ignorant peasant, and dares to break the rules because of what he believes in."

Murdock nodded. "I know what ye mean."

"So here I sit, ready to risk my backside for him. God help us, Murdock."

FOREST NORTHEAST OF HUNTLY CASTLE

The snow fell heavier, sticking to their hair and eyebrows. The young

Lord was chilled to the bone. He coughed until his lungs ached.

Blackheart frowned. "What's wrong with ye, lad?"

"My clothes are soaked to the skin. I'm freezing."

"Idiot! You nearly killed yourself."

Dughall sniffled. He felt his father's strong arms around him as he held the reins. The man's rage grew by the minute, penetrating his very soul. He shivered with the cold.

Blackheart stiffened. "You are so like your mother. You defy me with no mind for consequences, yet you shake with fear under my touch."

Dughall took a ragged breath. "I'm not afraid."

"Ha! You're not?" He made a small sound of disbelief.

"I won't run again. I promise."

"If I have to find ye again, I'll kill ye."

Dughall's heart sank. "Forgive me, Father. Beathag's dead. Isn't it enough?"

"That old crone was near dead already. Enough, lad! Bear your punishment in silence like a man."

The young Lord sniffled and wiped his nose. They rounded a bend and entered a clearing. Demon snorted and Blackheart pulled back slightly on the reins. The dogs ran in a circle and relieved themselves against a tree.

"Just a few more miles through those woods," Connor said as he pointed to a path. "We're almost home, m'Lord."

Blackheart stared at his hand as he flexed it. He leaned forward and growled, "Too bad. I didn't want to have to break ye, lad."

Dughall flinched. *He means to whip me. Ian... Help me to bear it.*

Forest Eight Miles West of Peterhead

They'd been riding for more than three hours. Snow fell steadily, making it hard to stay on the path. Alex and Klaas stopped and dismounted. Their breath hung in the frigid air as they looked around. Alex was anxious. "Are ye sure ye know the way?"

Klaas nodded. "I've come this way before, though not in winter." He noted a break in the trees and pointed. "There. See that mark on the oak tree? The path starts up again."

"Thank God." He waved to his family. "Ian. Jessie. Over here." They mounted their horses and waited for them.

Jessie reached back and pulled a scarf over her ears. Her nose and cheeks were bright red.

"Are ye all right, wife?"

She patted her thigh. "Aye, just a bit sore. It's been a long time since I've ridden a horse."

Klaas pulled on the reins. His brown-spotted mare trotted down the path.

"Go on ahead, Mother," Ian said. "I need to talk to Father."

Jessie pulled up her collar and guided the mare in Klaas's direction.

Alex stared. "What's wrong?"

Ian paled. "Dughall's in trouble. He's been captured."

"Dear Jesus. We're seven hours from Drake Castle, another four south to Huntly. We'll never make it on time."

"I can taste the fear in my throat. The Earl plans to flog him. He's asked me to help him bear it."

Alex ran his fingers through his hair. "Then that's what you'll do."

"I don't know how much I can stand."

Alex's nerves were raw. "Damn it, lad! If he can bear the lash on his back, then you can stand the thought of it."

"It's more than that, Father. I'm your son, too. Don't I matter anymore?"

Alex softened. "Oh God. You matter so much to me. At sea, I saw ye struggling with the rigging. You slipped and caught yourself, but I knew that I'd follow ye in the drink rather than lose ye."

Ian sighed. "I won't fail him, Father. When it happens, will ye hold me?"

"Aye. Your brother needs ye, more than ever. If we can get him to the Duke, he'll be safe. Pray that the Earl doesn't kill him."

Ian pulled on the reins. "I haven't stopped praying. Let's go. It's a long way to Drake Castle." They guided their horses through the trees and picked up the pace, catching up with Klaas and Jessie. They were about to cross a stream. As the horses entered the shallow water, Ian connected to his brother and answered his cry for help.

Face the fear, Dughall! It only exists when ye run from it!

HUNTLY CASTLE

Dughall's heart pounded as they reached the back gate. He knew that he was in for it and started to sweat. *Don't struggle or cry out. Act like a man. Oh God, not again.* He came to a sudden realization. *I must face the fear!*

Connor dismounted and pounded on the door. His breath was visible in the frigid air. "Open up, Troup!"

The voice was fearful. "Connor?"

"Aye, you idiot!"

"How do I know it's you?"

The Earl snorted.

Connor exploded. "God damn it! The Earl is waiting out here with his son. Let us in or I'll have ye taken below like Darge."

There was a sound of a lock being fumbled with, and the door opened slightly. Troup's terror stricken face appeared in the crack.

"Forgive me, m'Lord. I was trying to protect the castle."

Blackheart frowned. "Hmmphh... Open that door and let me pass."

"Aye, m'Lord."

Troup and Connor pushed open the heavy door in short order. The Earl loosened the reins and took Demon through. Connor mounted his horse and followed to the stables. They both dismounted.

"Take the dogs to their quarters," Blackheart commanded. "Reward them with meat and water."

"Aye, m'Lord."

"Come back here forthwith. We have ugly business to take care of."

Connor called the deerhounds about him. He ran towards their quarters with the dogs on his heels.

The Earl opened his saddlebag and took out a rope and a three-tailed strap. He ran his fingers through the strands and slipped it into his pocket. His voice was cold and deliberate. "Come on, lad. It's time."

Dughall was nauseous as he slid back on the saddle and dismounted.

The Earl held out the reins to Connor's horse. "Lead him in." The young Lord reached for the reins and staggered, resting his hands on his knees.

Blackheart frowned. "If you're that bad off, I'll put ye to bed. We'll do this tomorrow."

Dughall stared in desperation. "Father. Please... I'm sorry."

"Don't beg, lad. You'll not get away with this. The longer ye wait, the worse it will be."

The young Lord swallowed his fear as he faced the Earl. Suddenly, fear wasn't at all what he thought it was. Gilbert had endured beatings at the hand of his father, as well as Murdock and Connor. If they could bear it, then so could he.

His anger surprised him, "Get it over with." He took the reins and opened the door to the stables.

***

Murdock stoked the fire and poked it with a stick until the flames grew. "That's the last of the wood, m'Lord."

Gilbert leaned against a wall. "I'm worried. They should have returned by now."

"I was thinking the same thing." The door creaked open, startling them. They exchanged a furtive glance and flattened themselves against a wall, out of sight.

***

Dughall led Connor's horse to a stall that he shared with Black Lightning. He unsaddled him, stripped off his wet coat, and laid it over the stall door. The stallion cocked his head and nickered as the young Lord stroked his face. "I love ye too, Lightning." He watched his father put Demon in a stall and take off his saddle. A dark cloud hung over the man as he walked out of the stall carrying a rope.

"Get out of there, lad. Let's get this over with."

Dughall's anger grew as he slipped out of the stall. *He means to bind me.*

Gilbert came out of the shadows. "Father. You found him."

Murdock joined him. "My Lord."

"What in hell are you two doing here?"

Gilbert reddened. "We were worried. You've been gone a long time."

"Damn it! I told ye to wait in the castle." He took the strap out of his pocket. "Get out of here, lad! You don't want to see this."

Gilbert paled. "Father, don't beat him."

"This is none of your business."

"He's my brother." The two men stared each other down.

Murdock lifted Dughall's chin. The lad's jaw was swollen and there were bruises on his neck. He ran his hands along his arms. "You're soaking wet. Get these clothes off."

Dughall's eyes were glassy. "Nay! He means to whip me."

Murdock felt his forehead. "You've got a fever. Don't worry, lad. I'll take care of this. Just do what I say."

Dughall tried to object but he coughed uncontrollably and spit on the ground.

Gilbert frowned. "Father, have mercy. He's sick."

"This is between me and your brother. Get out of here!"

"I want to stay."

"Then be silent."

Murdock held his arm. "You're sick, lad. Sit down on this bale of hay."

Dughall sat and cradled his head in his hands. This was something he needed to face alone and the servant was in his way. "Leave me, Murdock. Take Gilbert with ye. I don't want ye to see this."

Connor entered the stables. He raised his eyebrows when he saw the strap in the Earl's hand. "My Lord. Shall we begin?"

Blackheart tossed him the rope. "Aye. Tie this to that iron ring on yonder wall. We'll bind him there."

"As you wish."

Gilbert flinched. "Connor, wait. Father, this wasn't his fault. Kate was after him."

"He ran from me! We searched for hours in the freezing cold. He deserves to be whipped. I told ye to be silent. Do it, Connor!"

Connor threaded the rope through the iron ring and left two ends dangling. He waited.

Murdock got down on one knee. "My Lord. I've failed the young master. I should have been at his side, protecting him from her. I ask ye to give me his whipping. It's my right as his manservant."

Blackheart placed a hand on his shoulder. "Are ye sure, Murdock? You're getting too old for this. I just might kill ye."

Murdock nodded.

Dughall wondered how many more would die on his account. The idea was more than appalling. "Nay! No one else suffers because of me. I won't allow it."

Blackheart reddened. "It's not up to you, lad."

"My Lord. Please. It will hurt him more to see me beaten."

"You could be right." Blackheart approached Dughall. "I have a better idea. Are ye afraid, lad?"

"Nay."

"You should be. Do ye know how badly I'm going to whip ye? I was only playing with ye before."

"Oh God."

"I'll allow Murdock to take your whipping under one condition." He laid the leather strap across Dughall's lap. "He's your servant. You do it."

Dughall's eyes widened with shock. He was prepared to take a beating, but could he stand this?

Murdock rushed to him, stripped off his shirt, threw it aside, and kneeled before him. "My Lord. I'd rather it be you. This is the best thing that can happen."

His emotions were raw. "Nay! I can't beat ye."

"I won't hold it against ye. Trust me, lad. I beg ye to do it."

Dughall ran his fingers through the leather strands. His heart thundered in his ears as he considered it. It would be so easy to let someone else bear the pain. Anger and outrage welled in his breast as he came to a realization. Father meant to turn him into a beast! He lay down the strap and spoke in a defiant voice. "I won't do it."

Gilbert pleaded. "Brother, please. Listen to Murdock. Give him ten hard strokes and we'll all go home. This is for the best."

Blackheart chided him. "Idiot! You're a lord. Your servant offered to bear your whipping. Let him do it. It's what a lord would do. It's what I would do."

"Nay!"

Blackheart frowned. "Connor! Tie Murdock to that ring. I'll do it myself."

This was the young Lord's responsibility and his alone. He couldn't let his servant suffer. Dughall stared at his father in defiance. "I can't be you! I'll never be you! I hate you."

Blackheart threw up his hands. He pushed Murdock out of the way and grabbed the strap. "So ye don't think much of me. You and your peasant morality. Take off your shirt."

Dughall stood and removed his shirt, and dropped it on the floor. Connor approached with a length of rope. The young Lord held out his wrists and allowed him to wrap the cord around each one and tie them together. "Do ye have to bind me?"

"Aye. Don't struggle, lad. It's for the best."

Murdock stood beside him with a look of pity on his face.

"Leave me, Murdock."

"Nay, m'Lord. I'll stay and care for ye afterwards."

Connor took the rope and led him to the wall. He lifted his arms above his head and tied the rope securely to the iron ring. "Forgive me, m'Lord."

Dughall felt the cold wall against his chest. Gooseflesh rose on his arms and legs. He glanced to the right. His father unbuttoned his cuffs and rolled up his sleeves, exposing his muscular forearms. The strap was in his hand. The young Lord prayed as his heart thumped against his ribs. *I'm so sick. Oh God. Help me to bear it like a man.*

Blackheart spoke in a threatening tone. "You don't have to like me, but you do have to respect me. First we'll settle this thing with my mistress."

Dughall tested his bonds. Blackheart watched him squirm. "Remember what I taught ye. A man must bear his punishment in silence and nay struggle or cry out." He ran a hand across his naked back. "Look at how strong you've become."

Dughall stiffened under his touch. "Get it over with!"

Blackheart laid into him with the strap, striking him hard across the shoulders. Leather tails blistered his back and brought tears to his eyes. "How dare ye hide things from me!" He struck him harder this time, raising welts. "Rutting with my mistress!"

Pain flooded his senses. "I didn't touch her!"

"Don't lie to me." He dealt him a sharp blow in the lower back.

Dughall chewed on his lip until it bled. The strokes continued, breaking his flesh. His breath came in ragged gasps as his back bruised and blistered. A rivulet of blood ran to his breeks.

Murdock made the sign of the cross and glanced at Gilbert. The young Lord watched intently, chewing his thumbnail. "You're a Lord," he whispered. "Do something."

Dughall cried out as a hard stroke was delivered. Blackheart stopped and took out his flask.

Oh God. Let it be over. A trickle of sweat ran down the young Lord's chest.

"Ten strokes," Blackheart said. "That's where we would have stopped had ye faced your problems." He drank a measure of whisky and put away his flask. "Now for the matter of running away."

Dughall's heart sank. It was far from over. Sweat beaded on his forehead as he waited for the next blow.

"Father, stop it. Isn't it enough?" Gilbert cried.

"Shut up, lad, or I'll haul ye up there next."

Gilbert flinched.

Dughall's voice was weak. "Leave, Brother. Don't watch it."

"Silence, lad. You'll never run from me again. Connor! Count the strokes."

The strap bit into his blistered shoulders, drawing blood. It whistled through the air and met his flesh again and again. Dughall groaned. "I'll go mad. Help me, Ian."

"Not another word!"

Connor counted aloud as the lash struck. Twenty, then twenty-five.

The Earl's face contorted with anger. "So ye hate me, do ye? I'll give ye a reason to hate."

The young Lord struggled in his bonds. His breeks were soaked with blood and tears streamed down his face. He pressed his forehead into the wall. Twenty-eight.

Blackheart grabbed him by the hair. "What's this? Tears? I'll teach ye not to cry. I can make this last a long time."

Dughall sobbed. "Oh God. Let me die."

***

Murdock winced as the lash struck again, drawing blood. Twenty-nine was counted. He looked at Gilbert expectantly. "Do something."

The young Lord fainted and slumped in the ropes. His arms and head twitched.

Blackheart snorted. "How dare ye swoon on me!"

"Father! He's suffering a fit."

"A sign of weakness! That doesn't run in my family. I'll beat ye awake." Blackheart raised the whip again, but a firm hand held his wrist.

"That's enough, Father! I won't allow it," Gilbert cried.

"Oh ye won't, will ye?"

"Nay."

"Don't make me hurt ye! I'll cut him down and haul ye up there in his place."

Gilbert reddened. "If you do that to me, it will be the last time."

"What do ye plan to do, kill me?"

"Nay. If you whip me again, I'll take my own life."

Blackheart lowered his arm. "What's wrong with ye, lad? I've whipped ye from time to time, but that's what's made ye the man ye are."

Gilbert scowled. "I'm who I am in spite of you. When you whipped me, I prayed that someone would stop it. I begged God to take my soul, and cursed him when he didn't."

"How dare ye. It's all part of being a father."

"I'll never do that to my sons!"

Blackheart threw down the strap. He made a fist and backhanded Gilbert across the face, knocking him to the floor. "Ingrate! Get out of here, before I kill ye. Connor, confine him to his bedchamber until I send for him."

Gilbert stood and massaged his jaw. "You don't deserve sons."

Connor's hand was on his arm. "Come along, m'Lord. You've said enough." He escorted Gilbert out of the stables.

Blackheart grabbed Dughall's hair and lifted his head. He let it drop. "He's out cold."

Murdock kneeled and offered him the strap. "My Lord. I beg ye to give me the rest of his beating."

"Hmmphh... He didn't want that."

"Aye. But he can't refuse now."

Blackheart took the strap. "God damn it! Have ye all gone mad, that ye don't care about your own skins? What is it about this lad that makes ye want to risk it?"

Murdock stayed silent.

He threw the strap on the floor. "Cut him down."

"Thank ye, m'Lord."

"Don't thank me! I'll finish this tomorrow." He picked up his coat and stormed out of the stables.

Murdock took out his dirk and looked at the young Lord. His body was limp except for his hand. The fingers extended and grasped something for dear life. As the servant cut him down, he heard the sound of the stable door being locked from the outside. "The Earl's gone mad. I'd best find something to stoke the fire with. It may be a long night."

***

Dughall sat on the point, watching the tide go out. It was a beautiful summer day and a light wind lifted his curls. Seagulls flew overhead, crying noisily as they searched for snails and mussels on the beach. The point was ablaze with wild violets and yellow buttercups. "I love it here."

Someone sat next to him. He turned to his right and smiled. "Aunt Maggie."

"Aye, lad. It's good to see ye again."

"You look so young. Your hair is brown and your skin is smooth."

Maggie held up a hand and flexed it. "My arthritis is gone, too. Here there's no old age, or pain, or sorrow."

Dughall reached out and took her hand. "Am I dead, then?"

She shook her head. "Nay, not yet."

"Where am I?"

"In that place that's in between. I'm here to help ye, should ye decide to pass."

Dughall squeezed her hand. "I love ye, Aunt Maggie. I'm sorry that ye died because of me."

"No matter, lad. I'd do it again, just to have known ye."

"It's not so bad being dead. I like it here." He looked at the sky. Scores of seagulls flew landward, approaching them. "They carry the souls of dead fisherman. They've come for me at last."

Maggie smiled. "Nay, lad. Ye have to go now. Ian's calling ye."

FOREST TWELVE MILES WEST OF PETERHEAD

They'd been riding for more than five hours. The snow stopped, making their passage easier. Klaas took the lead, with Jessie behind him. Ian's gray stallion followed, with Alex at the rear. They left the forest to cross a wind swept moor.

Ian cringed. He felt a cold wall against his chest, ropes on his wrists, and the wild thumping of his heart. *God help ye, Dughall.* He flinched as the strap bit into his back.

"Aye ye all right?" Alex asked.

"Nay. It's started. The Earl's whipping him." He felt another blow, harder than the last. Pain took his breath away. A man's angry voice rang in his ears. "That cruel bastard."

Alex's eyes were wild. "Should we stop?"

Ian's voice was weak. "Nay. We must get to the Duke." The beating continued. Ian chewed his lip until it bled and grunted as the lash struck. It stopped and he caught his breath. His eyes widened with shock.

"Is it over?" Alex demanded.

"Nay. He's sweating, but he's not afraid." He felt the strap fall heavily on his shoulders, blistering skin and drawing blood. "I've never known him to be this brave." He grasped the reins tightly, but swooned in the saddle.

Alex jumped from his horse. "Klaas, Jessie, stop!" He held Ian and eased him off the saddle onto the ground.

Ian grabbed his shoulders. "It's worse than before. Hold me, Father."

Alex held him and stroked his head. The lad's body flinched in pain as he cried out. Tears flowed down his cheeks and he closed his eyes.

"God damn it! Will the man ever stop?" Alex cried.

Jessie kneeled and took Ian's pulse. "It better be soon. We're going to lose both of them."

Visions of seagulls flying landward calmed Ian. He opened his eyes. "He's given up. He wants to die."

Alex panicked. "Nay! You mustn't let him." He held the lad's shoulders and sent him strength. "For God's sake, reach out to him."

Ian closed his eyes and held out his hand. "Take my hand, Brother." He felt his brother fading. "Dughall, take my hand!"

The gulls returned to the sea. Ian felt his brother's hand in his, holding on for dear life. He squeezed it and opened his eyes. "He's back."

RISKY BUSINESS

HUNTLY CASTLE
FEBRUARY 28 1637
ONE HOUR LATER - 8PM

Dughall lay on the cold stable floor, his bare back exposed to the air. Murdock had tried to rouse him, to no avail. He looked at his bloody back, covered with welts and cut through in places. He was desperate. "Perhaps it's best that he sleeps." The servant choked back a sob. "God help me, I love him like a brother. I hope he's not dead." Murdock kneeled and felt the side of his neck. "His heart still beats." The fear in his heart turned to anger as he held his face in his hands and sobbed. "How can he do this to his son?"

The young Lord opened his eyes. His voice was weak. "Murdock, are ye all right?"

"My Lord! Am I all right? I thought that he killed ye."

Dughall steadied his hands against the floor and tried to rise, but failed. "I'm not dead yet. Is it over?"

Murdock looked around fearfully. The Earl said he'd finish this later. "I think so. He hasn't come back."

"Thank God."

"Can ye sit up?"

Dughall took a shallow breath and gasped at the pain. "Not at the moment."

Murdock's heart was breaking. "My Lord. Next time, allow me to take your beating. I'm pledged to protect ye with my life."

Dughall sucked his ragged lip. "I'll not let ye suffer for what I've done. Father was so angry. Why did he not kill me?"

Murdock reached out to touch his shoulder, but it looked too painful. He stroked the back of his head. "You fainted and slumped in the ropes. My Lord, it looked like you were sufferin' a fit."

"Twitching?"

"Aye."

"It happened once when I was a child."

"The Earl didna care. He raised the whip and said that he'd beat ye awake."

"Dear God."

"Lord Gilbert stopped him. He fought with him terribly, even when he threatened to whip him. He called him a bad father, who didn't deserve sons."

"Did Father hurt him?"

"Aye. He punched him in the face and knocked him down. Connor escorted him to his bedchamber."

The young Lord shuddered. "Oh... Why did he not kill me then?"

"I begged him to give me the rest of your strokes."

"Murdock, are ye all right?"

"Aye. He threw the whip down and said we'd all gone mad, that we didn't care about our own skins. He stormed off." Murdock watched him try to rise up on his hands, his chest shaking slightly.

Dughall groaned. "Oh God, it hurts so much. Say no more."

"Forgive me my Lord, are ye all right?"

Dughall lay down. "Aye, it hurts to laugh."

"You're laughing?"

"He thinks *we're* mad."

Murdock chuckled in spite of himself. He sniffled and wiped a tear from his cheek.

Dughall gritted his teeth. "Tell me the truth. How does it look?"

"It's bad m'Lord. You're striped from neck to waist and you've lost a lot of blood."

His lids were heavy with exhaustion. "I need a healer. I'm getting hot."

Murdock felt his forehead. "I can't summon a healer. The Earl locked us in here. As soon as they let us out, I'll send for old Beathag."

Dughall's eyes filled with tears. "She's dead. Connor slit her throat."

"You saw this?"

"Aye. Father led me out of her cottage and sent Connor back. When I begged him to stop it, he choked me." Dughall coughed. "Is there any water?"

"Nay, m'Lord. Just what the horses have and it's not fit to drink."

His eyelids drooped. "How long was I out?"

"An hour, maybe two."

"I had the strangest dream. I sat on the point with Aunt Maggie watching the tide go out. She looked so young."

"Didn't ye tell me that she's dead?"

"Aye. She'd come to help me pass over."

Murdock shivered. The spirit world frightened him. He patted the young Lord's head. "You're not dead. You didna go with her."

Dughall sighed. "I wanted to. It was beautiful there. My brother Ian called me back."

"Thank God."

Dughall started to drift. "Murdock?"

"Aye, m'Lord?"

"I didn't bed the lass."

Murdock's eyes filled with hot tears. "I know, lad. I know."

"I'm getting sick. Make a bed of straw and wrap me in Lightning's blanket. I must sleep."

Murdock stood and looked around the barn. He gathered straw from the stalls to make a bed and spread the horse blanket on it. With an aching heart, he roused the young Lord and helped him onto the bed.

Dughall shivered. "God forgive me."

Murdock covered him. "For what, m'Lord?"

"Beathag's dead. Gilbert and Father are fighting, and you're locked in here with me. I'll never run again."

Murdock stroked his feverish head. "Sleep, lad. No one blames ye."

The young Lord slept fitfully, crying out in pain and terror. Murdock tore down a trough for firewood and stoked the dying embers. It wouldn't last 'til morning. The servant was desperate as he returned to the young man. He couldn't let the Earl beat him again. The faithful servant closed his eyes and prayed in the silences of his soul. "Dear God. I'll offer myself in his place; draw his anger if I have to. Take my life, but spare the young Lord."

***

Blackheart paced impatiently up and down the hall. Images of Gilbert and Murdock and Kate flooded his mind. "Damn it! What is it about that lad that makes them risk their own skins?" He drove his fist into the wall. "Ach! They've all gone mad!"

Connor gazed at the floor, avoiding his anger. "My Lord, is there something I can do?"

Blackheart glared. "Aye, indeed. Confine my mistress to her cottage. I'll deal with the unfaithful wench later. Where is Gilbert?"

"You said to confine him to his bedchamber, m'Lord."

Blackheart reddened. "Did I? That's a good place for him. Make sure he stays there 'til morning."

"As you wish. I'll station a guard at his door."

Blackheart flexed his hand, making a fist. "Good. I'll be in my study. Tell the steward to bring me a bottle of that twenty-year-old whisky. No one is to disturb me unless we're under attack. Am I making myself clear?"

"Aye." Connor hesitated. "It's getting late. Should I call a healer for the young Lord?"

"Nay. He's as strong as an ox. I didn't hurt him that badly. He'll get over it."

Connor stared.

Blackheart growled, "What are ye waiting for? Don't tell me that you have an opinion too!"

Connor flinched. "Nay, m'Lord. I will do as ye wish." He turned on his heels and ran down the hallway.

Blackheart groaned. "They've all gone mad." He pressed his back into the wall, sank to the floor, and cradled his head. "God in heaven. What have I done?"

LOUDEN FOREST - 9PM

Keira considered stoking the fire with a bundle of peat. It had been a difficult month, cold and stark, with waning stores of fuel and food. She threw the packet back on the pile and watched the dying flames. "I can bear it for one more night." She pulled on a heavy sweater and wool cap and kneeled. Her stomach grumbled. "Oh Goddess. These are the times that try our souls. The children are cold and hungry. I pray that Michael and Torry find a deer tomorrow."

Keira crawled into bed and pulled up the covers. Her breath hung in the frigid air. "Someday, Dughall will keep me warm." She kissed the fine scar that ran the length of her palm. "Think of me husband, wherever ye are. Spring will come and you'll find me in the heather."

The lass tucked her hands under her armpits and hummed one of her grandmother's tunes. "I love ye, old woman." She fell into a fitful sleep and dreamed.

In her imagination, Isobel stood by the bed and stroked her hair. Her hand was soft and warm. "Keira, child. I don't have much time."

"Grandmother. I've missed ye so much."

"Listen carefully. I've come to tell ye to pray. The man ye love is in trouble. His body is broken but his spirit is strong."

Keira's heart ached. "How do ye know?"

"Aunt Maggie and I were there to help him pass, but his brother called him back."

Keira touched Isobel's face. There weren't any age spots or wrinkles, and her hair was as black as the night sky. "Oh Grandmother. What shall I do?"

Isobel's image faded. "Ask the Goddess to heal him, child. The Goddess loves him."

DRAKE CASTLE - JUST AFTER MIDNIGHT

It was just after midnight when they arrived at the entrance to Drake Castle. Horses and riders were cold and exhausted. Alex dismounted and pounded on the heavy door.

A rough voice answered. "Who goes there?"

"Let us in! We must see the Duke right away."

"Go away. It's after midnight. Come back tomorrow."

Alex panicked. "For God's sake, let us in! The Duke's grandson is in trouble. He may be dead by tomorrow. Do ye want that on your head?"

Someone fumbled with the lock. The door opened a crack, and a man's heavily bearded face appeared. "Who are ye?"

"The Hay family and Klaas Van Dyck from Peterhead."

"Ah. Van Dyck. I was told to watch out for ye." He opened the door and motioned for them to enter. "My name is John Gilroy. The Duke will see ye right away."

***

They stood in the breakfast room, waiting for the Duke. Ian leaned against a wall with his arms folded across his chest. His back burned like it was on fire. "If I wasn't so hungry, I could sleep like the dead. Will we try to make it to Huntly?"

Alex nodded. "We're going whether the Duke helps us or not."

"This is as far as I go," Klaas said.

"What?"

"I agreed to take you to Drake Castle. The horses need food and rest. So do I. I'll head back tomorrow."

Alex reddened. "God damn it! What about my son?"

Klaas frowned. "I have no idea how to break into a castle. That's up to the Duke's men."

"Hmmphh..."

An elderly woman stoked the fire and lit wall sconces. "The Duke will be with ye soon. I'll bring some tea and cakes."

Jessie smiled. "Thank ye kindly."

Ian was finally getting warm. He looked around the room at the long table and counted ten padded chairs. A polished buffet stood against the wall, with silver candelabra on each end. It was unlike anything he'd ever seen. "Ha! A room just for breakfast. It's bigger than our cottage."

Alex grunted. "Never mind that. We need to leave for Huntly right away."

The Duke entered, wearing a silk dressing gown and slippers. He moved slowly, grasping a cane.

Jamison hovered around him. "My Lord. Are ye all right?"

"Aye! Let me be." His eyes widened as he saw the Hay family. "What's wrong with my grandson?"

"He's in dire trouble," Alex said. "The Earl whipped him. My son Ian said that…"

The Duke held up his hand. "Let the lad speak."

Ian was exhausted. He left his place against the wall and stood near his father. "My Lord. Dughall thought the Earl was going to kill him. He tried to run to ye."

The Duke's face fell. "Go on."

"The Earl hunted him down with dogs and whipped him."

"God damn it! I told that man…" Ian swooned and caught himself on the table. "You look like hell, lad. Are you all right?"

"I'm tired and in pain. I felt his beating, every stroke."

"Tell me the truth. How bad was it?"

Ian glanced at his mother.

"It's all right son," she whispered. "I can bear it."

Ian sighed. "He was tied like an animal, against a wall. The man threatened him again and again. I didna count the strokes. It had to be thirty, forty hard lashes. Some drew blood. He asked to die."

The Duke stared. "He's still alive?"

Ian's eyes were glassy. "Aye. He's sleeping now, but he's burning with fever."

"Why does he have a fever?"

"He was sick when the man whipped him."

"God in heaven! Jamison, ready a team of horses. Pack weapons and supplies. I'm getting him out of there. Have Madison relieve Gilroy. I want him, Pratt, and Suttie with us."

"You're coming along?"

"Aye. Have you got a problem with that?"

"Nay, m'Lord."

Klaas cleared his throat. "I can't go any farther, Sire. The horses need rest and I must return to Peterhead in the morning."

The Duke waved his hand. "My word is my bond. You've done your job, lad. Jamison, tell Bissett to provide for his horses and give him food and shelter. Pay him what we promised."

"Aye, m'Lord." Jamison led Klaas out of the room.

The Duke stared. "Can you show us where he's being kept, lad?"

Ian frowned. "I think so. We need to get closer."

"It will be dangerous. The lass can stay here."

Jessie interrupted. "My Lord. I must go with ye. Dughall needs a healer."

"You're a brave lass. I'd hate to think what would happen if the Earl got his hands on you. Can my grandson ride?"

Ian shook his head. "Nay. He's hurt too badly."

The Duke coughed until he choked. His voice was strained. "We'll take a wagon."

Alex stared. "You're coming with us, my Lord? You seem sick."

"God damn it! I'm an old man. I don't get any better than this. He's my grandson, I'd move heaven and earth for him."

"I know what ye mean."

"Jamison will be back soon. I'll go to my bedchamber and dress in my riding clothes. We'll leave as soon as the horses are ready."

Alex nodded. The Duke took his cane and left the breakfast room. The old woman returned with a pot of tea and a platter of sweet cakes. She laid out cups and knives and a crock of apple butter, and took her leave.

Ian's eyes grew wide. He grabbed a sweet cake, buttered it heavily, and popped it into his mouth. "Oh God. It's better than Maggie's sweet cakes." He reached for another.

Alex frowned. "How can ye eat at a time like this?"

"Father. I'm starved."

"Let him eat, husband. He deserves it." Jessie poured tea into the porcelain cups. "We have a long night ahead of us."

Alex picked up a knife and one of the cakes. "I guess you're right."

HUNTLY CASTLE - JUST BEFORE DAWN

The sky was beginning to lighten as snow fell on Huntly Castle and the surrounding forest. A faint smell of burning wood permeated the air. Jamison and Gilroy secured the horses in a wooded area, and covered the wagon with branches to disguise it. Suttie unpacked the weapons and handed each man a short sword and a dirk. Pratt stood by Ian. The burly man rubbed sleep from his eyes and yawned.

Jamison gave orders. "Stay awake, Pratt! Remain with the horses. Keep them saddled and ready to ride at a moment's notice."

Pratt frowned. "They'll be ready. What about the Duke?"

Jamison grunted. "I'll try to convince him to stay with ye. It's too dangerous for the man to go in."

"Aye," Gilroy said. "He'll only slow us down."

Suttie's beard was coated with frost. He stared at Ian. "What about him? He looks like hell."

Jamison nodded. "He's the only one who can lead us to the young Lord."

Ian's eyes were glassy. "I'll be all right."

"Listen up," Jamison said. "This is a dangerous mission. If the Duke follows us, it will be twice as risky. Protect him at all costs and kill anyone who gets in our way. We must get his grandson out. The young Lord is the man we will answer to some day."

Ian stared.

Jamison clapped him on the back. "It's your brother we're talking about."

"Aye. I know it."

"Come on, lads. It's getting close to dawn."

The four men walked into a clearing and joined Alex, Jessie, and the Duke.

Ian blew his breath out slowly. His skin was hot and his lips were dry. "We must hurry. He's weak and burning with fever."

Jamison watched the Duke. His face was pale and drawn and he coughed harshly, pausing for breath. "My Lord, it would be best if ye stayed with Pratt and the horses. It may be dangerous."

"I want to be there for my grandson."

"Your cough may give us away."

"I can control it."

"We may need to move quickly."

"Gilroy and Suttie can hang back with me. You and the lad's family can get him out."

"My Lord, please."

"I'm going with you."

Jamison sighed. "Stay back while we gain entrance. There may be a fight. I'll send for ye when we're in."

"How do we get in?" Alex asked.

Jamison spoke in low tones. "The rear entrance to the castle is ahead. It's not heavily guarded. Mills once said that a single guard mans it at night, Ty Atkinson. He likes his drink, but he likes the ladies more."

Alex frowned.

Jamison stared at Jessie. "We need a distraction. Lass, give me your healer's bag for safekeeping."

She handed it to him.

"Take off your coat."

She stripped off her coat and held it out.

"When the man answers, open your blouse and show him your breasts. We'll wait on either side of the door. Tell the man that you need a place to stay. Tempt him, play up to him, you know what to do."

Jessie nodded.

Jamison smiled. "Try to stay in the open doorway. Don't worry, lass. We'll get him off ye."

***

Jessie's heart was in her throat as they made plans. She didn't dare to look at Alex.

Jamison whispered. "I left the Duke with Gilroy. Walk softly."

They moved stealthily to the castle gate, so their footsteps wouldn't betray them. Suttie and Alex flattened themselves against the wall to the left of the door. Jamison and Ian hid in shadows to the right.

"Do it now, lass."

Jessie stood at the massive wooden door. Her heart pounded as she loosed her blouse and bared her breasts. *This is for you, Dughall.* She wet her lips and knocked.

"Who's there?" a rough voice demanded.

Jessie spoke sweetly. "My Lord, I'm a lost wench looking for a place to sleep." She trembled like a bride on her wedding night. Hands fumbled with a lock, and the door creaked open. A man's ruddy face, clearly blootered, peeked through the crack. Jessie licked her lips seductively. "I'm cold, sir. Do ye have a warm bed for me?"

The man opened the door and grabbed her wrist, pulling her to him. He pushed his lips against hers and thrust his tongue down her throat. She gagged and struggled in his arms. Alex and Suttie held the door as Jamison struck the man in the head with the hilt of his sword. He crumpled to the ground.

Jessie sank to her knees and reached out to touch the side of his neck. Her hand refused to do it. "He's so repulsive. Oh, God. I want him dead."

Alex helped her up and hugged her tightly. "God in heaven. What have we done to ye?" He closed her blouse and put on her coat.

"Forgive me, husband," she whispered. "I did it for our son."

Jamison surveyed the situation. "Looks like he was alone. Good job, lass."

Ian smiled. "Aye. Bastard's dead."

Jamison nodded. "One less problem for us. Alex, can ye get Gilroy and the Duke?"

Alex nodded and ran off.

Jamison wiped blood from the hilt of his sword. There was no time to waste. "Can ye lead us to your brother, lad?"

Ian closed his eyes and held out his hands. "Aye. I feel him nearby, lying face down in a bed of hay." His brow knotted. "A stable, perhaps. I smell horse dung. A man is with him, someone he trusts." He opened his eyes and pointed. "This way."

Jamison smiled. "Excellent, a stable! We won't have to breach the castle. God is with us today."

Alex, Gilroy, and the Duke joined them. Suttie closed the heavy door, leaving it unlocked. They propped the body against the wall and put a pint of ale in his hand.

Ian smiled nervously. "They'll think he's blootered."

Jamison drew his sword. "Aye. You're a quick study, Son. We're ready my Lord. Ian says he's in the stables. Lead us, lad."

Ian walked steadily to the west, between low stone buildings. The village was waking. A blacksmith worked at his forge, hammering a piece of iron. A servant lass opened a door and let out a flock of chickens. It was getting lighter in the east.

Jessie was worried. "How much farther?"

Ian breathed deeply. "It's just up ahead."

"Is he alive?"

"Aye, but he's weak."

"I see the stables." Jamison whispered. They hurried across a flagstone courtyard and approached the barn.

***

Murdock was exhausted from the long, cold night. He'd run out of firewood hours ago. The faithful servant held Dughall's head as he retched and agonized as he ranted in delirium. Murdock tore his shirt into strips to bandage wounds and kept him warm with a horse blanket. Though the young man burned with fever, he shivered with cold. Finally, he fell into a state of deep sleep or unconsciousness. The silence was frightening. "Dear God. There's nothing more I can do. Let him live."

Frigid air streamed through a crack in the wall. Horses snorted and stamped in their stalls. Lightning whinnied and hung his head over the gate. "The stable boy should be here soon." Murdock walked to the door and pulled on it desperately. It was securely locked. He pounded on the wall and cried out. "Open the door! For God's sake, the young Lord is dying. We need water. We need a healer. Please!"

To his surprise, hands fumbled with the lock and the door opened. Murdock recognized Jamison. He looked outside and saw the Duke standing with several men, a woman, and a red-haired lad, Dughall's brother.

Jamison frowned. "Where is he?"

Murdock hugged his bare chest. He knew that the Earl would kill him if he helped them. Yet, God had answered his prayers. "The young Lord is within. Take him away from here. The Earl nearly beat him to death."

Jamison's eyes narrowed as he fingered the hilt of his sword.

Murdock swallowed hard. *This is the end,* he thought. *He means to run me through.*

Jamison turned and barked an order. "Gilroy, Suttie. Stand guard at each end of the building. Hoot like an owl if anyone comes." Two men ran off to take their places. Jamison handed Ian a short sword. "It's yours to keep, Son. Stay with me and stand guard." He turned to Murdock. "Well. Show us where he is."

Murdock breathed a sigh of relief and stepped aside. "He's in the back of the barn."

The Duke stormed past the servant and hurried to his grandson. Murdock, Alex, and Jessie followed and kneeled at Dughall's side. Murdock pulled back the blanket and exposed his flayed back. "I tried to care for him, but I'm no healer."

Jessie felt his forehead. "Good man. You kept him warm in spite of the fever. How long has he been senseless?"

"Two, maybe three hours. Before that, I could rouse him."

Alex stared. "Is there anything else you can tell us?"

"It seemed like he was suffering a fit. Twitching."

"Did ye hear that, lass?"

Jessie worked quickly, removing the loose bandages. "Aye. No wonder he was senseless. I need to see his wounds."

Alex picked up the Earl's strap and ran his fingers through the bloodstained strands. "That cruel bastard."

The Duke paled. "Aye. What do you think, lass?"

Jessie frowned. "It looks bad. Open my healer's bag. Get the flask of water and the small bowl."

Murdock searched through the bag and found the supplies. He set them on the floor and watched as she worked.

Alex's voice was choked with emotion. "Will he live?"

She avoided his question and reached in her pocket for a packet of ground willow bark.

"You didn't answer me, wife."

"I won't lie to ye, husband. I don't know. He's burning with fever. Give me the flask and hold the bowl steady."

Alex cradled the bowl in his shaking hands. Dughall whimpered in his sleep. Jessie sprinkled bark powder into the bowl and mixed it with water.

"I can't boil it, but it will have to do." She glanced at Murdock. "Hold up his head, so his mouth falls open."

The faithful servant held the young Lord's head. She took some of the medicine in her hand and dripped it into his mouth. The lad's eyes were closed, but he drank the water. She tried it again. He swallowed the liquid and choked.

"Let him live." Murdock prayed.

***

Dughall fought his way back to consciousness. Hands touched him, uncovering him and tending to his wounds. It felt like his soul was being scorched. *I must be in hell.* He tasted bitter water, laced with willow bark. More water trickled down his throat and he choked. He opened his eyes and saw Murdock holding his head, Mother's face, full of concern, and Father, close to tears. "Oh God," he groaned. "I must be dead."

Jessie smiled. "Nay. You've come back to us." She soaked a cloth and stroked his forehead.

His voice was weak. "How did ye find me?"

Alex squeezed his hand gently. "Ian knew ye were in trouble. He led us here."

"Where is my brother?"

"Outside, standing guard."

Dughall tried to rise up on his hands and failed. His back felt like it was on fire. "Father may come back. He'll kill us all. Get me out of here."

The Duke balled his fists. "How dare he do this to my grandson! I'll kill that bastard with my bare hands."

Jamison entered the barn, a hand on his sword. "Not today, my Lord. We're in grave danger. We must get the young Lord away. You can take revenge later." He directed Alex. "You and I will carry him, one under each arm. It will be painful, but there's no other way. We can lay him down when we get to the wagon." He glared at Murdock. "What about him?"

Dughall's voice was weak. "Murdock stays with me."

The Duke frowned. "Speak to me man! Are you loyal to the Earl?"

Murdock shook his head. "Nay, Sire. I serve the young Lord."

"Are you an indentured man?"

"Nay, m'Lord."

The Duke kneeled at his grandson's side. "Can we trust this man?"

Dughall nodded. "With my life." The last thing he saw as he fainted was Murdock's smile.

***

Murdock was relieved. Once again, the young Lord had saved him. "I can help you get out. They know me."

Jamison tossed a sweater to Murdock. "Wear this. You and Alex can carry him." He brandished his sword. "If they try to stop us, they'll have to get through me."

Ian stood in the doorway holding a sword. "I'll stand with ye. Hurry! I'm seeing lights in the windows." The two men disappeared into the courtyard.

Alex took off his coat and removed his shirt. "We can't walk him out half-naked."

Murdock propped Dughall up. They pulled the shirt over his head and threaded his arms through the ample sleeves. "Thank God he's senseless. This would hurt like the devil."

Alex put on his coat. "Are ye ready?"

"Aye." Alex and Murdock lifted him under each arm. "You're his father?"

Alex nodded. "Aye."

"He's a fine young man. I'm his servant and his friend."

Jessie picked up the blanket and they hobbled out of the barn. Jamison and Ian met them at the door.

Jamison stared. "Gilroy and Suttie went ahead with the Duke. If we stay together, we'll attract attention. We're leaving the way we came."

Ian touched his brother's face. "God, he looks awful."

Jessie nodded. "Aye. It's a blessing that he's fainted. When we get him to safety, I'll treat his wounds."

They walked in silence between stone buildings, with Ian leading the way. A cooper holding a hoop driver and a hammer walked through a doorway and stared.

Murdock's heart pounded. "Ho Garrick! You know who I am. Nothing to worry about. The young Lord had too much to drink last night. I trust that you'll keep quiet."

The cooper's eyes grew wide. "Are ye sure, Murdock?"

"Aye."

"Who are these people?"

"Friends."

Garrick stared at Jamison's sword. The man's eyes were full of suspicion as he turned to look through oak staves leaning against the wall. Jamison drew his dirk. He grabbed the man's hair and pulled hard, exposing his throat. The blade cut him from ear to ear, splattering blood on the stone wall.

"Oh dear God!" Jessie cried, as the body crumpled to the ground.

"One less problem for us," Ian said.

"Ian!"

"Pretend ye didn't see it, Alex. Get your family out of here while ye still can." He crouched and lifted the cooper under the arms. "Take his feet, lad."

Ian bent over and took his feet. "Between the buildings."

Murdock watched as they hauled the body and dumped it behind a woodpile. He felt bad for Garrick and worse for his family, but he understood the danger. Jamison and Ian caught up.

Alex frowned. "God forgive us. Did ye have to kill him?"

"Aye. I saw the man's eyes. He would have sounded the alarm and we'd all be dead. Except your bonny wife. Gordon would have kept her as a plaything."

Murdock sighed. "He's right."

Alex reddened. They hurried past stone buildings and met the others at the back gate. Gilroy and Suttie supported the Duke as he limped toward the horses. Alex and Murdock carried Dughall, and Jessie followed with Ian and Jamison guarding the rear. As dawn broke, they lay Dughall in the wagon with Jessie at his side and mounted their horses.

Murdock's heart pounded with anticipation. He stood back, waiting for an invitation or death sentence. They'd let him live so far. Would they kill him now?

Jamison smiled. "Are ye coming with us, man?"

"Aye."

"The young Lord said that we can trust ye with his life. Take the lass' mare."

The faithful servant mounted the horse with a deep sense of relief.

Alex made the sign of the cross. "Forgive us, God, for what we did. Someday I'll understand it. Thank ye for protecting my family."

Murdock liked this man, already.

The Duke coughed into a kerchief. "Let's take this lad home. I'll need a week in bed when I get back. I haven't had this much excitement in years." They began the long ride to Drake Castle.

HUNTLY CASTLE - 9AM

Gilbert opened the door and looked into the hallway. Fang was gone. Last night he'd tried to sneak out to find Dughall, but Fang pressed him against the wall, threatening to beat him bloody. The young lord recalled the smell of his breath, as rank as rotten meat. "Forgive me, Brother. I tried my best."

He left his room and walked the hallway to Dughall's bedchamber. He hesitated, afraid of what he would find, and knocked softly. "Brother? Murdock?" No one answered. Gilbert opened the door and went inside. The chamber was stone cold and the young Lord's bed hadn't been slept in. His heart sank. "What did he do with him?"

Gilbert left the room and walked to his father's bedchamber. He considered his words as he opened the door and looked inside. The bed was made and the fire in the hearth was dead. A bad feeling gnawed at his belly. "Where are they?" He stood in the hallway, unsure of where to go.

Connor approached. "My Lord."

Gilbert reddened. "Connor. Why did you sic Fang on me last night?"

"Forgive me, my Lord. The Earl said to keep ye confined."

"Where is my father?"

"He's not in his bedchamber?"

"Nay."

Connor looked thoughtful. "Last night, he retired to his study with a bottle of twenty-year-old whisky. Perhaps he's still there."

Gilbert scowled. "How can he drink at a time like this? I think he's lost his mind."

"My Lord. Be careful what ye say. You're lucky the Earl didn't beat ye."

"I don't care any more. Someone had to stop him. He nearly killed my brother."

"Aye. I've never seen him that angry. He wouldn't let me call a healer for the young Lord."

"What?"

"Murdock and the young Lord are locked in the stables."

"God in heaven! There's no firewood in there. We used the

last of it before you came back. If they froze to death, I'll hold you responsible."

"Forgive me, my Lord. I'll get the Earl."

Gilbert's anger flared. "Forget him, he's likely hung over. Let's head for the stables."

"But my Lord…"

"Connor! Someday you'll answer to me! I won't forget this. Are you coming or not?"

"Aye."

They ran through the castle to the courtyard door. Gilbert's heart was in his throat. "My brother had better not be dead." They left the castle and crossed the courtyard to the stables. The wooden door was open a crack.

"Door's unlocked," Connor said.

Gilbert opened the door and they slipped inside. The fire in the hearth had been out for some time and it was ice cold. A young stable boy attended to the horses. "Lad, have you seen my brother and Murdock?"

The boy stared. "Nay, m'Lord. I came to tend to the horses. No one was here."

Gilbert looked around. There was a bed of hay on the floor and bloody strips of cloth piled next to the strap. He crouched down. Muddy footprints dotted the floor, from two men and possibly a woman.

A young tradesman in a leather apron entered the barn and waited to be acknowledged. "Forgive me, my Lord."

"Who are you?"

"George Marr, the blacksmith's apprentice."

"I'm busy here. What is it?"

"We found two dead men."

Gilbert stood. "Who are they?"

"Ummm… Garrick the cooper. His throat was slit, and Ty Atkinson."

"The night guard?"

"Aye, m'Lord. We thought he was drunk, sitting up as he was with a pint in his hand. But he wouldn't wake. His head was split open."

Connor frowned "I'll get the Earl."

"Nay. Come with me to the back gate. Let's get the whole story." They followed the young man to the guard shack, where John Barrie stood talking to a nervous Troup. The body of Ty Atkinson lay face down at their feet. Frozen blood crystals gleamed in a head wound. "Did anyone see what happened?"

Barrie spoke up. "Nay, m'Lord. But there's a stand of trees where a wagon and at least six men stopped. They got past Atkinson. I hear that Garrick's dead too. Are we missing anything?"

Gilbert nodded. "My brother and his servant."

Connor paled. "God damn it! Are there any tracks?"

Barrie shuddered. "Aye. They lead northeast, towards Drake Castle."

"How long ago did they leave?"

"Judging by those tracks they have two hours on us."

"We'll never catch them."

Silence was thick as each man considered the consequences. Connor winced. "Let's find the Earl. He's going to be angry."

Gilbert nodded. "Aye." Relief washed over him as he crossed the courtyard. *Thank God,* he prayed silently. *My brother got away.*

REUNION

DRAKE CASTLE THE HIGHLANDS
MARCH 2 1637

EARLY THE NEXT MORNING

Dughall slept on silk sheets, his arms wrapped around a soft pillow. As he woke, he felt a dull ache in his shoulders.

I'm alive and whole, he thought. *I faced my fear and survived it.* He called out faintly. "Murdock?"

The servant was at the hearth, stoking the fire with a bundle of wood. He hurried to the bed. "My Lord, you're awake at last."

"Where am I? This isn't my bedchamber!" Dughall focused his eyes.

"You're safe at the Duke's castle. The Earl can't hurt ye here."

He breathed a sigh of relief. "How did I get here?"

Murdock smiled. "I have much to tell ye. Can ye sit up?"

"Not yet." The young Lord glanced at his wrist, wrapped in a linen bandage. "You found a healer?"

"Aye, a special one." He reached out and felt his forehead. "Your fever's gone. Would ye like a drink?"

Dughall nodded. Murdock held a flask to his lips and poured water into his mouth. The lad was groggy. "I had the strangest dream. Father and Mother and Ian came for me. Perhaps if I sleep, I'll see them again."

"It wasn't a dream, m'Lord! Your mother spent the night with ye, tending your wounds. She's quite a lady."

His heart swelled with joy. "For true?"

"Aye, lad. They're having breakfast with the Duke. I'll fetch them." Murdock pulled up the sheet, covered his shoulders, and left the room.

Dughall drifted in a sea of exhaustion. "More strange dreams. I think I've gone mad."

***

The formal breakfast room was small, with tall windows that opened onto a large courtyard. Portraits of the Duke, his wife and children hung on the wall. The Duke sat at the head of the table, with Alex and Jessie on his right and Ian on his left.

Jessie was solemn. "Is that a portrait of your wife?"

"Aye, that's my wife Jeanne. She passed away sixteen years ago. My father wanted me to marry a cousin, but I had my eye on the schoolmaster's daughter. It was all they talked about for months when I married a commoner."

"You loved her."

"Aye. It's a shame she never saw her grandson."

Jessie pointed to another portrait. "Is that your daughter?"

The Duke smiled sadly. "Aye. Christal was the light of my life. She was beautiful and kind, and we thought that any man would cherish her. It killed my wife when she disappeared."

Alex pointed to a portrait of a young Lord in riding clothes, on a fine black stallion. "The young man?"

"My son Andrew. He was killed in a hunting accident not long ago."

Alex nodded. "Handsome children. I'm sorry to hear of your loss."

Wall sconces flickered, providing soft light. A serving lass took their plates and returned with a pot of tea and a tray of sweet cakes. Ian reached for one of the pastries.

The Duke smiled. "You eat like a horse, lad." Alex opened his mouth to scold him, but the old man raised his hand. "Let him eat. It does my heart good. My son Andrew ate like that."

Jessie sipped her tea. "My Lord, do ye have some honey? I want to use it to treat Dughall's wounds. It would be best if it's still in the comb."

The old man picked up a brass bell from the table and rang it three times. A matronly woman entered and bowed her head. "Anna is in charge of the pantry." The woman was in her sixties, with white hair tied back in a scarf. Her yellow wool sweater sat loosely on her plaid skirt. "Anna. This is Jessie Hay, our healer. She needs honey to treat the young Lord's wounds. I'll let her tell you the rest."

The old woman waited.

Jessie smiled. "Anna, do ye have any honey still in the comb?"

Anna nodded. "Aye, m'Lady."

"Good. Bring it to the young Lord's bedchamber. A knife, a pestle and a clean bowl would be helpful as well."

"Right away, m'Lady." The servant bowed and took her leave.

Jessie blushed. "I'm not a lady. I can't get used to this."

The Duke coughed. "I think you could, but we'll talk about that later. I must retire to my bedchamber for a while. This adventure took a toll on me. Will my grandson be all right?"

"I think so."

"He's been asleep for a full day."

"Aye, that's a good thing. I gave him poppy seed tea to ease his pain and make him sleep. Then I stitched up his wounds and treated them with aloe. His fever's down and he should wake soon."

There was a timid knock on the door and Murdock entered. He bowed and spoke respectfully. "My Lord. The young Lord is awake. He's asking for his family."

Ian grabbed another pastry. "Dughall knows we're here?"

"Aye."

Alex smiled. "He's going to be all right. God has answered our prayers."

"Aye," Jessie said. "My Lord, can I make coltsfoot tea for ye? It will help your cough."

"Bring it later, lass. Go now and see your son. Tell him that his grandfather will visit this evening."

Murdock bowed. "My Lord."

The Duke pushed back his chair and stood up. He picked up the brass bell, rang once, and waited.

Jamison entered the room and handed him his cane. "M'Lord."

"I wish to retire to my bedchamber."

"As you wish." Jamison escorted the Duke into the hall.

Ian grinned as he snatched another pastry. "It will just go to waste." Alex shook his head. "Father. Can I spar with Jamison in the courtyard? He wants to teach me how to handle a sword."

Jessie frowned.

Alex squeezed her hand. "It may not be a bad thing to know, lass. Think of what we've been through."

Murdock smiled. "I hear that Jamison's an excellent teacher. I may take lessons from him myself. Come now, your son is waiting."

***

Dughall felt fingers on his forehead, a female hand soft and gentle. The scent of lavender lingered in the air.

A familiar voice whispered in his ear. "We're here, Son."

He choked back a sob. "Oh God, now I'm hearing things."

Jessie stroked his forehead. "You're not dreaming. We're all here. Your father and brother too."

Dughall opened his eyes. "Mother?"

"Aye. Can ye sit up?"

"I think so." He rolled on his side, steadied his hand on the mattress, and sat up. Dughall's eyes filled with tears as his family gathered around. "I've missed ye so much. How did ye get here?"

Ian frowned. "I knew ye were in trouble. I felt your fear and your flogging, every stroke."

"Oh Ian. I remember now, you took my hand. How did ye get here?"

"We sailed to Peterhead and got the innkeeper to take us to Drake Castle."

Alex nodded. "The Duke gave us horses and men and weapons. We rode all night to Huntly. Just before dawn, we broke into the courtyard and found ye in the stables. It was verra dangerous. God was on our side."

"Jamison gave me a sword!" Ian said. "We guarded the door while they got ye out and made sure that no one followed. You should have seen what Mother did, she was so brave."

"Mother was with ye?"

Alex reddened. "Aye, she offered herself to the guard to get him to open the gate."

Jessie blushed as she kissed Dughall on the temple. "It's all right; they got him off of me."

Ian chuckled. "We got him off of her all right! Jamison killed the bastard with his sword, then we propped his body against the wall and put a pint of ale in his hand."

"Ian!" Jessie cried. "The repulsive man is dead. We shouldn't talk about him that way."

Dughall laughed. "Mother, I've never heard ye say such things. Now I know I'm dreaming."

Murdock spoke up. "My Lord. You're not dreaming. If your brother hadn't led them to ye, we'd still be at the mercy of the Earl."

His expression darkened. "No mercy there."

Alex reached out to touch him, but hesitated. "The Duke says you'll stay here from now on. The Earl can't hurt ye anymore."

Dughall's eyes filled with tears. "Why will ye not touch me? I need ye."

Alex swallowed hard. "You know your real father. You're a Lord. I have no right."

"My real father left me to die in a stable!" Dughall cried, as he gripped the sheets. He reached out to Alex. "It doesn't matter who I am, you'll always be my father."

Alex embraced him gently, being mindful of his wounds. His voice was laced with emotion. "I love ye, Son."

Dughall wrapped his arms around him and drew him close.

"God in heaven."

Jessie smiled. "I need to dress his back and then he must sleep. Let Ian come closer."

Alex pressed his lips to Dughall's forehead. "God brought ye back to us. I knew he would." He stepped back from the bed.

Ian reached out and touched his brother's arm, completing the connection between them.

"I was ready to die," Dughall whispered. "Why did ye not let me go?"

Ian smiled. "You're my brother and my best friend. I'll never let ye go."

His eyes were heavy with exhaustion. "Thank ye, Ian."

Alex cleared his throat. "Come on, Son. Your mother will stay with him. He needs to rest. Jamison's in the courtyard. Perhaps he can teach us a thing or two."

"Goodbye Father. Ian."

"We'll be back later." They smiled broadly and left the room.

Dughall held out his arms. "Mother..." Jessie sat on the edge of the bed and embraced him. "I missed ye the most. Each time I saw a red-haired lass, my heart ached. I wondered if ye still loved me."

"We never gave up hope. Why did ye not come home?"

"The Earl said that he'd slit your throats."

"Oh... Like poor Maggie."

Dughall took her hand. "Mother, I saw her." Jessie's eyes grew wide. "I think I was dying. I sat on the point watching the tide go out and saw her beside me. I took her hand just like this."

"Did she speak to ye?"

"Aye. She said she was there to help me pass."

"You loved her more than anyone. It makes sense."

"Her skin was smooth and her hair was dark. She said her arthritis was gone. In that place there's no old age, pain or sorrow. I wanted to go with her. Then Ian called me back."

"She let you come back to us."

"Aye."

"Thank ye, Maggie," Jessie whispered. She felt his forehead. "Fever's completely gone. Murdock. Help me lay him down." They lifted him under the arms and turned him, lying him face down on the pillow. He moaned softly as his back burned. "Did Anna bring the honey?"

"Aye. It's on the long table."

She went to the table and saw the honey, still in the comb. A light coating of ice crystals covered it. "Good. It's been in cold storage." She used the knife to slice sections into the bowl; then picked up the pestle and pressed honey from the comb. She returned to the bedside with the bowl in her hand. Jessie stroked his forehead. "Try to relax, Son. I'm going to dress your wounds. This may hurt a bit."

Dughall sighed. "Mother, you have no idea."

Murdock watched intently as she treated his wounds. "Is there anything I can do, m'Lord?"

"My stomach's growling. I think I'm hungry."

Jessie smiled. "That's a good sign."

"I'll get something from the kitchen right away."

***

The Duke sat in an overstuffed chair in his study, dictating to the scribe. "He is alive and recovering from the wounds you inflicted. Since you are determined to take his life, my grandson will stay at Drake Castle." The old man hesitated.

The scribe waited with his quill poised. "Will there be anything else, m'Lord?"

"Give me a moment." He cleared his throat. "I will allow you to see him at a future date under my strict protection, but only if the young Lord desires it." The scribe finished writing. "Sign it as usual. Lord James Drake, Duke of Seaford. Bring it to me for my signature and seal it with my official seal."

"Shall I arrange for a courier, m'Lord?"

"Aye. The man must leave tonight for Huntly Castle. He's to deliver the letter at the main gate and return immediately. I don't want a horse returning with a headless rider."

The courier stood. "As you wish, m'Lord. I will return in an hour."

"Send Jamison in."

"Aye, m'Lord." He picked up his quill and notebook and left the study.

Moments later, Jamison entered the room and handed the Duke his cane.

"Sit with me, Jamison."

"My Lord?"

The Duke patted a chair next to him. Jamison sat down and averted his eyes. He was clearly uncomfortable.

"Thank ye for saving my grandson."

"I'm pledged to serve ye, m'Lord."

"I know that! My life is nearly over. I appreciate what ye did. I'm sure I made it harder by coming."

Jamison looked up and smiled. "Aye, a bit."

"After I'm gone, serve the young Lord as well as you served me. He's a principled young man. He'll need strong men at his side to protect and advise him."

"I'll be his right hand."

"Move your things out of the servant's wing into the bedchamber at the end of the main wing."

"Your daughter's chamber, m'Lord?"

"Aye, it's been empty long enough. I want you close to my grandson. Starting next week, I'll involve both of ye in the day to day operation of this place."

"Thank ye, m'Lord. Did you write your letter to the Earl?"

"Aye. I'd rather not tell that bastard where his son is, but if I don't he may blame the lad's family and kill them."

"What do you plan to do with them, m'Lord?"

"It would be good for my grandson if they would stay."

"The lad shows promise. He could serve his brother."

"Talk to him, Jamison. He admires ye. Appeal to his sense of adventure. Appeal to his stomach, he loves food."

Jamison laughed. "That he does, m'Lord. Give me a day with him, man to man. What about his mother and father?"

"We could use a decent healer around here. The man's stubborn. He'll never leave the sea."

Jamison looked thoughtful. "Don't ye own a fleet of ships on Moray Firth? You could move them closer, out of the Earl's reach."

The Duke raised his eyebrows. "Aye. It's a good idea. Tomorrow you can take the lad hunting and I'll talk to his father."

Jamison stood. "Can I escort ye to your bedchamber?"

"Nay. Send Murdock in."

"As you wish, m'Lord."

Moments later, Murdock entered the study and stood before the Duke. "My Lord. You sent for me?"

The old man stared at the servant with no small amount of suspicion. "Aye. Take a seat across from me."

Murdock's eyes widened. He sat in the chair and waited to be acknowledged.

The Duke coughed. "I'm trying to understand what happened at Huntly. Why did he beat that lad so severely?"

The servant began to wring his hands. "Oh dear…"

The old man scowled. "There's no need to fear me! Tell me what happened."

"My Lord. The Earl's mistress was obsessed with the young Lord. She constantly tried to get him alone. I slept in his bedchamber to protect him."

The Duke shook his head. "Go on."

"That day, the Earl sparred with his son in the weapons chamber. Afterwards, the lad retired to his bedchamber to change his clothes. Mistress Kate cornered the young Lord and the Earl found them together."

His head ached. "What a mess. Did he sleep with her?"

"Nay. He told me he was trying to get away. The Earl choked him and knocked him down. He said that he'd deal with him later and went to his bedchamber to beat his mistress."

"That's when the lad ran away?"

"Aye. He feared for his life."

"I can't say I blame him."

"He should have stayed. The Earl won't stand for anyone running from him. He hunted him with dogs and brought him back. I've never seen him so angry, except when his wife ran…."

The Duke's eyes narrowed. "Are you referring to my daughter?"

Murdock shook with fear. "Aye."

"We'll talk about that later!" The Duke frowned. "He nearly killed that lad. Why did no one stop it?"

"I tried, m'Lord. I offered to take his whipping and the Earl accepted. The young Lord wouldn't allow it."

The Duke blew his breath out slowly. "My grandson has much to learn about being a lord. Why did the Earl stop?"

"Lord Gilbert fought with his father, demanding that he stop. He told him he didn't deserve sons."

"Gilbert's his older son?"

"Aye. The Earl punched him in the face and threw him out of the stables." The old lord reddened and clenched his fists to control his temper. Murdock groveled. "Forgive me, if I failed him. The young Lord is the most decent man I've ever served. Don't send me away! I'd give my life for him."

"For God's sake, man! I'm not angry with ye. I've lost two children. It's hard to imagine how a man can do that to his own sons."

Murdock caught his breath.

"Is Dughall attached to his brother Gilbert?"

"Aye. They were verra close."

"That could be a problem. Has he talked about what happened to him?"

"Nay. I was hoping that he didn't remember."

The Duke frowned. "That's not something a man forgets. He'll need someone to talk to. You know my grandson better than anyone. What can we do to help him heal?"

"Keep his family here. He draws strength from them, especially from his brother Ian. He's a complicated man, m'Lord. Why don't ye ask him?"

"I think I will. Thank ye." The Duke stared. "I have too much on my mind right now. When the young Lord recovers, you and I will talk about what the Earl did to my daughter."

Murdock paled.

"I assume you know something about that."

"Aye, M'Lord. I will tell ye everything."

LATER THAT EVENING

Dughall sat up in bed, eating a hot supper of ham and potatoes. He dunked a piece of brown bread in ham gravy and popped it into his mouth. "Murdock, I was starved."

"That's a good sign, m'Lord."

"Are there any sweet cakes?"

"Nay, m'Lord. I think your brother has eaten them all."

Dughall laughed. "Well, I guess he deserves them."

Murdock gathered the dishes and took them to the table. He opened the chest and came back with a blue silk robe. "My Lord, the Duke is coming to visit. Can we slip this on so you'll be properly dressed?"

"Aye." The servant held out the sleeves as he slipped his arms through them. "Grandfather seems like a reasonable man."

Murdock tied the robe in front. "Aye. He was angry with the Earl when he saw your back. He threatened to kill him with his bare hands. Jamison kept him quiet so he wouldn't give us away."

"Grandfather broke into Huntly with the others?"

"Aye. It took a terrible toll on him. He's been sick ever since."

"Everyone risked their lives for me. You're my friend. I'm glad that he let ye come with us."

"So am I, m'Lord. I thought I was a dead man."

There was a knock at the door and the Duke entered, leaning heavily on his cane. He nodded to Dughall and hobbled across the room.

Murdock placed a padded chair next to the bed and helped the old man to sit down. "My Lord. Is there anything ye need?"

"Leave us now. I wish to speak to my grandson in private."

Murdock bowed his head and left the room.

Dughall studied the old man as he gripped his cane. His face was pale and his hands trembled slightly. "Are ye all right, Grandfather? You look tired."

"You're worried about me? He beat ye half to death."

"Aye, but it's over."

The Duke coughed. "Well, don't fret about me. I'll recover after a few days of bed rest." His hand shook. "You saw your family."

Dughall nodded. "Aye. It was worth what happened to me just to see them again."

The Duke's expression darkened. "The Earl can't hurt you ever again, lad. You'll stay here from now on and take my place when I die."

"Don't die, Grandfather. I need ye."

"I'll be around for a while." The old man considered his words carefully. "Would you like to talk about what he did to ye?"

Dughall's eyes grew wide. "Nay!" He was trying his best to forget.

"Are ye sure, lad? Left unsaid, these things have a way of stalking ye. They're like a poison you hold in your heart."

"I'm alive and whole. I don't want to talk about it."

"Hmmphh... All right. I won't ask ye today."

"Thank ye, Sir."

The old man looked serious. "I'm gathering an army of men and weapons to defend us against the Earl. I have half a mind to storm his castle for what he did to ye and my daughter."

"Please reconsider, Sir! I don't wish harm to come to my brother

Gilbert. I'm told that he saved me."

"Hmmphh... All right, but I reserve the right to strike him if he causes us trouble. In the meantime, is there anything I can do for you?"

There were so many things that he wanted now that he was free. But was he truly free? Dughall thought not. "I'm a Lord now. I can't go back to Whinnyfold."

"That's true, lad. Your destiny is to be a powerful man in Scotland. Besides, the Earl would take you again if he found you there."

Dughall sighed. "I've been thinking about that. He would make me watch while he killed my family. This is the only safe place for us."

"I'm impressed with your people, Son. They risked their lives and showed as much bravery as my own men. I will talk to them tomorrow about staying here."

"Thank ye, Sir."

The Duke coughed. "I must retire to my bedchamber. Your mother promised me some of her coltsfoot tea. Is there anything you want? Horses, swords, fine garments..."

Dughall thought for a moment. "I want to learn how to handle a sword like a Celtic warrior. I'll need books and lessons from a schoolmaster if I'm to be Duke. You must teach me to be the best Lord possible."

"I will. Is there anything else?"

"We could have poetry and music in the great room. I love harp and dulcimer."

The Duke smiled. "I'm pleased that you have a passion for so many things."

"There's one more thing. More important than all else."

"What's that?"

"There's a lass I love, a commoner from a forest village. We were to be married within the year."

The Duke nodded. "That we can do, lad. When you're healed, we'll send for her."

DREAMS AND SCHEMES

DRAKE CASTLE
MARCH 3 1637
NEXT DAY

Morning light streamed through a window in Dughall's bedchamber. He slept in the large feather bed, arms around a soft pillow, and dreamed of a familiar place. Sunlight warmed his face and made his heart glad. Crickets chirped and meadowlarks warbled in nearby trees. The meadow lay before him, moorland grasses bending in the wind, ablaze with heather. He walked barefoot through soft blades of grass, his fingertips brushing the purple bells.

"God granted my wish. Keira waits for me in a willow patch at the end of the meadow." In the distance he saw a figure sitting on a log under a rowan tree. Dark hair. Leaning forward, head down. Could it be her? Dughall hurried in that direction. A raven circled above, giving a warning cry. He watched the bird streak away and faced the tree.

Blackheart lifted his head and stared. "I'm disappointed in ye, lad. You ran away again."

Dughall's heart thumped against his ribs. "Father. I didn't."

The Earl stood. "Don't lie to me! Don't make me hurt ye." He walked towards him, fingering the strap in his hand. His voice was cold and deliberate. "A man must bear his punishment in silence and nay struggle or cry out. Take off your shirt, lad."

"I won't let ye take me!" He turned and ran through the darkening meadow until granite walls appeared before him. Dughall looked around in confusion. He was in the courtyard at Huntly Castle, in front of the stables. Heavy footsteps approached from behind.

Blackheart growled in his ear, "I'm not through with ye."

The young Lord turned and faced his fear. "Oh, aye. Ye are."

***

The young Lord sat up in bed and grasped the sheets. "Never again!" He saw a shadow on the wall of a tall and muscular man. "You'll have to kill me first!"

Murdock rested a hand on his shoulder. "My Lord, are ye all right?"

Dughall looked back. "Murdock? Is it you?"

"Aye."

"He's not here?"

"Who m'Lord?"

"Father! He had the strap in his hand."

The servant felt his forehead. "You don't have a fever."

"He told me to take off my shirt! He wasn't through with me."

Murdock placed a hand on the young man's chest. "Your heart is pounding like a drum. It was a bad dream. Take some breaths."

Dughall breathed deeply and let go of the bed sheets. "I need to use the chamber pot."

Murdock nodded. He drew back the sheets and pulled a robe around his shoulders.

Dughall slipped his arms through. He went to the chamber pot, relieved himself, and turned to the standing mirror, which was covered with a tartan. He grabbed a corner and slowly pulled it off.

"My Lord…"

"I want to see what he did to me." Dughall looked into the mirror and ran a finger along his jaw. It was starting to turn yellow. His neck was bruised with finger marks.

Murdock pleaded. "My Lord, please. Don't look at it."

"I want to see my back."

"It's bad. Best that ye don't see it."

The young Lord dropped his robe, turned around, and looked over his shoulder into the mirror. Angry welts and stripes marked his flesh, from neck to waist. Some were blue and others a sickly yellow. Mother had stitched some of them.

He gagged. "Oh dear God."

Murdock held the robe while he slipped it on. He took his arm and led him back to bed. "You're shaking like a leaf. Are ye afraid?"

"Nay, it's rage." Dughall sat on the side of the bed and rubbed his forehead. His head ached from the unfamiliar feeling.

"How's your back?"

"Better. It burns when I stretch my shoulders, but it's not as bad as before."

"Good. The Duke said that ye would need to talk to someone. Will I do?"

Dughall's emotions were raw. "Aye, friend. Tell me what happened. I lost a whole day. I don't remember being brought here from Huntly."

"Poor lad. It was God's mercy that let ye sleep. You burned with fever and your wounds were raw. Do ye remember much of what he did to ye?"

Dughall nodded. "Aye. I tried not to struggle or cry out, but he kept on striking me. He said he would break me and he did. I couldn't stop the tears. Murdock, how many strokes did he..."

"Twenty-nine."

He clenched his teeth. "God damn it! I'm his son. How could he do it?"

The servant shrugged.

"We had a good morning in the weapons chamber. I tried to please him. He's my father, why does he hate me?"

Murdock touched his arm. "I don't know much about fathers and sons, m'Lord. Didn't know my own father. The Earl's never cared about anyone. Not your mother, or Kate, or Gilbert. It bothers me that he left ye to die."

Dughall knew that the servant was telling the truth. He'd come to the same conclusion.

Murdock looked thoughtful. "My Lord. Could God grant but one father to love us? Alex risked his wife, his son and his neck to save ye. The Earl would have tortured and hung him like Mills. I read the man's eyes when he saw your wounds. He loves ye more than life."

The logic was inescapable. Dughall sighed. "You're a wise man, Murdock. And I am a fool."

"Is there anything I can do, m'Lord?"

"Send my father to me."

"Alex?"

"Aye."

***

Alex lay in a large feather bed on sheets of pure white silk. "It's so soft. Heaven must be like this."

Jessie snuggled closer. "Aye. This bed is larger than three of our beds. I get lost in it."

Alex rolled on his side and nuzzled her neck. "Ummm... Let's see if I can find ye." His tongue found a spot behind her ear and lingered there.

Jessie shuddered. "It's been so long." His hand slipped under her nightshirt and stroked her knee. She rested her thigh on his. "Take me, husband. You're hard already."

Alex lifted her nightshirt and knelt above her, entering her. She raised her hips to meet him and made a small sound. Inside, she was as silky as the sheets. "God in heaven," he groaned.

There was a knock on the door. Alex struggled to gain control. A drop of sweat fell from his forehead onto her face. He pulled out slowly and sat up. "Ach! Who is it?"

"It's Murdock. Your son needs ye."

Jessie giggled. "Just like when they were wee babies."

"Aye." Alex got out of bed, put on a robe and answered the door. Murdock stood in the hallway. "Alex. The young Lord needs ye."

"Not his mother?"

"Nay, just you."

"Give me a moment." Alex went to the bed and stroked her hair. "We'll finish this later, lass. Dughall needs me." He tied his robe shut and joined Murdock in the hall. "What's wrong?"

The servant frowned. "He's having nightmares about the Earl."

"I think I would too."

"That's not all."

"Well, what is it?"

Murdock sighed. "The young Lord looked at his back. He's distraught that the man hurt him so badly and left him to die."

Alex considered his words carefully. "I think I understand."

"Will ye talk to him?"

"Aye."

***

Alex ran his fingers through his hair. The beatings he withstood at the hand of his own father came to mind. "God help me," he whispered. He entered the bedchamber and cleared his throat.

Dughall sat on the side of the bed, cradling his head. He looked up. "Father?"

"Aye." Alex sat down and put an arm around him.

The lad sighed. "I love ye, Father."

"I love ye too, Son. More than you'll ever know."

"I need to talk to ye."

"I know it. Murdock told me."

"Thank ye for coming for me. I know ye risked your neck breaking into Huntly."

"You're my son. I would break into hell to save ye. What do ye want to talk about?"

"Ian once told me something. He said that your father beat ye when you were a lad."

Alex stiffened. "Aye." The memories were painful and cut him to the heart.

Dughall's eyes widened. "Nay bother. You don't have to tell me, Father."

He sighed. "Aye, I do. Perhaps that's why it happened to me. It's a long story and not verra pleasant. Would ye like to hear it?"

Dughall nodded.

"It's hard to talk about." Alex swallowed and took his hand. "We were a usual family until my mother died. I was nine years old. Father went mad and wandered the beach, ranting and cursing God. Finally, he took to the drink. I spent my days on the point watching the sea."

Dughall squeezed his hand. "Where I used to sit?"

"Aye. After a week, Father got drunk and dragged me back by the hair, saying it was time I became a man. He ordered me to take off my shirt and pulled down my breeks, laying me over a chair. I can still hear his voice, so cold and angry, like he hated me. He showed me a strap with three tails that his father used on him. Then he held me down and beat me until I had no strength to struggle or cry out."

Dughall stiffened. "I know how that feels."

"Father hung that strap on the wall. He beat me without mercy, seemed like every few days. Most times, he wouldn't tell me what I'd done. I lived in fear of the next beating."

"That's terrible. Did he stop?"

"Not entirely. During a vicious beating, Maggie came after him with a broom, screaming like a banshee. After that, he didn't beat me as often."

Dughall smiled. "With a broom?"

"Aye. Now ye know why I loved her. When he drank too much, I'd show up at her door with my bedroll. She never said a word, but set another place at the table. Bless her heart, she saved my life."

"Father. Did ye feel like it was your fault?"

Alex sighed. "Aye. I begged him to tell me what I did wrong. I would have changed it, just to please him. I was his son. Was I such a bad child? Why did he not love me?"

"Did he ever change?"

"Nay."

"How long did it go on?"

"He beat me without reason until he was lost at sea. I became a man that day. I was fifteen."

"Six years," Dughall whispered.

Alex wiped a tear from his eye. "As long as I live, I'll never understand it."

"It wasn't your fault. You couldn't change him. It was his loss."

This was a major breakthrough. Alex lifted his chin and gazed into his eyes. "I know that now, lad. Do you know it?"

Dughall smiled. "Aye. You did something good, Father. You didn't pass it on to your sons."

"I made sure of that. I took that strap and walked far out on the point. I rolled it in a ball and threw it into the sea."

"So you forgot about it?"

"Not for a long time. For years I woke from bad dreams, sweating and crying in terror. I heard his voice, telling me to take my shirt off."

Dughall frowned. "The same thing's happening to me. Oh God. This will haunt me forever."

"It doesn't have to, lad. I carried the anger in my heart for a long time. I knew I was safe, but it wasn't enough. I needed to forgive."

Dughall stared in disbelief. "What? You forgave your father?"

"Aye."

"I hate him for what he did to me! How can I ever forgive him?"

"I don't know, lad. Maybe ye can't. I didn't forgive my father for his sake; I did it for my own peace of mind."

"Hmmphh… Maybe I'll think on it." Dughall seemed eager to change the subject. "Let's not talk about him anymore."

"All right, lad."

"Thank God you're my father."

Alex smiled. "When you were born, I held you in my arms and vowed I would never hurt ye. It was my second chance at a father, son bond. I knew what whisky did to my father. I didn't touch a drop from that day on." They both stood. His heart swelled with love. "Did this help, Son?"

Dughall embraced him. "Aye."

Alex sighed. "There's one good thing. We're a family again."

"I can't go home, Father. The Earl would kill ye and take me again."

"Don't fret, lad. God brought us this far. He'll keep us together."

HUNTLY CASTLE

Blackheart and Gilbert sat at the breakfast table in stony silence. Gilbert poked at his eggs, unwilling to look at his father. *I hate him,* he thought.

Blackheart poured whisky into his tea and belted it down. "Are ye still mad at me, lad?"

"Aye."

"Well, get over it. Your brother's not dead. It appears he got away. We have to come up with a plan to get him back."

Gilbert reddened. "I don't want him back! You nearly killed him."

Blackheart frowned. "Now, I said that I was sorry about that. When have I ever said that?"

"Never before."

"I'll need your help with this. He likes ye."

Gilbert wanted no part of this. "I won't do it."

The Earl made a fist. "I promised that I wouldn't beat ye. Don't take advantage of my good graces or I might change my mind."

There was a knock on the door. Connor entered and bowed nervously. "My Lord. A courier dropped a letter at the main gate."

"Take him below! I want to talk to him."

Connor handed him the letter. "He left this outside and rode away before anyone could stop him."

"God damn it!"

Blackheart examined the letter carefully. It bore the red wax seal of the Duke of Seaford. He opened and unfolded it.

Gilbert watched as he read the letter. The man's eyes widened and his face flushed with anger. Was his brother dead?

The Earl pounded the table, shaking the glasses. "How dare that man speak to me in that way! He accused me of trying to kill my own son. He can't keep us apart."

"Dughall's alive?"

"Aye. He's a strong lad. I told ye he'd be all right."

Relief washed over him. "Thank God."

The Earl's eyes narrowed. "Connor! Have the scribe meet me in my study. Arrange for a courier to leave as soon as the letter's ready. I'll demand that the Duke let me see my son."

"Aye, m'Lord." Connor turned on his heels and left the room.

"You're coming with me, lad. You'll tell him that I promised not to beat ye anymore."

"It doesn't matter what you do. He won't come back with us."

"I think he will. I have one more card to play."

"What's that?"

"My mistress is carrying his child."

DRAKE CASTLE

Murdock leaned against the wall and waited. The Duke had just asked him to gather the Hay family for breakfast. Strangely enough, he was invited as well. "I wonder what the old Lord is up to."

Alex emerged from Dughall's bedchamber, looking content.

Murdock straightened up. "How is he?"

Alex smiled. "He's feeling better. Thank ye for calling me."

"The young Lord asked me to. He needed his father."

"Aye."

"The Duke would like us to join him for breakfast."

"Jessie and Ian, too?"

"Aye."

Alex looked down at his robe. "My wife and I will dress and meet ye in the breakfast room. I'll wake Ian so he can join us."

Murdock chuckled. "I hear he's not one to miss breakfast." The faithful servant rapped on the door and entered the bedchamber. The young Lord stood at the chest, searching through drawers. It was a good sign. "My Lord..."

"These aren't my clothes."

"They belonged to the Duke's son, Andrew. He was your uncle."

"Oh."

"This was his bedchamber, now it's yours. The Duke says he'll call a tailor for ye next week." Murdock pulled out a white silk shirt with ample sleeves. "I hope this fits. He was a big man."

Dughall dropped his robe, slipped the shirt over his head, and guided his arms through the sleeves.

Murdock buttoned the cuffs. "This will do." The servant searched through a drawer, took out a blue and red kilt, and pinned it around the lad's waist. "You don't need a sporran today. Sit down and I'll get some socks on ye."

Dughall sat on a padded chair while Murdock pulled up his socks and slipped on some shoes.

"Did ye have a good visit with your father?"

"Aye. He told me about what happened to him when he was a lad."

"What was that, m'Lord?"

"His father beat him many times, until he was lost at sea."

"He understands then." Murdock frowned. "Alex never beat ye?"

"Nay. He vowed that he'd never hurt his sons."

"It takes an unusual man to do what he did. You're lucky to have him."

"Aye. I know it."

The servant ran a comb through Dughall's hair and washed his face with a wet cloth. "Now ye look presentable."

Dughall's stomach growled. "I'm starving."

"That's good, m'Lord. The Duke expects us for breakfast. After that, I'll take ye on a tour of this place. It's bigger than Huntly Castle."

***

Dughall was uneasy as he entered the hallway with his servant. This was a large and foreboding place with scores of people who would expect him to be Lord. Perhaps Grandfather would allow some time before introducing him.

A chambermaid approached, carrying a mop and bucket. The young lass stopped and bowed. "My Lord."

Dughall nodded. She continued on, passing them. "Oh God, Murdock. They know me."

"Aye, m'Lord. The Duke held a meeting in the courtyard, where he told everyone. There aren't many who don't know who you are, as well as your family and me. Is it a bad thing?"

"I guess not. I just wanted to be invisible for a while."

"They're calling your mother my Lady."

Dughall laughed. "Well, I guess she deserves it." The granite walls seemed to stretch forever. Dughall counted doors. His bedchamber was one of twelve in this wing. He felt light-headed and grasped his servant's arm.

"Are ye all right, m'Lord?"

"Just a bit dizzy. I haven't been out of bed for days."

"Easy, lad." Murdock held his arm and led him down the hallway towards the wing that housed the breakfast room. Wall torches illuminated tapestries and portraits of lords and ladies. They stopped in front of one that pictured a handsome man in hunting clothes, sitting on a fine black horse.

"He looks like Lightning. God, I miss that horse. Was this Grandfather when he was young?"

"Nay. This was his son, Andrew. Your uncle."

"I have his bedchamber and his clothes."

"Aye. You seem steadier now. Can ye walk on your own?"

Dughall nodded.

Murdock released his arm. They turned a corner and watched a serving lass carry a steaming tray into a room. "Smells like ham and eggs."

"That's the breakfast room. They're waiting for us, m'Lord."

"Us? Will ye be coming in, friend?"

Murdock smiled. "Aye. I don't know why. The Duke invited Jamison and I to join ye."

Dughall was glad. This was a very different place indeed.

***

The breakfast room bustled with activity. The Duke sat at the head of the table, with Dughall and Ian to his left and Alex and Jessie to his right. He'd placed Jamison and Murdock at the far end of the table. Servants brought platters of eggs, ham, and sweet cakes. They left the room and returned with tea and honey, and crocks of jam and country butter. Some lingered as long as they could. They were eager to see what the young Lord looked like. A young lass with golden hair batted her lashes as she poured tea for the young Lord.

"Cora," the Duke said. "This is my grandson, Dughall."

The cup overflowed onto the tablecloth. "Oh goodness!" She wiped up the tea with a napkin. "Forgive me, m'Lord. Is there anything I can do to ye? Oh... I mean for ye."

Ian snickered.

Dughall blushed. "Nay, lass. I have everything I need."

The Duke shook his head. "The young Lord is engaged to be married."

Cora stammered. "Forgive me, m'Lord. I didna mean to offend ye."

The old Lord smiled. "It's all right, child. Now be off with ye."

The young lass fled from the room. "Not again," Dughall said.

Ian laughed. "It must be those dark curls. They always fall for ye."

The Duke sipped his tea. "From what I hear, you've had enough trouble with women. We'll send for your lass as soon as possible and arrange a wedding."

Alex raised his eyebrows. "You're getting married, Son?"

"Grandfather said I could marry Keira."

Ian reached across the table and grabbed a sweet cake. He picked up a knife and spread it with butter. "That should make ye happy. Do ye know how to find her?"

Dughall reddened. "I think so."

Jessie turned to the Duke. "My Lord. We've never met her, but I hear that she's a fine healer. She put Ian's shoulder back in place."

Ian snorted. "I thought she was trying to kill me. It hurt like the devil!"

"Don't complain, lad," Alex said. "You've got full use of that arm."

Dughall picked up a sweet cake. "It must have been painful. Ian fainted."

"I did not."

"You did too."

The old man laughed. "It's good to have a family around the table, arguments and all."

They finished their breakfast and pushed back their plates. Dughall cleared his throat. "I have something to say." They all stared. "Thank ye for risking your lives to save me. I won't forget it."

The Duke coughed. "See those men at the end of the table? They're pledged to protect ye with their lives. There were three others who went in with us. Gilroy, Pratt, and Suttie. Jamison will introduce ye to them in time."

Dughall nodded.

"Your family risked their lives for ye."

"Aye, and you Grandfather."

"Remember what we did. The Earl will try to talk ye into coming back. You must stay here, where you're safe."

"I won't go back to him."

"Good. Now it's time to get on with our day." The old man addressed his servant. "Jamison, I sent word to the stable lads. They have your horses ready. Take Ian to the wardrobe keeper to get some hunting clothes. Show him the weapons room; we have a fine selection of bows."

Ian stared. "We're going hunting?"

Jamison stood. "Aye, just you and me. That is if your father agrees."

Ian threw down his napkin and stood. "Father?"

Alex nodded. "Go on."

"Thank ye, Father. Thank ye, my Lord." Ian smiled broadly and followed Jamison out of the room.

The Duke cleared his throat. "Murdock, show my grandson the main wing of the castle. Take care that ye don't tire him out. I'll expect him back here for the midday meal."

Murdock stood and bowed. "Aye, my Lord. Thank ye for having me at your table."

The old man addressed Dughall. "I'll see you later, lad. I need to have a serious talk with your father."

Dughall glanced at Alex, then back at the Duke. "Thank ye, Sir." He stood and followed Murdock out of the room.

The Duke picked up a brass bell and rang it three times.

Anna entered the breakfast room and bowed her head. "My Lord?"

"Anna. Pour a hot bath for Mrs. Hay. She's worked day and night on the young Lord without much rest. Take her to the bath chamber and bring her some fine clothes from storage. Some of my wife's things will do."

"As you wish, m'Lord."

Jessie stared. Alex smiled nervously. "It's all right, lass."

"I could use a bath."

"There's lavender soap and perfumes, m'Lady."

"Thank ye, Anna." She stood and followed the servant out of the room.

The Duke sipped his tea. "At last, we're alone. I need to have a man-to-man talk with ye."

"Aye, my Lord."

"I appreciate what ye did for my grandson."

"He's my son. I'd do anything to see him safe."

"Dughall said that ye talked to him about what happened."

Alex sighed. "Aye. It's not just his body that's hurt."

"Is he going to be all right?"

"It may take time. He's never had someone hurt him with purpose. Certainly not his father. How can a man do that to his own son?"

The Duke stared. "I was thinking the same thing." They were silent for a moment. "I can see that you love my grandson. He's quite attached to ye. It would be best for him if you would stay."

Alex's eyes grew wide. "For how long?"

"For the rest of your lives."

Alex rubbed his forehead. "Oh God. I have a scaffie and a crew of four men. My cottage was left untended."

"It may not be wise for you to return to Whinnyfold. The Earl will threaten my grandson with your safety."

"I won't live in fear."

The old man nodded. "I sent the Earl a letter stating that I took his son. At least he doesn't think it's your doing."

"I appreciate that."

He played his next card. "It may not stop the man from abducting one of ye. Most likely the lass, if she's left alone. He'll do anything to get the lad back."

Alex frowned. "Hmmphh…"

"I'd like you to stay at Drake. You don't have to give me an answer today."

"I need to feel useful. What would we do here?"

"The lad could serve his brother. Dughall's a principled young man. When he's Duke, he'll need strong men to protect him."

"Ian is to be married in May, to the daughter of Andrew McFarlein of Peterhead."

"He can marry the lass and bring her here."

"Andrew expects him to work a share in a boat."

The Duke was amused. "The man will not deny his daughter a chance to live at Drake Castle. They'll never want for anything and their children will be properly educated."

Alex frowned. "I can't speak for my son."

"Of course. I'll ask him myself."

"What about my wife and me?"

"We haven't had a decent healer around here in years. It's no secret that I'm dying. Perhaps she can make my last days more comfortable."

"She would be pleased to serve ye."

The Duke stared. "You have more than one choice. I know that you love the sea. I own a fleet of boats that run out of Moray Firth. They sail to places near and far, to provision the castle. They're not scaffies, mind ye, but twice the size. I could use an honest captain."

Alex rubbed his temple. "My other choice?"

"You could serve the young Lord. He'll need advisors, some strong and decisive, others steady and moral like you. So what do ye say?"

"Hmmphh…"

"Take your time and talk with your family."

"I will. Thank ye, m'Lord."

The Duke picked up the bell and rang it three times. "Why don't ye join your wife in the bath chamber? I'll tell Anna to pour ye a bath."

Alex sniffed his armpit. "A bath?"

"Aye. One advantage to living at Drake Castle. Hot baths, even in winter."

✳✳✳

The bath chamber was warmer than the rest of the castle. A small fireplace heated the room and provided soft light. Lavender scented steam hung in the air. Alex sat in the copper tub and blew his breath out slowly. "It's hot."

Jessie leaned back in her tub. "Aye. It takes some getting used to." She rinsed the soap from her long hair and stood.

Alex watched as she stepped out of the tub. Soapy water dripped off her body and pooled at her feet. He smiled. "I like this part."

She grabbed a towel from a nightstand and dried off. "What did the Duke say?"

Alex picked up a bar of soap and lathered his arms. "He wants us all to stay."

Jessie dropped the towel and reached for a bottle of lavender perfume. She opened the bottle, poured fragrant oil onto her fingers, and dabbed it between her breasts.

Alex felt his loins swell. "Oh dear God. I can't control it. Latch that door, lass."

Without a word, she walked to the door and set the latch in place. She returned to his tub and stepped in, sitting between his legs. "You promised that we'd finish it later."

His breath was short as he kissed the back of her neck. "Aye, lass."

"Oh husband. Would it be so bad? How long does he want us to stay?"

He was losing control. "Forever," he whispered. "He wants us to stay forever."

***

It was a clear day in the forest near Drake Castle. An easterly wind blew across the moor, promising a spring thaw.

Jamison smiled. "What a difference a few days make." He watched as Ian kneeled by a pheasant and drew his knife. The lad stretched the neck of the colorful bird and slit its throat. The pheasant shuddered and kicked for the last time.

Ian placed his foot against the bird's body and pulled out the arrow. He cleaned off the tip, straightened the feathers, and slid it back into the quiver. "It's a big one."

Jamison threw him a length of rope. "Aye. Good job, lad. Tie the feet. We'll have the cook dress this one for dinner."

Ian tied the bird's feet and made a loop for the saddle. "My brother could never do this."

"What do ye mean?"

Ian stood. "Dughall's tender-hearted. He feels like he's part of every living thing."

Jamison frowned. "Well then. He'll need strong men like you and I to help him with unpleasant decisions."

Ian nodded.

Jamison thought for a moment. The lad needed to gain a new respect for his brother. "Have you talked to the young Lord?"

"Not alone. Mother's been with him, tending his wounds."

"You may find that he's changed. The lad's been through a lot."

"Because he's been beaten?"

"That always changes a man, causes him to look at things in a different light. But that's not what I mean. Murdock says he's been working with a tutor, studying history, numbers and the nature of the stars. The lad took to his lessons well."

"Sounds like my brother."

"He learned to ride a spirited horse and handle a long sword."

"For true?"

"Aye. Murdock said he could wield a Celtic sword with a fair amount of skill. Those swords are twice the weight of a modern sword. He faced down the Earl in the weapons chamber with it. Not many men can claim that."

Ian raised his eyebrows. "Maybe he has changed." He hung the pheasant from the saddle and stripped off of a few of its iridescent feathers. "For Mother. She loves pretty feathers."

Jamison knew it was time to make his move. "Do ye like living at the castle?"

"Aye. The food is good. My bedchamber is larger than our cottage and I haven't had to haul peat or water in days."

"I enjoy your company, lad. I'd like ye to stay and serve your brother."

Ian frowned. "Does Father know about this?"

"The Duke is asking him today. He doesn't think it's safe for you to return to Whinnyfold. He wants you all to stay."

"I'm to be married soon."

"You can marry the lass and bring her here."

"Her father expects me to work a share in a boat."

"Think lad. You could serve the next Duke of Seaford."

"Father will never approve."

Jamison mounted his horse. "I think he will. The Duke's a hard man to turn down. Come on, we have to start back."

Ian joined him.

The servant smiled. "Let me tell ye what lay in store should ye stay. I'll teach ye to handle weapons and face down an enemy. The young Lord must be protected at all costs. You'd be given your own horse and sword."

Ian stared.

"Your lass would have all the comforts of living in the castle. Your children would be taught to read and write." Jamison pulled on the reins and led his horse onto the path. Ian's horse followed along side.

"Do ye enjoy my company, lad?"

"Aye. I'd like to be your friend."

"Good. Tell your father that."

Jamison smiled. "Now explain this thing that happens between you and your brother. If I'm to serve the young Lord, I must understand it."

***

Dughall returned to his bedchamber after the midday meal. He felt exhausted and his feet ached from the strange shoes. "That was quite a walk. I can't take another step."

Murdock undressed him. "Aye. You seem a bit unsteady, lad. Rest in bed until supper."

The young Lord slipped under the covers. "I don't feel like sleeping. My mind is spinning with questions." He sat up. "This place never seems to end."

"That's what ye said about Huntly the first few days."

"I remember. We didn't get to the west wing. Tell me what's there."

"I haven't seen it all, lad. I saw a library, a study, and a sewing and fitting room. Ah ... and a ladies' retiring room."

"A room just for ladies?"

Murdock chuckled. "Aye."

"What's in the library?"

"It's filled with books and maps and things that look like old scrolls. They're under glass, of course."

"How interesting. I wonder what they are?"

There was a knock on the door and Ian entered. Murdock frowned. "You should rest, m'Lord."

"I want to see my brother."

"As you wish. I'll wait outside." Murdock went to the door and warned Ian. "Don't tire him out."

Ian smiled as he sat in a bedside chair. "They certainly like to protect ye."

Dughall shrugged. "It's their duty, I guess."

"Are ye feeling better?"

"Aye. I was having bad dreams. Father helped me understand it." Dughall looked down. "We should thank God. He never beat us like his father did."

"He talked about it?"

"Aye. It was worse than what happened to me and it lasted six years. He had nightmares for a long time."

"Poor Father."

They were silent for a moment. "Jamison and I went hunting today."

"I know it. Murdock said ye got a big pheasant."

"Somehow I think that trip wasn't about hunting. Jamison asked me to stay here and serve ye."

Dughall raised his eyebrows. "You're my brother. You don't have to think of it that way."

Ian smiled. "I think I would. Jamison told me that things were different, that you had changed."

"In some ways, I'm the same. In other ways, I'm different. What do ye want to know?"

Ian leaned back in his chair. "Tell me about the Celtic sword."

***

The Duke sat at his desk in the study, reviewing provision lists for the castle. He picked up a quill, dipped it in the inkpot, and signed a list. He put down the pen and studied his hand. It was shaking more than usual. "I'm getting worse."

Jamison frowned. "My Lord. These fisher folk have strange ways. Maybe the lass has something for that."

"I doubt it. My father had the same thing. It comes with old age."

"I'll ask her, m'Lord."

The Duke coughed. "Someone else needs to understand this. Next week, I'll turn over this duty to you and the young Lord."

The servant stared. "To me?"

"Aye. I'll teach ye what ye need to know."

"As you wish."

"I spoke to the lad's father today. I asked them all to stay. He'll give me an answer soon. Did you talk to Ian?"

"Aye, m'Lord. He's inclined to stay, but doesn't think his father will approve."

"I think he will. I made him see the danger in returning. The Earl will stop at nothing to get the lad back."

"Ian plans to marry soon."

"I discussed that with his father. He can marry the lass and bring her here."

There was a knock at the door. "Come in!"

John Gilroy entered with a letter in his hand. He handed it to the Duke and bowed. "My Lord. A courier dropped this at the front gate."

"Is he still here?"

"Nay. He left it outside and galloped away."

"Thank ye, Gilroy. That will be all." He waited until the man left the room. The Duke turned over the envelope, which bore the wax seal of the Earl of Huntly. "It didn't take him long to respond." He opened the envelope, unfolded the letter, and read it. His blood boiled. "He can go straight to hell! I have the advantage now."

Jamison frowned. "What does he want?"

"He demands to see his son."

"What do you plan to do, m'Lord?"

"My grandson's wounds are raw. The Earl's not seeing him until the lad is ready."

"What will ye tell the young Lord?"

"Only that his father inquired about him."

"What if he decides to return to Huntly?"

"I won't allow it."

Wee Maggie

CONFRONTATION

HUNTLY CASTLE
MARCH 17 1637
TWO WEEKS LATER

Dawn broke over Huntly Castle, bringing gray skies and cold drizzle. The courtyard was deserted, awaiting servants and tradesmen who were waking. Gilbert's boots clicked on the cobblestones as they approached the stables. He longed for his bed and resented being forced into this mission. "Father. This is insane!"

"Silence, lad! I'm going to claim what's rightfully mine."

They reached the stables, opened the door, and went inside. A sharp aroma of horse dung wrinkled their noses. Gilbert's stomach churned. "It's a raw day. We could ride for hours just to be turned away."

Blackheart reddened. "The Duke won't turn us away. The law of the land says he can't keep me from my son." He entered a stall and patted the horse's face. The magnificent stallion stamped his foot. "Easy Demon. You don't mind going out today. Not like this whining, scheming son of mine."

"Father!" Gilbert gritted his teeth as he saddled his horse. "Come on, Flame." His mind reviewed a thousand injustices as he packed the saddlebag.

"Well, lad. Are ye coming or not?"

"Do I have a choice?"

"Nay."

"Then I guess I'm ready."

Blackheart led his horse out of the stall. "Throw a saddle on Lightning. We're taking him with us."

Gilbert's nerves were raw. "Dughall won't come back with us."

"You're wrong. His peasant morality will make him do the right thing."

"How do you know it's his child?"

Blackheart scowled. "I don't know, but consider the odds. I slept with the woman for ten years. We thought she was barren. He bangs the whore and she gets pregnant."

"What will you do with the child?"

"Kate's alive because it gives me an advantage over your brother. I have no use for a bastard child."

Gilbert's eyes widened. How could he be so cold about his own flesh and blood?

"Do ye think that's my first bastard child? Never mind, lad. You don't want to know what I'm thinking. Neither of ye has a stomach for unpleasant things."

The young man saddled Lightning and tied a rope around his neck. He felt numb inside.

The Earl mounted his horse. "Let's go get your brother."

"Don't tell him about the child, Father. He's suffered enough."

"I say he hasn't. I'm not through with him yet."

DRAKE CASTLE

Gray light filtered through the window, promising an overcast day. Dughall stretched on soft sheets and focused his eyes. "Thank God. A night without bad dreams." He stretched his shoulders and smiled. "I'm getting better at last. It doesn't burn anymore." His eyes closed as he snuggled against the pillow. "Soon you'll be with me, lass. If I sleep, perhaps I'll dream of ye."

Dughall drifted and found himself in a familiar place. It was summer in the meadow surrounded by thick forest. A warm breeze washed over him, drying the sweat on his forehead. He looked around, squinting slightly in the bright sunlight. The meadow was ripe with sweet grass and heather. A wind brushed past, whispering his name and drawing his attention to the west. Martins darted and swooped, picking tiny insects out of the air. "Wee birdies. Just like on the cliffs back home." He looked at his bare feet and wiggled his toes. "It's so peaceful. Why am I here?"

Dughall heard a child's laughter, musical and full of wonder. In the distance, a young girl picked flowers and put them in a basket. She held out her hand and giggled as a copper butterfly landed on it. "Such a bonny lass. I must talk to her."

He walked through the field, humming a tune. Drawing near, he saw that dark curls framed her delicate face. She looked up and smiled, her face glowing with recognition. Light shifted, as though the sun peeked out from behind a cloud. It illuminated the area around her. *How Strange... It's not cloudy.*

She seemed oddly familiar. Dughall knelt beside her and spoke gently. "I won't hurt ye, child."

Her blue eyes sparkled. "I know it."

"You're a bonny wee lass. Do I know ye?"

The little girl smiled, her nose wrinkling slightly. "Of course silly, you're my father."

Dughall stared as she reached out and held her palm against his cheek. Her hand bore a birthmark, the head of a stag. "Oh God," he whispered. "It can't be true."

"It is, Father. My name is Wee Maggie."

The love he felt for her surprised him.

Her lower lip trembled. "Save me, Father. He means to cast me away. You must stand up to him."

***

Dughall woke with a start, sat up in bed, and rubbed his temples. "Oh God. Tell me it's just a dream." His heart ached as he struggled with the memory. "She looks so familiar." Suddenly, he remembered. "The child's portrait in the library. My mother Christal." His head throbbed painfully. "She could be mine. I think I've gone mad."

FOREST BETWEEN HUNTLY AND DRAKE

The ride through the forest was cold and wet. Gilbert had been silent, thinking about how he could help his brother. He was getting desperate. There was just no good way to stand up to his father. They reached a clearing.

Blackheart dismounted and took three apples out of his saddlebag, tossing two to Gilbert. "Feed the horses, lad. It's another hour to Drake."

Gilbert tied the horses to a tree and held out the apples while Lightning and Flame crunched them. His thighs ached. "It's a long way. We should stretch our legs for a while."

"Nay. I want to get there early to catch them by surprise."

Drizzle turned into cold, steady rain. Gilbert stared as Blackheart unlaced his breeks and relieved himself against a tree. The bitter taste of bile rose in his throat. "To hell with his ideas!" he whispered. "I hate him!" His thoughts turned to Dughall. *Brother. No matter what he says, don't trust him.*

DRAKE CASTLE

Dughall lingered at the breakfast table with the Duke and Jessie. He poked at a broken egg yolk on his plate and gagged. "I can't eat this."

"What's wrong, Son?" Jessie asked.

His stomach churned, making him nauseous. "I'm not hungry."

"I thought you were going hunting with Ian."

"I must stay here today."

The Duke stared. "What's wrong with ye, lad? You look like hell."

Dughall cocked his head and listened. "The Earl's coming and my brother Gilbert as well."

"How do you know?"

"I can feel them."

"Dear God." Jessie's eyes widened with fear. "It must be true. He's always right."

"Damn that man! I told him not to come yet. You don't have to see him, lad."

"I have to talk to him. There's something I must know."

The old man picked up a brass bell and rang it once.

Jamison entered the room and came to his side. "My Lord."

"My grandson thinks that the Earl and his son are on the way. Alex and Ian went hunting. Find them and keep them inside today."

"As you wish, m'Lord. Shall I alert the guards?"

"Aye. Post armed men at each entrance. Tell them to watch for the Earl and his son. They're not to admit them until I say so."

Dughall rubbed his forehead. "Oh God. My head hurts like the devil. I need to get ready."

"How long do we have, lad?"

"An hour at most."

The Duke's eyes narrowed. "Leave us, Jamison, and take Mrs. Hay with you. I need to talk to my grandson in private. Find Murdock and Gilroy and report back."

Jamison nodded and escorted her out of the room.

The Duke poured tea. "Drink something, lad. You're making yourself sick."

Dughall lifted the cup to his mouth. "I'm not sick and I'm not afraid of him."

"You don't have to see your father. I can turn him away."

"I have to talk to him. There's something I must know."

The Duke sighed. "You may never understand that man."

"I have to try."

The old man removed his spectacles and polished them with a

napkin. "The Earl will do anything to get you to return with him. You can't trust what he says. He'll lie to your face."

"I know it."

"Then why see him?"

"I need to ask him why he did it. How could he beat me and leave me to die?"

"I doubt that he sees it that way. He was outraged when I accused him of it. Let me send him away."

Dughall reddened with shame. "I have to see him. There's something else, more important."

"What?"

"I'm embarrassed to tell ye."

"Why, lad?"

"It's a private matter. His mistress and I…"

"Murdock told me what happened. It's not your fault."

"I may have fathered a child."

The Duke frowned. "Hmmmphhh… What makes you think that?"

"I saw her in a dream."

"Her?"

"My daughter. She looks exactly like the picture of my mother in the library."

The old man blew his breath out slowly. "These things are far beyond my understanding. Yet there's substance to them. I won't let you go back with him. He'd beat you to death."

"I won't go back." Dughall took a ragged breath. "One thing bothers me. What kind of father chooses his own safety over that of his child? What if he kills her?"

"Calm down, lad."

"Help me, Grandfather. I want my daughter. What can I do?"

The Duke leaned forward. "Listen carefully, Son. You have the upper hand. After I'm dead, all of this will be yours. Not just the castle, but land that stretches northwest to Moray Firth. Horse farms and orchards and fleets of boats. Nearly a thousand men under your command."

Dughall's eyes widened.

"The Earl wants to be part of that, but he can't if you don't allow it. Deal with him from a position of power. That's your weapon."

"Aye." Dughall nodded. "Thank ye, Grandfather."

"Now here's what you tell him…"

✳✳✳

Jamison found Alex and Ian hunting in the forest. "We must hurry. The lad said that we had less than an hour."

Alex mounted his horse. "Do ye think he's right about this?"

Ian grunted. "I've never known him to be wrong about a feeling." He shouldered his quiver and mounted a horse. "God damn it! Dughall's not going back with him."

Jamison shook his head. "Nay, lad. The Duke won't allow it."

"My brother needs protection. I'll get my sword and stand with ye."

"Not this time. The Duke wants you both to stay out of sight. It's best if the Earl doesn't know you're here."

Ian frowned.

"You'll get your chance, Son. You need more training."

They tapped the reins and guided their horses through the woods. "Is my son all right?" Alex asked.

"He seems upset."

"I would be. The man's his father, no matter what he's done."

They passed two lads cutting firewood. The castle was just ahead, through a stand of pine trees. "The Duke wants ye inside today. Stay away from the Earl and his son. They may recognize ye."

Ian frowned. "How will ye protect my brother?"

Jamison waved to the guard to gain entrance. "He won't be alone. Murdock and I will stay with him."

***

Dughall spread a sweet cake with butter, popped it into his mouth, and washed it down with tea. "Thank ye, Sir. I feel better now."

There was a knock on the door. Jamison entered with Gilroy and Murdock. The Duke's face turned a dusty blue as he wheezed into a kerchief.

"Are ye all right, m'Lord?"

He gasped for air. "Never mind that! Are we ready?"

Gilroy nodded. "Aye, my Lord. I've got six armed men at the front gate, Pratt and Suttie among them. Four at the back gate. The Hays are in the library."

"Good. Join the men at the back gate. I don't want them slipping through."

Gilroy bowed and took his leave.

The Duke frowned. "Jamison. Have they been spotted?"

"Nay."

"When they arrive, I'm to be told immediately. Strip them of their weapons. Take care that you get all of them, even the small knives in their boots."

"The Earl will never submit to a search," Murdock said.

The old man smiled. "Then he won't be admitted. Return his weapons on the way out. Would ye like me to stay with ye, lad?"

"Nay, Sir. I must face him alone."

"Jamison and Murdock will stay with ye, armed with dirks. I'll allow one visitor at a time, the Earl, and then your brother."

"I want to see Gilbert. He saved my life."

"We owe him that."

There was a knock on the door and a young man entered. His cheeks were ruddy from the cold. "My Lord."

"What is it, lad?"

"Pratt sent me. The Earl of Huntly is at the front gate with his son. They're demanding to see the young Lord."

The Duke stood. "You were right, lad. Jamison. Search them well; then bring them here. Under no circumstance is my grandson to leave with them. I'll wait in the library with the Hays."

"Aye, m'Lord." He fingered the blade of his knife as he left the room.

The Duke leaned on the table and gasped for breath. He coughed hard and spit up phlegm into a napkin.

"Grandfather, are ye all right?"

The old man's face was ashen. "Nay, lad. But don't fret. I do this every day. Remember what I told ye."

"Aye, Sir."

The Duke grabbed his cane and slowly made his way to the door. Dughall's head pounded as he watched him leave. Soon the Earl would come through that door, determined to take him back to Huntly.

The young Lord turned to his servant. "Tell me something good, Murdock."

"The Earl can't hurt ye, lad. Jamison and I will see to that. But get ready for a fight. He's going to be angry."

***

It was muddy and wet outside the main gate. Rain was falling, soaking the Earl and his son. "God damn it!" Blackheart grumbled. "Is this any way to treat a Lord? Let us in!"

Pratt stared. "Nay, Sir. I have orders from the Duke to keep ye out."

"He knows we're here?"

"Aye."

Blackheart reddened. "How the hell did he know we were coming?"

"I don't know, Sir. I've sent for his manservant."

"Hmmphh..."

Jamison arrived and took charge of the situation. He opened the heavy gate. "Pratt! Take their horses." The servant took the reins and tied the horses to a hitching post.

"God damn it! I want to see my son."

Jamison put a hand on the Earl's shoulder and nudged him towards the wall. "Turn around."

"Don't touch me!" Blackheart cried.

"I must search ye for weapons. Do ye want to see the young Lord or not?"

"Aye."

"Put your hands against the wall, legs apart."

Blackheart complied.

Jamison patted him down, removing a dirk from his belt and a small knife from his boot. He reached between his legs and felt the bulge in his breeks.

Blackheart pounded the wall in frustration. "I'm an Earl. How dare ye treat me like a common criminal!"

Jamison searched his pockets, removing a three-tailed strap. "What were ye planning to do with this? Beat him bloody again?"

Gilbert paled. "Father! How could ye?"

The Earl scowled. "Shut up, lad!"

Jamison slipped it into his pocket. "You're not getting this back. Now for the young Lord."

Gilbert put his hands against the wall and spread his legs. Jamison searched his body, removing a dirk and a boot knife. "Pratt, keep their weapons inside the gate. Take their horses to the stables and give them hay and water." His brow knotted. "Why three horses? The young Lord's not going back with ye."

Gilbert swallowed hard. "The black stallion with the white streak belongs to my brother. We brought it to him."

The Earl stared. "What!"

"Lightning belongs to him, Father. It was a Christmas gift."

"I'll deal with ye later, Son. You'll be sorry you were born."

Jamison cleared his throat. "Follow me. The young Lord is waiting in the breakfast room."

"Hmmphh… Will the Duke be there?"

"Nay. If you wish to see him afterwards, ye can."

"I'd rather not."

They skirted mud puddles as they walked towards the castle entrance. "We'll be seeing my son alone?"

Jamison smirked. "Nay. He'll be under guard. One of you goes in at a time. You first, then the young Lord."

Blackheart's eyes narrowed. "God damn that man! He knew we were coming."

***

Dughall held his breath when he heard familiar voices in the hallway. He strained to hear what they were saying.

Murdock's hand trembled as he poured the tea. "My Lord, they're here. Remember what he did to ye. You're not thinking of going back?"

"Nay."

"Good. He'd kill us both for running away."

There was a knock at the door. Jamison entered and surveyed the room. "They're outside. Sit here, my Lord. I'll seat the Earl across from ye."

Dughall took a seat and swallowed hard against a growing lump in his throat.

Jamison continued. "I've stripped him of his weapons." He took out the strap and threw it on the table. "Including this one."

The young Lord flinched. He'd hoped never to see that again. "Take it away and don't return it to him!"

"Forgive me, m'Lord. I thought you should know what his intentions are." He slipped it into his pocket. "Murdock and I will protect ye. We'll be armed with dirks."

"Thank ye, Jamison."

Murdock stood behind him and squeezed his shoulder. "I'll protect ye with my life. I swear it."

Jamison left the room and returned with the Earl. Blackheart's face was grim as he took a seat across from Dughall. His eyes flashed as Jamison leaned against the wall, a hand on his dirk.

The Earl growled, "God damn it, man! Do ye have to stand next to me?"

"Aye."

He clenched his jaw. "Son..."

Dughall's nerves were on fire. "Father..."

Blackheart noticed Murdock. "God damn traitor! I took care of ye for years, even saved ye on the battlefield. What loyalty is this?"

"You gave me to the young Lord. I'm loyal to him now."

"Hmmphh..."

"Father, you've come a long way. What do ye want?"

"Tell them to give us some privacy," Blackheart demanded. "Send them away."

"Nay. I want them here."

"Hmmphh..."

The Earl's voice was cold and deliberate. "We have a score to settle. You ran from me again."

"Nay, Father. They took me out of there. I was out cold."

"If that's the truth then I won't punish ye. Come back with me."

"Nay."

"Why not, lad?"

"You left me to die, locked in the stables."

"Lies! Is that what they're telling ye? I didn't hurt ye that bad."

Dughall searched his father's face. Did the man truly believe that? He glanced at the rope burns on his wrists and unbuttoned his cuffs.

"My Lord," Murdock begged. "Don't do this."

"I want him to see it." He stood and pulled the shirt over his head, exposing his wounds. Scars and stripes covered his back from neck to waist.

The Earl stared.

The young Lord slipped on his shirt and sat down. His voice was cold. "You hurt me bad. I didn't wake up for a full day."

Blackheart drummed his fingers on the table. "I admit that I may have gone too far. It's what my father would have done to me." The Earl leaned forward and spoke in low tones. "I promised your brother that I wouldn't beat him. I'll make the same promise to ye. I'm your father. Come home with me."

Dughall didn't believe him for a minute. "Why then, did ye bring the strap? I won't come back, Father. I belong here."

Blackheart jumped to his feet and pounded the table. "Don't make me hurt ye! I'm not through with ye, lad."

Murdock put his body between them, keeping a hand on his knife. "Stand down, Sir!"

Dughall flinched and pushed back his chair. His heart thumped against his chest.

Blackheart made a fist. "How dare ye defy me, Murdock. I'll kill ye with my bare hands!"

Jamison drew his dirk and held it close to the Earl's breast. "Sit down, Sir! Or I'll be forced to restrain ye."

Blackheart sat down and scowled. "So this is what it's come to."

"Father, please. It's their duty to protect me. Be reasonable."

"All right. Let's be reasonable. You have to come back! My mistress is carrying your child."

Dughall burned with shame. "Oh God. It is true."

"Come back and I'll let the child live."

His heart sank. The wee lassie was right.

Murdock gasped. "My Lord! He slept with Kate, too. It may not be yours."

The Earl clenched his fists. "Silence, Murdock or I'll give ye to Fang for a week before I hang ye!"

Grandfather's right. I can't even protect Murdock. Dughall summoned his courage. "I won't go back with ye under any circumstances."

"What?"

"I said I wouldn't go back."

"What about your child?"

Dughall hardened his expression. "Look around ye, Father. Grandfather is dying as we speak. Soon, all of this will be mine. Not just the castle, but land and ships and men to command. Send my child when it's born, or you won't be a part of that."

The Earl stiffened. "How dare ye dictate to me! I meant what I said." He jumped to his feet and reached across the table, grabbing the young Lord's shirt. "Come back with me now or the child dies."

"Father, stop this! We're your flesh and blood."

Jamison drew his dirk and held it to the Earl's breast. "If you value your life, let him go!"

"This is an outrage!"

He pressed the tip of the knife to his chest. "Stand back, Sir! Your visit is over."

Blackheart released the young man and spat on the floor. "Insolent bastard! If the tables turn, I'll see that ye suffer a slow and painful death."

Jamison's eyes narrowed. "We'll see that the tables don't turn. I trust you can find the door."

"Aye."

"Shall I get your brother, m'Lord?"

"Aye. Send him in."

Blackheart reached the door. "It seems you've become a man. You have me to thank for that. Sometimes that's what it takes, a sound whipping." He opened the door and left the room.

Dughall blew his breath out slowly. "Father got the last word."

Murdock nodded. "He always does."

Angry words came from the hall. The Earl's voice; then Gilbert's. A fist pounded the wall.

Dughall's stomach churned. "Poor Gilbert. I've caused so much trouble."

The door opened. Gilbert entered the room, his face flushed with anger. "I don't have much time, Brother. I think Father's gone mad."

Dughall embraced him. "Murdock told me what ye did. Thank ye for saving my life."

Gilbert sighed. "God in heaven. I should have stopped him sooner. He nearly killed you."

"I'm alive and whole."

"I tried to return to the stables, but Fang had me under guard. I went mad when Connor told me you were locked up all night."

"You did what you could."

"Father expects me to convince you to come back. He promised not to beat us, but don't trust him. Stay here where it's safe."

"I intend to."

They were silent for a moment. Dughall had a hundred questions, but time was short. "Gilbert. I have a favor to ask."

"What's that?"

"Let me know when Kate's time is near."

Gilbert frowned. "That woman is nothing but trouble. You know that the child could be his."

Dughall sighed. "It doesn't matter. The child is our flesh and blood. I'll raise it as my own."

"Father has no use for a bastard child. He says he intends to kill it."

His heart was breaking. "I know what he said. Give me some time.

I'll find a way to change his mind."

"How will you do that?"

"God brought me this far. He won't abandon me or my child."

"I wish I had your faith, little brother. In any case, Father doesn't need another son to ruin. The child will fare better with you."

Jamison opened the door a crack. "The Earl wants to leave."

Gilbert flinched. "He likely needs a swig of whisky from his saddlebag. I must go." He reached in his pocket and took out a hair from a horse's mane. "A gift from me."

Dughall sighed. "From Black Lightning. God, I miss that horse."

"He's in the stables, Brother. I'll make sure that Father leaves him."

They heard a loud voice beyond the door, berating Jamison. A fist pounded the wall. "I'm going to miss ye, Gilbert."

"I'll miss ye too, lad."

"If there's anything I can do…"

"Someday brother. Take care of him, Murdock."

✻✻✻

Dughall and Murdock stood at the iron-grated window. At last, they saw Blackheart and Gilbert on horseback, leaving through the main gate. Lightning wasn't with them.

Dughall's heart ached. "I'm going to miss my brother."

"So will I, m'Lord."

"I wish I could understand it. He's my father! Why does he hate me?"

Murdock frowned. "He's angry because he didn't get his way. I've seen this before."

"Will he kill the child?"

"The way I see it, the child's worth more alive than dead."

"How so?"

"He can use it to influence ye."

"Oh…"

Murdock smiled. "At least they left your horse."

"Can I go to him?"

"Not yet. We should join the Duke in the library."

"Are my parents there?"

"Aye."

Dughall swallowed hard. "I'll tell them the truth, that I fathered a child out of wedlock."

"It wasn't your fault."

"She didn't force me, Murdock. I must accept responsibility for what I've done. My parents will be disappointed."

"I don't think they'll be angry. It's their grandchild at stake."

"Father taught me not to take advantage of a lass."

"Kate is hardly an innocent lass."

Dughall smiled. "Ach! Now that's the truth."

"My Lord. Your parents will accept it in time. There's someone else you may have a problem with. If you manage to get your child, what will ye tell your lass?"

"Do ye think she'll be mad?"

"I don't know, m'Lord. I can never understand women. Is she bonny?"

"Aye."

"Like I said before, those kind are the worst."

Dughall rubbed his temples. "Oh God. My head hurts just thinkin' about it."

***

They walked the hallway to the wing that housed the library. Dughall tried to think of something more pleasant. "Will ye come with me to find the lass?"

"Aye, lad. The Duke says we'll travel to the eastern forest and split up. Jamison and I will accompany ye to the lass' village and the Duke will go with your family to Peterhead. Gilroy, Pratt and Suttie will guard them. We'll meet in Peterhead at The Crack. Your parents have matters to settle there."

"Will we go to Whinnyfold?"

"Maybe the next day."

"I've dreamed of those cliffs and the sea birds as well." They reached the library and met Ian coming out of the door.

Ian smiled broadly. "Brother. Jamison said you were safe. So you're going to be a father. Better you than me."

Dughall stiffened. "You know about that?"

"Jamison told us. Mother smiled, but Father got verra quiet. He wants to have a serious talk with ye."

"Oh God. I hope he understands. I want to bring my child here."

Ian whistled. "Forget Father. What will ye tell your lass?"

"The truth, I guess."

"Think of an excuse, Brother. Mary would kick me in the ballocks."

"I won't lie to the lass I mean to marry."

Murdock interrupted. "Is the Duke in the library?"

"Nay. Jamison took him to his bedchamber. He's feverish and coughing. Mother went along to tend to him."

Dughall raised his eyebrows. "Father's alone in the library?"

"Aye."

"Best to get it over with. Murdock, I need to see my father alone. He can accompany me to the stables."

"My Lord, allow me to stay and protect ye."

"I'll be all right. Take my brother to the kitchen, he must be starving."

The faithful servant nodded.

"Good luck, Brother," Ian said. "I'll save ye some sweet cakes. You'll need them."

***

Dughall steeled himself against his father's disappointment as he opened the door and entered. It was quiet in the library. The desk was unoccupied and the overstuffed chairs were empty. He looked for his father and found Alex kneeling near the window, his eyes closed and hands folded in prayer. Dughall didn't want to disturb him. He tiptoed across the room and stood beside him.

Alex's face was solemn. His lips moved silently, forming the words 'Thank ye for protecting my son'.

Dughall's heart swelled. *I am such a fool. This is my true father.* He touched his shoulder. "Father..."

Alex opened his eyes, his face a jumble of emotion. He stood and embraced his son. "God forgive me. I was afraid that you'd go back with him."

Dughall's voice was tight. "I won't go back there. Ian says that ye know about the child."

"Aye."

"Aren't ye going to say something?"

Alex sighed. "I should scold ye, but I'm so glad to see ye I could cry."

Dughall's eyes filled with tears. "Father, they left my horse in the stables. Will ye come with me to see him?"

"Aye, lad."

"Good. I think ye should have a serious talk with me."

***

The courtyard bustled with activity. Children played with a black terrier, shrieking as it ran between their legs. A wee lass rolled a barrel hoop with a short stick.

The terrier howled. "Ah-r-r-r-r-o-o-o-o-o."

The laundry doors opened, allowing steamy air to escape. Aggie and Celia shook out a sheet. The hoop rolled between them, splattering mud on the sheet.

Aggie grabbed the hoop and tucked it under her arm. "Awww... Look what you've done to me laundry! Be off with ye, bad child."

Wee Mary pouted. "Gimme hoop."

"Nay. You're nothin' but trouble."

Tears rolled down her dirty cheeks.

Celia frowned. "Give it back, lass. The young Lord's coming. He's a tender hearted one with children."

Aggie stared. "Are ye sure it's him? I can't see that far."

"Too bad for you. He's a handsome one."

Aggie dropped the hoop and squinted, hoping to catch a glimpse. Wee Mary snatched it and ran away.

***

Alex and Dughall walked across cobblestones towards the stables. They stopped at a stone bench and sat down. Pounding echoed from the blacksmith's lair, along with a man cursing.

Dughall frowned. "That man shouldn't swear in front of those children. I'll speak to him later."

They were silent for a moment. Dughall's head ached as he gripped the bench. "I'm ready, Father. Let's get this over with."

Alex sighed. "You're giving me white hair, lad."

Dughall reddened. "Forgive me, Sir. There's no excuse for what I did."

"I taught ye not to take advantage of a lass. What were ye thinking?"

"She said she was barren. I never thought I'd get her with child. I slept with her twice."

"How did ye know the lass?"

"Kate's the Earl's mistress. He was mad that I was a virgin, so he sent her to me for my birthday."

"Like a cow to be bred. You could have sent her away."

Dughall nodded. "I wasn't myself. He insisted I drink whisky with him."

"Hmmphh... The devil's drink."

"I'll never touch another drop."

"What about the last time you bedded her?"

"She entered my bedchamber at night. I woke with her naked atop me, grinding against my manhood."

Alex reddened. "Enough said, lad. Weren't ye afraid of the Earl?"

"Nay. I thought that he sent her again. When we were done, Kate told me she'd come on her own. I told her never to come back."

"So, ye can't do right by this lass."

"She belongs to the Earl. I can't marry her."

"Jamison said the Earl threatened to kill the child."

"Aye. I'll have to convince him to send the child to me."

"God will show us the way. The man must have some good in him."

"I've seen glimpses of it."

"So the child will be taken from its mother."

"She's mine too. I saw her in a dream, a bonny wee lass with fine black curls. I love her already."

Alex smiled. "Your mother's happy about it. She's yearned for grandchildren."

"I'll do my best to make things right. Teach me to be a good father."

"You will be, lad."

Dughall's expression darkened. "Sometimes I wonder. His blood runs through my veins. Is there a cruel man inside me waiting to get out? I don't want to be him."

Alex squeezed his hand. "You don't have to, lad. We all get angry. God knows I could have beaten ye, especially when Ian lied. I saw the fear in his eyes and remembered what it was like."

Dughall nodded. Father always had good advice.

"You're a man now. Yesterday I watched ye sparring in the courtyard, standing tall and wielding a sword like a warrior. Soon you'll be a Duke, commanding hundreds of men. It humbles me to think I raised ye."

"I'm still your son."

Alex swallowed hard. "Aye."

Dughall smiled. "Come with me, Father. I want you to see my horse, his name's Black Lightning."

***

Dughall opened the stable door and hurried inside. "Lightning? Where are ye?" In the first stall, a horse nickered and stamped his foot. His heart soared. "Is it you?" He opened the stall and went inside. Lightning stood against the wall, a blanket over his back. They'd brushed him and braided his mane. "I love this horse. He's in here, Father!"

Dughall ran a hand between the horse's ears and stroked his forehead. The stallion's nose wuffled against his shirt, searching for an apple. He laughed. "I love ye too, Lightning. You missed me." The horse shivered under his touch.

Alex took an apple out of the trough. "Here, Son. He's a beautiful stallion. Worthy of a Lord."

"He's the best horse, a bit high-spirited, but strong and fast."

Lightning crunched the apple and licked his hand. "Ha! He wants more. I owe Gilbert for bringing him."

"I'd like to meet your brother someday, to thank him for everything."

"Someday you will. I promise." The horse whinnied and nudged his hand. Dughall stroked his nose. "Oh God, Lightning. We'll always be together. Tomorrow I'll take ye on a ride through the forest. Will ye come, Father?"

"Aye."

Dughall smiled. "It's been a hard day, but it ended well."

BLESSED EVENT

LOUDEN WOOD ABERDEENSHIRE
MARCH 21 1637
FOUR DAYS LATER

It was early morning in the stone cottage. Light streamed through a crack in the door, illuminating the rumpled bed. Keira slowly became aware of her surroundings. Sleep had been elusive, due to an empty belly and the bitter cold. The peat pile was empty and the firewood was soggy. "Dear Goddess. Help me to bear another night."

She snuggled against the pillow and listened to snow buntings twittering in the pines. The old rooster usually greeted daybreak, but he was gone now. They'd made a stew yesterday with the last of the root vegetables. "Poor Fowler."

Keira pushed back the blankets and got out of bed, resting her feet on the dirt floor. She sank to her knees and prayed with all her heart. "Goddess, hear me. Today is the spring equinox. At full moon, we sow the seeds of the harvest and honor the rebirth of mother earth. Truly a blessing as food is scarce. Still, we are grateful. Michael and Torry brought back a doe, sustaining us for a few weeks. There is hope we'll survive this difficult time. My mind spins with questions that cannot be answered. The children stare as I dole out the remaining flour, their faces pale and gaunt. Will they starve before my eyes? Janet's belly swells, the position of the child suspicious. Will it be breech? My dreams are filled with Dughall Hay, singing and reciting poetry. Will he come for me soon? I pray fervently, intent on changing what will be. You speak to me in whispers, telling me to be still and listen."

She stood and slipped on her brogues, digging her toes into the fur lining. A mouse scurried across the floor, searching for crumbs. It stared boldly, with whiskers twitching and black eyes shining. "Ach... You know I won't hurt ye." She poured water into the bowl and splashed her face. The icy liquid brought gooseflesh to her thin arms. Keira stripped off her nightshirt and dressed in woolen tights and a shift. She slipped on her coat, picked up a milk bucket, and went to the door. Someone knocked. She opened it and saw Aileana, her red hair peeking out from under her cap. The young lass looked gaunt.

"Priestess… Can I walk with ye to the barn?"

"Aye. What are ye doing out so early?"

"Michael took Torry and George bow hunting. He wants to bring back a deer or a boar."

Keira's stomach growled. "An honorable task. We'll ask the Goddess to help them." She came outside and faced the young girl, holding her hands. "Lady of light, Goddess of the hunt. Drawn bow, silver quiver, dogs at your side. Help our men sustain us for another moon. Grant them strength and skill."

Aileana smiled. "Blessed be." They hugged and started towards the barn. "Priestess. Is today the day?"

"What day, child?"

Aileana frowned. "I'm not a child. You said that Janet's baby would be born after the equinox."

"Ah that. You have to be patient. Only the Goddess knows when the child will come."

"I want to watch."

"You'll do more than that. You and Morgaine must help me to birth the child. The next one will be up to you."

"I've never birthed a child."

"You've come a long way, lass. I've taught ye to treat wounds and set bones. It's time that ye learned about childbirth." They reached the barn and opened the heavy door. The cow bellowed in her stall. "Hold on, Bessie. I've come to milk ye." Keira entered the stall. The cow snorted as she put a handful of oat straw in the trough and patted her side. She sat on the stool and braced her shoulder against the animal, gripping the front teats.

"Can I help?" Aileana asked.

"Nay. But you can share some porridge with me afterwards." She squeezed down and heard the milk hiss into the bucket.

"Priestess… You can't leave us."

Keira swallowed hard against a growing lump in her throat. "I must."

"Why? I love ye like a mother."

"I love ye too, honey, but I'm marrying a man who lives on the seacoast."

"Can I go with ye?"

"Nay. Who would take care of Torry and George?"

"I don't know. They don't like me much."

"Sometimes that's the nature of brothers and sisters." Keira switched to the back teats. Warm milk squirted into the bucket. "I thought you wanted to be the village healer."

"I do, but you're my best friend. I don't want to lose ye."

Keira made a promise she hoped to keep. "You won't lose me. I'll visit in summer when it's easy to travel. It's close enough that if you have a problem, you can send for me."

"What if something happens to ye? Michael says that it's dangerous to live among outsiders."

Keira touched her cheek. "I know what he says. Don't worry. The Goddess will protect me." Milk covered the bottom of the bucket. Keira stood, patted the cow's side, and gave her a handful of oat straw. "Thank ye, Bessie."

"Priestess... Why do ye thank the cow?"

Keira smiled. "We honor the animals that sacrifice themselves so we can live."

"Oh... Like poor Fowler."

Keira sighed. "Aye. I feel bad about that, too."

Aileana picked up the bucket and they left the stall. Barn swallows twittered overhead, stuffing their nests with mud and straw.

"It's a sure sign of spring," Keira said. "Soon, they'll be laying eggs and raising little ones."

"Aye." They left the barn and headed for the cottage. Aileana's stomach growled. "I'm so hungry I could eat some of that awful rooster stew."

Keira smiled. "I just happen to have a handful of oats and a pinch of salt. If we look hard we might find a crock of rhubarb jelly, just the thing for our porridge. Grandmother hid some away last winter in the loft."

***

After breakfast, they hiked into the woods to look for dead branches. The forest was damp and the oak trees were bare. Wind whispered through the pines, making them shiver. Keira and Aileana left the path, hoping to find a fallen tree. So far, their baskets were empty. Keira was getting desperate. "Goddess help us. We can't go back empty handed."

Aileana's face was grim. "Priestess... Is there no more peat?"

"None to speak of. What little there is we left with Janet and Alistair."

"Oh... I was so cold last night that I slept next to Georgie."

"Be grateful, child, that you have someone to sleep with." They walked a mile and came upon a clearing littered with dead trees and rotted logs. Keira's heart lightened as she took out her knife. "Look, friend. Dead oak trees and they look dry. Let's cut some of the smaller branches. They'll burn better than green wood."

Aileana braced her foot against a log and stripped a branch. She broke it in half and put the rods in her basket. "Janet is so lucky, about to have her first. Alistair is such a kind man."

Keira smiled. "Aye. They're good friends." She took off her mittens and used the knife to saw through a branch. "Bless the Goddess for this dry wood."

The young girl climbed a tree to shake down dead branches. They stripped and broke them into short lengths, then bundled them with twine. Keira straightened her back and groaned.

"Are ye all right, Priestess?"

"Just a bit stiff. This winter has taken its toll on me."

"When we get back, I'll make a tea of willow bark."

"Thank ye, lass. You've learned your lessons well."

Aileana rubbed her hands together to get warm. "Michael will be pleased. There's enough wood to last a few nights."

"Aye. We'll send the men for the rest of it. I want to go back and check on Janet."

In the distance, a familiar male voice called. "Priestess! Priestess!"

"Over here!" Aileana cried.

Kevin rushed into the clearing with young Robbie in tow. His forehead was wet with perspiration. "I'm glad we found ye! Janet is having pains, not too far apart. Morgaine is with her, but she's not sure what to do."

"Did her water break?"

Kevin shrugged.

"Is there any blood?"

He pulled on his beard, unsure of what to say.

Keira was anxious. "Where are the pains? How far down?"

"I don't know, lass. Alistair sent me."

Robbie held his lower belly. "Down here, Priestess. She was crying."

Keira piled bundles of wood into his arms. "Kevin, take these and remember this place. You must come back for the rest of the wood. Let's go. We must hurry!" They hiked the baskets on their backs and followed Kevin through the forest. In a distant pine, a raven called out a warning. A feeling of dread overcame her. The last time this happened, a woman lost her newborn son. Moments later, they cleared the dense woods and ran for the village.

Keira's lips moved in silent prayer. Her hand rested over her heart.

Aileana caught her breath. "Priestess, is there something wrong?"

"The raven's a bad sign. Pray to the Goddess, young one. We're going to need her help."

***

Alistair's heart ached as he watched his wife struggle. He sat by her bedside, wringing his hands.

Janet lay in bed, gripping the sheet as a wave of pain washed over her. "Dear Goddess! I can't bear it much longer. Where is Keira?"

Morgaine sponged her forehead. "I don't know, lass. We sent Kevin after her."

Janet gasped. "Ach! Something bad just happened. I'm leaking. Is it blood?"

Morgaine paled as she pulled back the sheet. "Your water broke. It won't be long now."

Alistair chewed his thumbnail until it bled. His heart would break if he lost her. "What should we do?"

Janet gripped her thighs and rocked. Her jaw clenched as the pain came. "Help me, husband!"

Alistair frowned. "You're the midwife. Do something."

Morgaine's eyes widened. "I've never done this before. Her pains are coming closer. Find the Priestess!"

Alistair stood and stroked Janet's hair. "Forgive me lass, for doing this to ye. I love ye so much. Don't die." Shaking with fear, he pulled on his coat and went to the door. As he lifted the latch, it opened.

Keira stood before him, her face flushed from running. Young Aileana was behind her.

He grasped her hand in desperation. "Priestess! You're here. Thank the Goddess. The child is coming."

Janet screamed. Alistair's eyes were filled with tears. "Tell me what to do."

Keira nodded. "Get the healer's bag from my cottage. I'll need blankets and clean cloth as well."

He took a deep breath and set about the task, running down the path.

***

Keira entered the cottage and took off her coat. Her nerves were raw. She sniffed the air, sensing that her water had broken. This was her dearest friend. For a moment in time, she was frozen.

Ailie's voice was hollow. "Priestess?"

She steeled herself and walked to the bed.

Janet looked up, her eyes wild with pain. "Oh dear Goddess, they found you."

Morgaine spoke up. "Her water broke. I don't know what I'm doing."

"It's all right, lass. Someday you will. Show me what's happened."

Morgaine pulled back the sheet to reveal a puddle on the mattress. Janet moaned.

Keira stroked her hair. "Easy, lass. Your water broke."

"Is it supposed to hurt this much?"

"Where does it hurt?"

Janet grasped her lower belly. "Down here. In waves... Ach! A pain so sharp I can barely stand it."

Keira's suspicions grew. She had to put her feelings aside and concentrate on the birth. "Do ye trust me?"

"Aye."

"Good. You must sit up and hold your knees."

Janet nodded.

"Ailie... Help me sit her up."

Aileana got on the other side of the bed. She supported Janet while Keira took her arm. Together, they slid her up against the wall.

"The pain's coming again," she panted. "Help me."

"Easy, lass. I'm going to see where the baby is. Take small breaths. That's it..." Keira placed a hand between her legs and felt for the head. She chewed her lip and tried again. It was a bad sign. "Morgaine, Aileana. Come here. I want ye to feel this." One by one, she guided their hands. "Feel this? Not very hard, is it? It's the child's bottom."

Janet groaned. "Have ye ever done a breech?"

"Aye. Just once with Grandmother."

"Did the child live?"

"Never mind that. We must have faith. Let's see if we can turn it."

Alistair entered the cottage and handed her the healer's bag. He put down an armful of blankets. "I got a blanket from your place and one from Michael's. How is my wife?"

Keira spoke in low tones. "I won't lie to ye, friend. We have a bad situation. The child is breech."

Alistair's lip trembled. "Will my wife be all right?"

"Only the Goddess knows. We'll do our best to save them both."

"What can I do?"

"Leave us women folk alone. Go outside, boil water for the cleanup, and pray to the Goddess." Alistair nodded and left the cottage. "Poor man. Best that he's out of our way. It wouldn't do to have him faint. Help me lie her down."

Morgaine stood on the other side of the bed and helped Janet lay flat.

"Get as many blankets as you can. We'll prop her hips up on them." They rolled blankets into tight pillows, propping them under her hips and knees. Janet groaned as the last pillow was placed. "Are ye all right, lass?"

"Aye, just sore. Do what ye must to save my child."

Keira remembered to teach the others. "Keep her head lower than her hips. With luck, the child will pull back from the bone. Then we can try to turn him."

"Turn her," Janet insisted. "It's a lassie, I know it."

Keira smiled nervously. "Then a lassie it is. Try to relax friend. This may take some time. Ailie, get my massage oil."

Aileana rummaged through the bag and took out the bottle of oil. "Here, Priestess."

"Pour some oil on my fingers, and then do the same for you and Morgaine."

Aileana poured.

Keira ran her fingers across Janet's belly, identifying the child's head and bottom. She found what she thought might be a foot. It was definitely breech. She guided Morgaine's fingers, showing her what each part felt like. Then she did the same with Aileana.

The young girl was entranced. "Priestess. It's amazing. I feel the life within her."

"It's a miracle of the Goddess."

The young girl's eyes widened. "It moved! The head's here, now."

Keira felt for the position of the head. "The baby must like your touch. It just pulled back from the bone. Now we have a chance for a normal birth." She placed one hand on the head and one on its breech, applying gentle pressure. "Don't force it, mind ye. The trick is to coax it. Come on, wee one."

The child changed position slowly. Each time, Keira applied gentle massage in the right direction and whispered to the child. At last, it was time. The head was close to the bone. Keira breathed a sigh of relief. "The Goddess is with us today. I need your help, friend. We'll get you up quickly and then I want ye to squat."

Janet nodded. They sat her up and helped her off the bed into a squatting position. Janet gripped the side of the bed to steady herself. Her legs shook. "It burns."

"That's a good sign. The child is ready to be born." Keira placed her hand between her legs and felt for the baby. "Now, that's what the head feels like, as hard as a rock." She let Morgaine and Aileana feel the crown.

"Is that the scalp?" Ailie asked. "It's so creamy."

"Aye. That's what protects the baby when it's inside."

Janet panted. "Are ye done with your lessons? Can I push now?"

"Nay. Give me a moment. I don't want ye to tear." Keira oiled the perineum, stretching it until it was supple, and placed a clean blanket under her. Morgaine and Aileana kneeled and supported Janet on both sides. "Bring your daughter into the world, lass. Push."

Janet bore down and groaned. "Dear Goddess."

"Good one. Wait for the wave and push again."

She gritted her teeth and pushed harder this time. "Ach!"

"You're doing fine."

"I'm tired."

"Labor is hard work. Accept the pain. Use it! Push again."

Janet's eyes widened as the next wave hit. She bore down and pushed harder.

Keira felt a chill. "I see the head."

"Is it a lassie?" Aileana cried.

"Well, I can't tell from the head." Keira touched the tips of her fingers to the scalp and felt for a heartbeat. "The child's life force is strong. Give us another hard push."

Janet's eyes burned with determination. She felt the wave and bore down, grunting at the worst of it. The baby's face appeared.

Keira eased her fingers eased along the cheeks and beneath the chin. "The child will usually come on its own. You can help it to turn, like this." She guided the baby in a slight turn until the shoulders were out. One more push and the child's body eased into her hands.

Aileana squealed. "'Tis a lassie!"

"Thank the Goddess it's over," Morgaine whispered.

The young mother trembled. "She's so tiny. Can I hold her?"

"Not yet. I must clear her passages and cut the cord. Morgaine, Ailie. Support her until the afterbirth comes." Keira worked quickly. She lay the child down and cleared her mouth and nose with her fingers. The child cried lustily. "There, there wee lassie. I'll give ye to your mother soon. It's a good sign when they cry." She took a piece of deer sinew from her bag, tied the cord close to the baby, and picked up a small knife. "Watch closely. I've tied the cord. Now I'll cut it." Blood spurted from the cord onto the blanket, but the sinew held fast.

Morgaine gagged and looked away. "There's so much blood. I can't do this."

Aileana watched intently. "I can."

Keira dampened a cloth, cleaned the baby's head and face, and bundled her. The young mother rocked on her knees, blood pooling under her. A spurt came out, followed by the afterbirth. "It's out, lass. Put her to bed." They helped her into bed, placed the wee child in her arms, and put a lamb's wool sponge between her legs. "This much bleeding is normal. Any more, and you must wonder if you got the whole afterbirth." She covered her with a blanket.

Janet cuddled the little one. "She's so bonny. Dark hair like her father and deep blue eyes. Look, she's moving her lips."

"She wants to nurse."

Janet pulled back her shift and let the child find a nipple. The baby began to suck. "Goodness! She's not shy about taking the nipple."

Aileana smiled. "Alistair will love her to death. Oh dear! We left him outside. Shall I fetch him?"

"Aye. Ask the poor man to bring in some of that hot water. We'll clean up."

Aileana ran off, her red hair flying. Keira smiled.

Morgaine hugged her. "Priestess... I'll find Michael for the blessing."

"Thank ye, lass."

Keira stood at the bedside, expressing gratitude to the Goddess. She never tired of the sight of mother and child or the earthy smells of birth. Guilt washed over her like a spring rain. "I don't want to leave this place. I love ye all so much. Do ye hate me for leaving?"

Janet looked up and smiled. "Nay. I'd beg ye to stay, but it wouldn't be right. You'd never hold your own newborn. Marry that handsome fisherman."

"You mean that, friend?"

"Aye."

"Dughall will come for me soon. I've dreamed of it."

"Then peace go with ye, Sister."

The baby let go of the nipple with a wet popping sound. Janet patted her back until a tiny belch came forth. "I've named her Keira. That way, you'll always be in my heart."

PREPARATIONS

HUNTLY CASTLE
MARCH 28 1637
ONE WEEK LATER

Blackheart and Gilbert sat at the breakfast table in stony silence. Their relationship had been strained since they returned from Drake. Gilbert was weary of his father's moods. He steeled himself and offered an olive branch. "Father. I'm taking Flame out to the moor. Would you like to come?"

Blackheart took a swig from his flask and belched. "Aye. I suppose I could. Demon is getting restless."

Gilbert stared. "How can you drink that so early in the morning?"

"Hmmphhh... You're just full of criticism lately. I can't do anything right in your eyes. Someday you'll understand what it means to be a man with responsibilities."

Gilbert burned with anger. Maybe he shouldn't have asked him.

There was a knock on the door and Connor entered. "My Lord. I have word from our mole in Drake Castle. The Duke is taking the young Lord to Peterhead to settle some business."

"When are they leaving?"

"Day after tomorrow."

"Excellent! This is our chance to get him back."

Gilbert's stomach churned. "Father! Leave my brother alone. He's suffered enough."

"Silence, lad! Connor, do we know how many men will be guarding him?"

"The man didn't say, m'Lord. He's just a tradesman, probably doesn't know. We can assume that there will be at least two, Jamison and Murdock."

"I wouldn't mind sending those two back to their maker."

"Father!"

"Perhaps we can abduct his family to get his attention. Aren't they from a fishing village south of there?"

"Aye, but they might be with the Duke. Rumor has it they've been living at the castle."

"God damn it! That man's played all of his cards."

"Father, let's stay out of it."

"Nay, lad. We'll leave tomorrow. Connor! Prepare the horses, pack supplies and weapons, and bring some gold coin to spread around. I'll need you and another master swordsman, Hawthorne will do. We'll take them by surprise."

Connor bowed and took his leave.

Gilbert paled. "Why are you doing this? We don't need to bring him back here. You read Dughall's letter. He said he'd deal with you if you send the child."

Blackheart drummed his fingers on the table. "Maybe he will and maybe he won't. In any case, I'll have another card to play. The red-haired lad or his bonny mother."

"God in heaven. My brother will keep his word."

"We shall see."

"How is Kate?"

"Sinking into madness. She hates her swollen body, and I have to agree. What a waste of a beautiful woman! She begged me to let her get rid of the child, but I can't allow it."

"Thank God."

"God has nothing to do with it. The child's worth more alive than dead, at least for the moment. I've placed maidservants with her so that she doesn't do anything foolish."

"Does she know that you're sending the child away?"

"I'm not going to tell her. I doubt if she'd care, anyway."

"Will you let her live?"

Blackheart stared. "Don't be an idiot. She made me look like a fool. Cuckolded me with my own son! She deserves to die."

Gilbert's face fell. He didn't like her, but he couldn't bear another execution.

"It's a long way off, lad. I might have a change of heart when the birth nears."

"Father, don't kill her."

"It's not your affair, Son."

DRAKE CASTLE

Morning sun beat down on the courtyard, promising a fine spring day. Swallows and robins flitted about building nests in beechnut trees. Children watched as four men practiced swordplay in the center of the courtyard. One of them was the young Lord.

Dughall stood with legs apart, one foot slightly in front of the other, and held the sword in both hands. He stared at Jamison and swallowed hard. *Oh God. He's such a fierce fighter.*

Jamison gripped his sword. "Come on, lad! We've practiced for weeks. Show me what you're made of. Don't hold back."

"I don't want to hurt ye."

"See if ye can. Try to wound me!"

"Come on, Brother!" Ian cried. "You can do it."

Murdock stared. "It's all right, lad. Remember what I taught ye."

Dughall's heart pounded. He raised the broadsword and lashed out in a thrust, slash, and overhead cut.

Jamison raised his sword and warded off the blow. Sparks flew and metal clanged. "Good try, lad!"

"All right, Brother!"

Jamison drew back and prepared to attack. Dughall closed in, bringing his sword down in a diagonal strike. The servant's eyes widened with surprise. He jumped back and blocked the cut with his sword, sending vibrations down their arms. "Good move! Did the Earl teach ye that?"

The young Lord smiled. "Aye, the hard way."

They sparred lightly, their swords clanging in the air. Jamison smiled. "All right, lad. Now try to anticipate my next move. Use your Second Sight!"

"Do it, Brother!"

Dughall reddened. He'd never thought of using the Sight in a battle. "Nay. It's an unfair advantage."

Jamison picked up the pace, challenging the young Lord. Their swords clanged. "In a fight to the death no advantage is unfair. This is your secret weapon against a stronger opponent." He taunted him, blocking his sword. "Now, don't let me block ye. Use your Sight!"

Sweat trickled down Dughall's back. Was the man serious?

"Do it, lad!" He withdrew his sword and waited.

The young Lord took a deep breath and went within. He connected to the older man, feeling the fire in his belly. He was about to raise his sword. Dughall's heart pounded as he raised his blade and lashed out in an overhead cut. "Is this what ye were about to do?"

Jamison ducked and swerved to the right. "Aye!"

"And this?"

"Aye! Now, don't tell me. Block me and take me down!"

They sparred in earnest, swords clanging loudly in the air. Time after time, Dughall anticipated his next move and blocked it or attempted it himself. Finally, their swords met with a sharp sound.

Jamison grunted. He bore down until the base of his blade met his opponent's crossbar. They were locked.

Dughall's muscles burned. "Dear God!" He read the man's intentions, pulled back slightly unsettling him, and watched him fall to the ground. He held the tip of his blade to Jamison's throat. "I win. Drop your weapon!"

Jamison's eyes widened. The sword clanged on the cobblestones. "Excellent, lad. You handle that sword like you were born to it."

Dughall offered a hand and pulled him up. "It's not as heavy as the sword I was using."

"The Celtic blade?"

"Aye. I love that sword. I wish I could get it back."

Ian spoke excitedly. "You were awesome, Brother!"

"Did ye follow it?" Dughall asked.

"Not just the moves, but the feelings! Surprise? Embarrassment?"

Jamison stared. "Aye. You can do this too, lad?"

"I've blocked it all my life, but it's coming back stronger than ever."

"Excellent. When we get back from the trip, I'll work with you."

Ian beamed with pride. "After that, I'll spar with my brother. We'll see what two fighters with the Sight can do."

"As long as it's not for first blood," Dughall said.

Ian's eyes widened. "What's that?"

"The match continues until one of ye draws blood. When I faced the Earl, he held the tip of the blade at my throat, threatening me. I thought he was going to slit my neck. Then he ran it down my shoulder and sliced my arm."

Murdock nodded. "Lucky it wasn't your throat. Come on, lads. I see the kitchen lass waving. It's time for the midday meal."

Jamison wiped his blade with an oiled cloth. "Lesson's over. My Lord. This afternoon we'll work on honing your form."

Dughall sheathed his sword. "Grandfather will tell us about his plans for the trip. I can hardly stand it. Day after tomorrow, we go home and pick up the lasses."

Ian sighed. "I hope Mary's father lets her come back with me."

Jamison smiled. "The Duke will persuade Andrew McFarlein. It's your job to convince the lass. What's she like, lad?"

Ian's eyes were dreamy. "Bonny and sweet."

Dughall's skin flushed as he connected to his brother. Ian was thinking of the big-breasted lass with yellow hair. She'd gone with him to the drying shed, where he'd lifted her petticoat and found her naked underneath. The patch between her legs was silky against his hand. She unlaced his breeks and he took her against the wall. "Brother! You took her."

Ian reddened. "Aye. You're not the only one who might be a father." He struggled with the bulge in his breeks. "I'll take Mary for a walk and tell her how much I need her."

Murdock chuckled. "You're bursting out of those breeks, lad. I think she'll know it."

Dughall rolled his eyes. "You need to be married, Brother. So do I."

***

Alex stared out the window of his bedchamber to the courtyard below. He saw the lads pack up their weapons and head for the castle. *Dughall fought well,* he thought. *He had Jamison on the ground. I can hardly believe he's my son.*

Jessie was busy selecting clothes for the journey. "I packed ye a kilt and a linen shirt, some breeks and sweaters too. I haven't packed mine yet. There are so many dresses." She looked up. "Are they done with their practice?"

"Aye. Dughall fought well. Come here, wife."

She left the chest of drawers and stood before him. "What is it, husband?"

The day was filled with signs of the earth waking to a new season. It filled his heart was gladness, but it couldn't take away his longing for the sea. "This is a grand place, lass. But I miss the sea. I need to be on the point, watching the tides come and go. And the gulls! I even miss their raucous cries."

Jessie pulled him close. "I know what ye mean. Last night I dreamed of it."

Alex sighed. "On a day like today, I'd be caulking the hull of the 'Bonnie Fay', getting her ready to sail. The cod and haddock will be running soon. I'm going to miss my boat."

"The Duke says that you'll be sailing boats twice that size."

His heart ached. "It's not the same thing. I've sailed that boat since I was a lad."

"Oh husband. Do ye have regrets?"

"Nay, lass. God answered our prayers. I lost the 'Bonnie Fay', but we're a family again. I would have traded that boat for Dughall any day."

"We're leaving the day after tomorrow for Peterhead. You'll sail her one more time to take her to Whinnyfold. It's been four long weeks. It will be good to see Robert and Colleen again."

"Aye. I was thinking of letting them use our cottage for their son and his family. It's the Christian thing to do."

"His son can take your place on the 'Bonnie Fay'. That way, you won't lose the boat." Jessie hugged him. "Will Andrew let Mary come back with us?"

"Aye. The Duke's a hard man to refuse. Andrew will insist that Ian and Mary are wed. I would if it was my daughter."

"Then a quick wedding it will be. I'll need to take a fancy dress."

"Aye, and the harp the Duke gave ye."

"I hope that Dughall finds his lass. His heart is set on marrying her. Ian says that he's not sure where she lives."

"Dughall has ways of knowing things that we don't understand. If she's alive, he'll find her."

Jessie smiled. "Maggie once told me they were meant to be together."

Alex's heart ached. "Oh God, lass. I miss her so much. So many changes in so little time. How can we bear it?"

"Think of the grandchildren, husband. Just think of the wee bairnies."

Alex loved this woman more than life. "It will do my heart good to see another generation. Perhaps we'll even have a wee Maggie."

Jessie smiled. "I'd like that."

He took her hand. "It must be close to midday. The Duke wants us all in the dining room. Let's go find the lads."

JOURNEY

DRAKE CASTLE
MARCH 30 1637
TWO DAYS LATER

It was dawn at Drake Castle. Light streamed through an open window in the candle-lit bath chamber. Dughall sat in the tub, pondering the letter. He'd thanked his father for leaving Black Lightning and apologized for his rough treatment. He told the Earl that Grandfather was dying and restated his intentions to stay at Drake. Lastly, he promised to deal with him if he'd spare his child. *It was so easy being a fisherman,* he thought. *I wish I could go back to being a simple man.*

Ian undressed slowly and prepared to get in the tub. "Dawn's breaking. Are ye all right, Brother?"

"The Earl didn't reply to my letter. Yet my daughter still lives. I feel her presence."

"Perhaps he's still angry."

"I keep praying that he'll understand we're his flesh and blood. When we get back, I'll invite him here to settle it man-to-man."

"That's daft! Jamison said he tried to strangle ye."

"That's true."

Ian reddened. "Next time, I want to be in the room with ye."

Dughall nodded. "All right." A feeling of dread overcame him. "Oh God. I just got a bad feeling. The Earl's up to no good."

"Wouldn't your half-brother warn ye?"

"Gilbert would if he could. It's hard to challenge the man when he's bent on something. He'd be risking his backside."

"Hmmphh... The way I see it, we'd all be better off if the Earl was dead."

"Ian!"

"Well, we would. I can't see where there's a bit of good in him.

Unless you feel him on our tail, let's not think about it." Ian hissed as he settled into the copper tub. "It's too hot. I'll never get used to it."

Dughall remembered his first time in the bath. "You will, Brother."

"Why must I take a bath? I took one last week. Do I stink?"

Dughall laughed. "I wouldn't be the one to tell ye." He rolled the soap between his hands and lathered his chest. "Don't ye want to smell good for Mary?"

"Aye. But it's ten hours to Peterhead. I'll smell like a horse no matter what I do."

The young Lord rinsed his chest and soaped his hair. "Wash up, Brother. We're men. Sometimes we don't know how bad we smell. The lasses will notice."

Ian smiled. "I guess I have to listen to ye. You'll be Duke someday."

Dughall rinsed his hair and stood up, letting the water drip off. "You're my brother. You don't have to think of it that way."

Ian was pensive as he washed his chest and arms.

Dughall stepped out of the tub and stood in front of the long mirror, drying himself with a towel. He turned around and looked over his shoulder. His heart sank. "The wounds are gone, but I'll always have these marks. My back looks so ugly. Do ye think she'll want me?"

Ian frowned. "If the woman's worth marrying, she will. This bothers me. What do ye know about her?"

Dughall wrapped the towel around his waist. "Enough. She's kind and beautiful, and a fine healer."

Ian stood and grabbed a towel. "Then she won't be bothered by your back. Do ye know where she lives?"

Dughall had been thinking about this for a while. "Not exactly. She said her village was ten miles north of the meadow in the Forest of Deer. Somewhere near the banks of the Ugie."

"There are a few settlements up there. Even an abbey at a place called Deer. Does her village have a name?"

"Nay."

"Jamison has a map. Before we leave, let's see how far that abbey is from the meadow. It might be a good place to start."

"Aye. Perhaps if I think of her, she'll know I'm coming and meet me."

"I thought that only worked between us. The lass left with that odd man. She could have married him. How do ye know that she's waiting for ye?"

Dughall held up his palm. "I got hand-fasted to her in a dream."

Ian stared. "That's daft. Are ye sure ye didn't cut yourself on that Celtic blade?"

Dughall's frustration grew. "Brother..."

Ian dried himself off with the towel. "Well, you can't get married in a dream. Start thinking about her now. You have to find her in the flesh."

There was a knock at the door. Ian wrapped the towel around his waist. "Come in."

Murdock entered the chamber with an armful of clothes. "My Lord, I brought riding clothes for you and your brother. Your boots are outside the door. Gilroy and Pratt are readying the horses, and the Duke requests our presence in the breakfast room."

"Are there sweet cakes?"

"Aye."

Ian smiled. "Ah, breakfast. I love this place."

LOUDEN FOREST

Keira snuggled under a pile of blankets, trying to stay warm. For the third night in a row, she'd given her firewood to Janet and Alistair and gone to bed without stoking the fire. "I survived another night. It's not so bad. In a week, spring will come and we won't need so much wood."

She fluffed her pillow, went back to sleep, and dreamed of a warm place. It was summertime in the meadow where she'd met Dughall Hay. The grass was almost to her knees and fragrant heather was blooming. Her heart soared. "Dear Goddess. Allow me to see him, even if it's a dream." She walked through the meadow towards the willow patch where they'd met. In the distance, a wee lass no older than four picked wild flowers and put them in a basket. As Keira neared, the child cupped her hands around a flower, brought them to her mouth, and blew copper butterflies into the air.

Her laughter was musical. "All creatures of the Goddess! That's what Mother would say."

Keira approached and touched her shoulder. "I won't hurt ye, little one."

"I know it."

"You're a bonny lass. Do I know ye?"

The little girl smiled in recognition. "Of course, silly. You're the one my father will marry. Kind and beautiful, and a fine healer. Will you be my mother?"

Keira studied the child's dark curls and full mouth. The face of the man she loved stared at her. Suddenly, she understood. This was his child, who needed her as much as he did. She picked her up and held her close. "I'll be your mother, lassie. What's your name?"

"No matter what they call me, my name will always be Maggie."

Her heart smiled. This truly was his child. "And your father?"

"He comes for you today."

Drake Castle

The Duke sat at the head of the table and said grace, "God in heaven. Today we gather to partake of your harvest and prepare ourselves for an important undertaking. Give us strength to endure the journey and protect us from all who seek to harm us. Amen."

"God go with us," Dughall said.

Silverware clanged against plates as they ate a hearty breakfast of ham, eggs, and brown bread. A pot of tea was passed with a platter of sweet cakes. Dughall sat next to his grandfather, with Ian next to him. Alex and Jessie sat across from the lads. Five men sat at the other end of the table, Jamison, Murdock, Gilroy, Pratt and Suttie.

The Duke put down his napkin. "Are the horses ready?"

Gilroy nodded. "Aye, my Lord. Pratt and I took care of it this morning."

"What's the weather look like?"

"It's a clear day, but quite cold. If all goes well, we should make Peterhead by nightfall."

The Duke coughed. "Jamison. We'll travel together until we reach the Abbey of Deer. From the look of that map, her village is somewhere near there. You and Murdock will stay with my grandson until he finds his lass. The rest of us will go on to Peterhead and get accommodations. Find the young woman and bring her to The Crack. We'll expect you late tonight or tomorrow morning."

"As you wish."

"You're all dismissed to bring the horses to the courtyard. I need to talk to the Hays." The servants got up and left the room. "Well, lads. Are you pleased?"

"Aye," Dughall said. "I haven't seen Keira since last summer."

Ian nodded. "My Lord. Do ye think that Andrew will let Mary come back with me?"

The Duke smiled. "Aye. Weeks ago, I sent him a letter stating my intentions. He has a matter of importance to discuss, but I'm sure it's nothing more than social or economic considerations."

Alex cleared his throat. "Andrew will insist that they marry. I would if it were my daughter."

"Not a problem. We can arrange that in Peterhead."

Ian swallowed hard. "Oh God."

The Duke chuckled. "What's wrong, lad?"

"I didn't expect it so soon."

Alex frowned. "You were to marry in a month, anyway. Will Dughall be all right with Jamison and Murdock?"

"Aye. They'll be armed and ready for anything that may happen. I doubt if it will, everyone knows that Jamison is my right-hand man. They won't want to incur my wrath."

"Good. You've been quiet, lass," Alex said.

"Just thinking about home. I can't wait to see Robert and Colleen."

The Duke stood. "Then let's be on our way. The journey will get no shorter by us sitting here."

PETERHEAD

Blackheart and Gilbert emerged from the fish-house tenement, looking tired and disheveled.

"Father. Why are we staying here? It's nothing more than a common alehouse. Last night, I slept with one eye open and a hand on my sword."

The Earl chuckled. "That crew from the Indies was pretty rough."

"Drunkards and thieves! Why don't we stay at the Dutchman's inn?"

Blackheart grunted. "Connor was told that the Duke would be staying at The Crack. I don't want to spook them."

Gilbert's head ached. "Can't we make peace with the Duke? The old man will be dead soon. Dughall said it in his letter. My brother will form an alliance with us if you send him his child."

"I read his letter. Either the Duke helped him with it or he's getting much better with his command of the King's English. I don't trust it. If the man's near death, why is he traveling such a distance?"

Gilbert sighed. "I know my brother. He'll keep his word."

"I want him back. I'm not through with him yet."

Connor approached. "My Lord."

Blacheart took a swig from his flask. "What did you find?"

"There's no sign of them, but they've got all the rooms at The Crack for the next three nights."

The Earl frowned. "Hmmphh… That's six rooms. I wonder who they're bringing with them. Or who they're meeting."

Connor stared. "Do ye want me to return to Huntly for more men?"

"Nay. They don't know we're here, so we have the element of surprise."

"What do you wish me to do?"

"Ask questions. Be discreet. Spread some coin around if necessary. I want to know why they're here. Where is Hawthorne?"

"Practicing swordplay in the field near the south pier. He says he wants to run Murdock through, make him suffer."

Blackheart smiled. "Good. That's the only way to handle a traitor. The young Lord and I will stay out of sight. Now be off with ye."

Connor bowed and headed for the pier.

Gilbert's heart sank. "Father, I can't be a part of this."

Blackheart reddened. "You will lad or I'll beat ye bloody when we get home."

"It will be the last time," Gilbert growled, as he turned away.

"Come back here, Son!"

"Nay!" His hands shook as he ran towards the pier. "God, I hate him. I'd rather be dead."

LOUDEN FOREST

Keira ran to the riverbank and stripped off her clothes. She stepped into the icy water and held her breath. "Great Goddess! He comes for me today, the child said so." She shivered as she lathered her hair and rinsed it clean. Her anxiety grew as she washed her chest and arms, noting how bony she was. "I'm so thin. I hope I please him." The lass finished her bath and stepped onto the riverbank. She dressed in fresh clothes and ran a comb through her hair.

"Priestess?" Aileana emerged from a stand of trees. "What are ye doing? It's too cold to take a bath!"

Keira smiled. "My husband is coming for me today."

"How do ye know?"

"I saw it in a dream."

Ailie frowned. "You can't leave us now! Janet just had a child. She'll be so disappointed."

Keira touched her cheek. "Janet understands, honey. She told me to go. If I stay, I'll never hold my own newborn child."

"But I thought that you and Michael..."

"Will never marry."

"Oh..."

Keira's heart ached. She would miss this young lass, as well as the others in the village. She vowed to say goodbye to every one of them. "You'll see me again. I'll visit in summer after the first harvest."

Ailie sniffled. "Are ye sure?"

"Aye. Come with me, young one. I have a bag to pack, and then I want to visit everyone."

"Can I help?"

Keira smiled. "Aye. You're my special friend."

ABBEY OF DEER - ABERDEENSHIRE

The Duke dipped his fingers in the font and made the sign of the cross. "In the name of the Father, Son, and Holy Spirit. Amen." His heart swelled with reverence in this holy place.

The old monk stood before him in a white cloak, emanating concern and kindness. "Forgive me, Sir. The Brothers live simple lives, worshipping God and working with our hands and hearts. I have no knowledge of the surrounding villages." He gestured at a long corridor. "If you need lodging for a night, we can accommodate you. The fare is Spartan at best, but that can be good for the soul."

The Duke smiled. "Thank you, Brother, but we must continue on. They expect us in Peterhead this evening. Perhaps my grandson and his men will join ye this evening."

The monk nodded. "They are welcome."

"Goodbye, Brother." He turned and walked down the marble steps to join his party.

Jamison cleared his throat. "My Lord. Did he have any information about the lass' village?"

The Duke coughed. "Nay, but he said that this entire area is called the Forest of Deer. You'll have to search the surrounding woods."

"The young Lord says that he has a way to find her."

"I wouldn't doubt that."

"You look tired, m'Lord. Will you stay here tonight?"

"Nay. The monk offered, but it's best that I continue on to Peterhead with the Hays. You three are welcome to stay the night. Dughall!"

Dughall left his family and joined him. "Grandfather?"

"The monks are not aware of any villages. Don't take it to heart. They rarely leave this place. We're going to Peterhead now. Jamison and Murdock will help you find your lass."

—"Thank ye, Sir. I'll say goodbye to my family."

The Duke watched as the young Lord stood in a circle with his family and prayed.

His heart was glad that they were back in his grandson's life. It was important to have a spiritual and moral base. "Gilroy! Pratt! Suttie. Ready the horses."

The men packed the horses and waited as the Duke and the Hay family mounted. They watched for their Lord's signal, mounted, and formed a protective ring around the group with Gilroy in front and Pratt and Suttie in back.

As they left the Abbey, the Duke looked back at his grandson and his men. The old man prayed. "God in heaven. Grant me one more wish. Keep them safe and allow him to find his true love."

LOUDEN FOREST

Keira sat in a rocking chair, holding Janet's newborn daughter. The child's skin was soft and sweet. "She's so bonny."

Janet sat across from her, knitting booties. "I love her so much. I didn't think it was possible to love someone more than Alistair, but I do."

Keira smiled. "Mother used to say that there's no love as strong as a woman's love for her child. Someday, I'll understand."

Janet sniffled. "Are ye sure he's coming today?"

Keira's heart ached. "Aye. A messenger told me in a dream. I'm going to miss ye, friend."

"You're like a sister to me! I'll miss ye, too. Where did Ailie go?"

She stroked the baby's face. "To tell Michael. I'm afraid to face him."

"Remember, lass. He was the one who backed out of the wedding."

"I guess so." The baby fussed and sucked its hand. Keira passed her back to her mother. "She needs to nurse. I'm afraid she won't get anything from me. I'm so thin I barely have breasts."

"Do ye think he'll mind?"

"Nay. Dughall is the most compassionate man I've met. He'll understand that we've been starving. At least you'll have one less mouth to feed."

"How can ye say that?"

Ailie entered the cottage, her red hair peeking out from her cap. "Priestess. Michael wants to see ye alone."

Keira felt a tug at her heartstrings. She kissed Janet on the cheek and smoothed the baby's hair. "Goodbye, friend. I'll visit in summer after the first harvest."

"Don't forget us," Janet whispered.

She picked up a bag containing her possessions and followed Ailie out of the cottage.

Michael was leaning against a tree, his arms folded across his chest. He looked like he had something to say. "Leave us, young one."

"Priestess?"

Keira embraced her. "Goodbye, lass. I left my healer's bag for ye. Take care of Janet and the baby."

Aileana gave a long look and entered the cottage.

Keira's knees knocked as she stared at the man who had almost been her husband. They'd spent time as priest and priestess, worshipping the Goddess among the stones. Would he support or berate her?

"Let's walk to the stones," he said. They walked in silence through the forest, stepping over dead branches and decayed leaves. Trees were budding, promising an early spring, and birds flitted about making nests. He picked up a stone and tossed it off the path. His voice was tight. "I'll clean this up for Beltane, so the young ones don't fall."

She swallowed hard. "I suppose you'll have Morgaine help ye."

"Aye."

They reached the stones and walked into the center of the circle. Keira's heart fluttered erratically, making her lightheaded. She looked at Michael. There was a tension between them that made her forget their differences. She took his hands. "I'm leaving, Brother."

His eyes filled with tears. "I know. Great Goddess, lass! I wish I knew that you'd be safe. How can he protect ye?"

She swallowed hard. "I don't know. I've prayed for reassurance, but none comes. The Goddess whispers that it's meant to be."

"He'd better take care of ye! I want to talk to him when he comes."

"You're frightening me."

"Someone has to worry, lass. You're safe here. Out there, you're likely to share your mother's fate."

"Dughall will protect me."

Michael sighed. "I won't scare him off. I'm your spiritual leader. Let me marry ye according to our customs."

Keira nodded. What he said made sense. "All right."

He kissed her forehead. "Bless ye, lass. Now, let's kneel and ask the Goddess to protect ye."

***

It was late afternoon when Dughall and his men left the road and entered the Forest of Deer. They followed a horse path for miles through dense woods and stopped at a stream. "The horses are thirsty," Murdock said, as he picked a burr from his shirt. "Let them drink. It's getting thick in here. Some of these narrow paths must have been made by deer."

Dughall nodded. "Aye. One leaped across the path as quick as a jackrabbit. Tiny thing, with a white patch on its tail." They dismounted and led the horses to the water.

Jamison scratched his head. "My Lord. This stream runs off the Ugie. We should be close to the village if her description was good. What else did she tell ye?"

Dughall was nervous. These men would follow him to the ends of the earth. How could he find her in miles of thick forest? Suddenly, he remembered. "She said that the village was near a circle of standing stones."

"Hmmm... Stones from the ancient people. Some of those are taller than a man." Murdock raised his eyebrows. "They should be easy to find."

Dughall's head ached. There was something important about those stones. "Tend to the horses. I need time alone to think."

"Stay in sight, lad."

The young Lord gazed at the surrounding forest. The trees were larger than any he'd ever seen. He guessed that two men holding hands couldn't wrap their arms around a trunk. He sank to the ground and sat with his back against an old pine, allowing the energy of the tree to renew him. "This place has the reverence of the sea. How can ye leave, lass?" He closed his eyes and prayed. "Dear God. Sweet Jesus. Great Goddess. I think it's all the same thing. I sit here among the gifts of nature, looking for the lass I love. Give me a sign."

Dughall shivered with knowingness. He opened his eyes and

noticed a narrow deer path to his right. On the trail, a large brown hare regarded him curiously. It stood on its haunches and twitched black tipped ears. In a blink of the eye, the hare whirled on hind feet and hopped away at a frantic pace. He stood and followed it down the path, oblivious to his servants.

"My Lord!" Murdock yelled. "You mustn't run off by yourself. Wait up."

The young Lord walked faster, unwilling to let the animal out of his sight. The hare stopped abruptly and ran off the path. Dughall's heart pounded as he arrived at its last location. He looked on the ground. An arrow made of sticks and twine pointed down a footpath. In the distance he saw a clearing with a circle of stones. His heart soared.

Murdock caught up and grasped his knees, trying to catch his breath. "My Lord. Why'd ye run off?"

Dughall pointed to the clearing. "Look friend, the standing stones. God answered my prayer. Let's get the horses. I think we're in the middle of it."

Peterhead

Blackheart entered a tavern and spotted his son at a table in the back. His blood boiled. The Duke and his party hadn't arrived yet. Could nothing go right? He walked to the table and knocked off a row of empty glasses.

Gilbert flinched as the glasses shattered on the floor.

"God damn it, lad! I've been looking all over for ye."

Gilbert stared through glassy eyes. "Why don't ye just run me through right now and get it over with?"

Blackheart sat down and chuckled. "I've never seen ye like this, lad! You're blootered."

Gilbert's speech was slurred. "I wish I was dead."

"Maybe this is what ye needed, Son. Loosens up your inhibitions. The world always looks better through a glass of whisky."

"Oh God…"

Blackheart snapped his fingers. "Lass! Bring two more whiskies."

The serving lass came with two glasses, setting them on the table. She frowned when she saw the broken glass. "Now, who's going to pay for that?"

Blackheart growled, "Do ye know who I am, lass?"

"Nay."

He remembered to keep his cover. "Never mind. I'll pay for it!"

She pointed at Gilbert. "He looks bad. You should take him home."

"My son's learning to be a man. He has a long way to go. Now get out of here!" The lass snorted and went back to the bar. Blackheart pushed a glass across the table. "Have another drink, lad. God in heaven! Is that what passes for a woman around here?"

Gilbert picked up the glass and took a sip. "Kate looking better to ye, Father?"

Blackheart reddened. "My God! I thought I'd never see it. You've grown balls between your legs."

"Father!"

"Why you're the mirror image of me."

The young Lord belted his whisky and turned green. He doubled over and vomited on the floor.

The Earl reached in his pocket and slapped a gold piece on the table. "Ach! The first time's always the worst. Come on, lad. I'll put ye to bed." He supported Gilbert under one arm and helped him out of the tavern.

Connor met him outside. "My Lord. What's wrong with him?"

The Earl shook his head. "Only God knows. We had a disagreement and he drank himself under the table." Gilbert moaned. "God damn it! He's likely to vomit again. Let's get him to bed."

Connor slipped the young Lord's arm over his shoulder. "I've been looking for ye. The Duke arrived with his party. The young Lord's not with him."

They started towards the fish-house tenement. "Hmmphh... What about Murdock and Jamison?"

"They're missing as well. The stable lad said that they're expected."

"Who's with the Duke?"

"Looks like three of his bodyguards and the lad's family."

"Hmmphh... The fisherman too?"

"Aye. Would ye like me to abduct one of them?"

"Nay. Let's wait until my son shows up. I'm not through with him."

LOUDEN FOREST

Keira and Michael kneeled in the center of the circle and held hands. Her heart was breaking for the loss of her friends. She loved this man, as father and brother. "Dear Michael. Can you forgive me for leaving?"

His voice was tight with emotion. "There's nothing to forgive, lass. Let us pray." He sniffled. "Great Goddess. Protect our sister, priestess, and spiritual heart! Sent on a dangerous journey to do your work. Enfold her in your wings of love and comfort her in times of sorrow." His voice cracked. "Allow her to return and if not, reunite us in the Summerland. Blessed be."

Keira trembled. "Oh, Michael. I'll be back."

"Let's hope so, lass." Words failed them and the sounds of the forest filled their ears. They heard squirrels chattering, birds chirping in the pines, and horses snorting. Michael released her hands. "Someone is here on horseback. Stay behind me and act like my wife."

They stood and faced the entrance to the clearing. Keira's heart raced. She heard voices, two men maybe three, and excited laughter. She pressed her face into Michael's back and felt him stiffen.

"They're coming, lass. Don't fret. I'll protect ye with my life."

Three men walked into the clearing, gazing in wonder at the eleven stones of granite. Two were commoners, dressed in breeks and linen shirts, and carried swords at their side. The third was a young man, well dressed in clothes fit for royalty. They came closer.

Michael's eyes widened with anxiety. "Ho! Who comes to the place of the ancients?"

Dughall smiled. "Michael. Don't ye know me?"

"Nay! Stay back."

Keira's heart fluttered at the sound of his voice. Could it be? She stepped out from behind Michael and saw that it was true. "Great Goddess!"

"Lass, no!"

"It's all right. My husband has come for me at last."

The young Lord's face lit up with recognition. He opened his arms. "Come to me, lass!"

They ran to each other and embraced. Keira held her breath as he lifted her into his arms and kissed her. She put her arms around his neck.

Dughall's eyes widened. "You're so thin, lass. I feel like I'm holding a child."

"There hasn't been enough food. Even the children are starving."

"I'm a Lord," he whispered. "I can change that."

Michael reddened. "Who are these men who come into the circle with weapons?"

Jamison cleared his throat. "The young Lord's bodyguards, sworn to protect him with our lives."

"The young Lord?"

"Aye. He's heir to the Duke of Seaford."

Michael frowned. "This marriage will never work! The nobility support the church that has tortured and killed so many of us."

Dughall put her down and held her hand.

Michael's face was full of concern. "Speak to me, lad! Do ye know that she worships the Goddess?"

Keira paled. She didn't understand what it meant to be a Lord, but she knew this young man. Would their love withstand these differences?

Dughall nodded. "I know that she worships the Goddess. I saved her at her mother's hanging and I mean to protect her now."

"But your church will…"

"I will support no church that tortures and kills in God's name."

"Do ye believe in a higher power, lad?"

"Aye. Look around you. The spark of God is in everyone and everything. Whether we worship Jesus, the Goddess, or the Gods of the Celts. It's the same thing."

Michael was stunned. "You speak the words of the ancients."

Keira's heart soared. "Don't you see? It's the end of the burning times."

Murdock raised his eyebrows. "My Lord. We must leave if we're to reach Peterhead tonight."

Michael sighed. "Before you go, I must marry ye according to our customs."

"My Lord!"

"It's all right, Jamison. I mean to make her my wife."

Murdock shivered. "This place frightens me."

"Then wait by the horses. I'll be all right."

***

Jamison and Murdock tended the horses and waited at the entrance to the circle. Murdock stared. "We can see him from here and rescue him if he gets into trouble."

Jamison chuckled. "He's already in trouble, friend. How long has he been like this?"

"Like what?"

"You know. This talk about religions and the church. His idea that it's all the same God."

Murdock sighed. "Ever since I met him. He got worse when he studied ancient religions in the Earl's library."

"She's a witch, ye know."

"I can see that. A bonny one."

Jamison rubbed his hands together. "I could never understand religion. Serving this man will be a real challenge. He's likely to get into trouble."

"Aye."

"Will he listen to reason?"

"He might."

"I'll ask him to keep it from the Duke. We should let the old man die in peace."

***

Dughall's heart pounded as she took his hands. Her skin was soft and fragrant. "Is it a dream?" he whispered. "Can it be my wedding day?"

She spoke softly. "It's not a dream. Do ye love me?"

"Aye. More than life." She was thin and fragile, in need of his protection. By God's grace, they'd survived the separation.

Michael reached into his pocket and took out a black ribbon. "Come to the center of the circle and face each other." They walked to the center and stood slightly apart. Michael tied their hands together; his right to her left, and began the ritual. "We stand in sacred space, witnessed by the powers of the four directions and Spirit, the center. In the beginning, forests and fields were the first temples. Therefore 'tis right that we come together in nature's temple to join this man and woman in wedlock. Let this be their first day of growing, learning, and loving." Michael continued. "Let us pray. Great Goddess, whose gentle breath formed all things, bless this sacred union. We ask that this man and woman walk in peace and beauty, forever in the light of your love."

Keira smiled. "So mote it be."

Dughall blushed. "So mote it be."

"Spirits of nature, powers of creation, cherished ancestors. Bear witness to these vows. Do you wish to be joined as one with the blessings of the Goddess?"

"Aye."

"How do ye come to each other?"

Dughall smiled as Keira whispered in his ear. They answered in unison. "In perfect love and perfect trust."

Michael had tears in his eyes. "From this day forward let these words guide you, in sickness and health, scarcity and abundance, sorrow and joy. I proclaim you man and wife. So mote it be."

Dughall's heart fluttered as he kissed her. "You were right, lass. We believed it and it happened. It's truly magic."

Michael cleared his throat. "Promise me you'll take care of her."

"I promise, friend. Now, we must go."

Keira's voice was soft. "Dughall, the children."

His heart told him that it was the right thing to do. "I'll give ye gold coins to buy provisions for your people."

Michael shook his head. "Gold is of no use to us. We don't trade with outsiders. It's too dangerous."

"Then allow me to bring a wagon of provisions. My men will acquire it in Peterhead and return in three days."

Michael hesitated. "No one knows we're here. I can't let them near the village or the stones."

"We'll leave it next to the stream at the base of largest pine tree."

"Thank ye, lad." He took Keira's hands and kissed her cheek. "Farewell, sweet lass. We will miss ye."

Murdock approached. "My Lord. We must go if we wish to leave these woods by nightfall."

Dughall nodded. They picked up her bag, left Michael in the circle, and mounted their horses.

CAT AND MOUSE

PETERHEAD
MARCH 31 1637
NEXT MORNING

Dawn broke over the seaport of Peterhead. Gulls perching on rooftops took to the air, their raucous cries mingling with the crash of waves. The Crack was waking to a new day, preparing to serve the important guests who'd arrived the day before. Klaas stoked hearth fires and tended to horses. His plump wife Maartje boiled water for tea and cooked the morning meal.

Dughall lay in bed, watching his woman sleep. He saw a heartbeat in the small of her neck and got lost in the rhythm of her breath. "Sleep, lass." He whispered. "We have the rest of our lives together." He thought of last night's journey, cold and exhausting. They'd left the forest by nightfall, determined to make Peterhead. Black Lightning had carried them both, she on the saddle in front of him. He remembered how frail she felt as he wrapped his arms around her to hold the reins. When they'd arrived at midnight, she swooned as he helped her from the horse. He carried her upstairs to his room, removed her shoes and coat, and put her to bed. The room was as cold as a barn. He'd started a fire in the hearth, stripped off his boots and cloak, and crawled into bed to keep her warm.

Keira opened her eyes and smiled. "It wasn't a dream. You kept me warm last night."

He stroked her hair gently. "Aye."

She touched her blouse, realizing that they were both still clothed. "Husband... It was our wedding night. We should have ..."

"Shhh... I can wait. We have the rest of our lives."

There was a knock. Dughall threw back the covers and walked to the door. He ran his fingers through his hair and opened it. Alex stood in the narrow hallway with Jessie. He raised his eyebrows when he saw the lass in bed.

"It's all right, Father. We were married according to her customs."

Alex nodded. "Thank God. The Duke expects us for breakfast. After that, I plan to sail the 'Bonnie Fay' to Whinnyfold. Would ye like to come?"

Dughall's heart smiled. "Aye. I've missed that place."

Alex sighed. "As I have, Son. I talked to Jamison. Your men will meet us there with horses so we can return by nightfall."

"Will Ian come with us?"

"Nay. He and the Duke will be talking to Andrew about his daughter."

Jessie took his arm. "Come on, husband. Let them freshen up so they can join us. I want to meet this young lass." They turned and walked the hallway towards the stairs.

Dughall smelled breakfast cooking as he closed the door. His stomach growled. They hadn't eaten since leaving the Forest of Deer. "Breakfast, lass! I smell ham and fresh bread." He pulled back the covers and sat on the edge of the bed.

She sat up and ran her hands around his neck. "You came for me."

He kissed her gently. "Aye. I keep my promises. Let's have breakfast; then I'll show ye where I was born."

"Husband... From what you've said, I recognize your father and mother. But who is the Duke?"

"The Duke is my grandfather. I'm heir to his title and estate."

"I thought you were a fisherman."

Dughall sighed. "So did I, lass. A lot of things have happened, some good and some bad. I'll tell ye everything tonight."

***

Gilbert woke with a splitting headache. He sat up slowly and groaned. "God in heaven. My mouth tastes like a herd of cattle walked through it."

Hawthorne sat on a chair, sharpening his dirk on a flat stone. "Had too much to drink last night?"

Gilbert stared. "Aye. What are you doing here?"

"Protecting your life and property, m'Lord." He put down the knife and tossed back his stringy hair. "A one-eyed man was searching your pockets."

"Then I guess I should thank you."

Hawthorne snorted. "No need, m'Lord. It's my sworn duty. Would ye like some water? Or some hair of the dog that bit ye?"

Gilbert gagged. "Water, please. I'll never drink whisky again."

Hawthorne looked amused as he handed him a flask. "Ha! That's what they all say after a night of heavy drinking."

The young Lord wondered where that flask had been. It looked like it hadn't been cleaned in a season. He took a swig anyway. "Where is my father?"

"He went off with Connor. Seems your brother got into town last night with his bodyguards. Don't worry, m'Lord. I've been sharpening my weapons all morning. I'll kill that bastard Murdock and get your brother back."

Gilbert's headache flared. That was the last thing he wanted. "Help me up."

Hawthorne stood. "The Earl wants ye to sleep it off."

The young Lord got out of bed and grasped his head. "I can't stay here. I have work to do. Ach! I can't bear it!"

The servant helped him back to bed. "Don't worry, m'Lord. Your father will take care of everything."

Gilbert's heart sank. There was no doubt of that. He turned his head and vomited on the bed.

✶✶✶

Blackheart sat in a tavern, eating a hearty breakfast with Connor. He put down his fork and stared. "Tell me again."

"My Lord. The stable lad said that they got in late last night. Your son, Jamison and Murdock, and a young lass."

"That's what I thought ye said. The Duke's not crazy enough to let him marry a commoner! Who the hell is she?"

"Don't know, m'Lord."

"God damn it! Spread some coin around. Maybe the innkeeper's wife will be willing to talk."

"As you wish. I've seen the red-haired lad and his father. They walked to the pier this morning and checked out one of the scaffies."

"Did they prepare her to sail?"

"Don't know, m'Lord. I stayed my distance so the lad wouldn't recognize me."

"Hmmphh..."

"Do ye want me to abduct one of them?"

Blackheart grunted. "Not yet. I don't want to alarm them. They have more men than we do. I'll trap my son and his brother at the same time."

"What about Murdock?"

"I want him dead."

✶✶✶

The Duke sat at the table, having breakfast with the Hays. He gazed at his grandson and the young lass and thanked God that he'd found her. *I see true love in their eyes*, he thought. *She's bonny, but the lass is too thin. These remote villages lack resources to make it through winter. We'll put some meat on her bones in no time.* He passed a plate of brown bread. "Eat some more, child. You're far too thin."

Keira blushed. "Forgive me, kind Sir. I'm not used to this much food."

Dughall squeezed her hand. "Grandfather. Her village is starving. Even the children have gone without. I promised to drop off a wagon load of provisions on our way back."

The Duke smiled. Charity was an admirable pursuit for one so young. "Of course, lad. It's the Christian thing to do. Let's put some men to work on it right away."

Alex nodded. "How many live in your village, lass?"

Keira counted silently. "Thirty-seven, nay, thirty-eight with the newborn. There were more, but we lost the old ones last year."

Jessie smiled sympathetically. "It's hard to lose the ones we love, especially the old ones. They have so much knowledge and wisdom."

"Aye. My grandmother was one of them."

Jessie touched her hand. "We lost our dear Aunt Maggie as well. I hope we can be friends and support each other in our loss."

Keira nodded. "I'd like that. Dughall said that ye were bonny, but your soul is beautiful as well."

Ian snorted. "That's Mother all right. So, Father. You're taking the boat to Whinnyfold."

The Duke felt uneasy about that. "My grandson will be aboard. Is it safe to sail today?"

Alex nodded. "Aye. The sea is calm and the sky is clear. You don't have to worry. We'll hug the coast."

Dughall spoke up. "We know how to sail, Sir. I helped Father for years on that boat."

"Are two men enough to handle that scaffie?"

Jessie smiled. "I can help as well."

The Duke chuckled. This woman reminded him of his wife, Jeanne. "You're a woman of many talents, lass."

Alex reddened. "My Lord. With your permission, Jamison and Murdock will meet us in Whinnyfold with the horses. That way, we can return tonight."

"A good idea." He rubbed his hands together. "Let's get started. I'll put Suttie and Klaas on the provisions. Then we'll see Andrew McFarlein about Ian's wedding."

Ian swallowed hard. "Oh God."

***

Alex and Dughall walked towards the boat, their boots clacking on the wooden pier. The women followed at a distance. Alex was torn by conflicting emotions. He was glad to be in Peterhead, about to set sail on the North Sea. His family was safe and his son was married to a lass he loved. But it was all bittersweet. This was the last time he'd sail the 'Bonnie Fay'. When they reached Whinnyfold, he would turn it over to Robert and wish him well. They reached the boat.

Dughall placed a hand on his shoulder. "Father. You're upset about the 'Bonnie Fay'. You gave up the life you loved to be with me. It doesn't seem fair."

Alex swallowed against a lump in his throat. This lad could read his soul. "You're my son! I would lay down my life for ye. The boat is dear to me, but it's just a thing." He embraced his son.

Dughall's voice was heavy with emotion. "Let's sail this boat with joy in our hearts and thank God that we're together again." They boarded the boat and raised the sails. Jessie and Keira were almost there.

"Look at them talking," Alex said. "They'll get along well."

Dughall smiled. "I always wanted to marry a woman like Mother. I think I have." They helped the ladies onto the boat and prepared to cast off.

✳✳✳

Ian left The Crack and walked along Keith Inch. His mind was spinning with possibilities as he turned onto King's Common Gate. The Duke was busy arranging for provisions for the lass' village. After that, they would meet with Andrew to work out the details of his marriage. "Andrew wants to talk about a matter of importance. What could it be? I have a bad feeling about this. Oh God, lass. I hope you're not with child." In the distance, he saw Mary in a lavender dress, running towards him. Her yellow hair was tied with ribbons, and flowed in the breeze.

Her face lit up with recognition. "Oh dear God. Ian!"

"Lass!"

They met in front of the fish-house tenement, and stopped to catch their breath. Mary grasped his hands. "Oh, Ian. I thought you were gone for good. I couldn't bear it."

Ian stared. Her breasts strained against the bodice of her dress. They were bigger than ever. He took her in his arms and kissed her. "Don't fret, lass. I mean to make ye my wife."

They separated and sat on a stone bench, holding hands. "Father told me that you're staying at Drake Castle."

"Aye, lass. It's a long story. My brother is heir to the Duke. I'm one of his protectors."

She sniffled. "You want me to come with you? To live at the castle?"

He smiled. "Aye. It's a wonderful place. You'll never have to empty a chamber pot or cook a meal. Servants take care of everything. Our children will be educated."

She held him close and shuddered. "That's a good thing."

"What's wrong, lass? You're shaking like a leaf. Don't ye want to come?"

"Aye. I love ye so much I can't think of anything else. But ye must convince Father. He's angry."

Ian's heart pounded. "Why, lass?" In his heart, he knew what she'd say.

She took his hand and placed it on her belly. "I'm with child."

***

Blackheart pounded his fist on the table, upsetting a water glass. "Where the hell is my son? If he got in last night, he must be in town."

Connor blanched. "I don't know m'Lord. The innkeeper's wife refused to talk to me."

"Does she know who ye are?"

"Nay. I was discreet."

"Good. Is his family in town?"

"I lost track of his mother and father, but the red-haired lad is with the Duke, talking to one of the local landowners."

"Who might that be?"

"Andrew McFarlein."

"Never heard of him. Probably a big fish in this stinking little pond. Where is Gilbert?"

"My Lord. Last I heard; he was sleeping it off. Hawthorne was watching over him. A man from the Indies was trying to rob him."

"God damn it! It's almost noontime. Get him out of bed! We have to be ready when my son shows his face."

***

Dughall's jaw tightened as they approached the Bay of Whinnyfold. The water was calm, but the harbor was narrow. He felt the power of the wind and sea as he manned the rudder. The young Lord glanced at his wife. She was sitting on a crate, her delicate hand gripping the side of the boat. This was her first time at sea, yet she trusted him totally.

Keira smiled. "Oh, husband. It's wonderful."

He was distracted by the sound of her voice. Rocks appeared portside, as jagged points rising out of the water.

"Watch out for the Skares!" Alex shouted. "Pay attention, lad."

Dughall's heart raced as he snapped back to reality. "Sorry, Father. Trim the mainsail! Slow her down."

Alex manned the rigging and trimmed the sail. They sailed on a starboard tack close to the wind, avoiding rocks, and turned into a port tack. Nearing the shore, Alex dropped the sail. The boat scraped the rocky beach and thudded to a stop. "Thank God for a safe journey. Pull her higher and tie her off." They jumped out of the 'Bonnie Fay', secured the sail, and pulled the boat onto the sand.

Dughall took Keira's hand and helped her out of the boat. "You're safe, lass."

She smiled. "Forgive me, husband. I distracted ye from your duties."

Dughall reddened. "Aye. That's why we don't take women to sea."

Alex helped Jessie out of the boat and kissed her tenderly. She dropped her pack and wrapped her arms around his neck.

Keira smiled. "Look, husband."

Dughall pulled her close and kissed her forehead. "I want to be like them," he whispered. "In health and sickness. Through joy and sorrow. In love, forever."

✳✳✳

The Crack was almost empty, being midday and the Duke's party the only guests. Three men occupied a table. The Duke, Ian Hay, and Andrew McFarlein.

Ian's heart pounded in his ears. Andrew seemed cordial when he talked to the Duke, but his eyes narrowed when he stared at the lad. *Oh God. He wants to kill me for what I did to his daughter. I guess I deserve it.*

The Duke coughed. "Pardon me. The sea air gets the best of me sometimes. Now, McFarlein. We've come here to settle the details of Ian's marriage to your daughter."

Andrew sipped a glass of whisky. "My Lord. What exactly are ye proposing?"

The Duke cleared his throat. "My grandson is Ian's brother."

"How did that happen?"

The Duke reddened. "Let me finish. It's a personal matter, far too complicated to explain here. Nevertheless, the young Lord is heir to my title and estate."

Andrew raised his eyebrows. "Just what does my daughter have to do with this?"

"I've asked Ian to stay at the castle and serve as one of his brother's protectors. Since he's engaged to your daughter, we'd like to bring her home with us."

Andrew reddened and took another sip. "My Lord. That being said, we have a matter of importance to discuss."

"Go on."

Ian felt like his insides were being torn out. Mary had begged him to make peace with her father. Yet he felt like an outsider in this conversation. "Oh God."

Andrew gripped the table. "Damn it, lad! Where was this belief in God when ye got my daughter with child? Then ye disappear for a month, leaving her in tears!"

Ian blanched. It was time to grovel. "Forgive me, Sir. I didn't mean to hurt her. With your permission, I'll make her my wife. Tomorrow, after my parents return from Whinnyfold."

Andrew grunted. "Hmmphh... Then tomorrow it is." He slapped the table. "You look like hell, lad. Have a glass of whisky with me."

Ian was too nervous to argue. He signaled to the serving lass.

Andrew stared. "My Lord. Tell me what this means for my daughter and my family."

The Duke shook his head. "You drive a hard bargain, McFarlein. We'll see them married tomorrow. In two days, your daughter will accompany us to Drake Castle. She'll be well cared for and will rarely have to lift a finger unless she wants to. Your grandchildren will be educated."

"This will break her mother's heart. Will we have access to my daughter?"

The Duke pushed his spectacles up on his nose. "Aye. You and your family will be welcome to visit. Do we have a bargain?"

Andrew nodded. "Aye."

The whisky arrived. Ian took a sip and felt the fiery liquid warm him down to his belly. "Thank God." He belted the rest.

The Duke chuckled. "Easy, lad. It's settled now."

Andrew stood and stared. "I'm going to church to talk to the minister. Tomorrow you will marry my daughter. Don't run away again, lad."

Ian swallowed hard. "I'll be there, Sir."

***

Dughall stood alone on the point, watching the tide come in. Kittiwakes and gulls wheeled on updrafts, filling the air with raucous cries. A scaffie moored just beyond the harbor, bearing two men casting small lines. The young Lord closed his eyes and prayed. "God in heaven. My soul swells with the sights and sounds of the sea. Thank ye for my life, my family, and this sacred place. Amen." He felt another presence and opened his eyes.

Jamison appeared at his side. "You sent for me, my Lord."

Dughall nodded. "Aye. Did you bring it?"

Jamison raised his eyebrows. He took the Earl's leather strap out of his pocket and placed it in the lad's hands. "Is there anything else I can do?"

Dughall's heart pounded erratically. "Aye. Send my father to me."

Jamison left him alone to ponder the instrument of torture. The young Lord ran his fingers through the strands, remembering the last time his father had beaten him. Bound like an animal and burning with fever, the Earl kept striking him. With no end in sight, he begged God to take his soul and fell senseless. The strap was streaked with his own blood. He would bear those stripes forever. His heart ached. *I'm shaking like a leaf. He really did break me. How can a man do this to his son?*

Alex laid a firm hand on his shoulder. "You sent for me, lad?"

His voice was laced with emotion as he held out the strap. "Father. I don't want to pass this on to my sons. Help me!"

Alex had tears in his eyes. "You must do it yourself. Roll it into a ball and toss it into the sea. It's part of the healing."

"Stay with me, Father."

"Aye."

Dughall's hands trembled as he rolled the leather strands into a ball. He leaned back and tossed it as far as he could. They watched the strap bob on the surface of the water and sink into the sea.

Alex smiled. "It can't hurt ye anymore."

"Or my children," Dughall whispered. "It's gone forever."

Alex embraced him. "Come on, Son. The horses are ready. It's time to return to Peterhead."

Dughall sighed. "Thank God you're my father."

✳✳✳

Blackheart and Gilbert sat in the tavern, eating a light supper. It had been an uneventful day. Connor and Hawthorne failed to find Dughall, so all they could do was wait. Gilbert picked at his food. The fare was poor and it didn't help that his stomach was glassy.

"What's wrong, lad? You look like hell."

Gilbert shivered. "I'm sick, Father. I can barely hold up my head."

Blackheart chuckled. "You're hung over." He pointed at a glass. "Drink some more of that rot-gut whisky. A hair of the dog that bit ye will help."

Gilbert gagged. "I'll never drink again."

"Ha! I said that once."

Connor entered the tavern and came to their table. "My Lord."

"What did ye find out?"

"The young Lord's brother is getting married tomorrow at the church."

Blackheart slapped the table. "Excellent! They're here for a wedding. It's all starting to make sense. Find out what time it's being held. After the wedding, they're sure to disperse. We'll follow my son and take him home."

Connor frowned. "It might not be that easy. He'll be under guard."

"Most of those men will stay with the Duke. They don't suspect that we're here, so they're likely to let him roam with one or two guards. You and Hawthorne can take them down."

"What about his family?"

"Kill them if they get in the way." He belted his whisky. "You can't have two families."

Gilbert was revolted. "Father! Leave his family alone. This is nothing short of murder."

Blackheart dismissed him with a wave of his hand. "Have a whisky, lad. I liked ye better when ye were blootered."

Connor chuckled. "My Lord. What will we do if Murdock is with him?"

"I don't care if ye cut his balls off and stuff them down his throat."

Gilbert stared as the two men plotted. He wondered if he could warn the Duke, but decided it was too risky. His father would skin him alive for treason. He swallowed his fear. *I'll find a way to stop this, even if it means my life.*

***

The ride back to Peterhead had been uneventful. After the long trip from Drake, it seemed like a short stretch. They'd taken a late supper and retired to their rooms to rest up for the next day.

Alex stoked the fire and got into bed. His emotions had run away with him today. Sailing the North Sea had been a joy, laced with sorrow when he had to leave his boat with Robert. His heart warmed when he saw the love between Dughall and Keira, yet he was concerned about the lass. She was far too thin. When they'd returned to the inn, they learned that Ian was to be married. Good news that was tempered by the fact that Mary was with child. "Hmmphh.."

Jessie rolled over and faced him. "Are ye still angry?"

"Just a bit disappointed and embarrassed. I taught that lad not to take advantage of a lass."

Jessie smiled. "Perhaps that's not how it happened. Mary's a headstrong lass."

"He could have stopped her."

She took his member in her hand and stroked it. "Has that ever worked with us, husband?"

Alex groaned. "Oh God. Nay, lass."

"Make peace with Andrew in the morning. Tonight I want ye in my bed."

***

Dughall and Keira sat on the bed holding hands. He'd told her about his mysterious birth, his life as a fisherman, and being abducted and taken to Huntly.

Her voice was full of concern. "The Earl beat ye on the first day?"

Dughall sighed. "Aye. That time wasn't so bad. He was giving me a taste of what was to come." He continued on, telling her about the castle, his brother Gilbert, and how strange it was to have servants. He talked about his education and learning to ride a horse and wield a sword. Lastly, he told her about running away, his capture, punishment, and rescue. His heart pounded. He didn't know how to tell her the rest, but it had to be done.

She grasped his hands. "Are ye going to tell me about the child?"

Dughall reddened. "You know about her?"

"Not really. I dreamed of a wee lassie with long dark curls. She said I was the one her father would marry and asked me to be her mother. Is this your child?"

Dughall held his head in his hands. "Aye, lass. Oh God. I'm so ashamed of myself! The Earl said I couldn't marry ye, it was beneath my station. He was angry that I was a virgin, so he sent his mistress to teach me how to make love."

She raised her eyebrows. "This woman carries your child?"

"Aye."

"You plan to take it from her?"

"Aye. Gilbert says she doesn't want it. I must convince the Earl to send the child to me."

Keira frowned.

Dughall's head ached. She would be in her rights to leave him. He took her hands and squeezed them. "Don't leave me, lass! I love ye more than life. Give me a chance! From this day forward, I'll be faithful until my death."

"Dughall..."

"Oh God, lass. I'll do whatever ye want!"

Her voice was soft. "I'm your wife. Make love to me."

***

Ian lay in bed, thinking about the day. Andrew had torn him apart in front of the Duke, who had allowed him to take his medicine. "Oh God, he was so angry." He expected more of the same tomorrow, until he finally married his daughter. If that wasn't bad enough, his father was angry and disappointed. "Ah, well. I guess I deserve it."

Suddenly, his skin flushed with pleasure, causing his loins to swell. He sat up in bed and connected to his brother. His eyes widened with anticipation. "Dughall, lad! You know what to do. Take her!"

Ian gasped and buried his head under the pillow. "Oh God," he groaned. "This is pure madness! I need to be married."

***

Dughall watched as she stripped off her skirt and socks and dropped her petticoat. His heart pounded as she pulled her blouse over her head. He took off his socks and dropped his breeks. When he looked up, she was sitting on the bed naked, holding her arms across her chest. There were tears in her eyes. He sat beside her. "What's wrong, lass?"

She trembled. "I'm so thin. I barely have breasts. I wanted to please ye."

Dughall stroked her cheek. "It's all right. I love ye so much, it doesn't matter. "

"But you're so perfect."

His face fell. "Nay, lass. Someday you'll have breasts. I will never be perfect." It was time to show her. With a heavy heart, he stripped off his shirt and threw it on the floor. Then he turned around and allowed her to see his back. The room was silent. *I'm so ugly,* he thought. *I'll always have these stripes.* He felt her kneel behind him and her soft fingers tracing the marks on his back.

"Your father did this?" she whispered.

"Aye."

"Did it hurt?"

"Oh, aye."

"I can imagine."

"Nay, lass. There's imagination. Then there's bein' there and havin' it done to ye. Two verra different things. I have black dreams about it." Dughall held his breath as her lips touched his wounds, one by one. Tears of joy streamed down his face as he realized that her love was unconditional. When she reached his waist, he threw back his head and groaned. "God in heaven."

The young Lord turned and lifted her, kissing her deeply. He stroked her hair and laid her on the pillow. "Lay back, love." His heart fluttered as he pressed his body against hers. This was his wife, the woman he loved. He would use his skill to give her pleasure.

***

Ian took the pillow off his head and sat up. "Thank God! They're done at last. I can't bear any more." He threw back the covers, went to the chamber pot, and relieved himself. When he got back to bed it started again, stronger than ever. He held the pillow over his head and ground his manhood into the mattress. "Ach! This is torture."

He got up and pounded his fist on the wall.

***

Keira lay back, trying to catch her breath. In her dreams, she'd been the aggressor with the shy and handsome lad. Tonight he'd surprised her by yielding to her desires. "Great Goddess! Did she teach ye that?"

Dughall lay on his side, stroking her hair. He reddened with embarrassment. "She did."

"Then I owe her that."

Dughall kneeled above her and steadied his hands on the bed. He kissed her gently on the forehead and whispered, "Let's not talk about her."

Keira closed her eyes and nodded. She felt his soft lips at her neck, and fingers caressing her face in a slow and tender exploration. He seemed to be waiting for permission. She placed a hand on his chest and felt his heart beat. Keira loved this man more than life and there was nothing she could deny him. She arched her hips to meet him and met his gaze. "Again?"

His beautiful smile rewarded her as he entered and pumped slowly. For once he was without words.

Her heart pounded like a drum as he increased the rhythm. A bead of sweat dropped onto her forehead and she knew that she was close. "Now, lad." Keira shuddered as a climax rolled through her like a wave and felt him explode inside of her.

Dughall pulled back and they lay together in contentment. He traced the contours of her face. "Happy, wife?'

She could barely speak. "Aye."

His cheeks flushed. "Will ye accept my daughter?"

"Wee Maggie?"

He raised his eyebrows. "That's a good name for her."

Keira sighed. "She's your flesh and blood. I'll be her mother." There was a loud knock on the wall, followed by a groan. "What was that, husband?"

Dughall chuckled. "My brother Ian. There are some things, wife, that are stranger than truth."

"Mmmm… Will we do this again soon?"

"Aye, lass. This and more. Tomorrow I'll show ye what they do in France."

TURNING POINT

PETERHEAD
APRIL 1 1637
EARLY NEXT MORNING

Lord James Drake woke at dawn, after a night of intense suffering. He'd managed to hold together during supper, suppressing his cough with a glass of wine. The talk had been exhausting, from wedding plans to provisions for the forest village. On top of that, Alex was angry with the lad for getting the lass with child. "Ah! The challenges of family life."

The Duke tried to rise, but was seized by a coughing spell that ended in wheezing. He steadied his hands on the mattress and caught his breath. "God in heaven! It must be the sea air. I'm getting worse." He coughed some more, losing control of his bladder. "Ach!" His spectacles were on the nightstand. Without them, the world was hazy at best. He found them and put them on.

The old Lord stared. His pillow was stained with mucous and blood, some red and some black. He recalled that his father died this way. "It won't be long, Jeanne. Give me strength to survive a few more days and see our grandson safe." He sat on the bed and prayed. "Dear God. I'm as weak as a baby. Have mercy on me."

There was a knock on the door. Jamison entered and came to the bedside. "My Lord! What happened here?"

"No one tried to kill me! I'm dying."

Jamison's eyes widened. "I'll get the lass. She'll know what to do."

The Duke sighed. "Let her be. It's her son's wedding day. She doesn't need an old man to care for."

"My Lord, please."

"Nay, lad. Help me get dressed and down to breakfast. With luck, a dram of whisky in my tea will keep the grim reaper away."

Jamison poured water into a bowl and bathed his master, then helped him into clean clothes. "Are ye ready for breakfast?"

The Duke kneeled by the bed, clutching rosary beads. "Not yet."

"Shall I leave ye alone, m'Lord?"

The old man smiled. "Nay, lad. Pray with me."

Jamison sank to his knees and folded his hands.

The Duke was solemn. "Our Father, who art in Heaven, hallowed be thy name. Thy kingdom come. Thy will be done. On earth as it is in heaven…" He grasped the servant's arm and gazed into his eyes. His voice cracked with emotion. "You've been like a son to me. Thank ye, lad."

Jamison had tears in his eyes. "Oh… Is there anything I can do, m'Lord?"

"Promise me one thing."

"Anything."

"Take me home tomorrow. I want to die in my own bed."

* * *

Ian stood outside the church with his parents, waiting for his bride to be. His heart pounded with anticipation and his stomach was in knots. He saw the McFarleins in the distance, a large party consisting of Mary, her parents, and her sisters' families. There were at least ten children. He remembered that he was going to be a father. "Oh God." Sweat trickled down his back.

Alex kneeled on the ground, straightening the lad's kilt and sporran. He stood up and stared. "They're almost here, Son. What's wrong?"

"My heart is beating like a drum. Andrew was so angry yesterday. I thought he wanted to kill me."

Alex chuckled. "Don't worry, lad. I talked to him this morning. Marry his daughter and he's willing to make peace."

"Thank ye, Father." He was truly grateful.

Jessie's face lit up with recognition. "There's Mary! Oh, Ian. She's so bonny in that white dress."

Ian's heart raced as he saw Mary in a wedding dress, yellow hair flowing. She was carrying a bouquet of daffodils. "Oh God. I love her with all my heart."

Alex grunted. "Tell her that, lad."

"I will. Where's Dughall?"

"Your brother is waiting in the church with his wife. The Duke and his men are with him."

The McFarleins arrived and crowded around the Hay family. Andrew held his daughter back. "Stay here, lass. I need to talk to the lad."

"Father!"

Andrew's face reddened as he grabbed Ian's collar. "Hmmphh...
Well, lad. At least ye didn't run away."

Ian flushed with embarrassment. "Nay, Sir. I kept my word. I mean
to marry your daughter."

"Father, please!" Mary was about to break into tears. "Let him go."

Andrew released him. He took his daughter's hand and put them
together. "I give ye my youngest daughter. See that ye treat her well,
Son."

Ian could hardly believe it. He was standing in front of the church
on his wedding day and Andrew had given him his daughter, even
calling him son. It was more than he'd hoped for. He faced his beloved
and took her hands.

Mary blushed. "Oh, Ian. I love ye so much, I can't think."

Mindful of the women and children, he kissed her forehead. "I love
ye, lass. With all my heart." Her hair smelled of rosemary and lavender.
Ian smiled and lifted her into his arms. "Come on, wife. The minister
is waiting."

The crowd parted and he carried her up the granite steps.

**

Dughall sat in the front pew with his wife and grandfather. He
could see the minister waiting at the altar, holding a prayer book. His
heart was glad for his brother, but he couldn't shake the feeling that
something bad was about to happen. Last night, he had black dreams
about the Earl and his strap and woke in a cold sweat, crying out for
mercy. The lass held him until he stopped shaking and fell asleep in
his arms.

Why am I dreaming of him? Oh God. He said he wasn't through with me.

The Duke took out a kerchief and coughed violently. The old man's
face turned a dusty blue as he struggled for breath.

Dughall grasped his arm. "Breathe, Grandfather. Oh God. Shall I
get Mother?"

The old Lord caught his breath. "Nay, lad. Don't worry about me.
Your brother's about to be married."

Dughall's heart ached. *Grandfather's dying. This must be what I'm
uneasy about.* The young Lord took a moment to look around the
church. He'd been here once for a cousin's wedding, but forgotten
how beautiful it was. The walls were made of stone and decorated
with tapestries depicting the life of Christ, and an elaborate wooden
crucifix hung over the altar. Tall pillar candles provided light for the
ceremony.

"It's beautiful," Keira whispered. "What does it all mean?"

Dughall smiled. "I'll tell ye later, lass. Here comes my brother."

Keira touched his arm. "Look, husband. Your brother' wife. She's
so bonny."

"Aye. That she is." The church doors had opened, admitting a large group of people. Ian carried Mary to the altar and set her down.

The minister cleared his throat. "Family, friends, and honored guests. Welcome. Gather 'round so we may witness this joining."

Ian and Mary stood in front of the minister, while the family gathered. The servants stayed at the back of the church, standing guard.

He opened his prayer book. "Heavenly Father. We are gathered here today in the eyes of God and family to join this man and woman in holy wedlock. Marriage is a serious commitment, not to be taken lightly. If any man can show just cause why they may not lawfully be joined, let him now speak, or else hereafter for ever hold his peace."

Dughall felt his brother's apprehension and held his breath. There were no objections, so the minister continued.

"Who gives this woman to be married to this man?"

Andrew nodded. "I do. I am her father." He took Mary's right hand and joined it with Ian's.

"Do you, Ian, take Mary, to be your lawfully wedded wife, to have and to hold from this day forward, for better or worse, for richer or poorer, in sickness and in health, to love and to cherish, 'til death do you part?"

Ian smiled. "I do."

"Do you, Mary, take Ian, to be your lawfully wedded husband, to have and to hold from this day forward, for better or worse, for richer or poorer, in sickness and in health, to love and to cherish, 'til death do you part?"

Mary blushed. "I do."

"Is there a ring?"

The Duke opened a velvet box and handed it to them. "A gift from me, lad and lass." The box contained a gold wedding band, intricately engraved with their names and the year.

Ian smiled. "Thank ye, m'Lord." He took the ring and placed it on Mary's left hand. "With this ring, I thee wed. In the name of the Father, the Son, and Holy Ghost. Amen."

The minister smiled. "Bless, O Lord, this ring, that he who gives it and she who wears it may abide in thy peace, and continue in thy favor, until their life's end, through Jesus our Lord. Amen. I now pronounce you husband and wife."

Mary threw her arms around Ian's neck and they kissed deeply.

Dughall breathed a sigh of relief. Nothing had gone wrong. He wrote off his anxiety to the bad dream and Grandfather's illness. He congratulated the happy couple and excused himself to talk to his mother. The old man needed care. He was sure he was close to death.

***

Blackheart and Gilbert waited in a tavern near the fish-house tenement. Connor and Hawthorne had informed them of the wedding party and gone back to watch the church doors from a distance.

The serving lass brought two glasses of whisky and set them on the table. She smiled at the young Lord through missing front teeth. "Feeling better, lad? You looked like hell the other day."

Blackheart scowled. "Leave us alone, stupid lass." He was too busy scheming to deal with this ugly woman. She left their table and headed for the kitchen. "My God! She's a young lass, but she looks like an old hag. Drink up, lad! We're about to get your brother back."

Gilbert stared. "Nay, Father. How can ye drink at a time like this?"

Blackheart ignored his question. The lad would never understand the value of a glass of fine whisky. Not that this was fine. The whisky in this town was enough to rot your gut. He checked his sword and the dirk in his belt. "Check your weapons, lad. They'll be back soon."

Gilbert paled, but he appeared to go through the motions.

The door opened and Connor entered. He scanned the tavern and came to their table. "The wedding is breaking up, my Lord. It's time to make our move."

"Where is Hawthorne?"

"I left him near the church. He'll tell us which way the young Lord went and how many men are with him."

Blackheart stood and grasped his shoulder. "Good. We'll abduct him and leave this place. One more night in that flea-bitten inn and I'll go mad."

✳✳✳

Dughall stood in the church with Jessie and Keira, discussing the Duke's deteriorating condition. He knew in his heart that the old man was dying, but hoped he could hang on a while. "He's near death, Mother. I'm sure of it."

Jessie frowned. "Poor man. This was a harsh trip for someone in his condition. Can we get him into bed? I'll prepare some tea to help him rest."

Keira nodded. "I'll go with ye, Mother. Coltsfoot and willow bark can ease his pain. Will he permit me to touch him?"

"I don't know, lass. What can ye do?"

"I can ask the Goddess to guide my hands and give him strength."

Jessie stared. "Hush, child. Don't say that in public, especially in a Christian church." She lowered her voice to a whisper. "Will ye teach me how to do that?"

Keira blushed. "Aye. You can watch."

Jamison and Gilroy approached, supporting the Duke under each arm. He was nearly unconscious. Pratt followed behind. Jamison's face was full of concern. "Can ye help us, lass? He collapsed. I want to put him to bed."

"Aye."

The wedding party had left the church and was headed for the McFarlein home to celebrate. Suttie and Murdock went along to stand guard. The young Lord was expected to join them. Dughall's heart ached for the old man. "Pratt. Find my brother and tell him that I will be along later. Grandfather is gravely ill."

"Aye, my Lord."

Jessie nodded. "Tell my husband that I'll stay with the old Lord as well."

"Aye, my Lady." Pratt turned and left the church.

Jamison and Gilroy firmed up their support and hobbled out of the church with the Duke between them. Dughall and the lasses followed close behind.

***

The Duke's room was cold. They'd made his bed, but the old sheets were in a pile on the floor. Jessie retrieved the healer's bag from her room and searched through it, removing several pouches of herbs.

Dughall stoked the fire in the hearth, coaxing the dying embers. He was determined to make the old man comfortable. "Get him to bed. I think we can help him."

The servants laid the old Lord on the bed and undressed him. They pulled a nightshirt over his head, wool socks on his feet, and tucked him under the covers. Jamison felt his forehead. "He feels hot."

"He's running a fever," Jessie said, as she picked up a soiled pillow-case. "Oh dear. That's a bad sign. He's been coughing up blood."

Jamison nodded. "Aye. He didn't want me to tell ye. He wants to go home tomorrow and die in his own bed."

Dughall's heart sank. "What can we do?"

"Coltsfoot and willow bark will ease his suffering, but our best hope is with your lass."

There was a loud noise from the tavern below. Jamison frowned. "Gilroy. I don't like this. There's too few of us guarding the Duke and the young Lord. Stand outside the door and keep your weapons handy. I hope Pratt has the sense to come here." Gilroy nodded and left the room.

The Duke stirred. "God in heaven. My whole body aches. Where am I?"

"In your bed, m'Lord," Jamison said. "You swooned after the wedding."

"Forgive me. Did I spoil the festivities?"

"Nay, m'Lord. They'd all gone on to the young lass' house."

He coughed. "Who's here with us?"

"Mrs. Hay and the young Lord's wife. They can help ye."

The Duke sighed. "Thank God."

Dughall came to the bedside and held the old man's hand. "I'm here as well, Grandfather."

"You should be with your brother, lad."

Dughall smiled. "It's all right, Sir. I'll stay a while and join him later." He turned to Jamison. "Tell the kitchen to boil water for tea and bring it as soon as possible."

Jamison fingered his sword and left the room.

Dughall stroked his forehead. *The man's feverish, yet his skin is clammy.* His nostrils flared. *He smells like death.*

"Grandfather. Do ye trust me?"

"Aye, lad."

"My wife knows things about healing that I don't understand. She can help ye, but you must allow us to touch ye and run our hands along your body."

The Duke groaned. "Oh God. Do what ye must. I'll do anything to stop the pain."

Keira came to the bedside and took his hand. "Rest easy, Sir. Close your eyes and drift away to a beautiful place. We're here to help ye."

The old man closed his eyes. "You have a gentle touch, lass. Just like my wife." Within minutes, he was sleeping peacefully.

Keira uncovered him. "Gather 'round the bed and watch what I do. Then help me."

Jessie and Dughall stood on the other side of the bed.

Her voice was soft. "I ask the blessed Goddess to come through me and provide healing for the higher good of this soul. Guide my hands and give him strength. Blessed be." Keira placed her hands on the crown of his head and prayed silently. She made circular movements around his face and head and lingered over this throat. "No problems here." She continued on, outlining the shoulders and resting her hands gently on his chest. "Here is the source of his weakness. Join me, husband, and imagine the healing energy of the Goddess coming through your hands."

Dughall was transfixed by her gentle touch and the love that flowed from her hands. He joined her, placing his hands over hers. He closed his eyes, uttered a silent prayer, and went within. Energy pulsed through them until his hands were numb. Suddenly, it was clear. "We helped him rest," he said, lifting his hands. "But we can't do more."

Jessie whispered. "Is he dying, then?"

Keira smiled. "Aye. His soul yearns to pass. A woman waits for him beyond the veil with a love so strong it transcends death." She removed her hands, rubbed them together, and covered him. She bowed her head. "I thank the Goddess for coming through me."

They were quiet for a moment. Jamison entered with a tray and put it down. "My Lord. The kitchen prepared a pot of hot water. There's tea and scones as well." He looked at the old Lord. "He looks so peaceful.

You got him to sleep."

"Aye." The lasses set about making a healing brew.

"My Lord. Your father and Murdock are downstairs, inquiring about ye."

Dughall smiled. "Grandfather will rest easy for a while. I should join my brother."

Jamison frowned. "It's too dangerous to be walking about on your own. Wait until Pratt shows up and I'll accompany ye."

"Murdock and Father will be with me. Is Murdock armed?"

"Aye, but my Lord…"

Dughall felt like he was floating on a cloud. Nothing bad could happen tonight. "Don't worry, friend. There's no danger here. I'll return later with Pratt and Suttie."

"As you wish."

Dughall stroked his grandfather's forehead. He hugged Jessie and Keira and said goodbye. "I love ye both with all my heart." He left the room and went downstairs to join his father and Murdock.

***

Blackheart and Gilbert waited in the shadows, watching the door to The Crack. When they'd reached Hawthorne, he wasn't sure which way the young Lord went. The wedding party went to the McFarlein house, while a smaller group returned to The Crack. Hawthorne admitted that he hadn't been close enough to identify Dughall.

Blackheart guessed that the young Lord would stay with his brother, so he sent Connor and Hawthorne to stake out the McFarlein house. He forced Gilbert to accompany him to the inn, expecting that the young man wasn't there. Now, they spotted two men standing in front of the inn. They had a friendly discussion, laughed out loud, and walked up the steps to the door. Blackheart's blood boiled. "God damn it! Was that Murdock?"

Gilbert's eyes widened. "I think so."

"Who the hell was with him?"

"I don't know, Father. It could be one of the Duke's servants."

"He didn't appear to be armed."

"Nay. What will we do?"

"Idiot! We'll wait here until they come out. Chances are my son will be with them. Murdock is no match for the two of us. We'll follow and take them down in a deserted place."

Gilbert paled. "Father. In the name of God, I beg you not to do this! This is wrong."

The Earl reddened. "Silence, lad! Do what I say or suffer the consequences." They waited in the shadows until three men emerged from the inn and walked downstairs. Blackheart's eyes widened. "There's Dughall! Carrying on with servants like they're old friends.

He thinks he has the upper hand over me. I'll take pleasure in tanning his hide when I get him home."

The three men started walking along Keith Inch towards King's Common Gate.

The Earl fingered his sword. "Excellent! Stay in the shadows as we follow. We'll take them before they reach the fish-house tenement."

***

Dughall's heart was light as he walked between Murdock and Alex. The women were getting along like mother and daughter and his grandfather was resting easy. He felt truly blessed.

Murdock smiled. "I've never seen your brother so happy, m'Lord. He looks at that lass like he worships the ground she walks on."

"I think he does. Is Andrew still angry at him?"

Alex chuckled. "Nay, lad. As soon as he married his daughter, all was forgotten. He's been calling him son ever since."

Dughall was relieved. "Thank God."

"Jamison said that the Duke is resting."

"Aye, Father. We eased his pain, but he's dying. He wants to go home and die in his own bed."

Alex nodded. "He's a good man, Son. If he's strong enough, we'll leave tomorrow. Perhaps we should look for a coach."

As they turned onto King's Common Gate, Dughall was struck by a bad feeling. Images of a dream flooded his mind, the Earl cornering him in the stables and choking him. He'd reached in his pocket, taken out a length of rope, and tied his wrists.

"My Lord, are ye all right?"

"I can't shake a bad feeling."

Murdock paled as he looked behind them. There was no one on the road, but something moved in the shadows of the trees. "My Lord, there's someone following us. Are ye armed?"

"Nay."

"Alex?"

"Nay."

"God help us."

Dughall searched his pockets for his ivory handled dirk. He usually carried it on his person, but not today because of the wedding. He swallowed hard against a lump in his throat. "Murdock? Is it the Earl?"

The faithful servant drew his sword. "I don't know, lad. But I'll defend ye with my life."

They moved quickly along the road, hoping to outrun the outlaws. Two men emerged from the shadows and blocked their way. Dughall found himself staring into the eyes of the Earl, glittering with anger as he drew his sword. To his left, Gilbert pulled a knife and blocked Alex.

He looked utterly miserable, but he obeyed the Earl.

"Father! What are ye doing here?"

"You're coming home with me, lad. I'm not through with ye."

It was just like the dream. "Never again! Murdock, give me your weapon!" He started to sweat.

The servant brandished his sword. "Nay, m'Lord! I'm pledged to protect ye with my life." He pushed the lad behind him and challenged the Earl. "Stand back or I'll fight ye!"

Blackheart chuckled. "Really, Murdock. You're no match for me. This will be a pleasure. Gilbert, keep that one under guard."

"He's not armed, Father."

"Good." The Earl gripped his sword and glared. "Well, well, if it isn't the traitor. So ye think ye can take me down?"

Murdock stood his ground, but his body betrayed him. He was as pale as a ghost. "I'll die defending him."

"That ye will. I'll split ye from neck to belly like a hog."

Dughall's heart was in his throat. He knew that Murdock was no match for his father. The man would be cut to ribbons. He glanced at Alex. Gilbert had a knife at his throat. Swords clanged.

✳✳✳

Connor grew tired of waiting in the shadows. "We've seen men come and go, but no young Lord. I don't think he's in there."

Hawthorne looked up from sharpening his knife. "Shall we try to find the Earl?"

Connor grunted. "Hmmphh... He said to stay here until we're sure. There will be hell to pay if we don't."

"The Earl could be in trouble. Lord Gilbert's been useless since he got blootered."

"Don't let him hear you say that."

Hawthorne ran a finger along the blade. "I won't. Why don't ye walk to The Crack and look for the Earl. I can watch for the young Lord."

Connor checked his sword. It was hard to know what to do. "All right. Stay here, lad. I'll be back." He walked down King's Common Gate, hoping that he wouldn't incur the wrath of his master. So far, he'd managed to keep all of his fingers.

✳✳✳

Dughall was desperate as he watched the fight. His servant was a poor match for his father, and he wished he had a sword. Murdock fought bravely, dodging the Earl's blows, but he couldn't land any of his own.

Blackheart played with him like a cat with a mouse. "Traitor!" They locked swords in a deadly embrace.

Murdock grunted. "I can't hold him, m'Lord. Run to the Duke!"

"Gilbert! If he runs, slash that man's throat."

Dughall paled. "Nay! I won't run."

Blackheart's eyes narrowed. He feigned fatigue, lowered his sword, and brought it up in a quick slash across Murdock's right shoulder.

The servant cried out as his blade dropped. He grasped his upper arm and bloodied his hand. "Ach! Run, lad!"

Blackheart kicked the sword over to Gilbert and knocked his opponent to the ground. He waited until the servant opened his eyes and stomped him hard in the stomach. "Say your prayers, Murdock." He opened the man's shirt and ran a finger along the edge of his knife. "Like slaughtering a hog... I can make this last a long time."

Dughall dropped to the ground and blocked the blade with his fingers. His heart was pounding like a great drum. "Nay! I won't let ye do it. He's my friend."

Murdock's eyes were awash with pain. "Run to your grandfather. Don't let me die in vain."

Blackheart locked his fingers in Dughall's long curls. "Get away from him, lad!" He lifted him and wrapped a hand around his throat. "Or I'll choke ye to death."

The young Lord struggled to pry the fingers off and saw stars before his eyes. His body shuddered as it started to shut down. Would he suffer a fit?

He heard Alex cry out, "Leave my son alone! Let me fight ye."

Blackheart grunted and released him. The young Lord dropped to his knees, holding his throat and gasping for breath. The Earl approached Alex. "So this is the fisherman."

"Aye."

He drew his knife. "I should have killed ye months ago when I sliced that old hag's throat."

"That woman was dear to me and an aunt to my son."

Blackheart exploded in anger. "He's not your son! You raised him, but I made a man of him." He grabbed Alex by the hair and held the sharp blade to his throat. "Join the old witch! Say your prayers, fisherman."

Dughall's anger ignited like a torch. Even death by the whip would be better than this. "Let him go! I'll fight ye. It's what ye want, isn't it?"

Blackheart smirked. "You don't have a sword, lad."

Gilbert reached down and grabbed Murdock's sword. His face was solemn as he threw it to Dughall. "You do now, Brother. Good luck."

"God damn it!" Blackheart cried.

"What's the matter, Father? Afraid to fight a mere lad?"

"You'll suffer for this, Son. I'll beat ye 'til ye can't breathe."

Dughall stood and picked up the weapon. He glanced at Murdock, who was losing blood at a steady rate. When he looked back the Earl was in his face, armed and ready to strike. He swallowed hard and faced his fear. "First blood, father?"

"Nay, lad. You'll have to kill me."

"What happens if I lose?"

"You come home with me."

"And Murdock?"

"He's a dead man."

The young Lord stared. "What about my father?"

"You can't have two fathers, lad. He dies as well. I'll try to make it quick."

Dughall's heart sank. It was wrong to kill a man, but there was so much as stake. Fate had prepared him for this moment from the day he was born. Like a warrior of old, he hardened his expression into a living war mask and raised his sword.

"Use your gift, m'Lord," Murdock whispered.

Dughall took a deep breath and remembered Jamison's words. "In a fight to the death no advantage is unfair. This is your secret weapon against a stronger opponent." He went within and connected to his father, feeling the anger in his heart. The man assumed he was facing a lesser opponent. That could be his downfall. Dughall stood with legs apart, one foot slightly in front of the other, and held the sword in both hands. Blackheart gripped his sword and prepared to attack. They sparred at first, testing each other. The young man used the Sight to anticipate his blows and parried successfully.

The Earl grew impatient. "You've improved, lad. But you're still no match for me!" His eyes glittered with malice. "Prepare for defeat."

Sweat dripped down the young Lord's back. *God in heaven! He's a fierce fighter.* Dughall raised his sword and lashed out in a violent thrust, slash, and overhead cut.

Blackheart warded off the blow, sending sparks into the air. "Ha! At last, a man worth killing. Do your damnedest, lad!"

Swords clanged and sparks flew.

Dughall shouted a war cry as he hacked and lunged, opening a gash in the Earl's right arm. For a moment it seemed like the man would stop, but when the shock wore off he fought harder. The young lad's nerves were on fire. He knew he had to kill his father, so how could he gain an advantage?

The young Lord went within to find the answer and was surprised by what he saw. He was on a dark moor, fighting a fierce battle. Thunder rolled and lightning lit up a battlefield, littered with bodies of his clansmen. His village burned in the distance, and women and children screamed. The sword of Red Conan was in his hand. At once, he understood the meaning of the symbols on its hilt. "Great Goddess

Morrigan!" he roared. "Protect me." A blue-faced warrior attacked him, uttering a blood curdling war cry. Anger blinded him as he ran him through with the sword and cried out, "Revenge is mine!"

Dughall came to his senses just in time.

The Earl charged with sword held high, preparing to bring the blade down on his head. "Take this, ye raging lunatic!"

Gut instinct guided him. Dughall raised his blade at the last moment and parried the blow, unsettling the older man. With hot blood coursing through his veins, he whirled the sword above his head, slashed the air from side to side, and struck downwards. The cries that he made didn't even sound human.

Blackheart's eyes widened as the blade struck the side of his neck. He tried to raise his sword, but the wound got the best of him. Blood spewed from his mouth as he fell backwards onto the ground. "Kill his father!"

Gilbert stared in disbelief. "Nay. It's over." He dropped the knife in the dirt and released Alex, who rushed past his son to attend to Murdock.

Blackheart lay on the cold ground, grasping his throat and moaning. He reached out to Gilbert, but the young man refused to come to his side.

Dughall stared at the bloody sword and kneeled to examine Blackheart's wound. It was deep and bleeding profusely. The Earl coughed up blood and his breathing was erratic. It wouldn't be long before death took him. The young Lord felt numb.

He took the dying man's hand so that he wouldn't have to die alone. "Father, I didn't want to kill ye. Oh God. Please forgive me."

"Rot in hell." Blackheart squeezed his hand as he struggled for breath. His eyes opened wide and he shuddered for the last time.

Dughall rocked on his knees, wailing in agony over what he'd done. His sword lay on the ground, beckoning him to take his own life. Surely, he deserved to die. He felt a familiar hand on his shoulder.

"Son..." Alex squeezed gently. "Murdock's losing blood. He needs ye."

Gilbert kneeled by his father's dead body, looking for signs of life. "He's gone, Brother. Attend to your servant."

Dughall crawled to Murdock and put pressure on the bleeding wound. He pulled out a kerchief and wrapped it around the shoulder. "It's all right, friend. Thank God you're still alive."

Murdock's voice was weak. "My Lord."

"Shhh... Don't try to speak. He can't hurt ye anymore. It's over."

"You were awesome, lad."

Connor arrived, kneeled at the Earl's body, and felt for a pulse. He stood and drew his sword. "My Lord. Who did this?"

"My brother."

"Murder is a capital offence! I'll see that he rots in the tollbooth. Traitors who kill their masters are drawn and quartered."

Gilbert's voice was cold and deliberate. "Put down your weapon. My brother defended himself in a fair fight. I'll not contest this."

"But my Lord! Your father is dead. This ungrateful peasant…"

"Connor!" Gilbert snarled. "Am I not the new Earl? You answer to me, now."

The servant paled and bowed his head. "My Lord, forgive me. I will do as ye wish."

"Then be off with ye. Find Hawthorne so we can move his body."

Connor turned and ran towards the fish-house tenement.

Gilbert's face was sheepish as he approached the young Lord. "My behavior was unacceptable, Brother. Can you find it in your heart to forgive me?"

"For what Gilbert? You saved me."

"Ah, the sword. I wanted him dead. It was a coward's way out."

"It took courage to do that. He threatened to beat ye."

"You're the one with courage, lad. No one's ever defeated him."

Dughall squeezed his shoulder. "Thank ye, Brother. What will ye do now?"

"I'll bury our father and take my place as Earl. It's best that you stay away from Huntly for a while. Some will hold it against you."

"Will I see ye again?"

Gilbert smiled. "In a few months, when I marry my mistress."

"And my daughter?"

"I'll send the child when it's born. Is there anything else ye want?"

Dughall thought for a moment. "The sword of Red Conan."

Gilbert raised his eyebrows. "Are ye sure, lad? I've heard it's cursed."

Dughall nodded. "Cursed to all but me. This is different, Brother. It belongs to me."

"Then you shall have it."

They shook hands and Dughall turned to his father. "Father, this is my brother Gilbert."

"I know it. Thank ye, Sir for what you've done. Perhaps we can meet one day under better circumstances."

Gilbert nodded.

"Come on son," Alex said. "Help me carry Murdock back to The Crack. Your mother can treat his wounds."

***

It was late evening in the tavern at the inn. They'd brought Murdock back to his room, where Jessie dressed his wound and put his arm in a sling. The Duke was resting peacefully, gathering strength for the trip home.

Dinner was a somber affair, with talk of gathering provisions and leaving the next morning. Fortunately, Jamison had found a coach to transport the Duke. They'd been careful describing the confrontation to the women, who had enough on their hands tending to the Duke and Murdock. After dinner, Ian and his bride joined them and retired to their room upstairs. As midnight approached, four men sat a table, drinking ale. Alex, Dughall, Ian, and Murdock.

Dughall was thankful as he looked around the table. By God's grace, these men were still alive. Murdock and Father had offered their lives to protect him. He saw that his servant's face was haggard, his eyes laced with pain. "Murdock. You should be resting in bed."

"Nay, m'Lord. Now that he's done with his husbandly duties, your brother should hear about how awesome you were."

"Murdock!"

"Well, he should. I could barely keep the man at bay. You turned into a wild man and took him down."

Ian raised his eyebrows. "What did ye do, Brother?"

Dughall's head ached. "I don't remember all of it. I had to kill him, so I went inside to gain an advantage. I found myself on a dark moor, in a fierce battle with an opponent. The Celtic blade was in my hand and I ran the man through."

"That makes sense."

"What did I do, Father?"

Alex frowned. "Hmmphh… Maybe we shouldn't tell ye."

Murdock sipped his ale. "You screamed like a banshee, called upon a goddess of war, and started slashing like a madman. The Earl was quite unsettled."

"Just like the vision. When I came to my senses, he was about to kill me, so I parried the blow and brought my sword down on his neck."

"You swung that blade over your head like a warrior of old."

"Awesome, Brother!"

Murdock smiled. "Ye know what I liked best?"

"What?"

"When ye cried out, 'Revenge is mine!'"

Dughall groaned. "Oh God."

Ian stood. "I have a new respect for ye, Brother. Soon you'll be famous, like that bible story. What was it? David and Goliath? Come on, Murdock. I'll put ye to bed. You look like hell." He helped Murdock up and led him towards the rooms.

Dughall sighed. "How can God forgive me? I've taken a life. Worse yet, I've killed my own father."

"God won't condemn ye, Son. You were protecting your life and your family."

"Even so, it pricks at my soul. I wish you could understand how I feel."

Alex sighed. "I do, lad. In a sense, I was responsible for my own father's death."

"You were?"

"Aye. I hated him so much. I let him drown."

"What could ye mean?"

Alex reddened. "We were fishing off the coast near St Fergus, when we were hit with a sudden storm. The boat rolled and three men went overboard. Father was one of them. The night before, he'd beaten me to within an inch of my life."

"What happened?"

"He was too drunk to swim back to the boat. Father called out to me to save him, but I jumped in the water and pulled out my friend Robert instead."

"Uncle Robert?"

"Aye. By the time I looked for Father, he'd disappeared under the water." His voice cracked with emotion. "I never told anyone. I hope ye don't think less of me."

Dughall swallowed hard. "We all do things that haunt us. It doesn't mean that you're a bad man."

Alex sipped his ale. "I know it, Son. Do you?"

Dughall nodded.

TRIAL BY FIRE

PETERHEAD
APRIL 2 1637
EARLY NEXT MORNING

Lord James Drake woke at dawn, after a good night's sleep. His head was a bit foggy, but his chest felt better. He vaguely remembered that young Lord's wife had laid hands on him. "Strange people, these rural folk. But it seems to have done some good." He stretched under the covers and noticed that he was wearing a nightshirt. They must have undressed him after the wedding. "How embarrassing. I wonder where Jamison is?"

The door opened and the servant entered. "Good morning, m'Lord. Are you feeling better?"

The Duke nodded. "Aye. There's nothing like a good sleep. Are we going home today?"

Jamison smiled. "Aye, m'Lord. The horses are being groomed, the wagon is loaded with provisions for the village, and I found a coach to make the journey easier."

"Excellent. Tell me. Did I spoil the lad's wedding day?"

Jamison frowned. "Nay, Sir. The festivities went on long into the night. But there is something I must tell ye. We had an incident with the Earl of Huntly."

The old man sat up, clearly alarmed. "The Earl? God in heaven. What was he doing here?"

"He came to abduct the lad."

"Is my grandson all right?"

"Aye, m'Lord. There was an ambush on the road between here and the fish-house tenement. Murdock was wounded, but he's still alive. The Earl threatened to slit him from neck to belly and tried to kill Alex as well."

The Duke polished his spectacles on the bed sheet. "Dear God. Who stopped him?"

"Your grandson. It's said that he turned into a madman and ran the Earl through."

"He's dead?"

"Aye."

"Hmmphh... I can't say that I'm sorry about that. How is the young Lord? He's a sensitive lad."

"My Lord. You can ask him yourself. He's waiting outside to see ye."

His bladder was about to burst. "Help me out of bed, Son. I need to use the chamber pot and get dressed. It seems the world has gone on without me."

***

Dughall waited for Jamison to finish the Duke's morning ablutions. He'd checked on the old man's condition sometime after midnight and found him resting peacefully. Mother and Keira were busy preparing a healing brew for the trip and dressing Murdock's wound. His head ached. "How will I tell Grandfather? I'm sure that it will cause him embarrassment."

Last night he'd dreamed of the moor, drenched in the blood of his clansmen. Lightning flashed and fires burned, as invaders set roofs ablaze. He'd kneeled and checked on the body of his son, a mere lad of twelve, speared through the heart by an enemy sword. He stared at his bloody hand and roared in anger, brandishing the Celtic blade. Dughall sighed. "Sheer madness. Perhaps I had reason to do what I did."

Jamison opened the door. "My Lord. The Duke is ready to see ye. Don't tire him out."

"Does he know about the Earl?"

"Aye."

Dughall reddened. "Oh God."

"Don't fret, lad. No one blames ye." Jamison ushered him to the Duke and left the room. The old man sat in an armchair, with a hand on the head of his cane.

"Grandfather. How are ye feeling?"

"Well rested, lad. Your mother and wife took good care of me."

"There's a long trip ahead. Is there anything I can do for ye?"

The Duke raised his eyebrows. "Aye, lad. Pull up that chair and talk to me. I hear that you had a problem with the Earl."

Dughall moved a chair and sat down opposite the old man. He wondered about how much to tell him.

"Don't worry about me, lad. I need to know what's going on if I'm to take action."

"There's no need, Sir. He tried to abduct me, but Murdock got between us. My servant fought fiercely, but was no match for my father. The Earl wounded him and threatened to slit him open."

"Who else was with ye?"

"My father. Alex. Oh God. It's so confusing. And my brother, Gilbert. He didn't want to be there, but he obeyed the Earl."

"God damn it! I'll send an army against his castle."

"Nay, Sir. When it was darkest, Gilbert tossed me a sword and I faced down the Earl."

"We owe your brother that. So you killed the man?"

Dughall sighed. "Aye. I didn't want to, but so many lives were at stake. Afterwards, a man tried to throw me in the tollbooth, but Gilbert stopped him. He said that he wouldn't contest it."

"Then we're safe for the moment. One more thing. The Earl was a master swordsman. How did ye do it?"

The young Lord reddened. "I used the Sight to anticipate his moves and called upon the memories of a Celtic warrior. God forgive me, but it was the only way to defeat him." His eyes glistened with tears.

The Duke patted his hand. "Poor lad. It's hard to kill a man, no less your own father. This isn't the last time you'll make decisions affecting lives. Are you all right?"

"Aye. I was lost in despair, but my father helped me think it through."

The Duke smiled. "Alex is a good man."

Dughall nodded. "He said that someday God will give me a chance to make things right."

"A sound philosophy."

"Come on, Grandfather. They're waiting for us at breakfast."

***

After breakfast, they left Peterhead and headed west over well-traveled roads. The day was crisp and sunny, with a few clouds overhead. Everywhere Dughall looked, he saw signs of an early spring. Trees were budding and birds were building nests in branches. The heather was brown, but that would change. Soon, purple flowers would set the hills ablaze. The young Lord sighed. It would feel good to get home and sleep on silk sheets, with the lass by his side.

The coach was a primitive affair, no better than a covered wagon, but it served to keep the Duke comfortable. Jessie and Keira took turns at his side, encouraging him to drink a healing brew. Now and then, he wheezed and coughed up blood. It was early afternoon when they neared the Abbey of Deer.

Dughall recognized a beechnut tree and pulled back on the reins. "Whoa, Lightning."

Pratt snorted. "What is it, m'Lord?"

"Beyond that tree lies a path that will take us to a stream. I told

Michael that we'd leave the provisions under a large pine."

Keira sat behind him with her arms around his waist. "Oh husband. This will mean so much to them."

"Stop the procession!" Jamison called. "This is where we leave the wagon." They dismounted and gathered around the cart of provisions.

"That forest looks thick. Can we take it in with the horse?" Pratt asked.

Jamison scratched his head. "Aye. The path's wide enough. Let's give it a try."

Dughall was uneasy. He thought it unwise to bring too many people into the forest. Michael was leery of outsiders. "There's no danger here. Jamison, Keira and I will take the wagon in. The rest of you stay and guard Grandfather."

Murdock frowned. "My Lord. I'm pledged to protect ye. I should be at your side."

Dughall smiled. "Stay here, friend. Your arm's in a sling and you need to rest."

They entered the forest with Dughall and Keira in the lead. Jamison walked behind, guiding the horse. The wooden cart groaned as they traveled over uneven ground. They found the path and headed towards the stream.

Dughall took her hand and held it to his heart. "Stay close, lass." His apprehension grew by the minute.

Keira's voice was soft. "What's wrong husband? You're shaking like a leaf."

"I don't know, wife. Something's not right."

* * *

Torry sat under a large pine, contemplating his unfortunate situation. He felt like the weight of the world was on his shoulders. *I'm not ready to be priest. I'm only fifteen. Goddess help me. We have to get Michael back.*

Ailie crouched in front of him and broke his reverie. "Hey, Brother! Did you hear me? I've been up and down the stream twice and I don't see them. I'm so hungry, that I could die. What will we do if they don't come?"

Torry's bowels churned. "I don't know, lass."

She frowned. "You're supposed to know what to do. Aren't you the priest now? Great Goddess! We're all dead."

Torry could hardly blame her. He was scared to death, but didn't dare show it. "I'm hoping that we'll get Michael back."

"Oh come on! He's likely dead already. Just a pile of cinders! Think of something else."

Torry heard a horse snorting and voices in the distance. It seemed as though they were approaching the stream. Hope and fear blossomed in his gut. Would he be the next to be taken? He stood and stared at the path. "Hide behind that tree, lass. If they take me, don't make a sound."

Ailie stomped her foot. "I'm not a child! I'll die with ye, Brother."

"Sister, please!" Sweat trickled down his back as footsteps sounded on the path. There were at least two, possibly three people. Keira walked into the clearing, holding a man's hand.

Torry breathed a sigh of relief. "Priestess! You came back."

Ailie squealed. "Thank the Goddess! We're starving."

Keira came closer and hugged her. "We brought a wagonload of food and provisions. There's honey and dried cranberries, too. It should last until summer."

"Thank ye, Priestess. I'm so hungry, that I could eat an old rooster." She looked up at Dughall and gasped. "Is this your husband?"

"Aye."

"He's young and handsome."

Jamison led the horse and cart into the clearing. He threw his jacket on the ground, rolled up his sleeves, and started to unload the wagon.

Ailie watched as he lifted sacks of grain, barrels of honey, and boxes of dried fish. "You're strong."

Jamison smiled. "Aye. That I am."

"Handsome, too. Are ye married?"

"Nay, lass. No time for marriage. I serve the young Lord."

"Oh." She put her finger in a flour bag and stuffed her mouth with the coarse meal.

Torry silently thanked the Goddess. With this food, his people would survive another season. "Thank ye, lass. I don't need to tell ye that we're starving."

"I know, lad. Torry. This is my husband, Dughall. We don't have much time. Where is Michael?"

Torry prepared for the worst. If this man wouldn't help them, Michael would die. He swallowed hard. "I pray that you can help us. Michael and I were hunting yesterday, about ten miles west, when he asked me to gather firewood. It was midday, time for his prayers to the Goddess, so he sank to his knees. When I returned with the wood, I saw three men beating him and calling him witch."

Keira paled. "Oh dear Goddess."

"I stayed out of sight, and watched as they bound him and took him away. I followed for miles to a town and tried to find out what was happening. A man said they'd torture him, to force him to name others. Then they'd burn him at the stake."

Keira nearly swooned. "Nay! Not like my father."

Dughall supported her. "Easy lass. We won't let that happen. Can you take us there?"

Torry was hopeful. "Aye. I remember the way all too well. But we must hurry. I don't know how much time he has left."

Dughall ran his fingers through his hair. "Jamison. A good man's in trouble. Are you up to an adventure?"

"Aye, m'Lord." The servant turned to the red-haired lad. "Can this bonny young lass get the provisions to your people?"

"I think so. She can fetch men from the village."

"Good. Can ye handle a sword, lad?"

Torry smiled. "Aye. Michael taught me."

"Let's be on our way. If the man's alive, we'll get him back."

✳✳✳

It was late afternoon when they joined their party at the Abbey of Deer. The Duke had gone inside to receive a blessing and retired to his wagon.

Dughall felt uneasy about leaving the old man. His cough was worsening and he longed to be in his own bed. The young Lord treaded carefully. "Grandfather. A man from my wife's village has been falsely accused and condemned. They've taken him away to execute him."

"What's he accused of?"

"Sorcery. But it's not true. These rural folk have superstitions and rituals, but they're good people. My poor wife is stricken with grief. I ask permission to go after him."

The old man hesitated. "I don't know, Son. It could be dangerous."

Dughall reddened. "Please, Grandfather. God is giving me a chance to make things right."

"Then go, lad. Take Jamison, Pratt, and your brother. Don't worry about me." He slid an ornate ring off his finger. "Here. Wear this on your right hand. That way, there will be no question of your birthright."

Dughall slipped it onto his finger. "Thank ye, Grandfather."

"Jamison is well known in this area as my right-hand man. Let him negotiate a deal. Take a sack of gold and buy the man's freedom if necessary."

"Thank ye, Sir. We must go, now. A man's life is at stake."

"Good luck, lad. We'll continue on to Drake and see you there in a few days."

Dughall left the old man and approached his wife. He took her hands and kissed her forehead. "Sweet lass…"

Keira's eyes glistened with tears. "What did he say?"

"We can go."

"Can I come with ye?"

"Nay, lass. It's too dangerous. Go with the others to Drake and take care of my grandfather."

"I will."

He squeezed her hands. "You're shaking, lass."

"I would die if I lost ye. I love ye with all my heart."

Dughall smiled. "Sweet lass. As the river returns to the sea, I shall return to you."

"What about Michael?"

"I promise ye this. If he's alive, we'll bring him home."

Jamison shouted, "My Lord! We must hurry. It could be far. The lad says he walked all night to get home."

Dughall nodded. They mounted their horses and headed west, following Torry's lead.

ELGINSHIRE – SCOTLAND

NEXT MORNING

Michael woke at the crack of dawn, anticipating his death. He was cold and thirsty and surprised that he'd slept at all. Days ago, they'd brought him to this frigid room, chained him to a wall, and beaten him. The next morning a priest demanded that he name twelve others, but he stayed silent. The black robe left him with two men, who tortured him until he was senseless.

Light streamed in a small window, illuminating the room. Michael looked down at his manacled hands, swollen and bloody. They'd pulled out his fingernails, one by one, each time demanding a confession. He sniffled. "Dear Goddess. May they cut my tongue out before I betray my people." His heart ached. "I've been such a fool. I should have married the lass and kept her safe. The young Lord can't protect her from this. Now my people have no priest or healer. I hope Torry has the sense to stay away."

He heard voices outside and stiffened. Soon they would tie him to a stake and burn him alive. He remembered standing on Agony Hill, staring at what was left of his friend. Michael's fear blossomed. "Kale, old friend. Stand with me in my hour of need and help me to die as you did, without malice in my heart." He held his breath. Someone was at the door. "Dear Goddess. I'm so afraid."

***

The young Lord's party arrived in town just as dawn broke. They'd traveled all night without stopping to sleep and were running on their nerves. Jamison was eager to get to the bottom of this. "Torry. Where is the inn?"

The lad looked perplexed. "I don't know about such things."

"It's a public gathering place where men drink and eat."

Torry nodded. "I think I know what you mean. Over this way."

They followed the lad to the other end of town and found a rough wooden structure with a large porch. A drunk slept in a chair with a pint of ale in his hand. "This must be it. Now, remember what we agreed upon." The five men walked into the local inn with their hands on their swords, startling the innkeeper's wife.

"What do ye want?" she cried. "What is the meaning of this?"

Jamison relaxed his grip and laid a gold coin on the desk. "Do ye know who I am, old woman?"

"Nay, Sir."

"I am Lord Drake's manservant and this is his grandson Lord Dughall Gordon."

She stood. "My Lords. Forgive me. I will get my husband."

Jamison slapped the desk. "Not yet! We need lodging for our horses. Is there a stable available?"

"Aye. 'Round back. The stable lad just arrived."

"Pratt. Torry. Take the horses to the stable and see that they're fed and watered. No grooming. They must be ready to ride at a moment's notice."

The two men left. Jamison motioned to a table. "Sit down, mother. We need information about the witch trial and the man in custody."

The old woman paled as she took a seat. "My Lords. What can I tell ye?"

As agreed, Jamison, Ian, and Dughall sat down and stared until she squirmed. Ian drew his knife and ran the blade along his thumb. "Let me ask her."

"Dear God! Don't hurt me."

Jamison slapped five gold coins on the table. "Put that away, lad. I won't let him hurt ye, mother. Is the prisoner alive?"

"Aye. They're burning him this morning."

"Hmmphh... There's been a terrible mistake. The man is not a witch, but a dear friend of the young Lord. Who do we see to stop it?"

The old woman picked up the coins and smiled. "You've come to the right place. I can help ye."

***

Michael's heart was in his throat as the door opened and three men entered. He hung his head and pretended to be asleep. *Dear Goddess. It must be time.*

The black robe approached and pulled his hair. His voice was ominous. "Look at me, witch. Sleep well?"

Michael looked up. "Nay."

"I didn't think so." He released his hair. "I see they bloodied your hands. Are ye ready to talk?"

"Nay."

"You're a tough bastard. They're erecting a stake and piling it with wood and pitch. Have ye ever seen a man burned alive?"

Michael's heart throbbed in his ears. "Aye."

The priest frowned. "It's a slow and painful death. Don't be a fool.

Name twelve others and I'll hang ye."

Michael was silent. Nothing was worth betraying his people.

"Answer me, witch!"

"I won't name them."

The priest turned to the two men. "Tear off his shirt and flog him bloody. Then take him outside. A crowd is gathering." He left the room.

Michael struggled as the men stood him up and tore off his shirt. "Brothers, please! I beg ye." They turned him around, manacled him to the wall, and took out a whip. The granite stone against his chest was as cold and gray as death. "Have mercy! You don't have to do this."

A man laughed.

Michael gasped as the whip bit into his back.

* * *

Outside the church, a stake had been erected. Young men piled faggots of wood around it and painted pitch on sticks. One lad drove a burning torch into the ground. A crowd gathered to watch the gruesome event, mostly men and young boys.

Jamison and the young Lord stood talking to the constable.

Dughall was pleased so far. *What luck! The constable is the old woman's husband. A handful of coins changed his mind.*

Jamison stared. "So you'll let him go?"

The old man scratched his belly. "Don't matter to me. You say he's not a witch, and I believe ye." He looked around. "The crowd will be angry. They expected some entertainment."

Dughall's stomach turned. How could they burn a living man for entertainment? "We'll provide it. Does the inn have a tavern?"

"Aye, m'Lord."

"Give him enough gold to provide ale and whisky for all. They can drink themselves silly. After we leave with my friend."

Jamison dispensed the coins into the man's open hand. "Now will ye let him go?"

The innkeeper slipped them into his pocket. "My Lords. I'll release him if the priest agrees."

Dughall had a bad feeling about this. "Where is the priest?"

"Father Ambrose is coming this way."

The church bell rang, calling the townspeople to order. Women and children came out of buildings and gathered in the churchyard.

Ian and Pratt joined them. "My Lord," Pratt said. "We left Torry with the horses. It's best that he stays out of sight."

The young lord watched as the priest approached. The crowd parted as he walked among them, a striking figure in a flowing black robe. He was remarkably erect and had an appearance of authority.

Dughall's blood boiled with the realization. *I know this man. I was only seven, but I remember it well. Except for white hair, he's the same. He hanged Keira's mother.*

"Father Ambrose," the innkeeper said. "These important men have a request to make."

The priest looked them over, lingering on Dughall's ring. "What do they want?"

"Your prisoner, Father."

"This is outrageous. Who are ye?"

Jamison fingered his sword. "The townspeople know me well. I am Lord Drake's representative."

"The Duke's servant?"

"Aye. This is his grandson and heir, Lord Dughall Gordon."

"Where is his Lordship the Duke?"

"His health is failing. He's not expected to live."

The priest glared. "My Lord. We gather here today to dispense justice. You mustn't interfere with local decisions."

Dughall's eyes widened. "You intend to burn a man to death. What has he done?"

"He's a witch!"

"I ask ye again. What has he done?"

The crowd gathered around, curious about a man who would challenge a priest.

"We found him in the forest, worshipping a Goddess."

Dughall's anger grew. "For this, you'll burn him to death?"

"Aye. The Bible says that thou shalt not suffer a witch to live."

"God in heaven! I don't care what it says. Jesus would be appalled."

The priest's eyes narrowed. "How dare ye twist the words of the good book! The witch will die according to scripture."

"Damn it man! Where is he?"

"He's being flogged."

Dughall felt nauseous as he grabbed the priest's collar and pulled him close. "I won't allow this! Jamison, is this town under my rule?"

"Aye, m'Lord."

"Then I say he lives. You will turn the man over to me immediately."

Father Ambrose freed himself and straightened his robe. "I will not. You can't tell the church what to do!"

Dughall tried another approach. "Very well. I will support no religion that kills in the name of God. We tithe a great deal of gold to the church. If you kill him, I'll withdraw my support."

The priest reddened. "You invite eternal damnation, sir. The Bishop will excommunicate ye.'

"Then so be it. At birth, I was baptized a Protestant. They'll be happy to take me back."

"You would forsake the one true religion?"

Dughall shrugged. "There is no one true religion. As far as I'm concerned, it's all the same God."

Jamison surveyed the situation and drew his sword. "My Lord. The crowd is growing restless. Be careful." Ian and Pratt followed suit, fingering the hilts of their swords.

The priest fumed. "You dare threaten me? Lord or no. This man has the devil in him! I challenge his honesty."

Dughall's mind flooded with images of fraud and debauchery. "Honesty? This from a priest who sleeps with his brother's wife?"

A man gasped. "Brother. Is this true?"

"Nay. The man must be daft."

"Not so, sir. I have the gift of the Second Sight." He pointed to a young woman holding a baby. "This is the lass and child at her breast is your son."

The woman gathered her skirts and ran off in tears.

"Brother! Is it true?"

The priest massaged his temple. "Nay. He knows nothing."

Dughall stared. "Nothing indeed. Shall we talk about the letter opener you stole from the church in Edinburgh? The one with the ruby stone? There's more…"

"Enough, sir! This is sheer madness. Cease and desist!"

"Then turn the prisoner over to me."

Father Ambrose mopped his forehead. "Release the witch. The Bishop will visit your grandfather, Sir. There will be hell to pay."

"I'll deal with that later. Where is the prisoner?"

The constable spoke. "In the bowels of the church. I'll take ye there."

The crowd grumbled. Jamison whistled. "Good people. There will be no execution today. In honor of this, the young Lord will provide ale and whisky for all."

"As much as we want?"

"Aye. The tavern will open for business as soon as we leave." A cheer went up. "Pratt, Ian. Get Torry and the horses. I will accompany the young Lord."

***

Michael writhed in pain as the lash bit into his back. How much longer could he bear it? Tears streamed down his face, clouding his vision. In the recesses of his mind, he heard the door open and the men being called away.

One of the lads unlocked his manacles and let him drop to the ground. "Witch."

Weak and exhausted, he rose up on his hands and kissed the floor. "Return my body to the earth to be reborn." He kneeled and prayed.

"Forgive them, Mother, for all life is sacred. Purify my heart, that my soul may enter the Summerland." Michael felt a hand on his shoulder and knew it was time to face the fire. Someone spoke his name.

"Michael…"

No one knew his name. Had he betrayed his people in his sleep? He stiffened and looked up.

Dughall's eyes were full of compassion. "I've secured your release, friend. We must hurry."

Michael swooned and dropped to the floor. He vaguely heard a voice directing another.

"He's badly hurt. Can ye carry him?"

"Aye, m'Lord." Arms lifted him. "He's as light as a feather."

Someone carried him into the cold and helped him onto a horse. After days in that dark hole, the sunlight blinded him. The man wrapped a blanket around his shoulders and mounted behind him. "Hold him tightly. He looks bad."

Michael thought he was dreaming. That sounded like Torry's voice. He felt strong arms around him, holding him close, and knew he was safe. He blacked out as they left the village.

HOMECOMING

TWO MILES FROM DRAKE CASTLE
APRIL 4 1637
NEXT DAY

Dughall's heart was light as they approached Drake Castle. He was riding his beloved horse and life was good. A man's life had been saved and a village rescued from starvation. He'd grown up a lot these past few days, tasting the joys of marriage and agonies of battle. The conflict with the church had tested his moral fiber.

After the confrontation, they'd traveled for hours without stopping. Ian and Pratt made sure that they hadn't been followed. Soon they reached a crossroads and made a decision. Dughall wanted to take Michael to Drake to recuperate, but the man wanted to go home. By nightfall they arrived at the Abbey, took Michael to the forest village, and treated his wounds. The man expressed gratitude and hope that the burning times would end. The young Lord and his servants stayed the night at the Abbey, getting a hot meal and well-deserved rest, and left for Drake in the morning.

Now, the castle loomed in the distance. The young Lord rode with his brother at his side and the servants behind. Dughall was overcome by conflicting emotions. The castle represented home, a soft bed, his wife's touch, and the love and respect of his family. It also meant responsibility for the property and lives of others, and the possibility that he would be Duke soon.

Ian cleared his throat. "You've been quiet these last miles, Brother."

Dughall nodded. "I've been thinking."

"The last few days have been interesting. Not like the life of a fisherman. I'm grateful to ye for that."

Dughall smiled. "When I was abducted, all I thought about was returning to the sea. Now that I'm at Drake, it feels like home."

"I don't blame ye. The food's good."

Dughall laughed. His brother would be easy to please. "So many things have happened since we left. Thank God we got Michael back."

Ian snorted. "You were awesome, Brother. I thought you were going to choke that priest. Did he really sleep with his brother's wife?"

"Aye. The truth was like cherries to be picked from a tree. Did ye recognize him?"

"Nay."

"He's the same priest who hung that poor woman in Newburgh."

"Ach! You have a better memory than me, Brother. Do ye think they're all like that?"

Dughall frowned. "Nay. But there's probably a few more, willing to twist God's words. I'm concerned about the village. It's not in my territory and those rituals may attract attention. Next time, we may be too late. Could I convince them to come here?"

"I don't know, Brother. They like that stone circle. Can ye build one?"

"It's not that easy. My wife says that the stones have markings that track the moon and the stars."

"Hmmphh...."

The entrance to the castle was just ahead. Gilroy had spotted them and opened the gate. "My Lord. You must go to your grandfather's bedside immediately. They say that he's held on just for you."

Dughall's heart ached. "Oh God. He's dying?"

"Aye. The priest just arrived to give him last rites."

The young Lord dismounted. "Ian, Pratt. Take care of the horses. Jamison, come with me to his bedside. He'll want to see ye one last time."

***

Dughall and Jamison entered the castle and took the steps to the second floor. They walked a long hallway and turned down a corridor that led to the old Lord's chamber. Dughall's mind raced. He'd developed a bond with the old man, based on love and respect. It was time to help him pass.

Jamison sniffled. "My Lord. I'm just a servant. I'll understand if ye don't want me there."

Dughall smiled. "Grandfather told me that you've been like a son to him. Come with me and say goodbye. I won't take that from ye."

"Thank ye, m'Lord. I do care about him."

They approached the Lord's chambers and saw two women waiting outside, Jessie and Keira. Their faces lit up with recognition.

"Son! Thank goodness you're here."

"Mother."

Dughall kissed her cheek and turned to his wife. He took her hands and squeezed them. "Sweet lass."

Her eyes glistened with tears. "Oh husband. You came back to me."

"I gave ye my word."

She trembled with anticipation. "What about Michael?"

"He's alive and whole. I'll tell ye about it later."

"Thank the Goddess."

"What's happening in there, lass?"

"Your grandfather's dying. There's a priest in there giving him a blessing. What do they call it, Mother?"

Jessie whispered. "Last rites." They were quiet as the door creaked opened.

The priest emerged, dressed in official robes and carrying a prayer book. "Are you the young Lord?"

Dughall nodded. "Aye, Father."

"You must hurry, lad. He's very weak. I will inform the Bishop of his impending death and arrange an appropriate service." He bowed. "Ladies. I'll take my leave now."

Dughall swallowed hard against a lump in his throat. It was time to face the death of a loved one. "Come on, Jamison. You and I will go in first."

The two men entered the chamber and went to the bedside. The Duke's eyes were closed and he was as pale as a ghost.

He looks dead already, Dughall thought. He took his hand and noted that it was cold. It wouldn't be long now. "Hold his other hand, Jamison."

The Duke opened his eyes. "Lads. You came back to see this old man pass."

"Aye, Grandfather."

"Did ye accomplish your mission?"

"God was on our side. We rescued the man and took him home."

"Good." He squeezed their hands. "I don't have much time, so listen carefully."

They nodded.

"Jamison. You've been a loyal servant and friend. I've bequeathed some land and a cottage to ye, near the castle. Marry a bonny lass and have some children."

The servant struggled to hold back tears. "Thank ye, my Lord. I won't forget this! I'll protect your grandson with my life."

"I know ye will." He gazed at Dughall. "The rest is yours, lad. Land, wealth, and power. Use it wisely. You're a moral man; don't let anyone take that from ye."

Dughall smiled through tears. "I won't."

The old man released their hands and gasped for breath. "I need to rest. Goodbye, Jamison."

"My Lord."

"Lad, tell your mother how grateful I am for her kindness. Then bring your lass in here. I need to speak to ye both."

Dughall brought Keira into the old Lord's chamber. They went to either side of the bed and took his hands. "We're here, Grandfather."

The old man opened his eyes and sighed. "When I look at you, I see the love that blossomed between my wife and me."

Dughall smiled. "We love each other more than life."

"That's how it was with Jeanne. Oh God. I stood at her deathbed, wondering how I could go on without her. She gave me a reason to live when she told me about you."

"How so, Grandfather?"

"Jeanne said that our daughter was there to help her pass. She spoke of an infant son and asked me to find ye. She said to look to the sea."

Dughall's eyes widened. "She was right."

"I wish I could see her again."

"You will, Sir."

Dughall felt a chill. Something cold and powerful moved through him and lingered over the head of the bed. He glanced at his wife. She seemed to feel it, too. "We're not alone," he whispered.

She nodded. "They've come for him, with a love that transcends death."

Dughall stroked the old man's forehead. He was drifting and breathing shallowly. "Rest, Grandfather. You've meant so much to me. I love ye."

His voice was weak. "I love ye too, lad." The Duke closed his eyes and whispered. "Oh Jeanne…" His body slackened as his spirit escaped.

Dughall was overcome with emotion. He dropped to his knees and thanked God for what he had witnessed. There truly was a Summerland.

A gentle hand rested on his shoulder. "Husband? Are ye all right?"

"Aye."

"It was beautiful."

He stood and held her close. "Amen, lass. That it was."

"Blessed be."

Dughall Gordon

LORD DUGHALL

DRAKE CASTLE
APRIL 6 1637
TWO DAYS LATER

It was a beautiful spring morning. Trees were budding and the air was lightly scented with daffodils. The family's private cemetery was quiet, in spite of the fact that hundreds of people gathered there.

Dughall watched as the casket was lifted off the wagon and carried to the gravesite. Over the past few days, his emotions had run the gamut from joy to sorrow. In private, he'd cried until there were no tears left. Today had been especially hard, with a high mass attended by visiting dignitaries and common folk alike. The young Lord greeted them all, giving them the comfort and reassurance they sought.

The pallbearers lowered the gold-rimmed casket into the ground.

Jamison, Gilroy, Pratt, and Suttie moved away from the gravesite and let the Bishop approach.

Dughall held his breath. The man looked regal in ecclesiastical robes and pointed hat, a silver crucifix around his neck. He glared at the young Lord, raised his mahogany staff, and went to the graveside.

The Bishop can't hurt me now, he thought. *I'll be Duke soon.*

Murdock stood next to Alex and Jessie, his arm still in sling. Ian and Mary held hands and bowed their heads. A piper stood at attention by the gravesite.

Dughall's heart was heavy as the Bishop took out his prayer book to begin the final benediction. Keira's arm was linked in his and she took the opportunity to snuggle against him. He glanced at her and saw her smile. *Thank God I have her. I love her more than life.*

The Bishop cleared his throat. "Almighty Father! We gather here to honor Lord James Drake. Grandfather. Leader. Benefactor. Brother in Christ."

A female voice, soft and comforting, followed his. *"Beloved child of the Goddess."*

"Into thy hands we commend his soul, to await final judgment."

"Step into Summerland and the arms of your beloved Jeanne."

The Bishop sprinkled earth on the casket. "Ashes to ashes. Dust to dust. In hope of resurrection."

"Thus the wheel turns. Return to the earth, rest, and be reborn."

He closed his prayer book. "Amen."

"Blessed be."

The mournful wail of bagpipes drifted through the air. Dughall looked around. No one seemed to notice the female voice, but he heard it clearly. He touched his wife's face and searched her eyes. "The Goddess spoke."

Keira smiled. "I heard her, husband."

His heart soared. "We were right, lass. It really is the same thing."

The Bishop concluded his prayers and approached the young Lord. "May we talk in private?"

"Aye." Dughall walked with him to a nearby tree.

The Bishop's voice was stern. "I've had disturbing communications about you from one of my parishes. I hope and pray that it's a misunderstanding. After an appropriate period of mourning, we will talk."

Dughall stared until the man flinched. "That we will, Father. You can expect that things will be different under my jurisdiction."

The man's eyes narrowed. "Good day, Sir. I'll take my leave now."

Dughall was calm as he watched him walk away. There was no point in getting upset over future confrontations. The young Lord felt a hand on his shoulder and heard voices behind him. He turned to see Jamison.

The servant waved his hand at the crowd. "Behold, my Lord. Your loyal subjects."

Dughall looked beyond to the cemetery. Family, friends, and servants stood before him, smiling with admiration. At Jamison's signal, every man, woman, and child dropped down on one knee.

Jamison kneeled. "Hail to the new Duke of Seaford!"

They shouted in unison, "Hail to the Duke!"

Dughall's heart swelled. These were his people. He would do all in his power to be worthy of his birthright.

Dark Birthright is book one in
the Dark Birthright Trilogy

other books
Dark Lord - book two
Dark Destiny - book three

Dark Lord

Dark Lord opens less than six months later, with your
favorite characters. Set during a time of political and
religious strife, it features action, magic, romance, and
politics. It's 1637 in Scotland. Dughall is settling into
his new role when the King imposes an Anglican liturgy
book on the Scottish church. Protests and riots plague
the realm, forcing lords and commoners to take a stand.
Dughall and Gilbert are placed in precarious positions,
torn between loyalty to the crown, their families, and
zealous subjects. To complicate matters, Dughall claims
the sword of Red Conan and inherits the curse that comes
with it. Challenged by real and supernatural enemies,
he must fight to continue his line. Conflicts pit brother
against brother and father against son. The National
Covenant is signed and war breaks out. Tempers run hot
and actions are rash. To maintain order, one brother must
take Blackheart's place. Which raises the question…
Who shall become the Dark Lord?

visit
www.jeanne treat.com
www.darkbirthright.com

Mini-Timeline of Scottish History
Dark Birthright takes place during 1619-1637

1597 Scottish Protestant Reformation, led by John Knox, occurs at a grassroots level.

1597 The future James VI of Scotland writes a treatise on witchcraft and demons called "Demonology", which fuels the hysteria about alleged "witches" and results in many witch burnings. This continues on well into the 1600's.

1603 Union of the Crowns of England and Scotland on the death of Queen Elizabeth I, and the succession of James VI of Scotland. This was not a welcome move in much of Scotland or England. James VI leaves Edinburgh to live in London.

1615 St. John Ogilvie, a Banffshire-born Jesuit priest is hanged for refusing to renounce the supremacy of the Pope.

1617 James VI, on his only return to Scotland, tactlessly lectures his countrymen on the "superiority of English civilization". Articles of religion, introducing Anglican principles into Scottish worship, are endorsed by Scottish parliament.

1618 The "Five Articles of Perth". James VI imposes Bishops on the Presbyterian Church of Scotland in an attempt to integrate it with the Church of England. This move was unpopular with the Scots.

1625 King James VI dies, to be succeeded by his son, King Charles I. Though born in Scotland, Charles had no interest in the country and dealt with Scottish affairs with less tact than his father, causing discontent.

1637 "Book of Common Prayer" introduced to Scotland. Charles I attempts to further Anglicanize the Church of Scotland with an English prayer book that creates social unrest and disorder.

Administration of Justice 1619-1637

Unless a crime was determined to be against the Crown, justice was administered locally by nobles such as Earls and Dukes. The common man was at a disadvantage, whereas a man of stature expected special considerations if charged with a crime. Lesser disputes could be handled by the clans or families themselves.

State of Medicine and Healing

If you lived in a major city like Edinburgh and had money and stature, you could have engaged a trained physician. Healers, midwives, and bonesetters would have been available for common folk.

In most of Scotland, local women served the population as healer, midwife, and bonesetter. This was a trade passed down from mother to daughter, or in rare cases from mother to son. They were skilled in the use of herbs and other natural materials such as tar or honey to cure disease or treat wounds.

In the book, I tried to make the healing and midwifery scenes authentic, given the time and place and resources available. However, my advice to the reader is to not try them at home without formal training or investigation.

The seventeenth century was a dangerous time to be a healer. The witchcraft hysteria created a climate where neighbor accused neighbor if they hated them or desired their property. A healer was especially vulnerable, as she affected lives and used seemingly magical medicines. In Scotland alone, thousands were accused, tortured, and burned or hanged.

THE GEOGRAPHY

"Dark Birthright" is a work of historical fiction. It takes place during 1619-1637, and is set mostly in Northeast Scotland. While not 100% true to historical fact, it reflects the political, religious, and cultural dynamics of 17th century Scotland.

The sea town of Whinnyfold exists to this day on the northeast coast, just south of Cruden Bay. Fours rows of stone cottages are still standing, though updated to today's standards. There is a relatively new house on the cliff side, built and once inhabited by none other than Bram Stoker. In the distance, one can see the ruins of Slains Castle.

Newburgh (where the hanging occurred) is a now a bustling residential village on the wide sandy estuary of the Ythan River. Nearby, the nature preserve of Forvie Sands comprises an area of dunes some three miles long and a mile wide. This would have been the place where Maggie and Jessie gathered mussels and the lads played in the rock pool.

The town of Peterhead serves as a seaport, dedicated to fishing and oil production. Greatly expanded from the days of this novel, the tavern on Keith Inch called The Crack is long gone, and King's Common Gate is now Longate.

Huntly Castle can be viewed as a tourist attraction. Although a ruins without a roof, one can tour the floors and enter the rooms, as well as see the prison and outbuildings like the alehouse and the stables. The rush of the River Deveron can be heard behind the castle.

Drake Castle is a fabrication of the author's mind. (Sorry...)

Louden Wood is a real place in the Forest of Deer. Located near the towns of Old Deer, Maud and Fetterangus, it features the ruins of an ancient recumbent stone circle. Standing in the middle of the circle, one can feel the energy of the earth and imagine the ceremonies that took place there. Although hard to find and quite a hike on foot, it is truly a treasure. There is an astonishing old growth forest nearby, with what looks like the ruins of a small village.

The ruins of the Abbey of Deer can be seen at Old Deer as well. In reality, its life as a religious institution came to an end with the Reformation in 1560, which would be shortly before the time frame of this book.

The Gordons - the Hays - and Lord Drake

"Dark Birthright" is a work of fiction. Names, characters, places, and incidents are either the product of the author's imagination or are used fictitiously. Any resemblance to actual events or persons, living or dead, is entirely coincidental.

That being said:

The Hay family did occupy the towns of Whinnyfold and Peterhead in the 17th century, and Alexander was one of their male names. There is no record of a strange birth, or a subsequent connection to the Gordon clan.

Historically, from 1562-1636, George Gordon served as the 1st Marquess of Huntly. The novel portrays an alternate reality for the Gordon clan if George had succumbed to the madness of the sword of Red Conan, to be succeeded by a mythical brother Robert. Robert then spawned a son named Robert, who became the cruel and powerful Earl of Huntly in this book.

Lord James Drake, Duke of Seaford, is a purely fictional character.

On my numerous visits to Scotland, I expressed concern that some of my fictional portrayals would offend the clans. An interesting Scot named Kenneth told me not to worry, because 'they enjoy being the bad guys'. Even so, I offer my apologies to the clans if I have offended anyone.

Note on the Use of the Scots Dialect

Some may wonder why I used only a bit of the Scots dialect in this book. Early on, I decided to lightly salt the manuscript with Scots to make it authentic, but easy for the reader. For two years, a focus group gathered at my home to read and criticize chapters. When I presented a piece with a lot of Scots, the focus became the translation rather than the story. In this novel, you will find a lot of ye's, a fair amount of canna's and dinna's, scores of lads and lassies, and a few self-explanatory words like blootered. Forgive me if it's not more widespread. I will leave that to Sir Walter Scott.

HONORABLE MENTION

SONGS

There are many songs referenced in this book, taken from traditional Scottish and Irish folk music. Most of these beautiful compositions are over 100 years old and in the public domain, with one exception. "Mairi's Wedding" was written by Johnny Bannerman in Gaelic in 1935 for his friend Mary McNiven, and translated into English a year later by Hugh Roberton.

CEREMONIES

The idea for the earth-based marriage ceremony was taken in part from *The Wiccan Book of Ceremonies and Rituals,* by Patricia Telesco.

Whinnyfold Today

Louden Wood Today

Huntly Castle Today

Stone Circle Today

Made in the USA
San Bernardino, CA
02 February 2014